I0590296

WHEN A DRAGON MEETS A PRINCESS

WHEN A DRAGON MEETS A PRINCESS

MIA BONES

Copyright

Copyright © Mia Bones 2025

All rights reserved. This book or any portion thereof may not be reproduced
or used in any manner whatsoever without the permission of the publisher
except for the use of brief quotations in a book review.

ISBN: 979-8-9991116-0-9
Front Cover Design by Etheric Tales
Printed by Endless Hells Tales, LLC. in
the USA.

Glossary

Angel- Divine beings created from gods to help fulfill their vision for whatever world they may call home. Can fall into the category of messengers, caretakers, or warriors. Because they are made from gods they contain a hint of their divinity. The stronger the god, the stronger the angel.

Cleansed- Anyone who is possessed by the power of a Cursed Object. If they experience any sort of remorse, there is a homing beacon attached to the soul of a Blessed that those Cursed will try to get to. The Cursed object will fight back against the Blessed even if the will of those they possess has changed. Many Blessed have perished when overcome by the power of a curse object. Though Cursed objects themselves have never managed to be cleansed, there is hope for the soul to be released from the collection and move on to wherever their after-life leads.

Cursed- Manifestation of intense trauma dispensed by the souls of mystics. Usually dumped onto objects that promise immense power to those who choose to wield it, in exchange for the portion of their soul that harbors their darkest bits. The more wielders a Cursed object has, the more power it can promise as it absorbs and amasses that potential from each previous master. God-level cursed objects refers to objects so drenched in cursed energy that their threats reach celestial level.
Also refers to the wielders themselves who are under the possession of the Cursed.

Demon- Dark beings first created in any pit of the endless hells. The more strength a demon has, the deadlier their poison is.

Djinn- A high dark and light magic being existing as checks and balances to all light and dark descendants.

Dragon- High-magical beast shape-shifters. At birth, dragons are assigned a specific element which they naturally excel with. Their element is usually visible upon colors of physical features such as hair color and eye color. Dragons who can manipulate multiple elements are eligible to take the position of Dragon King.

Elf- A limited earth-magic being known for their long lifespans and natural combat ability.

Kappa- Elemental based beings. Have a special relationship with weather and can either summon or disperse storms for a very short while.

Kitsune- High-magical shape-shifters. A fox-spirit shape-shifter. Proficient in elemental magic as well as beast magic.

Master Spellcaster- Any mystic who has attained a license from higher-education facilities like Spellcaster Academy. The requirements of the license are the attainment of at least four specialties offered by the academy ranging from conjuring to the healing arts.

Mate- The beast-side of shape-shifters is usually in a power struggle with their everyday counterparts. Mates soothe the struggle between the two sides of a shifter, most times leading to a balanced member of society. While there can be many candidates to a mate, a shifter can only choose one mate to tie their life to for the rest of their lives. When one half dies, so does the other.

Mystic- Any being who can take part in the mystical arts.

Shape-shifter- Any being who can shift into a different form of their natural state. Can have high or low magical abilities depending on species. All have a secondary persona that are usually referred to as their beast who more often than not fall into animalistic instincts.

Sphinx- High-Magical shape-shifter. Has the head of a human and body of a lion in full transformation mode. Proficient in beast magic and alchemy.

Succubus- Demoness' descended from Lilith (the first woman ever created). Must take in sexual energy from partners to survive. Usually have a second entity inside like the shifter's beast. Though much more subdued. Only come in the female variety.

Witch- A class of humans able to take part in the mystical arts through a combination of potion mastery, incantations, and sacrificial rituals.

Wolf-Shifter- Low-magic shape-shifter. Transform into giant wolves when in their beast modes. Highest ability of healing magic available to any shifter class.

Branches of Magic

Alchemic- Transformation that permanently changes the base composition of material from one form to another without the need for runes or magic circles.

Blessed- Rare magic that allows celestial beings to talk directly to those who carry this type of magic. Blessed are able to manifest a mixture of will and energy into weapons that can Cleanse a Cursed. (See more for Cleansed and Cursed in Glossary).

Blood- Allows for the manipulation of blood in others. Can be utilized to heal-- especially useful for poisoning- or harm--such as controlling bodily movements.

Celestial- Reserved for those who derive their magic from the faith of others. Human faith is the strongest source as it can create a being from nothing. Mystic faith can only create a celestial being out of an already existing being. Can only exist in the Celestial Realm. Creation or destruction incidents on great levels are works of Celestial beings.

Demonic- Magic that encourages the shedding of inhibitions. Gives those who have it the tools to best entice their targets. Allows the transfer of energy between two bodies. Most demonic beings require that energy as sustenance.

Divine- Creations of celestial beings. Can range from angels, messengers, demigods, and weapons. Can exist out of the Celestial Realm.

Elemental- Able to manipulate elements that come from the earth. Most mystics have a particular affinity to only one branch of elemental magic, but a few are known for being able to access more than one.

Mind- The ability to manipulate or read the dreams or minds of other beings even without their consent. Illusions stem from this form of magic.

Necromancy- Mostly used to communicate with the dead. Powerful necromancers can reanimate corpses but none can ever compel a soul to return if a soul doesn't want to.

Nulling- Ability to neutralize all other magic. Ranges in power as some casters can only null a small area while some can null a whole person.

Shifter- A soul fragmented into two different sentient beings in the same body. A beastly side that pursues base desires, and a sane side to temper those impulses co-exist.

Magic Practices

Alchemy Enchantment- Complex practice that requires an understanding of physics and chemistry as well as a proficient level of runes and spellcasting. Most modern advancement in technology stems from this form of practice, but also most magical disasters as people aren't nearly as proficient as they believe they are.

Nulling Enhancement- Can only be done by those with nulling magic. They're able to enhance physical objects to create a field of their power even without their presence. Because levels of nullers vary, so does the quality of these products. Nulling a material corrodes physical aspects, making material weaker than their natural state, but magic is able to flow easier through softer material. Gold is the most popular form of nulling enhancement.

Potion Making- Concoctions that can enhance targeted aspects. Most popular: healing, heightening sense, conjuring illness (poisons), protection from weaker magic, enhancement of magic capabilities.

Runes- Magic cast by designed symbols imbued with magic or blood laced materials. Casters don't have to have access to magic to use magic imbued materials.

Spell Casting- A combination of words, movements and ability to pull magic through the vishuddha chakra point. Most witches use this form of magic.

Summoning- Requires a physical sample of whoever is being summoned as well as intricate magic circles. Can be ignored if the person being summoned is more powerful than whoever does the summoning, or if they're wearing nulling jewelry.

Tracking- Requires a physical sample of whoever is being tracked. Can be avoided by using nulling jewelry or charms or if a person is behind a barrier of any sort. Can also be used to track objects to prevent theft.

Contents

For Cristina,
Who isn't the worst gift my mom ever gave me,
no matter how many times I've said it.
I love you, my unwilling shadow editor.

Also,

For the smut loving fans que no tienen vergüenza. <3

I

The first sign something was wrong was the uncommon rain that ripped through the skies of Black Cove.

Rowan Dahl might have noticed the even further unusual red streaks of light accompanying the storm if only she could fight against the overwhelming punishment of too many Bahama Mamas.

If she would have noticed the lightning, she might have turned on the TV or scrolled through her phone to find out what was going on.

But, as things stood, the Master Spellcaster was taking in the sound of the rhythmic droplets hitting her window to help soothe her hangover.

White-haired, fair-skinned, and pointy-eared, the woman fit the stereotypical description of an Eastern Elf to a tee.

As fourth in line to the Eastern Elven Kingdom throne, that's how Rowan liked to be perceived. No second looks underneath the glamor she wore.

The office assistant, a blue-haired fairy the size of an average hand named Dew, was pouring her a steaming cup of coffee with the aid of her magic while she went through her day's schedule.

"If you'd like, I can push the lunch meeting to Mr. Smith." The distaste Dew felt for her boss' condition was a sharp note in her normally chipper tone. "I think a nap would be best to get you prepared for Ms. Young's visit so soon after the Coven Elder's death."

Rowan, who already had the urge to vomit due to the constant spinning of the room, felt the bile in her stomach try to rise. "Today is the meeting with the Coven?"

"Yes." Dew's sharp tone softened. Visits from the Coven were the bane of Rowan Dahl's existence. "We already rescheduled her twice; a third time, and she might just walk in whenever she likes."

It took a beat for Rowan to signal her to continue.

"Also, Mitchell Tech left a couple of voicemails and a request that you're the one to call them back," the voice trailed off for a second then returned with a giggle, "Oh, wait-your mother asked me to remind you to make it to family dinner tonight lest you wish her to, and I quote, 'turn your apartments in the Eastern Elven Kingdom into an everlasting memorial.'" the fairy tinkled with full-blown laughter at the end of the message.

Rowan's attention split between her assistant's concerning reaction to her mother's genuine threat and a thunderclap that shook her teeth.

It was enough for her to wrench her eyes open and take in the odd color of the streaking skies. Her mind whirred past the hangover, searching for a plausible explanation.

The fairy floated toward one of the floor-to-ceiling window panes once she realized Rowan's attention was no longer hers alone. "Isn't that Draconis?" Her small hand spread out against the beaded glass.

Draconis was Black Cove's crowning jewel. The neighborhood was the only place in the world exclusive to dragon shifters—the oldest species of mystics.

Just outside its golden gates, which had remained open to the public as long as the town had become a bustling epicenter of trade and commerce, were streets of shops offering dragon wares and services.

The dragons welcomed everyone to their doorsteps. They had barter systems in place; more often than not, they preferred the chance to add to their hoards rather than accept currency.

Rowan herself had one chief interest in the neighborhood: Alessandro, the Dragon King.

The most powerful dragon to have ever lived.

He'd achieved godhood nearly three centuries ago, but, in a feat never heard of before, refused ascension.

He owned one of the private residences past a giant gate that was charmed to keep intruders out, even as it remained open.

For ages, she'd longed to come face to face with the shifter and to unleash her power against him, to see how she matched up to the most formidable Master Spellcaster of them all. But it was only a dream; she couldn't risk the consequences that came attached with showing her true prowess.

His magic, even without the godhood, was so grand that when he was in-house there wasn't an inch of the city or the suburbs she couldn't feel it from.

At that moment, she knew he wasn't in town, and perhaps that was the reason her sense of doom suddenly settled. Something was very wrong in Black Cove.

Rowan stood from her rolling chair as footsteps in the hallway approached her office, accompanied by two bickering voices.

"It was a fire dragon, look! The benches are melting!" The voice of Louisa Monterrey preceded the appearance of Rowan's two business partners.

Louisa was a fashionable, leggy brunette clad in a powder-blue three-piece suit with red stilettos that matched her glowing eyes. This, along with a pair of sharp incisors, was the dead giveaway of her vampire heritage.

Kin Smith—not his birth name, but the one he preferred—had already shed his suit jacket, rolled up his sleeves, and loosened his tie for the day.

His raven hair was as neat as his goatee, and his golden eyes, lined with an ever-present dark red kohl, cut a sharp look toward Rowan.

Had she not seen his transformation first-hand, she wouldn't have known that what stood before her was one of the largest kitsune shifters that had ever existed.

"I know you're going to want to get involved, but no one disturbs the dragons for a good reason." The lilt of his Japanese accent was only ever so prominent when his anxiety was up.

Rowan cocked her head to the side, and she leaned against her desk. "Get involved in what, exactly?"

Louisa dashed to her before Kin could hold her back, and she showcased the live footage of the mayhem that had been just out of Rowan's sight. Dew landed on her shoulder to watch.

Live streaming from the phone of an unfortunate bystander, sparring bodies of scaled dragons dotted the dark sky. Deafening roars and screams of the chaos made dread crawl up Rowan's spine.

Rowan glanced up. "Why are the dragons attacking?"

Louisa beamed at her, and Kin groaned.

"We cannot get involved with the dragons, Rowan." Kin clasped his hands, as if begging her to see reason.

Rowan only frowned. "There are people getting hurt. We have to help."

Louisa had a concerning shine of mischief in her eyes. "And maybe I can snag a dragon hottie to take out this weekend."

"They're going berserk. I think dating is the last thing on their minds." Kin snapped, but then let out a heavy breath. "I want it to be clear, when one of us dies, that I didn't want to get involved."

Rowan rolled her eyes and turned to Dew. "Sorry, it's an emergency. Take care of the office, okay?"

Dew, who was pale with fear, flew off her shoulder and gave a curt nod. "Please be careful."

Touched by her concern, Rowan smiled and gave her a reassuring nod.

The magic in the room tickled Rowan's nose as she gathered enough to send herself and her two partners to the heart of the battlefield.

-R-

The video did the fighting no justice. The roars of the dragons as they lunged for each other's throats and screeches of pain, combined with the scent of burning debris, pumped Rowan full of adrenaline.

"Communication established. Go for Louisa." Louisa's voice came through Rowan's head as they split up.

"I'll go for the bystanders and erect a blackout barrier. I'm guessing Rowan is going to try something she would rather the Coven not know she can do." Kin's voice rolled through her head.

Rowan's smile was unbidden. *"Kin, you're always two steps ahead of me."*

Magic thrummed in the air, slamming against her skin in the chaos of the dragons. It had always been eager to bow to her will, but Rowan recognized the abnormality of its desperation to sink into her pores.

To avoid overwhelming her body, she carefully opened herself to receiving a fraction of the power, enough to try to telepathically link into the mind of a nearby dragon. It was only half-transformed into its beast form, engaging in battle with a human form dragon who was attacking yet another, unaware of its impending doom.

The dragons were keeping the attacks amongst each other; anyone else who was getting hurt was collateral damage.

Where a mind should have been open to her request for communication, she slammed into a mental wall of musical notes as manic as the surrounding magic.

Her hangover reared its head with the sharp pain that split her skull. Groaning, she pushed past the discomfort to focus on the strange sound.

She poked at it with her magic, but she couldn't break through. The dragon took no notice of the normally offensive action.

"Kin, can you try linking with any of the dragons? All I hear is music when I try to tap in."

As a shifter himself, the kitsune had always been better at telepathic communication. As far as she knew, shifters were born with the gift.

"I hear the music, but I can't get access to them either. I see a fireball headed toward the gates, Louisa."

"I see it. On my way."

Rowan sidestepped the slicing power of air magic aimed at a blue behemoth of a dragon overhead; the force of it slapped her hair back in a wild torrent.

While it wasn't unusual for the dragons to take to the skies around Black Cove, seeing them engaged in battle rather than passing through was a much more horrific sight to behold. She couldn't imagine what the scene would be like if the biggest and baddest showed up and joined the fray.

His absence disappointed the part of her that yearned to meet, but the sane part of her knew it was better if the world never knew that kind of fear.

Underneath her feet, the ground trembled before piles of dirt exploded from the earth, became compact, and hurled toward a red, spiky-tailed dragon that moved through the sky with a speed that made her lose her breath as he passed next to her.

Rowan jumped from the debris before the makeshift weapons slammed against a fireball thrown from the back of a great maw five times the size of her body.

She landed on her feet, back in one of the newly formed craters. The rain was falling so heavily that pools of mud were being created.

Nausea from her quick descent rolled up in her throat. Rowan emptied her stomach, which eased a portion of the discomfort.

She cut her celebration short as a giant wall of fire appeared overhead and settled on the perimeter around the Estate and some portions of Dragon Alley.

Kin's spell was complete.

"These reporters don't seem to care if they get fried to get an exclusive look at the battle. Hurry with whatever you have up your sleeve."

Taking the words of her pseudo-PR manager into consideration, Rowan unclasped one of the two golden necklaces at the base of her throat. Her restrictions fell as she carefully tucked the piece of jewelry into her pocket.

Clarity rolled in as frantic magic filled her pores. It restored her body to the state before her intoxication. With unfiltered magic thrumming through her veins, Rowan was in peak form. Her senses kicked up a notch.

The smell of char was prevalent over the wet dirt. She heard the moment wings sliced through the air. Felt the magical signature of each creature alive on the field.

From the rain, the earth, the fire, and the howling wind, Rowan plucked even the tiniest morsels of elemental magic.

There was such a volume of it flying at her that her hands throbbed with their desire to lose it all back into the world. Her body was not used to accommodating so much at once, but she found it in herself to push past the discomfort until she absorbed every trace of magic around her.

A flash of her time at Spellcaster's Academy passed through her mind. As elementals, the dragons drew their power from these sources; it would take hours for the magic to fill back up. Therefore, it would take hours for the dragons to have access to their powers again.

In theory, it was a good plan. In practice, it was taking a lot longer than she expected for their already accrued power to run out.

It wasn't until a whole five minutes later, full of her casting spells of contrasting elements to divert some of the more lethal blows, that the rain pattered to sprinkles and the wind died down.

The howls and growls from the dragons turned into whines as the sky - bound bodies began to drop and transform mid-flight to the usual humanoid form dragons of modern times preferred. Wielding the enormous amount of magic she had taken, Rowan urged the Earth to beckon her call, and roots erupted from the grounds all over the estate, catching the bodies before they splattered on the ground. They retreated into their original pockets of earth as they laid the dragons down.

Even with their magic and energy wiped, the dragons were trying to crawl towards one another to sink their extended claws into each other's flesh. The oddest realization hit Rowan as she walked through their ranks, observing their half-hearted attempts.

Trails of tears rolled down splotchy red and purple faces.

It was only with the sudden silence following their onslaught that the notes of the song she'd heard in their minds hit her ear. She frowned as she walked past the bodies, pushing each of them apart with roots that re-emerged at her behest. It was the same song that she had heard rolling through their heads when she tried to communicate, full of notes so high and fervent it was a bid of desperation.

She had to launch herself past the dragons once she realized the sound was moving. As if it knew she was on its trail, it fell into silence.

Along with the sound leaving, the dragons also halted their attempts to harm each other. She watched as they fought against her spell and wailed through the silence, desperate to check on one another.

What in the endless hells?

Rowan had never been so confused in her 26 years of life. She, a Master Spellcaster from the top spell-casting academy, a pro at solving the most head scratching cases of magical incidents, had no idea what had just happened.

Slowly, the dragons seemed to realize there was an outsider in their midst, and they turned to her, weak but growing defensive. With practiced ease, she re-clasped the necklace, shrinking her connection to magic. She tried to ignore the hollow feeling the null charm filled her with.

Louisa appeared beside her in a smoky mist, her eyebrows coming together at the rise of the tension in the dragons.

"What's with the mood swings?" she scowled.

"Not sure." Rowan answered as she held her hands up in surrender, "We meant no harm; we just saw that your fight put innocent civilians in the line of fire. Your magic should return to normal within the hour."

A man with skin that reminded her of dark desert sand and bright emerald eyes was the first to stand up. It was only then that Rowan realized they had all reverted to their human forms completely naked.

The part of her kept under wraps during missions for work wanted to show her appreciation, but the professional side of her demanded she avert her eyes to focus on his face.

"How serious was the extent of the damage?"

Well, that made one thing clear: the dragons hadn't been aware of their destructive chaos. Rowan turned to Louisa, who was unabashedly roving her own ruby red eyes all over the naked man's body.

"How bad was the damage, Louisa?" Rowan repeated the question while she pinched the woman's arm.

Louisa sent her a glare as she rubbed the reddening spot before collecting herself enough to deliver the report, "The estate was in shambles by the time we showed up. The gate is obliterated, but you only got to two stores outside the entrance. No deaths. Two are in critical condition, and about a dozen civilians and police officers received treatment before being let go. As far as physical damage, that's it, but it's your reputation that took a much more serious hit. Dragons are protectors, not..." she trailed off, and her ruby - red eyes scanned the surrounding grounds.

"Not monsters out of control." The man finished, and he turned his fierce sight onto Rowan. "Who are you?"

She only then recognized the confusion in the man's eyes. A spellcaster who could accomplish what she just had should have been recognizable, but for as many years as she had been mastering her craft, she had been toeing a dangerously thin line of being anonymous or acclaimed. A chafing fact of her life that stung as she answered, "Just concerned citizens." Before waving her hand and phasing herself, Kin and Louisa back to the office.

Kin's usual attempt at staying incognito when they worked in the public eye was using glamor to change the appearance of his face. Much like Rowan, he kept a low profile whenever the cameras popped into action. His ability to remain totally anonymous made him indispensable in Rowan's life, as her pride sometimes begged her to reveal her name to the world despite the hovering circumstances.

"You can take people's powers?" His scowl was his sign of ultimate displeasure. Rowan was used to seeing it, so it didn't quite have the same effect it would on strangers.

Louisa slid into one of the two wingback chairs reserved for visiting guests and crossed her legs. "She didn't take their powers. She took the magic from nature itself, which is what juices up the dragons. The real question is whether they'll go berserk again as soon as they fill back up."

Rowan crossed her arms. "I heard some sort of wind instrument playing the same melody that was in their head. Once it stopped, so did the dragons. My gut says they're connected."

Kin's face rearranged itself to its natural state of sharp cheekbones and tidy goatee in an eerie, jigsaw fashion. "Do you two think you're just going to skate over the whole draining part of this?" he asked, placing his hands on his hips. "Since when have you been able to drain the power out of nature so completely that fifty dragons couldn't juice back up?"

"We've added two new nulling charms to my regimen. I think Master Japhet was right; my strength is increasing at an exponential rate."

It chafed. She liked the idea of being strong, but the true extent of her powers had been on lockdown since the first time she'd ever run into the Coven. They'd shown an uncomfortable interest in training her themselves. The last thing she wanted was to be a stooge for the world's biggest gang that ran under the cover of keeping the world "safe". In reality, they were just master hoarders of power.

"Do you think The Coven noticed?" She cringed just thinking about her visit with the Elder's granddaughter later.

"Maybe they weren't paying attention to your magical signature." Louisa tried to comfort.

Kin rolled his eyes. "Do you really believe they're not monitoring it with your meeting scheduled today?" He seemed taken aback by whatever crawled on her face at his words.

Years of witnessing stronger-than-usual mystics ripped from their families at the Coven's insistence that their lack of training and supervision would be detrimental to the safety of the public had filled her with nightmares.

Her father made sure she remained aware of the outcomes of each case since she'd been old enough to understand. Each time, it was as heartbreaking as it was enraging.

Kin's next words came out softer, "But they will have a hard time proving it when they hard-wire you to the power test unit."

Louisa sighed, "We really need to find a spellcaster stronger than you for that concealment charm."

Rowan's fingers touched the gold jewelry absentmindedly.

"For the moment, we have to hope what we have on it is enough. That's a matter for another day, though. Today, I need to make sure your combined client entertainment budget hasn't cut too far into our profits this quarter." He threw them both an icy glare before stalking out of the office.

"Didn't we dine and wine those jerks under his instructions?" Louisa stuck her tongue out at the empty doorway before her posture softened, and she turned to Rowan. "He is right. You've already surpassed my mother. It was a blissful two weeks when she wouldn't talk to me with how angry she was."

Rowan sighed. "I just hope when the Coven decides I'm too big a threat, that they leave my family out of it."

"Hey, if they make a move against you, they make a move against the North American Brood, the Eastern Elven Kingdom, and Master Jah. They know better."

Rowan smiled and squeezed the vampiress' hand as she walked to her own chair.

The Eastern Elven Kingdom would indeed go to war for one of its princesses. But the vampires and the excommunicated Master who had once been her mentor were up in the air.

The North American Brood held traditional vampire culture in high esteem. One of the most fundamental of those traditions was bleeding humans straight from the source, regardless of the havoc the act caused in human immune systems. The research that highlighted this side of vampire feedings had come out after Louisa had already begun practicing. While most new-generation vampires had no problem swearing off the practice, they had an easier time than the older generation, who had experienced the pleasure that came from drinking from a warm body. A pleasure comparable to when a succubus took in sexual energy. Warm, freeing, pure ecstasy.

Louisa was one of the few who'd experienced the high but walked away rather than risk the consequences. It wasn't in her nature to harm. This, above all, made her an unpopular choice for the North American Brood heir. It was only Louisa's above-reproach proficiency with the dark arts that earned her any morsel of respect. Talent, hand in hand with the fact that her mother, Rosario the Cruel-aptly named- was the current Grand Vampire, cemented Louisa's position.

Once, Master Japhet would have looked forward to declaring war against the Coven if they so much as breathed in Rowan's direction wrong. He used to look forward to a fight with the organization. But, in a recent development, he had found the love of his life. Years full of vacations alone with his beloved made him complacent and too happy to risk a back-slide into violence that he'd known too well.

Like Rowan's father, Master Jah had been through enough war to last a dozen lifetimes. Rowan would do everything in her power that all of her loved ones lived in days of peace if she could help it.

"It saddens me to ask this, after such sweet words, but what in the world did you do to make Mitchell Tech call me?"

Louisa grimaced for half a second before a cool mask slid into place. She stood. "Not the slightest clue. I really should get back to my work and follow our Kin's lead."

She was gone before Rowan could say another word.

Rowan groaned and turned to her phone. Sometimes, it sucked to be the point of contact for their minor operation.

II

Alessandro had only left Dragon City minutes after the news reached him. Still, he had been too late. By the time he arrived at the smoldering gate of Draconis, there was a barrier of fire installed that made the wrecked grounds past the gate invisible to outsiders.

The press, lined up behind metal dividers right outside of demolished storefronts, talked to a calm, black-haired dragon who was assuring everyone that everything was under control.

He stalked onto the grounds, and astonishment roiled through him as he took in the sight of roots as thick as some full-grown trees reaching towards the sky. He watched as several earth dragons worked in groups to get a single root back into its rightful place when it should have taken one dragon per tree.

No building on the estate remained intact, and a group of wind dragons manually cleared the debris-strewn ground instead of using magic.

Slowly, eyes turned to him, and as they realized who had arrived, they fell to their knees, casting their eyes away.

Alessandro scowled and crossed his arms, a tendril of smoke escaping his nose. "What happened?" He demanded.

From the group of dragons working on the roots, a woman with a honey-hued afro, dark skin, and glacial hazel eyes stood to address him. Alessandro wasn't surprised she was the first to stand. Terra was not only his Earth General but, as his younger sister and second-in-command, was best equipped to receive and temper his foul mood.

"My Lord, we have yet to find the cause. One second we were of normal temperament; the next, blinded by absolute rage, aimed toward each other. We would have resorted to killing, but a white-haired elf showed up and..." She was hesitant to continue. "She drained us of our magic."

Alessandro took a moment to process what she'd said. "An elf came and took down over 50 dragons with a bit of draining magic?"

"A bit?" Blaise, his Fire General and the youngest of the Draconian Thunder Elemental Generals, had pin-straight red hair that reached past his shoulder blades. His liquid amber eyes shone with irritation as he recalled the elf. "She damn near drained all of nature dry and..." He motioned towards the trees, "...left this mess for us to deal with, as if our own mess hadn't been big enough." He pointed toward the collapsed buildings of the estate.

Alessandro felt his hackles raise.

An elf, a fucking little elf, had come into his estate and eaten his dragons' magic? "None of you thought to stop her? Was she behind your madness?"

"No." Terra answered once again, and the shame behind her words was most highlighted in her hung head. Alessandro felt his shoulders soften a little at the raw display of regret. He wondered if she would ever stop being such a soft spot for him. "We were attacking each other before she showed up. The only reason we stopped was because she ate our magic stores. Even after that, we tried to kill each other with our claws if that's what it had to come down to, and so she wrapped us in roots to keep us from reaching each other. If she was behind the attack, I'm sure she would have just let us finish each other off, but she waited until we regained control to leave as quickly as she had come to our aid. We don't know what made us lose our minds, my Lord, but it was not the elf."

Alessandro sighed and rubbed his eyes. "Everyone broke out in this fury at the same time?" He asked, looking around the group. Heads nodded solemnly. Swallowing pride was difficult. Dragons had little practice with it. "No one has any idea what triggered it?" He asked again, hoping for a different answer, but no such luck. "Alright, healers, come to me. I'll speed along your recovery. Once I'm done, you'll do it to the non-healers."

"Yes, my lord."

Alessandro would never admit how creepy he found the unified response.

"Enough with the 'lords'. I despise when you all use that to appease me, and would you stand straight? You look like damn ostriches." Alessandro motioned the first healer forward and began trying to gather the natural magic in his practiced way. Trying being the operative word. The surrounding magic hadn't replenished. What elf could be so thorough in wiping out their source of power?

Though elves were elemental-based mystics, they were never so talented at wielding it at this level.

A chill went up his spine as he tapped into his celestial power and sped the replenishing process along until he had enough magic on his lands to heal his dragons.

Terra, who had stood up to her full, towering figure, watched over her king as he taught the healers what he was doing. He dispatched them to help the others, then turned to her.

"Who is the elf?"

Terra glanced over to his Air General, Naseem. Bald head drenched in blood and mud, the green-eyed shifter answered as if he'd been awaiting this question from the moment Alessandro appeared. "We believe her name is Rowan Dahl, my lord, but she didn't want to give it to us. She introduced herself only as a concerned citizen."

Alessandro snorted a laugh as he began walking through the crumbled remains of Draconis, sending out feelers for magic signatures that were not dragon, or—he still couldn't believe it—elven.

"And what do we know of Rowan Dahl?" He questioned as he worked, and both dragons fell into step.

Terra answered this time, and it occurred to Alessandro that the two were sharing the burden of responsibility. An indicator of how severe the case was, considering how every dragon always tried to avoid getting on Alessandro's bad side, even if they had to throw someone else under the bus to redirect attention. "She was in Stone's Spellcasters' graduating class. Apparently, the Coven has been interested in her since her entrance exam, when she used an unorthodox solution for the initial test."

"Which was?" He asked, annoyed he even had to prompt.

"They had to fight their way out of a water bubble surrounded by a barrier. Most people swam to the barrier's edge and broke it, causing the bubble to erupt. She changed the water into air. Without the pressure of possibly drowning, she established a record. It was the last time she displayed her abilities in public, though. She kept average grades and an average social life for a Spellcaster student throughout her time there. Stone says there were few instances that she did things normal elves were not capable of, but the most notable things that happened came after graduation. Master Japhet took her under his tutelage. That's all I got from Stone before I sent him to face the press. He's by far the most charming of us all."

"Indeed." Alessandro stopped over where the dining hall's patio had once stood in shining glory but now lay in shattered pieces of wood, glass, and concrete. There was an ancient signature of magic blended into the ground. Evidence of the caster trying to scrub their presence existed in the missing links of the magical signature.

His displeasure manifested in his scales roiling over his hands. He really didn't like unknown threats running amuck in his territory, and he realized even if the elf had saved his dragons from irreparable damage, she was one of two new threats.

-R-

Standing at well over six feet with a face of sharp angles that made her a very attractive middle-aged woman, Cherry Young instantly gave the impression that she was not to be trifled with.

Her hair, ginger and peppered with streaks of white, was coiffed neatly at the base of her neck. It matched her all-business attire of a navy pencil skirt and blazer set with a white satin blouse underneath. Her heels tapped on the hardwood floor as she entered the room, louder in Rowan's head than it probably was in reality.

The triumph in her sage green eyes was enough to let Rowan know the Coven had indeed felt her unleash her power with the dragons.

But as the woman sank into the chair on the other side of her desk, Rowan also noted a hint of sorrow.

The only explanation that came to mind was the recent death of Elder Henrietta Young. Though the woman had been Cherry's grandmother, the two had never seemed close on the few occasions Rowan had spent time with them.

"Was it worth it?" Cherry asked, without a single show of pleasantry. After all, she had what she had looked forward to for half a decade: a weakness in the lie that Rowan's true powers were ordinary.

Rowan shrugged, "I assure you, I don't know what you're talking about."

Cherry scowled, "We've only ever offered you membership to our community; it is not a punishment, but an honor to serve alongside us."

"Right." Rowan rolled her eyes and held her arm out. "You're more than welcome to test my blood. I am nothing but a slightly above average elf spellcaster."

Painful as the power test unit was, it was the quickest way to get the Coven off her back. The first time all seven needles attached to the black box had pierced all of Rowan's chakra points, she had almost passed out from the heat that traveled through her veins as the box tested every single node in her body. Two hours every month over the length of ten years had helped her develop mental barriers to the pain while it was happening, but the aftercare of the sessions wore her ragged for at least three days after.

Cherry shook her head and snapped her fingers. In her hand appeared a thick, brown, leather-bound book with glowing runes etched upon its spine. It filled the office with the scents of moths and spices.

Taken by surprise, Rowan leaned forward to examine the pulsing characters. "Is that what I think it is?"

The witch's eyes misted. Rowan feared the witch would fall into tears, but she regained control and slammed it onto Rowan's desk.

"If you think it's the Elder's Grimoire, then yes. Rowan Dahl, I, Cherry Young, am here to execute the last request of Henrietta Young; you are free, regardless of your true power levels, from the Coven's recruitment efforts. You are also here unto bequeathed with the Elder's Grimoire for fourteen days, which, when finished, you will return the grimoire to me, or so help me gods; I will raze this entire block and your familial palace to get it back."

Rowan's jaw dropped, and she looked from the book to the witch to the book again. "Um, I'll take the freedom part, but maybe you can keep the book?"

"No." Cherry pulled her hands back from the grimoire and curled them into fists at her side. "You take the freedom and the book together, or you get neither."

Still astounded by what she was being offered, Rowan narrowed her eyes at the witch. "Why in the endless hells did your grandmother want me to have it? I thought it was only supposed to pass on to the next elder."

"I do not know. I do not even really care. All I am concerned with is that you give it back. Do you understand me, Rowan Dahl?" Cherry looked as if she was imagining shaking the elf to make sure she understood the depth of her seriousness.

Rowan scowled and crossed her arms, taking a beat to think it over. It was enticing, the prospect of freedom from the monthly visits of witches determined to get her to work for the Coven. The grimoire not only held witch spells, but information Coven Elders gathered during their tenure and committed to pages, including, but not limited to: prophecies, recipes for potions, historic events, analysis on issues facing the mystic community.

But if she lost the book, the witches would make good on Cherry's promise. If word got out that the Elder's Grimoire had left the safety of the Coven Compound, she would have to beat off hoards of mystics who wanted a look at the damn thing.

Still, Henrietta had been a clairvoyant and a damn precise one. If her last request was for Rowan to receive a relic of the Coven, hand in hand with an offer she couldn't refuse, the witch would have had a reason for it. Could the elf trust these conditions to be in her favor?

Rowan sighed and dragged the grimoire closer to her, not missing how Cherry flinched.

"I'll take care of it. I promise." It was the softest tone she had ever used with the witch, and when she saw the woman relax, she knew it had been the right move.

-A-

Alessandro had used his proficiency with earth magic to help his dragons rebuild the Draconis Estate to its former glory of sprawling houses, libraries, and dining halls. He was sweating; the combination of physical action and the cold, ambrosia-laced beer in his hand had cooled his temper

Night was overtaking Black Cove, and lanterns were the only source of light as he wrapped up his speech to the Thunder.

Yes, they had been attacked, but it was only because they'd been unaware of a threat out in the world that would dare to entice their wrath. Now that they shook off their complacency, it was time to tighten security on Draconis Estate, and a select few would investigate more deeply into what had caused them to attack one another.

Naseem would lead that expedition, while Alessandro took charge of the other threat they faced, one that he hadn't voiced but one that his dragons had brought to his attention. What of the elven woman?

It had been too easy for her to take their magic, and if they hadn't been hurt from their battle with each other, he had to know if she was a threat against their physical prowess.

As he considered how best to test the woman, a familiar ripple of power hit the barrier he had reinforced around Draconis. With a wave of his hand the witch appeared before him, his bald head shining with the moonlight peeking through the redbuds, his eyes half hooded with drink and a goofy grin that didn't quite go with his giant viking beard or towering body lined with muscles.

"Japhet, thank you for answering my call."

"Of course, Dragon King, our friendship is worth too much for me to ignore you in your time of need."

Alessandro wanted to sneer. Friendship? Their relationship was just one favor, gained and paid for over two centuries, and Japhet knew it was Alessandro's turn to demand payment.

"The Coven has its eye on an elf. One who has powers beyond natural elven limits?" Alessandro went straight to the point. If he wasn't careful, the witch would go on a tangent that would last several hours.

Japhet seemed to only comprehend what he wanted after a minute of silence.

"Do you mean the Dahl girl?" His voice showed that he was reluctant to talk about her.

"Yes, your one and only apprentice."

Japhet, whom Alessandro had known as brash and impulsive, was behaving too calculated to fit his normal MO. "What did she do to bring the Dragon King's wrath to her doorstep?"

"Drained the natural magic reserves all over Draconis and called the roots from my trees like they were twigs."

Japhet's nose flared. "The Coven won't let her get away with that. Do you know how tenuous peace has been between them and the Eastern Elven Kingdom since that elf got into Spellcasters?" Japhet demanded "I keep telling them, they're going to provoke the Bloody Elf too much one day and I doubt they're going to let her just be now."

"Kyron, the Bloody Elf?"

During the elven-dwarf wars, the Bloody Elf had become well-known for his ruthlessness on the field. A war of territory. Alessandro doubted the Bloody Elf appreciated one of his subjects being eyeballed by the Coven.

"Is there another Bloody Elf I don't know about?" Japhet asked dryly, and waved off the glare Alessandro sent him. "Yes, Kyron the Bloody Elf. That's the one."

"So tell me about the woman, Japhet."

Japhet sized the dragon up, perhaps trying to determine his intentions. Alessandro was sure the witch counted on his massive body to be an intimidating factor to push people to do his bidding, but the Dragon King was full of his own muscle along with magic so ancient Japhet's would wither before he so much as finished his first spell.

"She isn't a threat to you, if that's what you're trying to figure out."

Alessandro raised an eyebrow. "I would prefer to be the one to determine that."

Taking a seat on one of the bistro tables, Japhet put his feet up and turned his head towards the sky, "When she was younger, she saved a witch. One of my wards. Perhaps you've heard of her? Chloe Darling?"

"The null." Alessandro nodded his head. He'd heard the woman's abilities to cancel out magic had been extraordinary, to the point she could null a Master Spellcaster's power at the tender age of six. As an adult, she had harnessed that power into everyday jewelry. Her Darling brand was a household staple among humans and weaker magicked mystics.

"During a visit to Incindria in the winter, Chloe had been playing in the woods that separate it from the Eastern Elven Kingdom with some children. She had gotten so lost that she found her way into troll territory during mating season. As I'm sure you know, aggression levels in trolls are high during that time, and one of them caught her."

Yes, Alessandro had an unfortunate memory of his own troll encounter tucked in the back of his brain. If he really thought about it too hard, the stench of their nests would come back to haunt him.

"Chloe is not a warrior, by any means of the word. Her physical strength is really quite lacking, and with nulling being her only magical ability, she was pretty much dead meat. Until, from out of nowhere, another girl shows up and starts demanding that the troll let go, lest she face her wrath." Japhet shook his head and laughed, still refusing to meet the Dragon King's eye, and Alessandro felt in that moment the fact that the witch had quite the soft spot for the elf. "As any self-respecting troll would do when threatened by an eight-year-old elf, the troll also took Rowan captive. Rowan didn't know she was in the presence of a null, so when her powers weren't coming to her as easily as they had in the past, she got angry; so angry that she cried. Her wails were so loud and shrill that we heard them from Incindria, and the elves heard them from the Eastern Elven Kingdom. By the time we arrived, three trolls had somehow been bound by vines that weren't native to that forest and had blooms of flowers that released a gas to put the trolls to sleep. Rowan had been undoing Chloe's binds with her magic."

The implication was blatant for Alessandro; at eight years old, Rowan had surpassed Master levels of magic.

"Just how did the Eastern Elven Kingdom keep her a secret for so many years? How has the Coven not gotten its claws into her?" The Coven had a nasty habit of poaching incredibly gifted spellcasters from weaker races, like the elves. It should have been easy, considering how much mistrust the public had against spellcasters left to their own devices. There should have been outcries for her to be kept in check by the many bylaws of the Coven.

"Well," Japhet groaned and turned his gaze to Alessandro, "Do you mind supplying me with some whiskey since your bloody barriers keep my powers nulled?" Alessandro scowled, but conjured a bottle and two glasses onto the patio table. He took the other seat and sat to pour them both drinks.

"Ambrosia-laced." Japhet sighed with admiration after his first sip. "You really want me jabbering away, don't you?"

"Well, she took on my dragons and won, so yes, I'm invested in your tale."

Japhet laughed, "Fair enough, I suppose. Where was I? Oh, yes, when the Coven heard of the situation from a witch that had traveled with me, they foamed at the mouth to get their hands on her. Everyone wanted to know what Rowan Dahl was about. But Rowan wasn't interested in those kinds of things. She was interested in fashion, cute boys, and sweets. In those days, you could ask her to do anything with the promise of a cannoli."

The twinkle in his eye was clearer now that Alessandro was closer. He had never seen the man so tender. Even if the woman had been an apprentice, it was strange for Japhet to express any sort of emotion like that.

"King Kyron knew if the Coven got their hands on her, the girl would change for the worse, so he hired me to protect her." He shook his head. "Can you imagine? He trusted a witch to hide his precious daughter's powers from more witches? I thought he was insane, but Rowan and Chloe had bonded from their near-death experience, and so Chloe also demanded it of me. With the help of a couple of witches who owed me favors, we fashioned concealment charms while a phoenix monk and I taught her how to access the bare minimum of her magic to show the Coven when they tested her. It worked. We convinced them it had just been a fluke when she could only light three of the ten bars on the Power Test Unit. It only rated her a step above a normal elf of her age. The Coven left her alone until Spellcasters Academy."

"One of my dragons studied with her. He said she revealed a bit of her true self when she took the entrance exam."

Japhet's anger lived in the fierce scowl that had his eyes glowing, it was a mark of the witch's magical aptitude for such a thing to happen within Alessandro's wards, "Someone rigged her test, the water burned her skin, so of course she got out of there as fast as she could. She only showed a portion of her talent, and the Coven knew it. The harassment began. They sent representative after representative for her until they got to Cherry Young."

"The granddaughter of the late Elder?"

"Yes, the compulsion master. She tried to use her powers on her, but Chloe had learned how to make nulling charms by that point. She gifted Rowan with a locket for her birthday. It stopped the attack, but Rowan had had enough. She agreed to go through PTU assessment on a monthly basis, and if it ever got higher than just above average for an elf, she would join, no questions asked. Cherry, unable to compulse her, agreed. Since then, the Coven has been keeping a close eye on the girl, and the girl has been stacking herself up with concealment charms." The witch looked almost miserable at his next words. "I don't know the limits of her strength. I doubt even she does, with how she's had to fly under the radar for so long. It's a pity. You should have seen the flowers on those vines, Alessandro. Now she's making a living cleaning up the messes of spellcasters who don't understand magic the way she does. Pretty profitable business of hers. You might have heard of it? RLK Magical Disaster Services, worth millions after only five years in business."

No, he hadn't, and his not knowing was a problem. He'd become too complacent in this age of peace. The oversight had hurt his dragons.

"You know." Japhet's eyes watered as he said the next words, "She's more than just that power."

"Do you love this woman, Japhet?" Alessandro was stunned. He had never seen the witch act this way. Was it the drink?

Japhet laughed, "I suppose I've never really considered that, but the brat is one of the few people I consider mine and precious in this damned world." Even drunk, Alessandro understood the witch's next words to be said with all the sobriety the world offered. "So understand when I say that if you make her life miserable, I will come to avenge her. Any pain you cause, I will deal threefold, and I won't care that I am marking my card for death; I will make sure I take you down with me."

III

Freedom.

Rowan laughed from her belly as she soared through the setting sun's orange skies at breakneck speed.

Just for fun, she stopped her forward propulsion and dropped like a stone over a roaring body of water, and as she saw it approaching, she tilted herself until she was diving headfirst.

Calling the wind to wrap around her in an air bubble, she penetrated the surface, coming into the midst of a school of bright pink fish. She took in the sea life as she continued forward — the coral banks, the stingray that soared along her side as if trying to race for a while. She broke the surface again and took off back into the sky, shouting her elation.

This is what she had been missing. Her connection to the surrounding magic was energizing. It made every hair on her body prickle to attention as it rushed into her pores, seeking to connect after years of sewing concealment charms into all of her clothes. After being afraid of taking too much magic to mold. She let it all in. Her skin glowed. The world around her sang.

By the time she zoomed over the Eastern Elven Kingdom, the sun had totally set, and the streetlights were embers in their casings.

Elves liked their starlight more than seeing each other on the cobbled streets.

The castle was no exemption. Only a few of the windows danced with light as nobles moved within their living quarters.

The royal apartment was the one on the highest tower, with carved French doors and billowing curtains on the balcony, which overlooked the kingdom from the top of a mountainside.

She landed on the rail; the aroma of oils and spices wafted into her nose as she entered a dining room holding six people at the table, who turned to greet her.

Manners instilled in her from her Southern Elven Kingdom mother, she had to stop by and hug each of her family members on her way to her seat.

King Kyron sat at the head of the table, wearing a black button-up with the sleeves rolled up to his elbows. Usually he hid the sprawling tattoos in the presence of his subjects. He had his white hair buzzed to the scalp, excluding the two inches he allowed on top. His beard was thicker and longer every time Rowan saw him, now reaching past his chest. He was the calm center of the family, tranquility contagious.

Rowan had only seen him shed the calm and become the Bloody Elf once in her life. It had been when she turned to him for help in cutting the monthly visit deal with the Coven.

She had brought him along for reassurance, more for the use of the calm energy he oozed than the rage he carefully kept tucked away within himself, but when Cherry attempted to entrap them in a more strict agreement, he lashed out and sent the guards accompanying the witch to emergency treatment as a warning.

As disturbed as she had been to see that side of her father, his blood-thirst was effective in securing a fair agreement.

He tapped her arm lovingly. "Hello, kiddo. You smell...like the sea?"

Rowan grinned down at him. "I took a little dip on my flight here."

Annabelle Dahl, her mother, had her black hair done in complex braids. Beads and hoops shone through strands. A practice from her birthplace that she'd passed on to her daughters. She was in a cotton wrap dress with a frilly pink apron Rowan had once gotten her as a gag gift. Annabelle loved it so much that she wore it to every family dinner, even if it wasn't her turn to cook.

"Flight?" Her mother's eyebrows furrowed as Rowan dropped a kiss of greeting on her forehead. "With your wings?"

Rowan shook her head, "No. Flight with my magic."

Axel, her second eldest sister, narrowed her eyes. "Magic flight? I thought you were supposed to be using the bare minimum outside of your work."

She was still in her military uniform, a forest-green, silken tunic embroidered with gold. Her collar had her commander insignia, a golden tree with five branches shining in the low candlelight. Thick curls braided away from her face, much like their mother's, Axel's tension set on her shoulders.

The most adept of the Dahl sisters in combat, both in strength and strategy, their father had employed her abilities to lead the intelligence division of his army, often sending her and his field division leader to take care of foreign enemies if things needed to be strong-armed. More nosy than overprotective, she asked uncomfortable questions without so much as a flinch.

On Axel's left, Rowan's eldest sister, Lexine, had her own white hair let down. It fell past the middle of her back in soft waves that asked to have fingers running through them by simply existing. She had donned a simple pink sundress that draped over her heavily pregnant belly, and she beamed at Rowan as she raised her hand when Rowan approached her and patted her hair. "Well, that explains the windswept appearance. Hun, will you go get Rowan a hairbrush?"

Rowan's fingers slid through her hair before she conjured her own brush.

Lexine's husband raised an eyebrow, already halfway to standing.

His black hair was a fluff of curls that Rowan had once run her hands through in childhood and swore that's what clouds should have really felt like. Initially, the son of a Stable Master, Rowan's close friendship with the man had lulled the royals and the common folk into a false sense of security that even if the friendship blossomed into something more, the Stable Master could not touch the throne with Rowan's fourth in line status.

Black-haired elves were rare in the Eastern Elven Kingdom. Superstitions painted them as ominous signs, even though their queen was also raven-haired.

When Rowan left for Spellcasters Academy, she'd asked her family to look out for her friend. Lexine found she enjoyed the company of the crass man so much that she decided they were to be married the next year.

Atlas didn't fight back. He'd spent their pre-teen years confiding in Rowan that Lexine was his dream woman, though he dared not approach. Years later, Rowan found it nauseating to be around the insufferable lovebirds for more than a couple of hours.

The relationship had sparked outrage and calls for Lexine's removal from the succession. Axel and Rowan extinguished the worst of the threats, particularly those that put violent plans to assassinate the heiress and her lover into action.

Critics of the relationship soon sang a new tune as Atlas and Lexine established new relations with foreign lands that brought more opportunities and gold to the common folk of the Eastern Elven Kingdom.

"What's changed?" Her mother's patience had run out. Not that it was long to start with.

"Well," Rowan began, as she curled her arms around Zeva, the second-youngest, who sat across from Lexine and hadn't torn her eyes from the book she'd been reading as Rowan said her hellos.

Her white hair was in a messy bun she had streaked with aquamarine dye, much to their father's disapproval. She wore a pair of jeans, an oversized hoodie, and a pair of new sneakers Rowan was sure cost as much as Lexine's high-end heels. Her collection of glasses was as extensive as Rowan's collection of daggers.

"I am officially free."

Zeva, who'd dropped her book and was trying to escape the playful chokehold by nibbling on Rowan's forearms, froze her attempts.

Zeva's superpower was her intelligence. Last time Rowan had checked, the woman had a dozen degrees from universities all around the world. They varied as much as her interests, and had taken her on expeditions all over the world. Whether it was an architectural dig or a scientific discovery, Zeva just wanted to learn new things all the time. She wasn't shy about sharing what she learned. She had helped Rowan master some of the more challenging spell works and through the summers held seminars to ensure the children of the Eastern Elven Kingdom all had equal access to education.

She was the first to react after Rowan's declaration. "Free?"

"One of the late Elder's last requests was for the Coven to leave me alone. I can use my magic without restraint now!" Rowan clarified. "I just flew here to test the limits, and no one stopped me."

"Really?" Lexine gasped.

"Does that mean I can have a tag-along flight?" Axel grinned.

"Does this mean you can set a permanent portal to your cabin so I can visit your library whenever?" Zeva gasped.

Rowan narrowed her eyes and reinforced her chokehold. "You mean visit me, right?"

Zeva laughed nervously, "Of course I did!"

"Absolutely not, it's already hard enough to get you out on the few occasions that you go." Annabelle's annoyance shone in the hint of a Spanish accent.

"It will be easier to get me out if I know I can return whenever I want. Please, ma?" Zeva clasped her hands together.

When Annabelle didn't seem to want to budge, Zeva turned watery eyes to her sisters.

"Well..." Axel began, "We could use the portal as an auxiliary escape route in case there's ever an attack on the castle."

"And imagine how easy it will be to visit anytime you want!" Lexine grinned.

Rowan glared at her sister and only got a laugh in response.

Annabelle seemed terribly tempted by the offer.

"Are you sure the Coven isn't employing an underhanded attempt to capture you?" Kyron asked, clearly concerned.

Rowan had considered this before even leaving the office, but shook her head. "I don't think so. They gave me the Elder's Grimoire as collateral."

Finally releasing her sister, Rowan slid into the chair between her mother and Zeva.

Blank faces stared back at her, and Rowan had to remember that her family didn't live in her world or have a common understanding of magic. With elves being so limited in their abilities with the stuff, they naturally were ignorant of one of the most treasured magical artifacts in the world.

"It's a really important book to the Coven, only passed between the previous Elder and the next. It's got loads of magical secrets etched into its pages."

"Ooh, do you think it has a recipe for how to find you a proper partner so I can finally have an army of grandchildren?" Annabelle's eyes shimmered at the prospect.

Rowan sighed, "Ama, I think there are a few more interesting entries."

"Well, I will just remind you that you have given me full permission to go to war with the witches if they decide to rescind their offer." King Kyron grinned. "I'm excited to see where your freedom takes you, little one."

There was something about his voice that sealed the deal as real to Rowan, and she grinned back. "Thanks, Dad."

The rest of dinner passed by as they caught up on each other's lives. Work stress mostly, and Zeva's divulgence of where she planned to head for her next expedition.

There were a few castle intrigues thrown in here and there.

Rowan was keen to keep up on Miasma, the phoenix medical healer who was Lexine's counterpart in the medical wing. While Lexine was the surgical and mundane wound expert, Miasma's focus was on magical maladies.

Lexine had brought Miasma on board after the first year Rowan went into business. While at that point, Rowan had already been living in her inherited cabin, she'd made several trips home to see Lexine for wounds that were out of her older sister's depth. As she and Atlas traveled for several diplomatic trips, she ran into the healer during a festival in Incindria.

She'd been homeless and so anxious that she began crying when Lexine approached her.

Rowan couldn't blame anyone for being anxious when Lexine first approached them. There was an otherworldly beauty to her eldest sister that took time to get used to. Even five months pregnant with twins, she was undoubtedly the most beautiful woman in the Eastern Elven Kingdom.

The rainbow-haired woman had caught the princess' eye. She'd been healing a cat, and her magic called to Lexine, who'd been on a float during the festival.

Her departure had caused the eyes of hundreds to follow her and doubled the shaking of the phoenix.

Axel had nearly imploded with rage when she realized her sister had dragged the girl from the streets of their neighboring kingdom.

Lexine ordered her to figure out how to make it okay while she worked on getting the phoenix settled.

It had been Axel's first day in charge.

It didn't take long for the rest of the family to see what had ensnared Lexine.

Music.

Lexine's love for the arts had decorated her entire wing with several collections of statues and portraits of her own creation. But she'd been abysmal at music.

Couldn't hold a note to save her life. As an elf, it was a real shame, as music was only below starlight on the list of what most elves adored.

The first time Rowan had heard the phoenix sing, she'd wept in her hospital bed, texting her family to come and listen. They'd all fallen asleep on her tiny recovery bed while Miasma sang to her heart's content.

Since then, they'd sent each other recordings of the phoenix when she slipped into song, convinced no one was around to hear.

They wrapped the evening up by crowding around Atlas, who had been the last one to sneak a recording in.

"It's a pop song." Lexine's eyes misted.

At the beginning of her stay, Miasma only sang sad songs that tore at Rowan's heart. Over the years, they'd become slightly less melancholy, but this was the first time she was singing something that was full of joy.

Zeva smiled softly, Axel looked awed, Atlas and Kyron both stood and held their hands out to their women.

The recording launched a playlist of songs that had the entire royal family dancing around the table, laughing with the simple joy of just being together.

The clock shone midnight when they called it a night.

Rowan's family watched as she took off into the sky from the railings of the balcony, and whistles of joy and approval reached her.

Rowan couldn't help but grin, which dropped after an insect flew into her teeth.

While flying from Black Cove to the Eastern Elven Kingdom was doable, because only a couple hundred of miles separated them, heading back home was a different story.

Rowan felt out the tendrils of her bonds.

Bonds were magic that kept her connected to her entire family, both chosen and born to. It allowed her to feel where they were physically situated in the world, allowing her to phase instantly to their side if she needed to. She could also feel their health in case it ever sharply declined, and if they were near enough, a chance to link mentally without the requirement of a spell.

Her bond with her cabin was unorthodox. Had it been a regular building it wouldn't have worked, but the Traveling Cabin was a space and time anomaly and had a shred of sentience to it. That shred allowed Rowan to connect it to a network usually exclusive to bio organisms.

She phased from the sky over the Eastern Elven Kingdom to mountain cliffs overlooking a twinkling town about 25 miles away.

The magical cabin she called home had a habit of moving on its own. That morning she'd woken up in the middle of a desert, settled next to a lush oasis, the day before in a humid swamp, nestled high in the branches of ancient trees.

Even with the size suggested by the ebony wood logs and floor to ceiling windows that sparkled with candlelight, the cabin was even bigger on the inside. It had once belonged to Rowan's paternal great Aunt Liza, an elf obsessed with magic. The mansion included hidden treasures like an endless library she hadn't finished exploring, a shrine to a goddess Rowan and Zeva had worked for years trying to give a name to and a maze of hallways that would sometimes give access to the room you needed rather than wanted.

The cabin concealed Rowan's powers better than any other charm and she found out she could cast any spell within its walls without repercussion. It sent a tingle of pleasure up her spine to realize that now she would be free to do what she wanted even outside of its walls.

The laugh that was on the tip of her lips died out as a torrent of icicles went flying past her face.

Her guard had been down.

Rookie move, Dahl.

She tasted her blood as she drew up a personal barrier, her eyes locking on the figure vaulting up with a fist pulled back, eyes swirling with all the colors of the rainbow. Dark curls danced behind him as his magic exploded against her barrier, sparks ignited from the friction and, seemingly with little effort, he shattered her protection.

Stunned with recognition, she almost missed the window to parry the punch before she launched into her own swing, which he blocked and then did the oddest thing by interlocking their fingers together.

Heat crawled up from her chest, her breath caught, disbelief prevalent in her mind.

She took a moment to take in the giant leather wings behind him, so dark they blended into the night, the solid chin she knew would break her fingers if she tried to land a punch and the deep pink color of his lips that struck a chord with something primal inside of her body.

Taken by surprise by the familiar feeling of lust rolling off of him in turbulent waves, Rowan froze; she stayed frozen even as his face got closer and closer and then his lips were on hers.

She stayed still until he pulled back and smiled down at her. "It's nice to meet you, Rowan Dahl. I am the Dragon King, Alessandro." His eyes landed on a glowing red as he stared down at her.

Rowan didn't know why, but her eyes were suddenly heavy and the center of her forehead was burning. She tried to say something cool, anything to break the unbearable tension inside, but darkness took her instead.

IV

There was something in the way the elf woman moved as she awoke that sent Alessandro's dragon into cautious overdrive.

Like water lapping on a lakeshore, the woman's softness was deceptive. The undertow was the reality of her immense magical capacity.

A magical capacity that was indeed unheard of in elf kind, but even more interesting, the woman's aura was glowing with a rare gift that he'd seldom seen in real life.

Bright blue eyes took in his visage. Confusion quickly morphed into something predatory.

It was beyond rare for anything to look at him with such eyes. He was Alessandro, king not only to his dragons, but to all beasts.

Yet, a woman of barely five feet tall stared at him as if he were a walking, talking piece of meat.

Her soft inhalation of the temperature controlled caves didn't go unnoticed, nor the lavender glow that passed through her eyes in a flash.

A fucking succubus?

"Alessandro the Dragon King." She spoke the words with a slight smile.

She was challenging him. Annoyance intermingled with his curiosity. Her magic level had seemed to diminish as she became more and more alert. Where it currently was, there would have been no way that she'd be able to do what she had in Draconis.

Suppression magic? If Chloe Darling was in the picture, it was no surprise.

Just how potent was that magic underneath it?

"Rowan Dahl, Princess of the Eastern Elven Kingdom."

She seemed annoyed by the title and Alessandro found he enjoyed inciting that emotion from her.

"Is this where I think it is?" She shed the annoyance in a split second. "Is this your hoard?"

He supposed he liked not having to encourage her to finish her questions. Her open nature would make it unnecessary to skim her surface thoughts and allow him to dig deeper to test her motivations.

"Yes. I would like to repay you for helping the Thunder."

Oh. That was an interesting bit of magic. A mental wall stopped him from getting too far, and the frown that sliced her face warned she was aware he was sifting through her mind.

"Why don't you try asking whatever you're wondering?" She suggested.

Her eyes locked onto his and he knew with a wave of irritation she'd noticed the subtle change of color. He collected his thoughts while she concentrated on his traitorous features.

"How did a little elf wipe magic so completely from the land of dragons?" He took her advice.

"Oh." She cleared her throat. Her eyes darted to a space behind his head. "Is that the shield of Aneas?"

Alessandro's magic reached out like a viper. The quick defensive barrier she erected impressed him. He pressed further and the unexpected scent of lust bombarded him.

Her eyes were now fully glowing, and he felt his knees buckle. The strength of the succubus blood running through her veins usually came with indicators the woman lacked. Yet he could scent the power as it tried to take over his will. His eyes landed on the necklaces against her chest.

They broke with the slightest tug of his fingers.

The extra limbs he'd been expecting popped into existence. Black fleshed wings with red inner folds spread out behind her. Delicate black horns curled gently up from her forehead, ending in deadly sharp points. A tail, as thick as her wrist at its base, thinned before flaring out into the shape of a spade, its tip just as sharp as her horns.

Her roar of rage shook him.

She clasped his wrist, her unleashed magic trying to force him to his knees.

He took a step back.

He, the motherfucking Dragon King, took a step back.

She used the slacked momentum to sweep his leg from under him, sending them both tumbling. She straddled his hips as she pinned him.

His dragon hissed at the alpha stare she threw down at him as if he was some simple victim of the demon she contained in her tiny body. His hand was around her neck and he was pushing her down to the floor, a growl ripping from the back of his throat.

"Are you really so stupid?"

In response, her hand wrapped around his forearm before slipping up to his wrist.

Her tongue snuck out to lick her lips, and his hold slackened with surprise.

She was clearly unbothered by any show of his power. In fact, her initial rage had simmered. She was now downright vibrating with desire.

"Was that nice?" She hissed as they both rose to their feet, glaring at each other in the next second.

"How did you get through Spellcaster's without showing your true potential?" He demanded.

"*I* can control myself if I wish." She stroked the side of her neck as if to emphasize that this restraint was something he lacked.

Under normal circumstances, Alessandro had immaculate control. He had honed it over years of having to deal with his people and keeping them under the strict lifestyle they'd had to adopt to keep their greatest secret.

But Rowan Dahl was more infuriating than those who showed him fealty and reverence.

It was a combination of both threat and asset that she presented. His greatest responsibility as Dragon King was to eradicate threats to the Thunder, and it was usually uncomplicated for him to reach a conclusion of where things landed.

He couldn't threaten her to behave, she seemed to... he couldn't fathom it, but she seemed to enjoy irritating him.

"Are you friend or foe?" He hadn't meant to sound so stone cold, but the scent of her lust was eroding the so-called control he possessed.

It wasn't his first dance with a succubus. He'd been in the company of their very creator more times than he would have liked, but none had ever affected him like this one did.

"Depends on what you make of me, and right now, it's more of the latter."

Heat crawled up his neck. He could barely contain the fury her words brought out of him, nor the lust the promise of violence enticed.

He'd always known equating the two states of being was fucked up.

Her lavender eyes lit up like neon lights that bounced off the space in front of her.

"Or the former, if I can rely on your scent." The pitch of her voice was low as a smile unfurled on her lips. "Can I rely on your scent, Dragon King? If so, I'd like to choose repayment from the Thunder for my earlier troubles."

Alessandro's low growl didn't stop her from gripping the throat of his cloak.

"Do I look like a prize?"

She only grinned, amused, as she pulled him down to meet her lips.

Physically, he dominated her, but fuck if he wasn't already hard from the moment that she parried his punch.

Even if violence turned him on, he never engaged it in his practice of intimacy. He had always executed a soft, careful dance. He was so used to taking care of others he couldn't imagine accidentally hurting them with the beast he kept carefully tucked inside.

But violence on the elf went hand in hand with her lust, just like it did with him. It had to be with how quickly she shifted from snarling to purring.

He let her kiss him. Curiosity over this new state of being drove him to meet her toe to toe.

The true depth of her power was palpable in the physical joining of their bodies. The potential the woman held mesmerized him. He couldn't deny that it was exciting to hold something so foreign to his usual partner in his arms, but even more, it made him feel an awe he couldn't quite understand.

He gave into her desire, allowing her entrance into the cavern of his mouth while he backed her up against a case of collections.

Her tongue was blazing heat and tasted of sweet berries she must've just consumed to be so potent.

Something in him snapped.

Was it his control? He couldn't identify it, and he had to concentrate on the hand that had trailed underneath the cloak and under his pants.

It had to be his control because he didn't move to stop her. In fact, his own traitorous limbs trailed along the curves of her body to the swell of her ass which he squeezed, pressing their fronts closer together, increasing the pressure her hand had on him.

He'd never bedded a succubus. His partners had been strictly dragons. For a good reason.

A reason he couldn't recall when her hands entangled in the hair at the base of his skull and tugged.

"No spell work." He hissed, pulling back. There was no way she could have already found his ultimate weak spot without magic.

"The Dragon King, afraid of his own desire. How long have you deprived yourself of sincere pleasure? Is this the first time someone is giving you what you crave? With me, you don't have to say a word." Her kisses trailed from the bottom of his chin, down his throat. "With me, shame doesn't exist."

He let out a throaty laugh that vibrated the walls of the cavern. "You might regret those words, little elf. It isn't shame that holds me in check, it's concern for your safety. Do you really believe you can handle all of me just because you're full of spirit? You're still just a mortal."

She scoffed. "I can take everything you dish out and maybe even teach you a thing or two, Dragon King."

Challenge after challenge. Alessandro's dragon roared, demanding to dominate the elf to put her in her place.

He hauled her over his shoulder.

"I can walk." She snarled.

"My cave, my rules, little elf." It was only a few steps to the pile of throws he had set up in case he ever needed to spend the night in the cavern.

"It's *my* prize."

"Take me as I am, or you don't get me at all." He murmured as he set her to her feet on the edge of the make-shift bed. "Once you cross that line, there's no going back."

She regarded him with calculated appraisal. Then she paced a tight circle around him, fingers grazing against his shoulders, down the chords of muscle on his back and over the curve of his ass.

He crossed his arms.

She wouldn't get any participation from his part until she crossed that line.

It was a concession his beast required.

She continued her leisurely perusal and finally stood in front of him once more. Her violet eyes were blazing.

Rowan Dahl's essence smelled like a field of flowers in fresh bloom mixed with the sweet heat of sunbaked sand.

"You'll do." She snapped her fingers and his clothes vanished.

Still. She hadn't crossed that line.

Bared to her hungry gaze, he felt his jaw twitch when her eyes landed on his length. He could feel the moisture from the tip tap against his belly. Could feel it throbbing in time with his heartbeat.

The glow of her eyes flashed in matching tempo. She bit her bottom lip as she finally took that step back and he was on her before her second foot could join.

She took his ferocity in stride as he fell to his knees with her legs spread over his thighs. Her still covered soaking wet heat was flush against his and he almost lost full control at the sensation.

She was steady under his kiss. She didn't bow or cower as his hand settled on the small of the back of her neck, a shifter trait of dominance that always had his partners going limp with submission.

Heat trailed through his chest and to the crown of his dick. His lust stretched like a rubber band, waiting to snap.

Aching.

Burning.

He brought her deeper into the kiss, while his other hand extended a claw to remove the layers of her clothes.

Her hands rested on his shoulders as they simultaneously pulled back to watch as he nudged the shreds of fabric to the side. She was pink and so wet. His fingers slid into her with an unintended speed and force that had her stomach quivering and her breasts tightening and his restraint disintegrating.

Her violet eyes fluttered close as his fingers railed into her and the other hand that still hadn't left her neck pulled her forward so he could seal his mouth around a peach colored nipple that tasted so much sweeter than he could have imagined. If this was her sweat, what would the slickness coating his fingers taste like?

Violent with desire, he squeezed the back of her neck and she let out a long sigh of contentment as her hands tangled in his hair.

She enjoyed his violence. Nothing about him scared her. He could lose himself if he wasn't careful.

A sensation curled around his dick and he pulled away once more to glance down and his breath caught when he saw her tail wrapped around his straining head.

"Be careful with that point." He hissed, his breath short. And he hadn't even started fucking yet. Endless hells.

"What's a little bloodshed between two lovers, Dragon King?" She teased, rocking her hips on his fingers as if to remind him to keep moving.

He had to close his eyes. This was too fucking much.

Her hands moved from his shoulders to his cheeks, and she retook his lips while her hips gyrated. She was as desperate for him as he was for her. Her tail stroked the length of his shaft, his pre-cum aiding the smooth movement.

"Your smell." She leaned her forehead against his. "Will you taste how you smell?"

He let out an unwilling laugh.

Fuck it.

He'd never looked a gift horse in the mouth and Rowan Dahl was the most unexpected gift he'd ever received.

His eyes snapped open and the sight of her tousled hair, flushed cheeks and swollen lips was fuel. Using his middle and ring finger, he applied pressure to the roof of her entrance as he moved back and forth.

Her nipple was back in his mouth, this time the left to spread the love, but he was through with holding back and his canine sunk into her flesh. The copper tang of her blood coated his tongue. It wasn't a deep bite by any meaning of the word. But it was a sting he knew she'd like.

"Yes!" Rowan's moans were the most addicting notes of sound he had ever heard.

"Cum for me, princess." His own release was mounting from the force of her tail. "Unravel for me."

Tears gathered in the corner of her eyes as her release mounted. He could feel her tightening around his fingers so fucking close.

"Let go."

And she did. So hard and so fast that he almost missed the chance to slide home when he'd been planning to.

Her sheath was the perfect fit, the perfect heat.

Her breath hitched, and her eyes were wide with shock. Her open expression lured a cocky smirk from him as his completion filled her walls, claiming it as his before he began a steady rhythm that had those orbs rolling to the back of her head and her claws sinking into his back.

His mouth peppered her collar bone with bites, leaving trails on every available expanse of skin as their bodies shifted with each new round they initiated on the heels of each release. His furs were so drenched their combined essence that they'd had to move to the floor, the bite of the stone on his back while she rode him without abandon was worth every moment of discomfort.

He still hadn't decided where she fell on his scale, but his suspicion melted into pleasure with every thrust. The hardness of his cock was everlasting. His hunger for her growing rather than wavering.

It was when she was on all fours, ass in the air, back arched low, that he realized what she'd been chanting under her breath.

'Dragon King.' Over and over again. An inexplicable irritation swept through him at the title.

"My name is Alessandro, slutty little elf."

Her laughter died as he gripped her hips and slammed into her with more force than he'd been using before. Her dazed, lavender eyes glanced back at him over her shoulder.

"Alessandro."

In the mystic world, names had power. His instruction for her to use his had a meaning he refused to acknowledge.

He emptied himself inside of her so many times he lost count, and by the time the succubus had worn herself out, she'd fallen asleep with him still inside of her. It took another hour for him to convince himself what had happened had been a mistake, for she was glowing with his celestial energy, covered in endless love bites and bruises, and he could swear there had never been a more beautiful sight.

Her powers had done their job and ensnared him.

He cursed and sent her away before he did something that he would regret even more.

V

"Fuck." Rowan shot up in her bed as a surge of magic slapped her. Cursing, she phased out of her cabin to a high-rise condo in the heart of Black Cove. A high-pitched scream and a blast of air threw her into the cabinets.

She cursed and glared at the two figures eating breakfast on the island.

"Master Jah. *You* should know better than to cast without verification."

"What the hell have you done with all of your charms?" The giant witch moved at a speed that didn't match his size to help her up.

She hissed. "I took a bite out of something bigger than I could chew."

The blonde woman who had remained at the counter giggled as Japhet took back his hand and promptly dropped her back into the pile of wood that used to be cabinets.

"Every day I know you is another day I am grateful for a daughter like Chloe."

"Lovely." Rowan whimpered, checking her new wounds. It was in trying to identify them that she realized the extent of damage her previous night had left her with.

Love bites marked her from head to foot. Her knees, palms, back, and the swell of her ass were scraped. Bruises bloomed from her wrists, forearms and ankles.

Chloe's fork clattered on the counter as she realized how hurt her friend was at the same time. "Rowan Dahl, who hurt you?"

"You smell...familiar. What exactly did you get yourself entangled with?" Master Jah asked as he conjured an oversized tee shirt for her privacy as he began casting healing charms to speed up her recovery. "You look like you just lost a fight to a giant squid."

"There was more pleasure than pain." Rowan ignored the warning noise that escaped Master Japhet. "Actually, you won't believe who it was."

"Who?" Chloe's face gained more and more disbelief as she turned her friend around to examine all of her bruises when Master Jah turned his attention to fixing the cabinets.

In her many years of feeding her succubus, no partner had been as satisfying as he had been. She'd never expected to fall asleep in the middle of a rut, nor had she ever been so unhinged and out of control. Never had she been so utterly full of energy she wasn't sure she'd ever need to eat again.

"Um, Rowan, do you want to talk about it?"

Rowan snapped her attention to the floating blonde. She looked amused. Master Jah, who the spell had also caught, floated in the background, irritation clear on his eyebrow.

"Sorry, I'm not used to having to put thought into controlling it." She recollected her excess energy as gently as possible and set the two witches on the couches.

"Even if the witches let you off the hook with recruitment, it is no permission to be sloppy with your magic. You still have a secret to maintain, Rowan." Master Jah scowled.

"I know." Rowan sighed as she swiped a piece of toast off an abandoned plate on the counter. "I just didn't expect the Dragon King to amp me up this much, okay? Though I should have, the dude's a freaking god walking amongst us lowly mortals."

"*What?*" The roar from Master Japhet startled both women in the room.

Chloe placed a calming hand on his forearm. "What's wrong?"

"You're sure?" He demanded.

"Well, I've only been obsessed with him for like more than half of my life, so I'm confident it was him." She placed a finger under her chin, considering she could have mistaken the identity of the man.

No. She knew what his magic felt like, and last night she'd rolled around in it to her heart's content.

"How am I supposed to keep you safe from the Dragon King, Rowan?"

Rowan furrowed her eyebrows. "Keep me safe? We just shared a night. I didn't run into him once in the last ten years that he's been living down the street from me. I'm sure there won't be another situation where we'll see each other again."

Disbelief was clear on Master Jah's face.

Rowan sighed. "Look, I'm able to protect myself now, Master Jah. I know it's new, but don't you trust that you've taught me enough?"

"Obviously not if on your first night of freedom you decide to bed the single-most dangerous entity in the world!"

She couldn't find an argument against that. "You worry too much."

"You don't worry enough!" Master Jah groaned and then his eyes slid to the clock. He cursed as he stood. "Halley and I are going on a cruise this week. Try to control yourself, won't you?"

Rowan promised to try her best.

"I like the wings." He said as a last-minute observation. "Perhaps keeping them out will aid you in keeping your other secret safe."

Rowan considered it.

It could also help her explain why she was so magically gifted when elves weren't.

Succubi, as a species, were mysteries. Few in numbers, there wasn't much documented about their powers, weaknesses or culture. She knew, because she'd scoured the globe trying to find information on them to explain why she had turned out so differently from the rest of her family. Not only on the magical side of things but also on the physical.

When Rowan's horns showed up as nubs as she'd entered her feeding age, her mother was beside herself with worry.

Neither Annabelle nor any of Rowan's sisters had attained the limbs of their ancestors. But Annabelle had once upon a time lived with succubi and seen how harsh the world was with them. It was why the succubi stayed in their corner of the endless hells, only coming up for their meals and heading right back home after.

Respect instantly went out the window at the sight of the wings, tails, and horns. The heavy sexualization of succubi to the public convinced Annabelle that the best way to protect her thirteen-year-old daughter was to commission glamour jewelry.

By then, Rowan's clothes were all lined with nulling charms to hide her magic. What was one more layer to her endless layers of masks?

Now she was old enough to protect herself.

Japhet was right, it would be a useful tool to deter anyone from looking too closely.

"I think you're right." She shrugged, "I guess it's time for the world to get to know the real me...well most of me, anyway."

Master Japhet grinned and wrapped her in a warm hug. "Make better decisions, kid."

He turned to his adopted daughter and wrapped her in the hug as well.

"Protect each other while I'm gone." Were his last words before he phased out.

"It's been a while since I've seen him so worried."

Chloe nodded before she let out a squeal. "Spill, How did you snag the Dragon King?"

"Well, he snagged me. He ambushed me on my way to the Cabin and took me to his hoard. He was sizing me up, trying to figure out how I wiped magic out of Draconis."

Chloe shuddered. "Ro, we have to figure out your true limit."

"I agree. Especially in this super powered up state after getting my fill of the Dragon King." Rowan held her arm out in front of her and noted that the glowing she thought she'd seen earlier was indeed there, though already muting.

Chloe sighed as she also took it in. "Do you want a full powered nulling chain, or one that'll just take the edge off your...energy?"

"Just enough for the edge. Think you can have it ready in like an hour? I'm already late for work. Kin's going to kill me."

Chloe nodded and motioned towards the door of her bathroom. "In the meantime, how about a shower? No offense Ro, but you reek of sex."

-R-

Kin glared down at her from the open second-floor landing as she entered the office an hour later.

As she was late, had missed a couple of appointments, and dressed in what he deemed inappropriate office attire, Rowan wasn't shocked by the annoyance he radiated. She'd even stopped by the donut shop next door in anticipation of it.

However, the predatory instinct that flashed in his red-rimmed eyes when they landed on her was unexpected.

It was the only warning she got before a fireball hit her square on the chest, making her crash through the sliding front doors and back out onto the busy cobblestone streets of downtown Black Cove.

She cursed and looked down at her torched shirt. It struggled to contain her privacy, and the skin underneath was already blistering. She crossed her arms, noting the small crowd forming around her.

"We have got to work on you using your words!" She hissed as she called forth a curtain of ice to halt his next attack. She phased away from the wreckage of glass and metal to turn her attention to the shifter stumbling down the stairs. Something was seriously wrong, but she hadn't the faintest idea what as she curled her arm around his neck and flung him into the front desk where Dew had evacuated from as soon as she realized the two powerhouses were going fist to cuffs.

"I got it!" Louisa appeared out of thin air and plunged a syringe into the side of the struggling kitsune's neck.

Rowan and the vampiress took a step back as white fur bubbled to the surface of his face.

"Kin! Get a hold of yourself, asshole!" Rowan held her hand out, calling for gravity to pin him to the granite. He howled against the invisible restraints, but he was slowing down. It gave her enough time to look around and realize she hadn't been his first victim of rage. Louisa was in a pair of shredded white leather coveralls, had several bruises to her face and dried blood on the corner of her lip.

The only thing that stopped Rowan from digging her own fists into Kin's face was his sudden lack of fight. Whatever had been in the syringe had finally kicked in and Kin was unconscious.

"It wasn't his fault." the vampiress groaned as she found an intact chair and sunk into it.

Dew fluttered down from the pendant light she'd been perching on and laid a hand on the deep gash the vampire had on her neck. The skin sewed itself back together and scabbed over before their eyes.

"Are you low on blood?" Rowan demanded, falling to her knee in front of her and examining her dilated pupils. If even the slightest flicker of crimson passed through, she would open her vein for the vampiress to suck on.

"No." Louisa waved her concern away. "He was more busy fighting his fox than me. The only reason I got tore up was that I got in his way of hurting himself by trying to inject him. The only reason you got tore up is because you have shifter pheromones pouring off of you. What is that? Dragon?" Her examination of the white-haired elf tore a gasp out of her. "You know your succubus is showing, right?"

Dew blinked and looked her over. "It isn't always showing?"

Rowan's lips twitched. Even knowing that fae had incredible senses, she'd never considered Dew knew of her true nature throughout their entire relationship. The faerie had never treated her as less than. A brief vision passed in Rowan's mind's eye of those she'd shown her true appearance to. Their disgust always felt like a slice to her soul.

"No, Dew, it isn't to other mystics."

Dew's bright eyes widened. "So they don't know how cool you really look?"

"Cool?" Louisa let out a laugh. "Dew, you know Rowan isn't cool."

"She's really cool!" Dew clenched her hands over her heart and closed her eyes as if the truth was too hard to take, and she fluttered around Rowan's entire body. "Look at these wings! They could carry at least twenty of my family members on one trip." She grabbed the horns protruding from Rowan's head as if riding a bull. "These horns are weapons ready to slash any dastardly enemy, even if she's tied up. I've felt blades duller than these wonderful tools!" She held her suddenly bleeding hands up, demonstrating the validity of her words.

Rowan gasped. "Dew!"

Dew ignored her and grabbed Louisa's face with her still bleeding hands. "And do you see that tail? I bet if you arm wrestled with it you would lose! My Rowan's body is a work of art! Every single part."

Rowan felt warmth spread throughout her entire being. Yes. Dew was right. Some of the trepidation she'd felt over her true appearance being out on display melted.

Louisa giggled, "Well, when you put it like that. Of course she's cool. I'm not sure how I didn't see it before."

Louisa had seen it before.

Rowan recalled the first time the succubus charm failed in front of the vampiress. It had been during a life or death test for Spellcasters Academy. Though they'd been in many of the same classes for nearly a year at that point, Louisa and Rowan hadn't actually exchanged anything more than greetings.

Dew's excitement over her wings had reflected Louisa's own reaction.

"How do you keep them so shiny if you don't let them see the light of day? I've never seen this color before. Would you call it black or red? Can I dye my hair this color? We can match without the world ever knowing."

From that moment on, Rowan had stuck to the girl like glue. Eventually she burrowed her way into her heart despite Louisa making it her personal mission to create and maintain a distance between herself and the whole outside world. Being the daughter of Rosario the Cruel hardly made Louisa an enticing companion.

The first time meeting the strict no-nonsense Grand-Vampire of the North American Brood, it had helped that Rowan had years of translating her mother's frustration through a language she used only when she was upset. She could understand every word the woman lashed her with, even as she stumbled over her own tongue to respond.

"It matters to me only that you try. Not that you're an imbecile at using the tongue your mother should have known better than to deprive you of. Our ancestors abandoned their native language, whether forced or by choice. Don't let anyone, not even your mother, keep you from your birthright."

Rowan returned to the present by the loud snore Kin gave. "Was he triggered by yesterday's attack?"

"Possibly, but I don't have time to analyze his blood." Louisa's eyes slid to the clock behind Dew's desk. "We each have five visits scheduled today. We're going to have to split up his work. You know he's going to be pissed when he wakes up and realizes you didn't kill him as he asked."

Rowan waved Louisa's concern away. "We'll cross that bridge when we get there. Today is the day with the leprechaun and phoenix wreck, right? I call the leprechaun."

Dew moved to her desk, looking at the schedule through the computer. "I'll call them to let them know."

"No! I want the leprechaun!" Louisa hissed.

Rowan raised her hand, moving her concentration to repairing the front entrance with a bit of earth magic.

"I have to catch up with my own missed appointments. Be a team player and give me the easy one."

Louisa rolled her eyes. "No, you were late. In Kin's honor, you must be punished."

Rowan grimaced, knowing she would have thrown the same words at Louisa if she'd been in her position. "Fine, but I get Dew."

Dew was indispensable with appointments like the one Kin had given them a heads up on. Dew grinned and gave her a thumbs up.

Louisa huffed, "Fine."

-R-

As a magical disaster expert, Rowan had seen her share of magic gone askew, but sometimes the oddities of the situations she tried to fix left her unsure of how to feel about them.

The phoenix, whose outrage had been audible through an entire flight of stairs when Dew had called to tell her about the switch, stormed into Rowan's office at 3 o'clock on the dot with a very obvious issue.

Everywhere the woman stepped, she left behind a trail of gold dust.

Though Kin had left notes about what to expect when Rehya Harper walked in, the leprechaun magic attaching itself to the very irate woman, both surprised and intrigued Rowan.

"Good afternoon Ms. Harper. We appreciate your understanding of Mr. Smith's absence. Please have a seat." Rowan pointed to the makeshift exam table in the corner of her office.

The phoenix looked like she was on the verge of declining the offer, but when the gold production increased in correlation with her anger, she gave in.

"So, from Mr Smith's notes in your initial conversation, it appears you may know exactly what's going on, but are a little stubborn in try-ing to accept it. The refusal is exacerbating the symptoms of your condition to correlate with your emotions." It was unusual for Rowan to be so blunt with her clients, but Dew was weaving her magic of calming through the room and she still had hours of catching up on her own work looming over her head.

The phoenix, though a lot calmer than Rowan suspected she could be, increased the amount of gold she had been producing, giving away her displeasure.

"What exactly do you believe I am trying to refuse to accept?" Rheya asked tightly.

"That you're pregnant." Rowan pointed at the small mountain of gold building on the wooden floor. "And the father is a leprechaun."

Rowan didn't blink even as streams of flame erupted from the hands of the woman that found themselves around her neck. It was more of a threat of violence than an actual attack with its lack of grip or actual heat.

"Take it back!" She hissed, hot tears falling down her cheeks. Rowan could tell this wasn't a surprise to the woman as much as it was painful.

A hot bubble of sympathy ballooned in the hollows of Rowan's stomach. She grasped her wrists and guided the woman's hands back down to her lap. "Miss Harper, I know this will be even harder to hear, but such an occurrence, while rare, is not impossible. If you don't mind me saying, it's proof of how much your soul and the soul of the leprechaun have bonded. Shifters are notorious for having a hard time producing offspring, even with their own kind. I know you know what this means."

"B-But how? How could it be him?"

Rowan wanted to shrug.

Love. While she had it in spades for her family and friends, she'd never been able to say that she'd fallen into it. Never been willing to make a fool of herself for the prospect of forever. She hadn't had time.

Between hiding her true self from the world and satisfying her desire to surpass each limit she reached with magic, then being a good daughter, sister and friend, she had been hurtling from task to task for so long that falling in love had fallen off her radar.

But now she had an opportunity.

Her inner succubus wouldn't allow for her horns, wings, and tail to be hidden. She didn't need to make herself smaller to avoid recruiting attempts from the Coven. She would have to be careful of how much she showed in public, but during private jobs, she could finally unleash her full potential. It was startling to realize how much hope it filled her with.

"Miss Harper. You have choices, and I can give you referrals to many who can assist you whichever way you choose."

The phoenix laid her hands over the belly that had yet to even show the slightest hint of pregnancy.

"This is really happening."

"Yes." Rowan glanced at the clock and steeled herself for Kin's plan. "By any chance is your leprechaun Mick McCormick?"

Tension rolled into the phoenix's shoulder. Her red wings quivered.

"He's due here in about fifteen minutes. Mr. Smith wanted to provide you the option of you two speaking with himself as a mediator. If that's something you want to pursue, I can facilitate in his place."

Rheya took a deep breath.

"If you're not ready, I can sneak you out the back."

Rheya shook her head with vehemence, "No, I'm ready. Let's do it."

-R-

"And you're sure it worked out?" Kin was finishing buttoning his shirt as Rowan and Louisa filled him in on the drama of the leprechaun and the phoenix.

As soon as Rheya and Mick caught sight of each other, it was instant tears for the leprechaun and an undeniable sense of relief for the phoenix.

The couple dismissed Rowan and Louisa within seconds. Though they hadn't been able to hear the conversation, through the wall that connected Louisa's office to Rowan's, the two had left hand in hand through the front door.

"Rheya took Miasma's number with her and they were both smiling in the end." Rowan shrugged as she handed over a blood red tie from her place behind his desk. "I can't believe this is the first time you've had to use your backup office outfit."

Kin's scowl should've been a warning Rowan heeded, "You two were lucky I didn't shred your throats out. I've told you to take me out the moment I lost control."

"We took you out of consciousness." Rowan shrugged. "Kind of the same thing."

"It is not the same thing!" He snapped. His eyes flashing red.

Rowan narrowed her eyes. "If you would like for me to finish the job now, I can do that."

His hands slammed on the desk between them, white fur dancing along his face. "You both could've died because you can't make the hard decisions, Dahl."

"It wasn't hard. It was wrong." Rowan was careful not to make even the slightest movement of domination. But the reason Kin had risked his lucrative career to join her and Louisa in their start-up year was because of her ability to chain his beast with her own control.

She could feel Louisa's anxiety rise from her seat on the soft maroon corduroy couch in front of the only fireplace in the building, threatening the very fragile balance of their interaction.

"It was what we agreed to."

"Before I could exert my full power. We are in different waters now, Kin. I can protect us. Will you continue to trust me, or not?"

A hiss left the back of his throat, but eventually his head dropped and Rowan shared Louisa's sense of relief.

"Thank you." The elven woman whispered and clasped her hands together, "Now, do you think Julio will care if you get after-work drinks with me and Louisa, or what?"

VI

It was rare for Alessandro's patience to be tested. Contrary to popular belief, it had been ages since he'd given in to his anger and ripped the wings off the backs of those who annoyed him. He'd grown.

He knew his long gone favorite punishment kept most of his dragons in line. His Elemental Generals were a secondary line of reinforcement of the rules and regulations that riddled the Draconian Thunder, but it was fear of his wrath that kept them a mostly peaceful race.

Now that everyone, including the generals, had lost control, there were many trying their hand at a shot for power.

The fire dragons were the most hard pressed. He'd extinguished too many runaway fireballs for his liking.

Blaise was the youngest of the generals and the most hot headed. His demeanor had been the reason his dragons lacked the discipline the other elementals had, but he was formidable. As one of Terra's top combat students, he never had his guard down, no matter how relaxed he seemed.

Alessandro glared over at him as he snuffed the life from the stray fireball he'd caught on his claw.

Blaise pressed the young fire dragon's face into the ground and bowed his own head. "Sorry, my king. The idiot sneezed wrong and accidentally shot that, right, Mateo?"

Deciding not to risk a mouth full of dirt, the dragon gave a sharp nod of his head, which Alessandro knew had to be just as uncomfortable, seeing as Blaise hadn't let up on his grip.

Alessandro growled his displeasure and continued his walk to Naseem's home.

The bald-headed dragon was pacing his balcony when Alessandro found him.

"That bad?" Alessandro asked, leaning against the door frame.

Naseem snapped his eyes in surprise towards the Dragon King. Oh yes, it was bad. Naseem, like Blaise, always had his guard up.

The air general grimaced, "Your timing astounds me. I've barely had a second to digest it myself."

"Who?"

Instead of speaking, Naseem extended his fingers. On the ground, Alessandro hadn't noticed the magic circle until the broken pieces of magic Naseem had collected from the scene of the crime crawled to show the unmistakable dark blue and purple streaks. Even unfinished, the purple circle of dragon magic was visible. The blue inside noted it even further as a water elemental. Tendrils of cursed magic that had shielded the pieces from immediate recognition skirted the border of the spell, contained, but not dissipated.

It wouldn't have been enough to determine which water dragon it had come from, but the Thunder only had one who had recently left home.

He had to pause before he lashed out his rage and alerted all of Draconis to his immense displeasure. The last thing he wanted was to see the woman again, but ignoring her had proven to be more dangerous than he could have imagined. To think an ex-lover would seek vengeance by trying to destroy his Thunder.

He scowled. He had known better than to get involved with Elaine Hitori, the Thunder's sweetheart, but she had been relentless in her pursuit of him and had gained the support of all but one of his generals.

Charmed by her drive, he had given in and they began dating. She'd been a great lay, but in the end, that was all she could offer him. Under the impression of an assured future together, Elaine began executing Dragon Queen duties, passing orders and convincing the Thunder that she spoke for him.

The manipulations on ensuring everyone she'd had the power to do whatever she wanted resulted in the only time he had to break a relationship off in public. Having gotten on the bad side of most of the Thunder through her abuse of power, she had only a few allies and he had assumed her recent absence in Draconis and Dragon City was her attempt to get back on her feet.

Apparently, she had been biding her time to attack the people who shunned her.

He cracked his neck as he stood to his full towering height and he reached out with his magic to get a lock on her signal. Surprise filled him as he realized where the dragon was situated. A few feet from the unique magical signature that was the Traveling Cabin.

"Your eyes are glowing crimson, Alessandro. Think before you react." Naseem's voice halted him from phasing out. "She is one of us. She has rights."

Smoke curled from his nostrils as Alessandro attempted to reign in his beast.

"Her rights were forfeit the moment she attacked Draconis." Was all he got out before the vision of Naseem's balcony crumbled away.

-R-

Rowan awoke to the sound of a dull thudding. For a moment, she thought it was a raging hangover she hadn't meant to bring on by trying to make Kin feel better about his loss of control. But as the pounding grew more insistent, then turned downright hostile, she shook off the dregs of sleep from her mind and gathered magic.

The cabin quaked as whoever was outside was trying to blast their way in. Her home fired back its own attack. Rowan heard the snap of trees. She could imagine a body being thrown across the mountain her cabin had settled in for the night.

Clad in only her silky pajama shorts and an oversized tee, she zoomed out towards the front of the house, giving the doorframe an appreciative pat as she slid into a pair of rain boots she left near the entrance.

The night had a new moon sky. Stars twinkled brightly with the lack of city lights, but they didn't make up for the absence of the lunar satellite.

It was so dark Rowan only saw the body shooting itself towards her because it had a fireball gripped in its talons.

Rowan dug her heels into the porch planks, crouching a bit to make sure she would actually stop the seething creature rather than letting it in through the open door. She realized a second later that the creature wasn't intending to meet her body to body, but to send the fireball to her face.

Rowan's water barrier ate the flame before it hit her square on target, but she didn't miss how much power it packed.

Who in the endless hells had she upset so much they were aiming to kill? Had her father been right, and the Coven had reneged on the agreement? She couldn't believe they would risk the Elder's Grimoire.

She stepped out onto the porch, her eyes locking on the beast. Its transformation seemed to have stopped halfway to completion. One giant horn erupted from its skull, curving back around its misshapen head. One eye was reptilian, the other blacked out. Its mouth was full of fangs, but the humanoid shape had them jutting out in all kinds of disturbing directions. On the opposite side of the horn was a giant bat-like wing bigger than the entire body of the thing. Only one hand was taloned, and a scaled foot was being dragged as the beast got closer.

So, not the Coven, but something much worse.

"What happened to you?" Rowan asked, her breath short.

The creature gave off a pained sound, so sorrowful and familiar. It wasn't as melodious as it had been in Draconis, but it was what had turned the dragons berserk.

The creature rushed towards her, sharp talons glinting with the sparse night light, taking advantage of the apparent second of indecision from Rowan. It wanted her dead.

Rowan sneered as she dodged deadly swipe after deadly swipe, careful not to stumble on the rocks underfoot while she struggled with doing what she knew she had to do. In a desperate attempt, she tried to drain the thing's energy source, but she found it wasn't feeding off nature's magic like regular dragons did. Instead, it was feeding off the source of its own pain, chaotic and full of dark ancient curses. The thing should've already been going cold in a ditch somewhere with the saturation.

Still hoping for an alternate answer, Rowan turned to the option of incapacitation, but a slice to her thigh and forehead when she attempted it made her realize a knockout spell would be ineffective.

Spell resistant creature. Rowan cursed as she summoned the only solution she knew.

Tears filled her eyes as light erupted from her hand. It took on the form of a blazing sword. It crackled through the air, lighting the edges of the forest as she fed it more and more power to make one slice all she'd need to finish it. She recalled the other broken creatures that showed up at her doorstep looking for release when they realized there was no return to their former life.

She looked into the reptilian eye for a breath, catching a bit of lingering consciousness, and she whispered an apology before she sliced through where she thought its heart would be. She watched as it convulsed after her strike. When it came down, it landed at her feet, breathing hard, the song fading into the wind.

Rowan released the sword and as it extinguished, darkness consumed them again. She looked down at the body as the cleansing took effect. A small object fell from where its talons transformed into a delicate hand.

So that's what had driven the dragons insane? Pan's Flute. The original.

She fell to her knees before the object and glared down at it. The first time she put on a nulling chain, a hatred for things that made people lose free will carved her soul. The deep-seated darkness had swelled in the following years. She wanted to stomp on the relic. To destroy it so thoroughly it would be a question if it'd ever existed, but it was impossible. Godly trinkets were impossible to destroy, and hundreds of curses saturated this one.

The body next to it stopped morphing, and a dragon shifter lay in its place.

She was beautiful. Long, dark blue hair fanned out around her glowing porcelain skin. Her eyes were about the same shade as her hair as they took Rowan in through the shadows.

"They're okay, aren't they?" She bit out in short pants.

Was she asking about the other dragons? If so, Rowan didn't think so, but she couldn't find it in herself to say so when it would bring the woman no comfort in her last moments. She briefly wondered how many lies she'd given over the years. "Yeah."

The dragon let out a gasp as her gaze settled behind Rowan's head. Tears filled her eyes, and she sobbed. "I'm sorry, my king."

Rowan didn't have to crane her neck to see who was there. She felt his immense power shroud her like a blanket. He didn't say a thing as the woman let out a final breath and was gone.

With her departure, the strength that kept Rowan's tears in check faded. She looked up, searching for the moon, but she had forgotten it was gone, and all she saw were the glowing silver eyes of the Dragon King staring at her.

She knew what that meant for normal shifters, but there was no way it could be the same for the Dragon King. His eyes had shifted colors before. That was proof that she couldn't expect him to follow the same precedent, right?

"I'm sorry." She repeated the last words of the woman before them.

Alessandro shook his head, his curls bouncing as he did so. He knelt down beside her and he reached a hand out to touch the other dragon.

An odd mix of relief and disappointment filled her. If the silver had been the sign of his beast's intent to mate, he wouldn't have been able to ignore the instinct.

Rowan watched as the body emitted a small amount of light before slowly combusting into thousands of light shards that dispersed into the air before them.

"I was the reason she felt she had to go so far." He spoke minutes after the last light went out. "This is the second time you've helped the Thunder out."

Rowan let out a hum before saying, "Are you going to spirit me away again?"

-A-

Alessandro turned to the woman. Never having had trouble seeing in the dark, he could see that her eyes were blank. Her bloody clothes were so soaked they clung to every part of her body. She was exhausted, and she was still cracking jokes.

"No." He held a hand out and a dark glass bottle appeared in it. He uncorked the top and took the first drink. Ambrosia laced wine, as sweet as pomegranates and honey crisp apples, melted on his tongue as he handed her the bottle. "Any time I make a kill, this helps me dull the sting."

Rowan turned to look at him, bright blue eyes wide. "You're going to drink with me?"

Alessandro smirked. "Yes. I am."

She took the bottle, and he watched with surprise as she chugged. He thought to warn her of the potency, but there was an ease in her body that assured him she had enjoyed the spirit more than once in her life. Perks of being an elven princess, he supposed.

She let out a sound of refreshed satisfaction, gave the bottle back, and turned to the lake behind them. Without warning, she shot up into the sky and dove deep into the dark water, still clothed.

Alessandro's eyes turned to the musical instrument that had cost him Elaine. How had she gotten her hands on such a thing? His curiosity was momentary because the elf had breached the surface and was floating face up, her moment of elation suppressed by a wave of grief.

It had been one thing to see the marks of a Blessed in her aura when he'd taken her into his cavern, another to see her perform a cleansing. How many times had she done it? It didn't seem to be her first.

He waved a hand over the flute, executed a precautionary sweep for tracing spells before he sent it to his hoard to be examined later.

"So, who was she?" She had moved to the edge of the lake where she could sit submerged to her shoulders. The water was so clear he could see she was sitting cross-legged and her arms were playing with the hem of her pajama shorts. He could also see through the white fabric of her shirt to two dark spots where her areolas sat puckered. It seemed she was unaware, so he averted his eyes.

Alessandro took a drink before he answered. It was difficult for him to talk about his dragons to those outside of the Thunder, but he supposed the woman had earned his trust twice over. "Her name was Elaine Hitori. She belonged to one of the Thunder's most prominent families."

"There was a more intimate history between you." He could see the waves forming on the hair plastered to her scalp as it slowly dried. She crawled out far enough to where she could reach the bottle and she took another chug.

Her tolerance amused him. For someone so small, she should've already been tipsy with the amount she was inhaling. "I saw it in her eyes when she looked at you. She was in love with you."

Yes. She had been, but he had a feeling that Elaine had loved the power that came with being his partner a bit more than she loved him.

"Like most kings, my people have wanted me to find a partner to make my Dragon Queen. Elaine was hopeful for the position, but before I offered it, she took it for granted. A side of her came out with the imagined power that let me know she would be a failure. As part of a powerful family of the Thunder, she had allegiances and she let them blind her. She could not make fair and rational decisions. Perhaps that would have been a bit more forgivable if she'd had the right. But she didn't, so I cut off the courting and she ran away." He shook his head, "Headlong into a cursed object that might have killed my dragons had it not been for—well, you."

Rowan blew bubbles in the water as she pondered her next statement, but he saw an opening.

"This isn't the first time, is it? That someone with an irreversible curse has come to you?"

-R-

Rowan's first instinct was to lie. Hadn't her godfather warned her to hide her true nature?

But he had seen with his own eyes what she'd done. She had no delusions that he hadn't already put two and two together.

Besides, talking to a spellcaster as capable and as old as Alessandro himself—three centuries' worth of life last time she checked—might give her information she could use to one day complete the first full cleansing.

As far as she knew, while many Blessed had cleansed the possessors of cursed objects, each possessor had ceased to live almost immediately after. Worse yet, the object had remained cursed, waiting for its next victim to fall into its arms.

"No. The Cursed often find themselves at my doorstep. The first time it happened, I was only nine. I had been playing in my mother's gardens with my sisters when he showed up. He was just a kid too, but he had been so malformed that he scared us all. To protect them, I needed a weapon and a sword of light appeared for me as soon as I reached that conclusion. I just wanted to scare him off, not kill him, but he thrust himself right into the tip while trying to claw my face off. He returned to his normal appearance, and he died right in front of us all." She shook her head. "Ever since then, I've tried to tear the curses off, to keep them alive, but nothing works. I've studied scroll after scroll, grimoire after grimoire, but I always fail." The word was more breathed out than said. Rowan Dahl was not used to failure.

-A-

Blessed. It was a term for those who could end the misery of the Cursed with a weapon made of a rare bit of magic afforded to very few individuals. Over the years, some could even hear the words of full-fledged gods. Powerful entities whose powers were so grand that they couldn't fit in the dimension their worshippers filled.

The Blessed had become coveted, their identities protected with utmost diligence. Connected to celestial power, he could see the marks of the Blessed, even as he refused his godhood candidacy.

When the world discovered the Dragon King had reached godhood but refused to ascend, it adopted a wide berth stance for the Thunder. The lack of documentation of Alessandro's strengths and weaknesses was an effective tool for protecting secrets as it should have been with Rowan Dahl.

In their first meeting, she'd been sealed shut. Giving him no information to help reach a verdict of whether she was a friend or foe, even as she spread herself open for him.

He couldn't be sure if she was giving the information so easily because he'd witnessed her using the power, or if it had to do with something else entirely.

Could it be the trauma from what she'd just done? Guilt begging to be forgiven for an action driven by compassion, an action executed over thousands of years?

Could it be the ambrosia? It certainly was messing with his own inhibitions.

"You know they're called irreversible for a reason, right?"

A flash of disappointment ran through her eyes before she shook her head. "So even you can't help me find the answer. In a world of magic, there is almost an answer for everything. Why not this?"

"Ah, you're one of those. A hopeful young girl that still hasn't realized how fucked up the world can really be."

Rowan shrugged. "Better than being a bitter old man who doesn't know how to try."

"You don't know a thing about me."

He realized too late it was exactly the reaction she'd been seeking for him when a smile curled on her face. "Who said I was talking about you?"

Alessandro bit his tongue before he burst into laughter. How long had it been since he'd been so challenged? Not an ounce of malice coated her scent. She was having fun. "Well argued, I apologize for assuming."

It made him slightly self-conscious as her teasing smile softened into an expression of pure contentment. It was almost as if his laughter brought it forth. He'd seen that look only once before. When the woman that had adopted him after the death of his parents watched him hold her daughter for the first time. It was still his favorite memory of the woman he called mother.

These were dangerous waters his mind had traveled to. Shifting his focus, he looked over at the building behind them. The slowly rising sun cast a spotlight on it. "How did you end up with the Traveling Cabin?" He had never been inside, only heard stories of the dimensional anomaly.

His magic allowed him to feel its contradiction against time and space.

"Before it was mine, it was my great-aunt's."

She stood and Alessandro found his eyes trailing beads of water rolling down her body, past the areolas, down to where her shorts plastered onto her belly. He recalled her softness as he'd bent her over the previous time they'd been so close. He continued his perusal over her curvy thighs, which he had nibbled at and down to her painted toenails. Was that a sunflower?

"Do you want a tour?"

Alessandro took another drink, though he could feel the effects of the booze already blurring his rational thinking if his leisurely perusal of her body was anything to go by. "I would love a tour."

VII

The rising sun's orange hued rays followed them as they walked past the threshold. The amount of plants that hung, sat or floated around the entrance way floored Alessandro. He felt like he was inside of a curated terrarium.

Light poured in through a giant skylight that he hadn't seen from the outside, bathing evergreen leaves with life. It smelled good, like a mixture of wood and grass and several decadent blooms. Rowan's smell.

He followed the white-haired woman past the room of floating plants through an open door, where all he saw was a giant bed with mussed sheets, scrolls, books, and clothes strewn without a care on the floor.

"Sometimes it likes to think for me." Rowan murmured, and she began taking her clothes off. "It's as maddening as it can be productive."

Alessandro felt his cock twitch at the sight of the two dimples at the base of her spine. His mouth went dry.

She was a forward little minx. He wondered how much of that was her succubus blood.

"I'm—uh" He stuttered. How much of the nervous energy he was suddenly full of could he blame on the ambrosia? He had never stuttered before in his entire existence.

Rowan turned towards him. Her breasts bounced. Her soft pink nipples stood puckered, hard as rocks.

"Yes?" She asked, and he realized with horror that he was staring at her breasts as if he hadn't seen thousands of them in his lifetime.

"We shouldn't." He whispered.

"I was unaware changing into dry clothes was such a big deal." She smirked and headed towards another door he could see was a walk-in closet about the same size as the bedroom.

What the hell was this? He felt the heat on his cheeks and he tried to steady his breathing. Hadn't he already had his way with the damn woman, tasted every inch of skin on top of his throws in his hoard?

Had she cast a spell over his libido so she could suck all his celestial energy, as if he was her personal collection of aged wine?

No. He knew how succubus magic felt, and this wasn't it.

She exited the closet in a flowing light blue dress, the fabric so thin he could see the outline of her curves just underneath. Her wings, tucked in to be as small as possible, helped create the sexiest silhouette he had ever seen. It was more of a distraction than her nakedness. If she voiced her desire, he knew he wouldn't have the strength required to decline his own.

"As I was saying." Rowan sashayed past, tail brushing lightly against his hip. "The Traveling Cabin likes to think for me. Whoever has ownership, the house shifts for." She went through the bedroom door again and when he followed, they stepped into the kitchen instead of back into the entrance hall.

White granite floors, black marble countertops and chrome cabinets were a sharp departure from the nature theme the two previous rooms had. "Are you hungry? A cheesecake sounds delicious."

"Cheesecake? This early in the morning?"

"Maybe you're right." She rummaged in the fridge before making a sound of elation and emerging with a cake box. "Carrot cake it is!" When she opened it, Alessandro didn't know whether to be amused or concerned that there was already a spoon inside and missing pieces that showed she didn't bother with slicing.

"I can make you some eggs if you'd prefer. With bacon and toast. I cook a mean breakfast platter." She motioned to the stove. From how clean it looked, Alessandro wasn't sure it saw much action.

He decided taking her spoon was the safest option. "Something tells me you didn't really intend on sharing this. It makes me want it that much more." He dug a giant piece out and shoved it in his mouth.

Rowan glared at him. "You need to savor the flavor, or else it's just a waste!"

Following her command and pairing the cake with ambrosia, Alessandro found it difficult to remember a time when a cake had ever tasted so decadent.

The next room they visited was a tearoom, where ornate portraits of elves hung. "According to my aunt's notes on the place, whoever owns the house gets this room rearranged with their family line." She pointed to her immediate family's portraits. "Look at all those good genes."

He had to admit the royal family of the Eastern Elvin Kingdom was indeed a good-looking bunch. But maybe he held a bias toward the youngest daughter.

Curiosity room after curiosity room they traveled through until they finally reached one that perked the interest of his dragon.

It was no wonder she hadn't been interested in anything in his hoard; the woman had one of her own.

"My sister Zeva travels everywhere and sometimes she asks me to come along." She held up a spear, a mischievous grin on her face.

"And how did you come across the Spear of Destiny?" He asked cooly.

"We are very good explorers." She answered just as cooly.

They perused through the rest of her collection, Alessandro growing more and more impressed by the wealth of knowledge she had on each item she possessed.

Then they came amongst a case with three protective barriers installed around it. Inside, he could see the dark energy of the cursed objects throbbing around a green stone, a jeweled belt and a simple golden ring. Her eyes seemed to harden at the sight of them.

"You kept them?"

He noticed the tension that straightened her back. "It's dangerous if they fall into the wrong hands. Concealment is the best way to deal with them." Just as she had been, she didn't need to say, but he heard it loud and clear.

"I heard the Coven has been looking for a way to sink their claws into you. As an actual repayment for helping the Thunder, I'd like to extend a sort of sanctuary over you."

The woman leveled him with a stare that shuttered her normally exposed thoughts. It was wildly attractive to Alessandro that she could jump from warmth to cold so quickly. "Sanctuary?"

"You'd be an honorary dragon. Fall under our laws and be our responsibility regarding your magic. No one would dare to question your ability to control yourself, or where you get your power from."

"So, instead of bowing to the Coven, I'd bow to you?" Her voice was sickly sweet and Alessandro understood his offer had offended her.

"In public. In private, your life would be your own." He intoned.

"Until you found a use for me that would benefit your Thunder." She shook her head as he was about to snap at her. "It doesn't matter. The Coven has promised to back off. I think I should make this clear, Alessandro; I will never be a damsel in distress."

Alessandro scoffed. "You dare use my name so easily?"

A mischievous glint took place in her eyes and the corner of her mouth, "Weren't you the one begging me to say it?"

Endless hells, he could feel his shaft throbbing as he recalled her moans.

"Careful."

"What exactly are the consequences if I choose to ignore your warnings?" She took a small step towards him.

It might have been an innocent movement, but the smell of desire she had been exuding since he'd eaten the cake had erased any idea of innocence from his mind.

"I was careful with you yesterday, little elf. If you tempt me into your bed again, I won't hold back. You've had your chance to run."

She took hold of his belt and yanked him closer. "My preferred cardio involves you underneath me."

He yanked her hair as he forced her to look at his face while his other hand curled around her throat, thumb against her already wet, pink lips. "I don't think I like you much, Rowan Dahl. You're greedy and full of nothing but lust."

She smirked. "I don't need you to like me. I need you to fuck me, Alessandro." His name on her tongue was fodder to his desire. His cock, strained towards her and he made sure she knew the consequence of that action by grinding it into the softness of the space just underneath her perky breasts.

Her eyes fluttered shut, and she took his kiss with an eagerness that stoked his dragon into roaring life.

How many times would it be until she no longer affected him like this?

He watched in fascination as her knees hit the floor. She tilted her head back and opened her mouth. Her breathing sped up as he grew closer, visible in the rhythm of her breasts rising and falling.

From his angle, even with her dress still on, he had a perfect view straight down to her heat.

His teeth ached to devour her.

Teasing her, he was slow to undo his fly. Her eyes pulsed with a purple glow he knew to be her succubus joining the fray as soon as his dick bounced out of its confinements. He reached down, sliding the tips of his pointer and middle finger into the wet heat of her mouth. His pads brushed against the points of her teeth and along the velvet walls of her cheeks. Her lips wrapped around his digits, and he could feel her tongue sliding over and in between his knuckles, a suction pulling him deeper.

He slid them back out and ran them along the entirety of his length. Her breath hitched, eyes locked onto the movement.

"Ask nicely, and it's yours."

"Fuck nice." She snarled.

"Then suffer." His fingers moved to tuck himself back in, but she let out a small groan.

Satisfaction rolled through him at the sound. Small wins mattered when dealing with her.

"May I please suck your soul out of your dick?"

He let out a sharp bark of laughter. "Rowan Dahl, you're playing with fire. My dragon wants to break you."

"Let him try." She shrugged.

He firmly grabbed her chin, holding her still as he traced the curve of those full, wicked lips with the tip of his length. "Ask nicely."

The warmth of her breath slid over his skin. Goosebumps crawled over his arms and down his back.

"Please." It was little more than a breath, but he would take it. Alessandro had reached his own limit.

"Open for me, Rowan."

He removed his grip from her chin and guided himself inside. Slow. Her tongue accommodated his girth, her violet eyes watered slightly at the stretch required.

He entangled his now free hand within her hair, slightly tugging as he settled for the ride.

Her moan vibrated around him, her tongue pulsing with her heart-beat. The warmth of her hands enveloped his balls.

Her eyes never left his as she pulled back and then slammed him in. He tried to keep watching, but the suction, wet warmth and her fingers, which were soaking up the saliva that ran down his length, overwhelmed him. He gave up the battle of keeping his eyes open as he gripped her hair even tighter.

A moan of appreciation encouraged him to take the next reckless action in which he rocked his hips in his own rhythm. She joined him with vigor. Her heat abandoning his sack as she gripped the back of his thighs, trying to keep her balance as he fucked her mouth.

He wanted to move on, to show her he was as good at giving plea-sure as she certainly was, but, when he tried to pull away, her nails dug into his thighs, her speed increased and she took him deeper than he thought possible.

Endless hells.

Her knuckles caressed the skin between his asshole and his shaft, and he could feel the pull in his belly. He didn't have enough time to warn her before he was spilling his seed into her mouth. Hard and hot.

Rowan drank every drop and licked her lips as she pulled back. When Alessandro looked down at her wet, swollen pink lips, the blush on her face and her hazy eyes mesmerized him.

Then his attention snapped on a movement down below. She was touching herself, sliding her own fingers in and out of her wet heat.

He growled with approval and he watched her for a few moments, before he had seen enough to know what she liked from the session.

He ripped the dress off of her in one fell swoop and cleared a table full of her collectibles. She glared at him, but he was unconcerned as he tested her flexibility on the edge of the table by spreading her legs apart and tilting her pelvis up for his viewing pleasure. She wasn't fully bare. An adorable patch of white hair shaped into a heart hov-ered over her soaking wet heat.

How had he missed that the night before? He couldn't help but ap-preciate the lovely surprise and he laid a soft kiss at the point before his tongue extended and he took his first taste of her.

She was spicy and herbal like her scent had suggested, and with the ambrosia in her system, she was also tangy. He grazed her clit with a fang and her gasp was enough to remind him that this woman, despite how soft she felt in his hands, liked it hard.

He smirked as her mewls of pleasure rose in pitch and whispers of encouragement joined as he added fingers in to stretch her. Gods, she was so wet he would happily drown in her essence. He was losing more and more control and though he had kept his size manageable before, he could feel it expanding as he drank her in.

His other hand worked on her breast, but as he could feel her first release coming, he reached past it, wrapped his fingers around her throat and gave a careful squeeze. Rowan's hands wrapped around his forearm, encouraging the action and even tightening, demanding more of a grip.

Alessandro complied with the demand and the reward for his efforts came an instant later with her climax. Heady and warm, he lapped at her until she caught her breath and reached down to entangle her hand with his curls.

He slowly made his way up her body, placed a kiss as he passed her navel, nipped at her perky buds, up towards her neck where he sucked and bit before landing on her lips.

They were as soft as they had felt on his dick, her mouth even hotter, if that was possible. Their tongues danced in their kiss as they poured their lust into each other. Alessandro felt her hands on his scalp, trying to bring him closer and he could understand her urgency. Something made him want to crawl into her skin.

He lifted her past the edge of the table; she spread her legs further apart, and he knew she was ready to take him in. Taking his cock into his hand, he placed its tip at her entrance. He refused to part with the decadent kiss that made him want to cum right there and then, especially when she nipped at his bottom lip.

"Fuck, you feel amazing." He hissed in between kisses. She was pulsing over his head, the warmth welcoming his entrance. He pulled back to watch her face as he sank in, watching for any sign of discomfort.

She bit her lip inch by inch, her breath coming shorter and shorter as he got deeper and deeper. "Are you bigger right now?" She asked, surprised.

"I said I wouldn't hold back." He watched as her eyes rolled back as he passed a certain point. He tilted his hips back a bit and brushed past it one more time. She hissed her pleasure.

He smirked down at her and her hands landed on his shoulders.

"Deeper!" She demanded and he once again complied until she took him to the hilt.

She took a shuddering breath, her eyes closed as she accommodated him. He leaned down and captured her still swollen lips, one arm wrapping around her waist, the other had his fingers playing with her bud.

When she rocked her pelvis against his, he began a slow steady beat, hitting that spot that made her breath catch. Soon he lost control and was driving into her hard and fast.

She pulled out of the kiss to catch her breath as he unleashed his full lust on her body. His teeth needed to feel her soft flesh. He found purchase on her shoulders and he applied enough pressure that she cried out.

Rowan's moans and yells tore at something primal in him. He was born to do this. To bring this woman to the edge. He had no other purpose. He looked at her as he worked.

Her eyes were now a steady purple glow as she took him in. Hair mussed, her face pink with their exertion. Her shoulders, neck and breasts marked by his bites.

She was gorgeous with the rays of the sun peeking from behind her head, which cast a halo that made him want to do the absolute filthiest things to ruin the image. He reached around as he felt his next climax building, grabbing her hair, making her arch her head back like how she had started this all, and his mouth worked on her nipples. She held onto his shoulders for dear life as he sped up and her breath shortened, signaling her nearness to completion as well. As she came, he bit down harder than he had before and she roared with a back-to-back orgasm as he spilled his seed into her pulsing cavern.

They continued like that, unburdened by the typical rules of new lovers. They unleashed their depravity onto each other. Faces they'd buried under the expectations of the Dragon King and an elven princess.

He was just Alessandro, as she had called him.

And she was Rowan.

Alessandro had never been so vicious with a lover, had never had so much demanded of him by someone who knew what they wanted and asked for it with no thought of shyness.

It was around the sixth round when he couldn't hold himself up any longer. Black edged his vision, watching as she also fought the losing battle of exhaustion. He was still inside her as they both closed their eyes.

He'd made a mistake, he thought as he fell unconscious. He'd let her crawl under his skin not only once, but twice.

He really had to do something about the woman. But perhaps it could wait until he showed her everything their bodies could do together.

Yes.

It could wait.

VIII

When Rowan came to consciousness, she realized she was in bed. Her bleary eyes looked around the room to see that the sun was working on setting outside. The blaring sound of her phone ringing near her footboard had woken her up.

Sighing, she tried to reach for it, but her aching muscles stopped her in her tracks. Her back, her abs and her vagina screamed their denial of her freedom and she cursed her inebriated alter ego for its recent reckless decision.

Yet, she couldn't help but smirk at some images that ran along her mind. Alessandro had proven to be as fantastic of a lover as she'd sometimes daydreamed. Actually, even more so because she hadn't expected him to be such a ferocious beast.

As she lay in the bed, worrying about if she could ever walk straight again, an unfamiliar plant on her bedside table caught her attention. She turned her head and saw a small card on its base with her name written in an ornate font.

Being within arm's reach, she grabbed the note and flipped it to the other side where in the same font it said, 'These two green pills will ease some of the discomfort. Your choice to take them or not, but it will be easier on your throat than my dick. Next time you want to test the limits of your succubus, here's my number. Thanks for the fun, Princess Rowan."

Rowan wasn't sure she'd ever get rid of the shit-eating grin she could feel on her face by the time she got to the end of the letter.

The sharp tones of her ringtone tore her attention from the scenarios of what else she could do with the Dragon King. She sighed and swallowed the pills.

It took less than a breath or two for them to kick in. She felt the throbbing pain ease until she could reach for her phone.

"Finally! Do you know how close fox-boy and I were to coming and kicking down your door?" Louisa's shriek filled Rowan's ear.

Rowan rolled her eyes. "If the sound of the lapping waves outside of my window are anything to go by, we could have had a beach day."

Kin's annoyance was palpable even with no facial features to underline his displeasure. "Could you explain why you went M.I.A?"

Rowan didn't really want to, so she remained quiet, knowing Louisa, uncomfortable with prolonged silence, would interfere.

A moment later the vampiress came through with the rescue, "What's really important is figuring out if you have some idea on how to deal with these wolves."

"Which wolves?" Rowan asked, only noticing then that she could hear a commotion in the background that wasn't Kin related and that Louisa sounded winded.

"What? Are you serious? What have you been up to? I'm talking about the wolves that are attacking the people in Greece. The Coven is here, but I can't tell if they're doing more harm than good."

Rowan, for her part, was still finding it difficult to move despite the speed she felt herself recovering. She had a thousand questions and her mind was working to figure out if there was a connection between this and the attack on the dragons.

Could Elaine Hitori not have been the only one responsible for it?

It could be a coincidence. Violent things happened every day, but her gut was telling her this wasn't the case.

"Louisa?" Kin's voice cracked. "Something's wrong."

Rowan's heart slammed to the bottom of her stomach. Her eyes darted around her room to find a tee shirt and a pair of cotton shorts not too far from her. They didn't match, but it would have to do. Pushing past the pain of her nether region, she vaulted from the bed and scrambled to put them on.

"Kin, Kin? Can you hear me?"

Rowan heard the phone clatter to the floor and Louisa's muffled curse as Rowan shoved on a pair of sneakers.

Faster than she'd ever managed, she located her bond with Louisa and phased before she even stood back up to her full height. She was once again on what seemed to be a battlefield. Screams ripped through the air in rattling unison.

Craters peppered what had once been cobblestone streets, white lime pieces of buildings lay in reminiscent fashion of the attack on Draconis. Rowan glanced behind her, catching sight of Louisa on the floor, her arms held up in defense as Kin slashed at her with extended claws. Blood dripped all over Louisa's white camo pants and crop top, her sobs muffled by the continuing mayhem around them.

Rowan moved behind the much bigger man, hooked her arms under his armpits, and could only take half a step back before he bucked her off and turned to face his new opponent.

Rowan's breath froze at the sight of his reddened conjunctiva, ruby slits that were his pupils and enlarged fangs that made an image of Elaine flash in her mind.

Had she not already proven she could take his beast going berserk, fear might have done her in. But as things stood, Rowan was the only one who could drag him back to his senses.

Trained in combat by her father since the age of seven, she dodged his attacks as they came, though he sliced off several locks of her hair with his extended claws.

He was faster this time, so fast she didn't have the time to mold the excess magic coursing through her veins to her whim.

She was stuck dodging and pulling back.

Catching sight of Louisa struggling to her feet behind Kin, Rowan shook her head when she saw the vampiress move to attack with a large piece of white rubble. "Draw a water prison circle. He's maintaining some control. I can keep him occupied for a couple of minutes." Though she still wasn't back to her full potential, the pills combined with the adrenaline that pumped through her veins had done a good job of numbing her pain.

If she died because of the most amazing sex of her life, Rowan would go to the grave in tears of humiliation.

She kept an eye around her, looking for anything she could use to help keep him at bay. But he was fast, and the town was in shambles.

As they cleared a large white stone building, she saw the first sign of what the call had been about.

A wolf was snarling, with his head low to the ground, sharp teeth bared as he and a dozen frenzied wolves stalked a large group of terrified civilians.

Unlike the Black Cove bystanders whose injuries were collateral damage from the dragon fight, the wolves were actively hunting civilians. They were herding them like they herded animals in the wild. The mass moved toward the harbor where boats and bodies were hurrying away from the shore, choosing the water rather than the teeth headed their way.

The observation cost her a sharp slice through her side. Cursing, she returned her focus to parrying his claws. Ducking and dodging the more critical hits and taking weaker ones for a chance at landing her own.

After the second hit landed, and her vision swam, she ditched her plan to focus on defense.

As she danced over piles of concrete, she picked up on his rhythm. The fox was much easier to read than the man was. It gave her the opportunity to check how much Louisa had progressed.

It was at that moment that Rowan caught sight of a child falling behind the still fleeing victims. She was reaching out. Her face was blood red and soaked with tears as wolves were inches away.

On instinct Rowan phased, landing in front of the girl and barely gathered enough energy to bring the water from the harbor in as sharp as a whip, keeping the wolves at bay.

"Get on!" She shouted as she crouched in front of the girl. The wolves were undeterred by the attacks of the whips and were still bearing down on them.

The girl scrambled on, the heel of her palm pressing into Rowan's eye so hard that she saw white for a second. It was a second she regretted losing, as she felt another slash of claws against her stomach.

She hissed and phased out back towards the screaming masses.

Pain was clouding her mind, making her sluggish, but the cries of fear from the girl were grounding her.

Dig deep, Rowan Dahl!

Cursing, she opened herself up to even more magic. It was more difficult than ever to regulate its entrance when she ached to heal herself, but her priority was the protection of the people behind her. She could hear them growing desperate as they ran out of space to escape. The sounds of more and more bodies splashing into the sea from the boardwalk grounded her even further.

Kneeling, she swung the girl around as her body vibrated with power.

"Cover your eyes and get at least two feet behind me."

Terrified, the girl took off.

Rowan faced the oncoming hoard of hundreds of wolves, catching sight of the Coven behind them. They were driving wolves towards the people rather than away with poorly planned spells that were the primary source of the ruined city. Were they unaware, or did they simply not care? She didn't have time to reach a conclusion. She molded the magic in her hands, setting parameters to a barrier that exploded from her. It would allow mystics and humans to pass through, but it locked out the witches and the wolves. She expanded it behind her to curve around the entire boardwalk and a few feet into the sea. She felt the bodies of sea life get pushed back by the limits of the barrier as she herself walked forward.

Carefully, she dragged walls of the land around each wolf, isolating them in high cells that they couldn't jump over, which only left her with one challenge. Kin could fly even without turning into his beast form. He was using the flames on the balls of his feet to get to her even as she threw wall after wall of water at him.

"Ready for our pissed off kitsune." Louisa's voice came through her head like a whisper.

Relief washed through Rowan and she shot towards the sky to get back to the vampiress as quickly as possible. The pain of her wounds knifed through her as she came upon the sight of her friend who was trying to catch her breath inside a blood circle.

The nut had used her own blood to map out the spell's intricacies perfectly. The woman never failed to impress with her precision.

Rowan landed at Louisa's side, wrapped a steadying arm around her shoulders and phased out moments before Kin landed in the circle. She heard Louisa murmur the activation words before a huge water bubble ensnared Kin.

They both held their breath as the torrents swirled him violently until his red eyes rolled to the back of his head, the flames on his feet extinguished, and the prison drew still.

Relieved, Rowan let out a shaky breath. It was short-lived as the sound of a familiar growl came from her side. She slowly turned her head, registering the bloodshot eyes and the elongated fangs too late. Louisa's teeth sunk into her neck.

Damn. She had fucked up. She was so tired, sore and wounded that she couldn't get a proper grip to get the vampiress off.

The energy that Alessandro had given her was endless, but as a half-succubus, she needed food and sleep to use it to its full potential.

Rowan traced a shaking, bloody finger on Louisa's exposed forearm. It took a moment for the rune to grip the vampiress and knock her out.

Woozy with blood loss, Rowan collapsed with the addition of her friend's unconscious weight to the debris filled street.

As they fell, so did the spell Louisa had erected to contain Kin, depositing the fox shifter right next to them.

As she had time to catch her breath, she allowed the magic to target the injuries she could take care of without a trip to her sister, noting that she really needed to brush up on battlefield first aid.

A slight groan caught her attention, and Rowan eyed Kin as he stirred to consciousness. Instead of the rabid kitsune she had been fighting, the golden eyed man stared back at her, horrified.

"It's okay." Rowan reassured as he looked them over while he scooped Louisa from on top of her.

She sat up on the cusp of her second wind. His face lost more and more color as he took in the bloody mess they both were. "We're going to be okay. I just need a second to catch my breath."

He gave a curt nod and then his eyes zeroed in on the still healing slash of her abdomen. "Ro." He gasped.

"It wasn't you. It was the wolves." She reassured him. "I need to get to the people. The witches were doing more harm than good last time I saw them. I need to make sure they're protected." He looked like he wanted to argue, but she narrowed her eyes. "You're a liability. I don't know what triggered your beast, but you're the only real threat to me here. Get Louisa to Rosario. I'll take care of getting this cleaned up."

Kin cursed before finally doing as she asked.

IX

owan hissed as she stood back to her full height. Even with the
help of her magic and Alessandro's pills, she wasn't healing as
quickly as she wanted. She needed to figure out how to deal with the
wolves and get to her sister in the Eastern Elven Kingdom as quickly
as possible.

She squared her shoulders as she rose to fly back over the scene. It
wasn't long before a black-haired witch with a silver goatee floated up
to meet her. The rest of the witches were working on healing wounded
civilians. As she passed some, she noted the witches looked a bit dazed
and confused.

She clenched her jaw, not sure how to take their sudden interest in
the wellbeing of the survivors.

"You are Rowan Dahl?" He asked, as he looked her over.

Years of avoiding using the full extent of her magic made her jumpy
about being up in the air with a member of the Coven beside her.

"I am." She answered with her head held high even though all she
wanted to do was crawl back in bed and lick her wounds.

"I'm Dae Kang, current Head of the Mediterranean Chapter of the
Coven. Great job containing the wolves and sorry we couldn't be of
more help. My A team is with the Elder in Brazil. We weren't ready
for four breakouts at once."

"Four?" She furrowed her eyebrows together.

Rowan didn't miss the confusion on Dae's face. "Yes, Greece, Brazil,
Egypt and Canada are all currently facing something like this. The
dragons are tidying up the bear shifters in Canada. The Elder is in

Brazil with the Snake shifters and the Atlanteans are in Egypt with the sphinxes."

What the hell had happened to the world while she had been asleep? Rowan shook her head and opted to concentrate on the one thing she could control. Helping the wolves turn back to sanity.

Unlike with the dragons, the targets of their bloodlust were the civilians rather than one another. She couldn't hear music or feel the darkness of a cursed object, but she could see and hear the desperation of the wolves to still reach their targets by bouncing off the walls in their make-shift cells.

"Do any of your people know what would trigger a wolf to go berserk?" She asked tentatively. Although she was uncomfortable working with the Coven, she would take all the help she could get with both of her partners out for the count.

Dae rattled off a list of triggers for a wolf, but they all seemed mundane and more of a one-on-one kind of issue rather than a pack. She hadn't realized how temperamental the beasts could be.

She held her hand up to stop the continuing list. "Sorry, I meant something rare, not day-to-day offences."

Dae put a hand on his chin and she could feel the slight buzz of magic around him, letting her know he was using a telepathic link to communicate with his cohorts.

"The only thing that really gets the wolves riled up is the full moon." He glanced up at the blazing sun. With the new moon just arriving the previous night, Rowan was finding the Coven about as useful as a bicycle without wheels.

Rowan examined the makeshift cells again, her eyes sharp to look for a piece that would finish the puzzle, then her sight settled on the largest wolf present.

At roughly six feet tall from paw to shoulder in its wolf form, the wolf's silver-white fur was a contrast to its sharp emerald eyes. Unlike the rest of the wolves, it wasn't trying to get out of its cell. Instead, it was low, its attention turned to the wall furthest from the bay, fangs bared.

She tried to establish a link with him, but she couldn't feel his mind out.

She turned to Dae. "Your telepaths, are they adept at connecting with shifters?"

Because of their beasts, shifters were notorious for being difficult to establish a link with. It was one of Kin's super strengths and Rowan felt the absence of her partners sting her.

Dae's shake of the head made her want to curse.

Instead, she took a deep breath and said to him, "I'm going to talk to that wolf. I don't think it's under the influence of whatever is happening. If it shreds me alive, wait for an adept telepathic to show up and try to talk to it again."

Dae raised an eyebrow. "You really are Rowan Dahl." Something about the way he said it suggested it wasn't a compliment. "Just so that we're both clear on this plan, I want to remind you that you're covered in blood and that wolf is in beast form."

Yep. Not a compliment. "Well, I am indeed Rowan Dahl."

As she approached the wolf, its brethren snarled, but her target looked up at her and sat back on its haunches.

She let out a sigh of relief. Dae's warning hadn't been totally unwarranted, but it seemed luck was favoring her for the day. "I won't be able to understand you, but maybe you can understand me?"

The wolf gave a slow nod to her question. Thrilled with the response, she shaped yes or no questions in her mind before she spoke again.

"All the other wolves are in bloodlust. Do you know why?"

The wolf gave another slow nod.

"Is that what you were just focusing on?"

Perhaps if the situation hadn't been so dire, Rowan would have found the 'so-so' head bob amusing.

"Is a wolf cursed?" She needed to get that one out of the way. She wasn't so sure it would allow her to do what needed to be done if that was the case.

It glared at her and shook its head.

Her initial reaction was to trust it, but if Kin were there, would he allow her to?

Deciding to deal with the consequences as they arose, she watched as the wolf turned to the sidewalls of his cell and made a motion of getting out, once again pointing his snout in the direction he wanted to go when she caught sight of him.

She considered her options. "If I drop your walls, you won't attack me, or your buddies, right?"

The wolf, if possible, shot her an annoyed look, and she raised her hands in defense, "Hey, I have to cover my bases here." She undid the magic holding up the surrounding earth, and he was immediately sniffing the air and curving around the cells of his brethren.

Dae was at her side as she tried to keep up with the giant strides of the wolf.

"What are you doing?" He demanded.

"He knows what's going on." She answered, "Just shut up and follow him." Dae looked like he wanted to argue, but she interjected. "He's being useful, so how about you let him work before you judge my decision?"

Dae cursed under his breath, but he followed.

They continued to weave around cells until they reached the furthest from the bay. The wolf pounced on the side, his massive claws gouging deep into the earth.

Rowan peeked over the wall, and her breath caught in her throat.

Inside there was a pup, maybe two feet tall if it stood on its hind legs. She could hear the weakened beating of its heart, and for a mystic whose heartbeat was supposed to be twice as fast as a human's, she knew it wasn't a good sign. Despite being in such a weakened state, it was still conscious, laying on its side staring up at Rowan as she popped over the wall.

Another thing she noticed were the similarities between the giant wolf and the tiny one; the green eyes and the silver-white fur. The pup seemed to reach out for the matured wolf on the other side of the wall once it realized it was there.

Rowan dismissed the magic keeping the two apart, and she watched with bated breath as the wolf sniffed around the pup. His teeth struck at the air a second later and, curiously, a piece of silky cloth popped into existence. Rowan felt the cracking of the barrier, keeping the magical signature of the godly treasure hidden. It seemed to burn the wolf, and he whined, turning to her with eyes full of concern.

She landed on the ground beside him without thinking and she fell to her knees to examine the cloth.

Somehow, the article had gotten so tied up with the pup that there were knots everywhere, sentience riddle the fabric as it tried to wrap tighter around the fading wolf.

"Kaguya's Robe." Dae's voice reached her from a distance, clearly still not trusting the wolves. Coward.

Rowan called forth a pair of gloves to cover her hands, raw from the heavy usage of magic, as she worked on the giant tangle that was the pup and the robe. Unlike Pan's Flute, the robe didn't carry a curse, but there was something undeniably menacing about it.

She recalled the tale of the bamboo cutter and the celestial moon princess. She supposed there might have been something malevolent as the princess returned to the moon after finding her true love, but her knowledge of Japanese mystic history wasn't as well versed as Kin's.

"If this were Kaguya's robe, why would anger be associated with it?"

Dae's answer sounded as if he enjoyed showing off his knowledge of things. "In some versions of the story, when Kaguya-hime returned to the moon, she left her robe with her earthly parents who fell ill with their grief over losing her. Perhaps the robe imbued their grief into dark energy. It's happened before."

Ah, so pain over loss.

A ballad from the Southern Elven Kingdom slid through Rowan's mind. She'd heard her mother singing it when she thought she was alone a week after news of King Lauricio's death reached them.

Rowan had never met the wispy black haired elf who was her maternal grandfather, but she'd caught glimpses of a picture her mother kept hidden behind a picture of her daughters in a pendant around her neck.

While Annabelle was unyielding and prickly when she had to talk about feelings, if one waited long enough, silence effectively turned the woman into mush.

The lyrics of a song her mother had once taught her from the Southern Elves that portrayed a story much like the moon princess' and her parents filled her head.

Rowan hummed as she worked. She poured magic into the notes like she would a spell. The robe became still, and she sang as she worked the knots.

The pup's whines calmed and soon it seemed to become putty in Rowan's hands. Its tension hadn't helped the situation.

It only took a few minutes to untangle the pup. Once it was free, the howling of the hundreds of wolves rattled her.

Rowan phased the robe away to join her collection.

The pup morphed into a girl with tight dark curls, emerald eyes and cinnamon brown skin that vibrated with life. She was also naked. Rowan held a hand out to summon a pink unicorn tee shirt from her bedroom and she quickly put it on the child, who giggled as her head and arms popped through their respective holes.

Rowan conducted a quick inspection over the girl looking for signs of burns or bruises, but wolves were the top healers of the world and the pup was undamaged.

Behind her, the grown wolf hadn't shifted forms, but she could hear a voice rush through her head.

"Who are you?"

The voice was so low and menacing that it sent shivers down her spine. She turned and saw that he didn't seem angry. Perhaps it was just in his nature to sound so rough.

"I am Rowan Dahl. Of RLK Magical Disaster Services."

"Harris Knox."

Comprehension grasped Rowan. "Ah, the Alpha of the Eastern Hemisphere Wolf Pack makes sense why you were a bit more resistant to falling in line with this mess. Do you have any idea how this adorable pup got a hold of such a thing?" The girl still hadn't let go of Rowan's leg, though she was now looking up at Dae as he made a descent.

"She found it in the forest during our morning hunt. As she was bringing it to me. I lost my reign on the hunting wolves when it began wrapping around her. The robe took advantage in a split second and took control." He hung his head in what seemed to be shame. *"They ran into the city and could not understand that we were out of the forest. I believe they only began hunting the civilians because they couldn't differentiate our usual prey against the adrenaline everyone was providing here. I tried to get them back under control, but the robe put up a barrier against me."* He growled at the memory, *"It isn't coincidence Rowan Dahl. Someone put that thing there for my daughter to find. There are few items that affect our wolves like that and the Robe of Kaguya is one of them."*

"I agree. Do you have any clue as to whom?"

He shook his head. *"I have to take my pack back home, but I can take you to the spot right after. Would you accompany me?"*

Rowan looked down at her wound, gauging how much longer she could go without seeking the right medical treatment.

"If you'll allow it, I could heal you."

Rowan raised an eyebrow. While wolves were known for their own healing abilities she had never heard that they could heal others. Their access to magic was as limited as most elves. "You're versed in healing?"

"Our saliva works wonders." He assured and Rowan felt heat crawl up her face.

Reminding herself that it was a simple medical procedure, and that she wanted to investigate the crime scene, she lifted her shirt to expose the wound.

"What are you doing?" Dae hissed.

She turned to glare at him. "Is that your catch phrase?" She didn't know if it was her prejudice against all Coven members, but something about Dae pushed her buttons. Even Cherry couldn't get her riled up so quickly.

He glared at her, but fell silent.

His tongue was hot and sticky. Rowan tried not to picture Lexine's disgusted face when she told her what first aid she had used. The tip of the tongue moved from her hip to under her breast, where she felt a bit flustered when the image of Alessandro, who had done something similar a couple of hours prior, popped into her head. The wolf's tongue faltered, and she knew he could smell her arousal. Heat traveled up her face; she would die of shame before she would die of an actual injury.

"Sorry." She whispered, refusing to make eye contact.

"It's an erogenous zone." His voice was softer and she could feel that maybe he was just as embarrassed as she was.

When he pulled away, she could see the skin stitching itself together again.

"Is it all shifter saliva that heals physical wounds, or is it special because he is the alpha?" Dae asked, making Rowan realize she had forgotten everything happening around them.

She could appreciate his curiosity. The same question had unfurled in her mind as she watched the effects.

"Let him know every canine shifter has their own power level, but even the youngest can cure the most dastardly of paper cuts."

Rowan snorted and passed the message. "I think the scene is secure, Mr. Kang." With her words, she dropped the cells. The wolves turned in their spots, looking around, coming to terms with the destruction they had ravaged. "Can you and the witches handle the resurrection of the city? The wolves are going to send me home."

"I think we'll manage. Thank you for your help, Rowan Dahl." The sincerity of his words surprised Rowan, who would have never imagined a Coven Witch saying anything of the sort to her.

She climbed onto the wolf's back and, with one last glance at the odd witch, she disappeared into the forest.

X

D raconis was a buzz underneath the pictures of Elaine Hitori that hung in ornate frames around the dining hall. It had been a long time since they had lost one of their own.

Alessandro sat through dinner with his people, some who were still recovering from their injuries from the fight wrought on by the wayward woman. Not one soul blamed Elaine for her part in the incident; they were too busy being in shock with her end.

Before the attacks on the other shifters, he'd found himself convinced that her connection to the flute was a tragic happenstance.

Now he knew better. Someone was targeting shifters and doing a thorough job at shattering every progress they had made to living amongst humanity in peace.

The face of the Ursine alpha, Willow, when she realized the extent of the damage their broken totem had caused, was stuck in a loop in his mind. The shadow of her beast pacing near the surface, ready to take over control, led to his decision to leave behind a set of dragons who would alert him if she fell victim to her grief.

She'd lost a daughter and five more of her bear shifters. Like the dragons, they'd turned on each other.

The news was spitting out stories and speculations from mystic races ranging from the average brownie to giants. They were riddling the media circus with conspiracy theories that he knew would have everlasting ramifications.

Tradition was the only thing keeping him from launching into a full investigation. The public mourning period for Elaine would be over in the morning, and he already had plans settling in his mind.

"She helped with the wolves too? You don't honestly think she's involved, do you?" His ears caught a snippet of a conversation between Stone, Naseem and Blaise, one table behind him.

"What if she's trying to make a name for herself? They were already calling her 'Dragon Hero.'" Blaise argued, "And now she's caught on live tape with the Eastern Hemisphere Wolves' alpha, riding his back through the woods after he drags his tongue all over her in broad daylight? You're really trying to tell me it doesn't seem fishy?"

What?

Alessandro controlled his face as he took in the information. The little elf had been in Greece? He had taken two hours to recover from their activities and he knew her healing abilities were inferior to his own. She'd gone to battle in that state? And the mutt of the Eastern Hemisphere Pack dragged his tongue all over her? As if she were some pup that the alpha needed to bathe?

Across the table from him, Terra had stopped her own conversation and was looking at him with concern. Her gaze slid discretely around to make sure no one else had seen before she motioned to her eyes. Alessandro glanced at his reflection in the glass cup before him and saw his own had turned red. A full on territorial red his people would recognize and question him over.

Terra had been the only one that had smelled the elf on him when he returned. She had helped him cover the rut markers, sure that the Hitoris would revolt if they knew he'd indulged in a quick round in the sack so soon after Elaine's death.

They hadn't asked for details. It was hard enough to face the fact that Elaine was gone. But he knew as time healed, they would come to him and ask him who had dealt the final blow.

It was something he had decided he wouldn't divulge. As soon as he'd seen that first tear trail down her cheek as she turned her gaze up to him, her secret had become his.

"First off, Rowan tried to maintain her anonymity when she was here. The only reason anyone found out her name was because two reporters slipped past a broken piece of the gate to overhear our conversation. Second, did you miss that giant slash across her stomach? The alpha was showing his gratitude to her for, you know, saving his entire pack from killing off everyone they saw, and it wasn't like she stuck around for interviews for that either."

Injured? How had she been injured? He burned to return to her, but what right had he? He needed to stay with the Thunder to mourn and though they'd crawled into each other's skin for two straight nights, he had no claim on the woman.

"If I didn't know any better, I would think it sounded like you're really interested in our elf friend Stone. Do you have a little crush?" Blaise joined in.

"I'm not blind. I'd give her the best weekend in bed if she'd allow it."

The brat had never sounded cockier or surer of himself, and Alessandro wondered if he'd made the right decision in naming him his heir. Not that he had much of a choice with the lack of multi-elementals in the Thunder.

"She would be the one doing the fucking if you got involved. What she needs is an actual experienced man to show her appreciation for helping us out. It's only right." Blaise laughed.

"Well, I think I could spare a weekend or three." Naseem's smirk was audible in his chuckle.

"I got the impression that you didn't trust her." Stone deadpanned.

"You don't have to trust to fuck. Not knowing that definitely puts you out for the count."

Alessandro was finding it more and more difficult to keep his full might muted. He knew how uncomfortable it made his subjects when he unleashed it. But, his dragon wanted them to know how inferior they were to him, the one who had already claimed her, the only one who ever could put a claw on her soft, flushed flesh.

"How do you idiots expect the elf to even get turned on by three dragons who fell to her feet so easily?" Terra cut in and Alessandro remembered why she was his favorite person in the world. An expert at reading her king, she had put two and two together and was cutting the problem at the root. "You would have a better chance of laying with each other."

"Terra, that hurts!" Blaise groaned theatrically.

Alessandro scoffed and turned in his seat to face the trio. "Does it hurt as much as it should, I wonder?" He asked. "After our mourning period is through, we will hold a physical readiness assessment for every capable dragon of the Thunder. If you don't meet my standards, I will allow Terra to whip you all into shape."

Color drained from the faces of the men, and Alessandro could all but see Terra's glee over his shoulder.

Deflated, the trio turned the conversation to scheduling mat time and Alessandro turned back to his dinner quite pleased with himself.

-R-

Rowan despised stopping by the North American Brood Estate, but her concern for Louisa outweighed her aversion to the place. As bad as the injuries had been, Rowan's primary intention revolved around checking on Louisa's mental well-being.

She'd bled a warm body, and she'd done it without express consent. It didn't matter that Rowan would cut herself a thousand times if it meant she could help the vampiress. Louisa held herself to a higher standard than her peers. And like Rowan, Louisa didn't take failure well.

Rowan passed the sprawling Spanish buildings of the estate in a blur, locating the magical signature of the vampiress and hoping to arrive without being stopped.

Wards kept her from phasing right to the woman's side as she'd have preferred, but if anyone stood a chance at getting there undetected, it was Rowan.

As an unfortunate regular of the Estate, she knew which parts would provide her with a bit more privacy. However, the security had gone up a tick since her last visit. She didn't know whether that was because of the shifter attacks, or because the Grand Vampire's daughter had shown up at home heavily injured.

Even with the increased security, she might have made it undisturbed if anyone other than the Grand Vampire herself had been the one to stop her. She was so unexpected that Rowan forgot to cast her eyes away. Rosario set her with a stony glare.

"Que haces escondiéndote en las sombras?" Rosario the Cruel demanded in her native tongue.

Rowan wasn't as practiced at using it as Rosario liked, but it usually garnered more favorable results if she at least attempted it.

"Estoy buscando su hija." Rowan cast her eyes to the floor, hoping it wasn't too late to show some reverence.

Rosario's voice was stone. "Do you think I should let you see her when you're the reason she ended up bleeding all over my carpet? And you sent ese zorrito who knows absolutely no Spanish or the slightest bit of manners to bring her to me?"

Rowan bowed her head. "Perdón Doña Rosario."

"Perdon? I thought I told you two to stop getting involved in matters outside of your business because you would end up dead. But no. Not only once, but twice in two days, you two tontas flew into the fray of danger without a single thought. Did neither of you ever grow up with any sense knocked into you? Shall I knock some sense into you now, Rowan Dahl?" Each moment that passed, Rosario's voice got lower and more furious.

Rowan kept her head bowed as the woman unleashed her anger upon her, nodding and agreeing when prompted to. Seriously, even her own mother never berated Rowan as much as Rosario did.

"And one more thing. Let me see the wound."

Rowan winced, but raised her shirt. Despite the effects of Harris Knox's tongue, it still needed proper medical attention.

She could feel the frustration coming off the Grand Vampire in waves.

"Your mother is going to hear about this," Were Rosario's last words before she phased away.

Rowan groaned but continued her way up the winding sidewalks until she came upon Louisa's apartment door. She walked right past the cozy living room, spotless kitchen and bathroom to the massive bedroom with a fourposter bed lined by thick curtains pulled shut around it.

Rowan slid them open. Louisa and Kin were both sound asleep. Caught in what seemed to be a battle over the blankets, they sprawled in two different directions. Her presence didn't wake them up, underlining their exhaustion. Conjuring a second blanket, she separated them. There wasn't a single flutter of eyelashes or groan as she worked.

Warmth and relief filled her to see them healed and comfortable. Satisfied, she backed out before her irate mother could call her and she stole out into the night as quiet as a burglar.

-A-

Alessandro lay in his bed, staring at the screen on his phone, inexplicably irritated.

Not one call. Not one text. It was as if the elven princess had forgotten he even existed. He, the mother fucking Dragon King.

He rolled his eyes at his own behavior before flinging the device across the room into a pile of pillows in the corner, disgusted.

He tried to fall asleep but his mind kept flying back to the vision of the woman laying in a pile of her own blood, the wolves idiotic enough to believe her if she said she was fine. Had it been any other time, he would have sent one of his dragons to check on the situation, but he didn't want them knowing he was interested in her beyond repaying the debt.

He also didn't want her to know that he was more interested in her than she was in him.

He supposed he could visit the astral plane. She would never know he even stopped by and his body would remain in Draconis. His dragons need not know he wasn't all there.

Mind made up after another half hour of fighting his sheets, he began his meditative journey. Magic wrapped him up in a wash of coolness, seeping through his scales as he gently slid out of his physical form. He searched for a hint of the woman, recalling the way magic zoomed to her beck and call at the slightest provocation. The golden glow that was a sign of a Blessed called his attention. He found her in a blaze of yellows and purples. Yellow usually denoted elven lineage, the purple her succubus, though he noted both colors were brighter than was usual. He supposed it could have something to do with her unnatural aptitude with magic.

She was laying in a bed he didn't recognize. It was small and barely big enough to contain her. Around the room, hanging posters caught his attention. Some were of bands he recognized, cartoonish ones he didn't. But his interest zoomed in on the one of himself.

He didn't recall posing for the picture, but he'd been coming out of the ocean on a rare day at Black Cove's beach with his dragons, water running in rivulets off his exposed muscles. He'd been in the middle of braiding his mass of curls into a manageable form, half grinning at what he remembered was something Terra had said just out of shot.

She was a fan? And hadn't even tried calling him once? Perhaps age had dulled the infatuation.

He moved on and took in the collection of second place trophies put on grand display shelves with her name carved into them. He couldn't help but observe that not a layer of dust existed on a single award.

"Alessandro?" Her whisper came from the bed. She wasn't asleep. He moved closer to her.

He should have been nothing but a passing shadow to her eyes, but he should have known magic wouldn't have worked as intended with her.

He noted her sharp intake of breath as she peeked around the room, as well as the scrapes and bruises all over her face. He also caught sight of the marks he had left along her neck and her arms where he had held her. How rough had he been?

"I heard of the injuries you received while working with the wolves. I came to make sure you weren't dead." Or worse off and mated off to the mutt, he added only in his head.

Rowan seemed surprised by the gesture. "I'm okay. A little banged up, but my sister was more concerned about your bite marks than the injuries from the fight."

"Your sister?" He asked.

"Lexine is the best healer in the Eastern hemisphere." Pride was obvious in her voice. She laid back down and patted the tiny spot next to her. When Alessandro sat, he felt the softness of her stomach along his leg. It was bizarre to feel the physical realm on the astral plane. "I would've gone home, but Rosario called my mom and freaked her out. Now she thinks I'm asking for death or something and insists I stay the night in the castle. I'm not sure what she's hoping to accomplish, but most times it's easier to just give her what she wants."

He trailed a finger on the wounds of her shoulder. He recognized the mark of a vampire bite, and whoever had done it hadn't taken care. "Who did this?"

He could feel the moment that tension entered Rowan's body. "It was an accident."

"It seems like all of your wounds were an accident." Alessandro was about to chide her but he recognized the signs of the woman expecting punishment for what she had done.

Shoulders hunched, head bowed. How many people had already gotten onto her for her recklessness? He softened his voice, thinking about how he would approach the situation if she were one of his dragons. "People lived through today because of you." He said, reaching out to pat her head, "But you must be gentle with yourself if you wish to continue to play the part of a hero."

Rowan turned to face him and the smile she threw at him brightened up the entire space around her. Rowan Dahl was literally glowing at the praise. His smile was unbidden, and he doubted she could see it, but there it was, anyway.

A knock at the door took the glow away. "I'm really not supposed to have boys in here." She whispered.

Alessandro laughed at the dismissal, but he faded out without a fight.

When he landed back in bed, he found sleep came to him much easier.

-R-

Rowan glared at the spot Alessandro had disappeared from. His laugh had been so loud her father had definitely heard it before he opened the door.

Kyron looked around the space, but once he found there was no one with her, he raised an eyebrow. "Should I even ask?"

She shook her head, "What's up Daddy-O? I thought you were already asleep."

He reached into the pocket of his robe, pulling out two packaged cake rolls and juice pouches.

She grinned and eagerly took one as he made himself comfortable at the foot of her bed. It took her a moment too long to realize she wouldn't be able to open the pouch without inflicting pain on herself, and she gave it back for him to help.

With the loss of the adrenaline pumping into her, Rowan was in so much pain it hurt to even breathe. It had been pure pride to not allow the Dragon King to see her so obviously beat up.

Wordlessly, her father rolled down the packaging and inserted the straw into her pouch before putting them on her lap for easy reach.

"How much did mom scream?" He asked after swallowing his first bite.

"She didn't." Rowan cringed at the memory. "She talked with that really quiet voice and almost started crying like twice. I wonder exactly what Rosario said to make her act like that."

"That doesn't sound like the woman I know and love."

Rowan giggled, "I wish she would've screamed. Maybe then I'd be in my king size bed instead of this twin. How did I ever fit in here?"

He laughed, "Once upon a time you were a kid. It's difficult for her to see you as a grownup. Honestly, it's difficult for her to see herself as a grownup."

Rowan snickered. Wasn't that the truth? There was an everlasting youth in Annabelle Dahl.

"So, you and the alpha?" Kyron raised an eyebrow.

Rowan huffed, reminded of the tabloid-like newsreels her sister had accosted her with on her hospital bed. "No, I didn't even see any reporters around when they took that video. I thought we were in the clear. He was just giving me a hand. I was ready to pass out before we even got to the clearing where his daughter had found the robe."

"Well, to anyone who saw it and knows even the slightest bit of mating culture, it looked suggestive, and that's without all the bite marks all over your neck. Isn't that a shifter thing, too?"

Rowan could feel the heat radiating off her cheeks. "That wasn't him."

Kyron didn't really want to know about Rowan's love life. He had shown up for another reason, and they both knew it.

Ever since the first Cursed incident, her father had been with her through them all. He was the one who had convinced her she was helping them by ending their pain and suffering. When she was younger, he had often held the sword with her as she dealt the last strike until she grew old enough to keep the weight on her own shoulders.

Cakes had once upon a time helped the bitter tears that fell into her mouth; she wondered where he had learned that and if maybe he did it by himself when he had been on the battlefield. Now, she seldom cried when it happened, but it still tore at her. Until she swung her sword, the Cursed still lived.

Sure, if the curse took them over, they would eventually disintegrate into something her godfather called worse than death, waiting to be released when the next soul fell victim to the object. That could take days or centuries depending on where the body fell. Even knowing that had never helped her feel better.

"She was a dragon." She whispered. "And she was beautiful. She had these dark blue eyes and really shiny hair. Her name was Elaine." She smiled bitterly.

"You've never known their names." He was concerned. "Was she a friend?"

Rowan shook her head. "No. The Dragon King saw me do it. He told me."

"Dragon King?" Kyron sat up straighter. Concern darkened his baby blue eyes as they landed on the poster across her room. "He didn't hassle you over the girl's death, did he?"

She shook her head. "No. He understood."

"It was your first time meeting a loved one. It must've been hard."

Had it been? Is that why she had done what she had done with him? Given herself so completely. He had lost a lover, so she became one?

No. Their first night together had been just as raw and uncontrolled as their second.

"It was different." She murmured, "I always envisioned the families of the loved ones to be angry with me. But he felt... grateful."

Kyron took a deep gulp from the pouch and asked, "How did you feel after experiencing that?"

"Less shitty. I'm glad he was there."

Kyron sighed. "So there's no way that he missed the fact that you're a Blessed?"

Dread curled into her mind. "No. There isn't." Especially not after she'd completely spilled her guts out to him about everything.

"Do you trust him?"

"I don't know yet." She admitted, her eyes catching on the poster across the room.

The first time she'd heard his name, it had been from Chloe that day the troll took them captive.

Before Master Japhet adopted her, the orphaned witch lived in an orphanage that Dragon King was a patron of.

Not only did he dole out money for them, but he went above and beyond by stopping by personally at least once a month. He ensured the kids had every resource available to them: food, education, safety, and even birthday parties.

"One day, you'll be more powerful than even him. I'm sure of it!" Chloe's words rang through Rowan's mind.

Before she'd seen the poster on a trip through the market with her godmother, she'd imagined the Dragon King to be an aging old man with silver hair and a soft smile.

When Lilith caught sight of it, she'd bought it, proclaiming she wanted it as a dartboard. Rowan had asked who it was and after a long breath of curses, her godmother finally told her it was Alessandro, the Dragon King, but that Dirty Worm King would've been a more apt name.

At fifteen years old, Rowan found her first ever crush, and her godmother wanted to call him a worm.

Safe to say, Rowan seized the suggestive picture as her own and pinned up the same night.

When she first felt his magic in Black Cove, the power gap between where she stood against him floored her. But she had also been thrilled.

Did she trust him?

The answer was that she didn't know. But she really wanted to.

XI

❦

Alessandro eyed the two greatest pieces of evidence he had at his disposal. The flute that had been the source of his dragons' madness and the totem that had caused the bear shifters to attack one another the day before.

Naseem, buried in scrolls in one corner of the office, was gathering information over the two pieces of treasures.

Aqua, Alessandro's Water General, a thin pale woman with hair the color of turquoise, was extracting all the physical evidence from the pieces. Though from the huffs and groans, she wasn't having the easiest time with her assigned task.

Blaise was tracking down the last known whereabouts of the flute, and Stone had gone to interview the Canadian bears over the history of the totem within their tribe.

Alessandro's focus was on dwindling down a suspect list. Over the years, he'd kept track of those he'd pissed off. He hadn't realized how long it had gotten, if he was being honest.

He referenced it against those who openly had grudges against shifters.

Creating a list of suspects that he would whittle down when his generals turned in their own data.

"There's nothing here." Aqua's irritation was palpable in the air.

Naseem and Alessandro glanced over their screens to the blue-haired healer, who was glaring at the two objects with unsheathed animosity.

Alessandro shifted his body so he could dodge the objects he could feel she was close to flinging.

"Perhaps that's a clue within itself." Naseem suggested. "What spells can erase traces? Magic always leaves a trail of some sort."

Aqua groaned. "Isn't that your area of expertise? My talents end at healing and water related magic."

Even if Blaise was the one general who received the most guff from his charges, Aqua was inarguably the least assured. Alessandro had confidence when things got dicey that she would prove that he hadn't been mistaken in choosing her over Elaine's mother, Mezine. But until then her insecurity over her position would hold her back.

"I could help you if you wanted me too, but I definitely will charge for my services." Naseem grinned.

Aqua squared her shoulders as she turned to face him head on. "What are your terms?"

"I want one of your rotations."

Alessandro raised an eyebrow when Aqua's pleading eyes turned to him to beg for his interference. "I am but a beacon of hope for my people, not a tyrant."

Naseem and Aqua both burst out into laughter.

"Half a week." Aqua offered.

"Done." Naseem agreed, and he moved his computer over to help her.

Alessandro resettled into his task. His dragon let out a breath of discontent. He had hoped the argument would have escalated so he could squash it.

His energy wanted a physical release. He'd prefer to seek the company of the white-haired elf that kept randomly crawling into his mind as he worked. But he would've taken a fight if only to take the edge off.

He wanted to curse. Instead, he adjusted his pants, leashed his beast and concentrated on the names rolling across his screen.

-R-

When Rowan walked into her office the next morning, she hadn't expected Louisa and Kin to be

in their chairs. Healed, and elbow deep into the work they had to catch up on.

It was a productive morning as Dew passed tasks out and kept them on schedule to be caught up by lunch.

As an incentive, Dew had threatened to take away morning coffees for a week from whoever failed to meet her expectations. It explained why Kin and Louisa had both been diligent in their work since the beginning of the day.

Rested, and a bit drugged with one of Lexine's medicinal teas, Rowan had enough energy at her disposal to get through her workload before noon hit.

After lunch they would have to continue business as usual, but the only thing on Rowan's mind was the plate of banh baos from the Vietnamese restaurant down the block.

"Finally, done!" She heard Louisa cry with relief.

Kin had finished before both Rowan and Louisa and was taking a well-deserved break by propping his feet up on his desk and catching up with the news.

"No new shifter attacks?" Rowan asked, passing his office. He was at her side a moment later, jacket draped over his arm.

"No, but you're all over the gossip rags. I'm actually surprised your mother hasn't stopped by to give you a good lecture." He extended his phone. The high definition of the image made it impossible for her to even try to deny it was her.

She was bloody, missing half of her shirt and slumped, drained of energy on top of the wolf.

"Apparently, a witch assured everyone that you said you were going home. I can't believe you never told us you were so close." Louisa joined them as they descended the stairs.

Dew fluttered around them before settling on Rowan's head as they headed out to the beautiful spring day Black Cove was experiencing.

Downtown had been one of Rowan's favorite spots during her time at Spellcasters Academy. The bars and restaurants catered not only to the young collegiate students, but to a more mature crowd as well. Each building was brick, but modern architecture had crept in. Floor to ceiling windows and neon lights married old class to new class.

Rowan's body still ached as her heeled boots hit the cobblestones of the sidewalks and she had a difficult time scraping out the pictures of injured casualties of the shifter attacks from her mind. The news wasn't being stingy with the more horrifying images. Though they had been sparse on information over the sphinxes.

"I'm not." Rowan bit out. "I was tired. He wanted to give me a ride."

"Oh yeah. I bet he did. On his back, on his dick, whatever worked." Louisa snickered.

Dew joined her laughter, but Kin glared at the brunette. "Must you be so crass?"

Louisa simply stuck her tongue out, "So where did lover-boy end up taking you, anyway?"

"To where his daughter found the robe." She sighed. "There were absolutely no clues on who could've left it. It was near a popular trail. Marissa seemed okay, though. I thought she might suffer from some trauma, but up to the point I left, she had been playing with the other pups her age."

"Ah, so you don't deny that he's your lover-boy?" Louisa waggled her brows, "Ten bucks, Kin."

Rowan gasped melodramatically. "I just met the guy yesterday. How easy do you guys think I am?"

Save for succubus meals and Alessandro—and come on, he was the freaking Dragon King—Rowan didn't just sleep around with anyone, thank you very much.

Kin rolled his eyes. "Yes or no?"

"No." Rowan growled.

A grin spread over the kitsune's face and he held his hand out for the ten-dollar bill. "Told you we were right, Dew."

Rowan gasped, reaching up to pluck the fairy off her head. "Dew, y tú?"

Dew escaped her searching hands and hid in Kin's glossy black hair. Louisa was laughing so hard she was clutching her stomach and wiping tears from her eyes.

"Kin promised me spring rolls if I sided with him! They're my weakness! And technically I was on the side that made you less...promiscuous." Dew cried from within the strands.

Kin grinned down at Rowan, unabashed. "Thanks for lunch."

The words cut Louisa's laughter off sharply.

Rowan caught her footing at the last second as Louisa attacked her with a side hug. "Ro, I am so sorry I attacked you yesterday. I don't know what came over me."

Rowan leaned her head against the cradle of the taller woman's throat and smiled. "You were bleeding out, Louisa. I think you had excellent control, given the condition you were in."

"You mean the condition I put her in." The ten-dollar bill crumpled in Kin's fist. "I've never lost control like that before. I don't know what is going on with my beast. The dragons or wolves shouldn't have affected it."

Dew peaked her head out of his hair and patted his forehead to comfort him.

"Well, you reacted differently. The first time it was a whole day later, the second time you snapped out of it before the pack did." Rowan pointed out.

Kin stiffened and froze in his steps. "I could snap again, at any time. How much longer until you have more potions to knock me out, Louisa?"

Louisa grimaced, "Ten days. It's unfortunate you destroyed my collection during your first rampage."

Rowan placed her finger on her chin. "It is strange. All the research we've done on beast interactions always highlights power structure and there are very few who can actually make you submit. Maybe we need to look at all of this from a new angle."

Her jaw popped open as a picture of the most in depth magical encyclopedia ran through her mind. "Oh, my gods. That bat knew I would need it!"

Both Louisa and Kin waved away some of the concern Rowan's outburst had attracted.

"Which bat?" Kin asked.

"Henrietta Young." Rowan waved the thought away, "First lunch and then research."

Dew's voice was soft with trepidation. "If they attack again, it's going to be on a grander scale. Surely every shifter group has their defenses reinforced at the moment."

"Yea." Rowan agreed, "Whoever's behind it all isn't done. None of the attacks reached their full potential. I think they're going to keep trying until they get what they want."

"Besides turning the world against the shifters, what could any of this do?" Louisa demanded.

"Maybe that's the goal." The fox shifter guided them around a huddled group of young mystics blocking the middle of the path.

Rowan held a bated breath as she felt the stares of the group follow them. "That's the fox shifter that was in Greece, I told you I'd seen him around here."

That was quick to reach back to their slice of the world. How many cameras had there been? How long had they been there?

"And I told you I'd seen that succubus around here too! But she didn't have those wings and horns before. Do you think she's really one? I've heard there are a ton of mystics getting procedures done to look more exotic."

Rowan felt her anger rise, she was getting ready to turn and lash out at them, but then Dew resettled on her head and a wave of calm rushed through her.

This was her new norm. She had to get used to anything that could be thrown at her. She had no doubt it could be worse.

"Louisa, if you get some time today, I want you to dig around and see who has a big enough grudge against shifters to target any race. Kin you focus on beast communication. I'll try and see if any of the leaders of the snake, bear or sphinx shifters are willing to tell me what their trigger source was and I'll look around their point of origin."

Louisa pouted. "But Romo is launching a new sweater collection and I cannot fall behind in fashion this winter, Rowan. I just can't."

Rowan scrunched her nose. "You're right, priorities are important. Sweater collection first and then trying to make sure people don't die.
"

"No." Kin cut in, "You are a princess and you are the heiress of the North American Vampire Brood. Get some servants to do your shopping and focus on saving people's lives first."

Rowan and Louisa groaned.

"You know, Ro, this is all your fault. I don't know why you couldn't have had your grand idea until after the release."

-A-

Alessandro was in the middle of a meditative bubble bath when the doors to his personal bathroom slammed open.

He glanced up through the steam as Blaise entered, cheeks flushed from exercise, his hazel eyes bright, "There's a mob outside of the gate."

Alessandro felt his jaw tighten. "A mob?"

"They're destroying the shops. They're calling us murderers." Blaise paced up and down the length of Alessandro's tub, his rage becoming more and more pronounced. "Aqua keeps putting fires out, but they keep making new ones, literal ones, not figurative ones. Naseem doesn't know what to tell Stone to say or do and the four heads of houses are saying they're in mourning."

Alessandro growled as he stood up to his full height. Trails of water and bubbles followed him as he swept out of the room. "What about Terra?" He demanded.

"She's already left for Dragon City to prepare defenses and beds in case we need to retreat that way."

It was a solid call on the earth-dragon's part, and he hated it. But he was Alessandro, and he did not back down. Stepping into a pair of black jeans, a white shirt and his favorite boots, he led the way back to the gate through the air.

The gate had been more for decoration than an actual barrier. It was ornate, extraordinarily difficult for it to move. The sight of it closed filled Alessandro's mouth with bitterness.

Throughout its life, the gate had remained open. Once upon a time, it helped soften the public image of the tight-lipped community that lived behind its walls.

Stone stood at the gate, a ball of flame jumping from one hand to the other. Though Alessandro had warned the younger dragon to not turn to fire when he was angry, it had become a tell that the Dragon King used to gauge him.

Alessandro was angry too, but as a leader he needed to show how calm he was even in the face of adverse conditions such as the ones they found themselves in.

"Aqua, Naseem, you two will take the east side of the street, Blaise and Stone you two will take the west. While Naseem and Blaise work on putting out the fires, Aqua and Stone, you are going to deep ice the stores. Mundane fire won't be able to ignite it if you do it right. Make sure you give it a bit of a soft finish. We don't want to seem threatening. I will shift the crowd towards the end of the street. Once you're finished with the task, I want you all to walk right back through the gates. No engagement with the press or crowd. Am I understood?"

The four dragons nodded.

Alessandro took a moment to cool his anger, observing the four following his lead before he threw the doors open in one push.

The crowd that had gathered outside had been bigger than he had mentally prepared for, but his plan took the numbers into account. Smoke had turned the street dark, the smell fueling the rage of the more infuriated individuals present. The hollers and threats enticed his dragon forward, but after years of having to deal with his Thunder, Alessandro knew how to put on a face of peace even if he wanted to break the offenders into tiny pieces.

The roots of the trees that lined the sidewalks danced around the crowd, easing those who were there more to gawk and say they were part of the movement towards the end of the shopping district.

He dodged debris the crowd threw, wares from the shops they'd ransacked.

Fury permeated his chest. How dare they? Creations his dragons had shed blood, sweat, and tears for, used as weapons.

"You're all monsters!" Echoed like a war cry.

Each spell felt like a step away from losing total control. But he couldn't afford to give in. It would play into the hands of whoever was behind all of this.

He created air bubbles that discombobulated the more rowdy participants in mini twisters before the branches guided the confused individuals with the rest of the crowd.

Questions from the press came as he worked, and the bright lights from rolling cameras filled his vision with momentary stars. None of the questions really stood out besides one; how could the public trust that the next time the dragons lost control, Black Cove wouldn't be in danger as it had been heading to with the first attack?

He bit his tongue as he thought, how were his dragons ever going to trust the public again after the damage they'd caused to the their collections? For something that they'd had no control over?

With Dragon Alley cleared, he cast his eyes away and turned his back to the world. The gates shut behind him with a resounding thunk.

XII

R owan was stunned into silence as she looked at the TV set in the corner of her office.

He was on the screen. His hair dripped water on his crisp white shirt as he worked his magic without missing a beat. He weaved spells so tightly and quickly that she missed moments when he alternated between wind and earth style. He removed the intruders of the shopping district with vines from the blooming trees that ran along the sidewalks and then confused others with mini tornadoes.

She was in absolute awe of the nuances she would have missed if she hadn't been paying such close attention to the events unfolding. The dragons fell into his rhythm, correcting steps by small signals he sent if they veered. It was a controlled dance. She could watch it for hours.

There was so much fear from the crowd, mingled with a hateful speech that enraged her as a spectator.

Dragons had always been the ultimate mystics. Their magic was so old it was a popular dispute that it was the first established art. Their casters were so well imbued, it was unheard of for any of them to not have established access to magic.

The impenetrable scales added yet another layer to their untouchable status, which made the incident that much harder to swallow. But these facts did not make it okay for the public to threaten their livelihoods. Fear was not an acceptable excuse for their actions.

There was no more trust on either side. She could feel it most of all when he turned his back on the world and shut the gates once and for all.

Something about his eyes, despite their solid state of steel gray, did something to her that had her reaching for her phone as soon as Draconis' barrier visibly erected.

"Hello?" His voice was rough with fury.

"Hi." She rolled her eyes at herself. Why the hell had she called him? A text would've been fine. "It's me."

The soft sound of an exhale preceded a small chuckle. "I know."

"You were great." She watched as the mob tried to reignite the flames. They were idiots for underestimating the power of the Dragon King and his dragons. Dragon Alley was impenetrable. "Deep ice?"

"A small trick I invented, of course." He seemed to have calmed a lot more than she would have at that point.

"Of course. You are the great and powerful Dragon King. Probably been alive for ages, naming and inventing all the cool magic tricks."

"The one and only."

"Come over tonight." She didn't know what she was saying. "To my office or home, whichever you prefer."

"I should focus on how to fix this mess that my Thunder is in."

Rowan had to swallow her disappointment. "Solid call. Before you go, I'm sorry, the world is full of idiots."

For a moment it felt as if he had hung up, but then his voice came through once more, "Thank you."

And then he ended the call without a single goodbye. Rowan glared at her phone and groaned, throwing her head on her desk.

"Was that a groan of longing?" Louisa asked from her doorway.

Rowan refused to pick her head up, and she groaned again.

"Nuh uh, get up, explain yourself. Who made you sound like a schoolgirl on her first call with a boy she liked?" Louisa sunk into the wingback chair across from her friend, a nail file in her hand, heels long lost somewhere in her office.

Rowan glanced up at the TV and saw the glimpses of Alessandro again. She pointed him out to the brunette.

"No fucking way, you hooked up with the Dragon King and kept it from me?" Louisa gasped.

"Things have been hectic lately." Rowan rolled her eyes.

Louisa tilted her head and raised an eyebrow as she examined the dragon, "He's kind of a meathead, isn't he?"

The disrespect! "He is not a meathead!"

"Did I just overhear that you slept with the Dragon King?" It was Kin's turn to stand at the door, arms full of his laptop, several hardcover books, colored pens and journals.

Rowan crossed her arms. "Yes, you did. Can you believe she called him a meathead?"

Kin sized the man up on TV and pursed his lips. "I suppose I can kind of see where she's coming from."

"What? Those eyes totally show he has so much more depth to him than just his insanely gorgeous body!"

Louisa giggled, "My goodness, what kinda skills must he have to make you so defensive?" Then she let out a gasp of enlightenment. "Wait, how long has it been since you've known him?"

Rowan shrugged.

"The dragon I smelled." Kin gaped. "Was that him?"

Rowan leaned back against her chair, a cocky smirk on her face.

"Did you meet him after the attack on Draconis? You *are* an easy slut!"

"Worth it," Rowan grinned as she pulled down the collar of her turtleneck to show the bites and slid the sleeves up to show where he had gripped her.

Kin's mouth fell open and Louisa's shaded eyebrows climbed into her hairline.

"Was he hungry?" Kin asked, recovering first.

Rowan waggled her eyebrows. "He was, and he got a full meal."

"We're going to have to establish an HR department." Kin sighed.

"Is that why you couldn't fight at one hundred yesterday?! How rough was he?"

Rowan frowned at Louisa's question, remembering that some of her injuries had indeed been a consequence of the coupling.

"Come on, let's concentrate. I need to get home before the sun sets or my dear husband will have my head on a platter. He was already upset that I spent the night at the Brood compound yesterday."

Rowan sobered up and nodded, "I see you've brought your own materials to class Kin, however, Henrietta Young also pitched in and sent us this." Rowan tapped the leather-bound book neither of her partners had taken notice of.

It took a second even after she directed their attention to the relic for them to comprehend what they were looking at.

Louisa let out a gasp.

Kin looked as if his eyes had landed on the most precious thing the world had ever beheld.

"Dead Henrietta Young?" Louisa asked.

Rowan nodded.

Louisa's eyes grew wide with shock, and she covered her mouth. "Rowan, did you kill Henrietta Young so you could get the Elder's Grimoire?"

Kin saved Rowan the energy from hitting her best friend by giving her a soft smack with one of his journals. "Why are you such an idiot?"

Louisa waved them both off and leaned over the book. "I never thought I would get to see it, let alone touch it."

"Do it." Rowan whispered conspiratorially as Louisa paused, her hand inches from touching the cover. As soon as her fingers stroked it, Rowan gave a shout and burst into laughter at the vampiress' terrified features.

Kin delivered her strike while picking up the grimoire.

Rowan rubbed the back of her head, sure that he had hit her harder.

"Well, I think it'll be more helpful to your role than ours. Perk up Louisa, time to get into the gossip reels."

Louisa pouted, "Fine."

-R-

By the time Rowan hung up the phone for her last call, the sun was close to being where Kin would have to leave.

She wasn't surprised that as he'd researched, Kin had also created a slideshow. As he set up, Rowan and Louisa took turns looking through the Elder's Grimoire, trying to find a rhyme or reason for its random entries. Kin had apparently got it down pat and was 'testing' their intellect to see if they could also figure it out.

"It's impossible." Louisa groaned, slumped over one of the five bean bag chairs Rowan had littered throughout her office.

Rowan turned to Dew perched on her shoulder, who had made her way in for moral support once she'd closed up the front office for the day. "Do you have any idea?"

"Well." Dew got shy when asked for input on things she considered way over her head. "It's not in any order that would make sense to us, because the Coven keeps their history pretty close to the chest. I think to decode it you would have to know which Elder had it and what events they went through and when they went through it."

"Yes, Dew. That's exactly what it is." Kin flung a chocolate in her direction and Dew caught it with a giggle.

"Lucky guess." Louisa grumbled.

"You really need to work on being such a sore loser, Louisa." Kin motioned to his prepared presentation. "So, according not only to the grimoire, but also a couple universities that have studied the relationships between shifters, hierarchies are the strongest determining factor in how we act. Hierarchies themselves range in structures between familial, to friendly, to romantic. Over this past year, a new study posed the question of how these hierarchies formed and what the most important factors were. They returned with an answer that the beast hierarchies aren't determined by race at all, but things such as age, physical prowess and—perhaps most important—magic capabilities while in beast form. The wolves shouldn't have affected me because I'm older and my magic capabilities as a kitsune overpower the typical wolf by tenfold, but because they were in a hive mindset, they counted as one giant threat to my beast."

Rowan didn't miss the annoyed tone Kin took on as he relayed this last part. "Still, they couldn't dominate me. I still maintained a relative humanoid form rather than going full fox, which was probably a mistake. If I would've let the beast take over completely instead of trying to hold on to my human reasoning, I could've made my own decisions and not hurt either of you."

"Is this hypothetical, or fact?" Louisa asked.

Kin scowled at the vampiress.

"Then we can't know. You could've ended up finishing us both off with a swipe of one paw." Louisa shrugged.

Enormous was a word for the behemoth that Kin was in his full fox form. Not only could he have wiped Louisa and Rowan out if he had lost control, but he would have wiped out the entire bay area as well.

"Is it possible someone is trying to start a war against the shifters? Paint them out to be bad guys?" Rowan asked, moving away from the grim hypothetical.

"Shifters are notorious assholes, present company included." Louisa eased the mood with a teasing nudge towards Kin. "But they've always been protectors, not attackers of the common masses. Still, I found some groups that hold something against them. My first inclination is, of course, the Order."

Rowan, like most mystic children, had learned of the Order in elementary school.

An organization stemming from an ancient group of monks that tried to justify their murders of Mystics by using the crimes as their proof that Mystics as a species were evil base creatures.

"Over the last five years, the Order has become more active and with a bunch of new recruits when vigilante movies and shows started gaining popularity. Their hate for all mystics isn't equal. I found a video of a rally which called for special attention to the shifters, calling them the ultimate deceivers because of their relative human forms when out of beast mode. Elves, us vampires, and most other species have distinguishing features that definitively sets us apart, but not them."

Rowan had yet to meet a member of the Order, but she figured whoever aligned themselves with such a group would've had to either be extremely vain, or extremely scared. Scared they were more dangerous, so the elf hoped for the former rather than the latter.

"There is also one more organization. It started off as a support group meeting for parents who had lost their kids to shifters infected with rage lust."

Rage lust, the name of a condition where shifters lost complete control of their beasts for a longer period than ten minutes. It onset after traumatic events the shifters couldn't deal with, or degrading mental conditions like dementia.

Four years prior, an unsettling increase in rage lust cases brought Louisa and Rowan's minor operation to Kin's familial doorstep.

In those days, it had only been RL Magical Disaster Services. Their office had been a room the Traveling Cabin offered, and they'd been functioning online, tracking down work through different chat rooms.

They'd been out of their depth trying to solve the root issues of these rages, mostly because of the shifter's tight-lipped attitude toward the issue. But they'd quickly discovered that Rowan's control over her magic made her an equivalent to an alpha for most shifter beasts. This allowed the inflicted to at least say goodbye to their families and gave them enough time to get set up with new lives in the wilderness.

The hardest cases had been those in which the afflicted took life from another being. Shifter law dictated these shifters to surrender their lives, as they continued drawing blood if just left alone.

Rowan's ability to dominate them allowed them to choose how to end it with whatever dignity remained.

If she closed her eyes, she could still hear the last gasps of breath that she was sure would follow her to the grave.

When the alpha of the Takamoto Kitsune Clan went into rage lust, they called Rowan and Louisa. Though the two young spellcasters had been making a ripple through shifter kind gossip reels, their odd situation of using a non-shifter to fix such a personal shifter issue had ensured their relative anonymity. An anonymity the clan desired above all.

As soon as they'd phased into the kitsune compound, both felt Kin's magic. He clearly should have been the actual alpha. In most other shifter societies, his prowess alone would have ensured that title for him. But, the Takamoto Kitsune Clan operated in the fashion of a bygone time that excluded branch family members from taking positions of power.

Rowan found it foolish that they looked down on someone who could have been a formidable asset. They'd been reduced to turning to the unconventional aid of an elf and a vampire.

Still, it had been only with the help of detailed notes Kin left in their room covering happenings around the Takamoto Compound a week prior to their arrival that gave the outside spellcasters the last puzzle piece of the mystery in hand.

At each hot spot location, a storm had preceded rage lust settling in. It only stood out in his notes because he also noted it had marked a low for his relationship with his mate. He'd been so angry at everything Julio had done that even he felt the urge to give into his beast so his heart could have a break.

It turned out that the ley lines in the sky had become entangled to where a simple storm passing through created fluctuating pressures that drove the inner beasts of shifters crazy. If they were even slightly uncomfortable, they faced the possibility of losing complete control of their beast.

He'd left the notes anonymously, but Rowan and Louisa tracked him down using unorthodox spells aimed at tracking the ink on the pages. They impressed him with their creative problem solving. He'd been shocked by their youth and inspired by their commitment to ensure he got credit and gratitude his family had always deprived him of.

Fixing the ley lines had been a monumental pain in the ass, but after the numbers of rage lust cases got back down to normal—about two every year — they couldn't say it wasn't worth the hours they put in. This was especially true because the experience convinced Kin that he wanted to help them get established in exchange for being a silent partner once they got the ball rolling.

It didn't take long for RL Magical Disaster Services to add a 'K'. Kin was literally the foundation for legitimizing their business, which had been, in his not-so-humble opinion, on the brink of financial ruin.

Along with the addition of Kin, the business established its long-term goal of creating either a cure or treatment for rage lust.

As tragic as the rise had been, good had come out of the situation. Because they were thorough in their record keeping, they understood the triggers of the condition even better than the common shifter.

They'd come up with a theory for prevention, though they had yet to actually encounter a rage lust onset in time to test it out.

"There was a fear that stemmed from the attacks of their loved ones, and a few of the members formed a compound to live together in what they considered safety from the shifters. They're pretty strict. They're not allowed to have any form of relationships with shifters and have kicked a couple of people out for even buying their produce."

Louisa frowned. "Not violent per se, but they've grown more into a cult than a support group. They live independent of any sovereignty by living on unclaimed grounds. A few undercover reporters have infiltrated their ranks and published a few documents of a doctrine the group follows. It underlines the shifters as their mortal enemies and compares them to demons. It's like they took a page out of the Order's modus operandi, but only applied it to shifters."

Rowan couldn't see the group having international capabilities like the Order did, but a motivated and grieving family member was liable to do anything they could to reach a goal. A goal Rowan was sure would spell disaster for the shifters.

Now it was Rowan's turn to relay her findings, "I got a hold of a friend in the Brazilian Pit and she told me that the witches found a gorgon head near their borders. No one died, but during their attack, she noticed something strange about the witches. They didn't jump into action to help them. Instead, it felt like they were just observing the chaos until they found the head." She templed her fingers in front of her. "I got the same odd feeling yesterday with the wolves. The witches were herding them towards the civilians."

Kin leaned back in his chair. "That isn't your prejudice against the Coven speaking?"

"I can't be totally sure." She admitted.

"We'll note it." Louisa said. "What about the sphinxes and the bears?"

"They both refused to talk to me, but that isn't surprising. The bears lost six members, they're grieving. The sphinxes just suck at freely exchanging information. But, I called The Griffin."

Kin grimaced. "How much did that cost us?"

"It cost *me* two golden rods from Tut's official tomb." Rowan sighed dejected, "But he told me what the sphinx were hiding. Only one of them had been affected, and it was their leader. He killed six sphinxes before the Atlanteans arrived. They're also in mourning and he has scheduled his own death two days from now."

Louisa covered her mouth in horror. "There wasn't a sign of what affected him? He must know that he couldn't control what happened to him."

"We shifters are all proud creatures. He wouldn't care about that, only that the blood ended up on his claws."

Rowan frowned, knowing it was the truth. Kin was still depressed about attacking herself and Louisa and they had survived the ordeal. "I want to visit him before the execution. I don't know if you guys want to come with me, but The Griffin didn't know what caused it and if we want a clearer picture, we have to get all the facts we can."

"If they don't want to let you in, they won't." Kin shot her a wary look.

"So then I won't ask for permission. Something bad is in the air and I'm not stopping until I find out what it is and fix it."

Louisa groaned. "And the bears, you can't ask your dragon boyfriend about them?"

The vision of him slamming that gate shut rolled through her. "He has a lot on his plate right now. The sphinxes are time sensitive. I want to focus on them first."

"Well then, we can get to the bears after the sphinxes. Don't worry." Louisa placed an encouraging hand on hers.

"If there's another attack, it could happen soon." Kin's voice was soft.

Rowan bit her lip, knowing she was about to reach a field full of emotional landmines. "We can't be sure if there will even be another attack, but if your family gets targeted, what do you want us to do?"

Kin's nose flared. "Your heroic tendencies wouldn't allow you to turn your back on them, but part of me wishes you would."

Rowan, aware that diversity made the world interesting and healthy, wished everyone had a family like hers. It wasn't always idyllic, but it was bursting at the seams with love.

While she didn't know everything about Kin's past with an abusive clan, she knew the man well enough to realize that whatever history lay was unforgivable enough to make a loyal person like Kin renounce his connection to them.

"If the time comes, I'll follow your lead. You're my priority, not them." Rowan reassured.

"And if she can't sit her ass down, I'll be happy to hex her." Louisa's ruby eyes glinted with mischief.

Kin rolled his eyes, but the small smile playing at the corner of his mouth allowed Rowan to know she had said the right thing.

XIII

If the elven woman hadn't called the moment she had, Alessandro would have gone back into the Estate and had the four heads of houses exiled from any Thunder land. But her awkwardness had amused so much that his breath was even by the time he hung up.

He had calmed down to the point of realizing his people were upset about something. They only ever behaved this way when he disagreed with something they believed was important. It was time to take a beat and listen to what that could be.

"Explain to me why mourning the dead is more important than protecting our living?"

Inside the depths of the library of Draconis, the audience chamber Alessandro preferred to dole out punishment in, was two floors underground. Anytime his dragons stepped through its doors, they knew they had reached a point to pay for the consequences of their actions. It was a recent realization that Alessandro hated it as much as they had.

Its stained glass windows, cement floors and stone walls reminded him of the old days while he liked to live in the present. Still, it had been a necessary move to remind his heads of houses that this discussion wasn't lax. What they had done had been serious enough to warrant a proper official response.

"My king, may I speak freely?" Gotan was a fire dragon. He was the head of House Ash, one of the wealthiest houses that made up the Thunder. He also was the thorn that wouldn't die on Alessandro's side. Over 500 years old, with silver hair that brushed the floor when he relaxed, Gotan never missed an opportunity to question Alessandro's decisions.

Alessandro inclined his head towards the man. "You may, but I warn you, Gotan, my patience at the moment is fragile."

The dragon scowled. "We grieve not only over the loss of Elaine, but of the prospect of our future. She is the only woman that you have truly considered as the Dragon Queen in the past century. We are not whole without a queen. Our balance is so disturbed our women are having a hard time having children. This is a punishment from our ancestors that we have warned you of time and time again. You *must* find a mate, my King. Without our children, we have no future, so why would we fight for it?"

Alessandro could hear a dull ringing in his ear. He could feel his power pour out of his concealment field, his claws elongated, horns protruded from his head. "You all agreed this was a justified reason to put your families of current relevance in danger?"

"We all can phase out, my lord. If it took the loss of Draconis the place to get you to think seriously about the needs of your people, we would give up a thousand Draconis'." Gotan dropped to his knees, and he pressed his forehead to the tile. "No dragons would have suffered."

Alessandro sneered down at the man. The temperature of the room plummeted and he could see his breath mist. "Draconis is not just a place. Since its founding, have you all forgotten why we have a dragon haven in the land of mortals? Why we, the leaders of this Thunder, spend the bulk of our time here instead of returning to our ancestral home? If they burned this place down and saw no dragons, they would hunt us down. We would lose the peace that comes with having one of the world's only intact histories of its people. And do not think they couldn't do it, find Dragon City. The technology of this time and age makes it near impossible for it to remain hidden. The only reason we have so far is because we have given them no reason to look for it." He could feel their instant remorse and it helped calm him down a bit.

"I understand your frustration with my lack of a mate. But if you think I'll just allow anyone to sit by my side for the rest of my life just so you can have babies, you're wrong. Picking the Dragon Queen is a job I take seriously. I kept this from the rest of the Thunder save for Elaine's family, but that has proven to be a miscalculation."

The water dragon tensed from her position, but she didn't speak out.

"Elaine was of sound mind when she found the flute. She made the conscious decision to not only touch the cursed object, but to bring it back here and play the forbidden melody. She made the choice to take on the full burn of the curse and take us all down with her if she couldn't have the Dragon Queen seat."

Gotan was now sitting up, looking horrified at the woman who refused to move a muscle. Besides her, the two dragons of the remaining houses sat up and shared Gotan's expression. "Mezine, you didn't say!"

Alessandro regained full control of the beast and he felt everything neutralizing around him.

"I do not say this to besmirch her name. Elaine was a promising candidate, perhaps the most promising, but she didn't stir my beast and she fell short of what I expect from my queen. I ask that you all give me your patience and believe me when I say I hear your concerns. I will give you a Dragon Queen and when I do, I hope you'll give me your full support knowing it is not a decision I will make without considering every aspect of that person and their role in our future."

Alessandro motioned for them to stand. "I expect none of you to breathe a word of Elaine to the rest of the Thunder. Let her die with honor. In the end, she regretted the betrayal, and I forgave her. Until time heals the mental wounds of those who drew blood from their fellow dragons, let us keep it between ourselves and the archives. Am I understood?" He wanted to make sure they knew this last bit was an order and not a request.

"Yes, your majesty!" All four heads of families chorused.

"As for your punishment, you four will return to Dragon City and fall under the command of our Earth General. She has a plan to protect Dragon City if the worse comes to worst. Leave your chosen heirs here. It's time to test them in times of peril. I do hope they do better than you have today."

He could see his heads of families were ashamed of their decision, and he dismissed them with a wave of his hand.

Stone stepped forward from the shadows, his face pale. "Is what you said about Elaine true?"

"Yes."

"Does that mean she died in a lot of pain?"

Alessandro studied the young man. He briefly recalled Elaine had been his age. They'd grown up in the same clutch even though they'd never hung out in public. Could Alessandro have missed something between the two dragons when he wasn't paying attention?

Elaine had been an oversight of the highest esteem. But Alessandro was hyper aware of every aspect of Stone's life. He'd considered the dragon a little brother. There was no way he'd missed him falling in love. Right?

"When I first saw her cursed form, she was full of pain, but in her dying moments, she was at peace. She even laughed a little. Was she a friend?"

Stone shrugged. "Sometimes it feels like I don't really have friends. I'm disconnected."

"That's the burden of dragons blessed in more than one element, Stone. Don't worry, you'll find a piece that grounds you."

Stone scoffed, "Like you?"

Alessandro's laugh was from the belly, a rare treat that removed some tension from the heir's shoulders. "The second I became the Dragon King, you all became my anchors. Right now I'm looking for a piece that makes me feel like I can fly, even with all of this weight." He cocked his head. "Come on, let's get some dinner. I think you're on the verge of another growth spurt."

"I told you five years ago, I think I'm done growing!" Stone called after his master as they walked out of the audience chamber.

XIV

R owan wasn't sure how she felt about this recent development.
Growing up without her tail, horns and wings out for the world
to see hadn't prepared her for the day Chloe's charms stopped working and exposed them to the world.

The stares that had followed her during lunch had made her feel
exposed. After years of living in the shadows, it was taking longer than
she'd imagined to feel comfortable.

Her mother and her sisters didn't share these extra physical traits,
but they'd helped her figure out how to keep them healthy and glowing, even if they weren't always out for the world to see.

She turned as she examined the rainbow hues threaded onto her
wings, falling more and more in love with her body the longer and
harder she looked. Fuck the world if they thought of her as less than
just because of their presence.

"Is this part of a nightly routine?"

Rowan's eyes snapped to scan her surroundings, only to catch sight
of his astral body in the corner of her bedroom.

The only difference from his physical presence was a faint glow
outlining his body.

"I thought you were busy." She had, of course, taken him at his
word that they wouldn't be seeing each other and felt more than comfortable in confronting her new truth. "Wait, the cabin let you in?"

Alessandro smirked at her and she could practically hear him
purring, *"Honey, I'm the Dragon King."*

She rolled her eyes.

"Wasn't it you who begged me to come?" He moved to her papasan chair and relaxed into its form.

"Does it really count when you're so ghostly?" She pouted as she slid into a red robe hanging on the corner of the mirror. "I wanted to have sex."

Alessandro used his elbows to prop himself up. "Is sex all I bring out of you, little elf?"

Rowan shrugged. "I mean, I *am* also a succubus."

He gave a low chuckle, then motioned towards the plant he'd left the day before. Small buds had emerged from the stalks, but not much else was different in terms of progress. "I see you've attempted to figure out how to make it bloom."

The elf groaned, "We had one at Spellcasters, but this one might be defective. I've tried every chakra point and I'm getting no action."

"Innuendo?" He asked dryly, "I thought you were above those."

She slid her gaze over his form. Her hunger had been growing since he uttered his first word. It was growing too quickly for her to be comfortable with.

Before he'd blasted into her life, she'd only required feedings every three months. She couldn't be sure if the new hunger was because of her heavy magic usage, or because she'd become addicted to the high of his otherwise neglected celestial energy.

Her eyes slid over the bulging erection just underneath the fabric of his pants. It was frustrating. She wanted to smell the usual sweet proof that his lust was stirring. The physical presentation did little to nullify her as she recalled how it felt in real life.

Alessandro's low growl raised her attention to his eyes, but it didn't help her situation as the sound only reminded her of the sweet noises he'd made while he slammed into her.

She couldn't tell what color his eyes were, but they were glowing as they locked onto the plant. Clearly, he would not be changing his mind on an impromptu visit.

His voice was strained when he spoke. "This plant gauges how efficient you are when you channel your magic, not how strong it is. I noticed the damage to your hands after you intervened with the wolves. It's worrisome if you've never actually channeled through the proper methods. Your gates could be close to collapsing and you've never even realized."

Forcing herself to change focus from her cravings to the plant, she felt the frustration the damn thing had incited in her flare back to life.

Most of her training had been untraditional. She had not only kept her true power levels a secret, but also half of her genetic makeup. Other than how to feed off sexual energy, neither her mother nor godmother had given her the tools she needed to use her succubus' side to filter magic.

But she wasn't willing to talk to anyone, much less him about that aspect of her life.

"You may have to go back to basics to cast the blooming spell." He moved from the papasan chair to beside her in the blink of an eye. "What's the first step?"

Rowan shook her annoyance with the man off as she recalled the baby steps of magic from her elementary school. There was no way she was going to pass up learning something from the most formidable Spellcaster to exist. This was what she'd wanted from him since she'd first learned who he was.

For the next hour they worked on meditation, then a bit of incantation until they began trying the different channels. Rowan found her mind sharpened by this point. Intentionally using the building blocks of magic was making her every move feel purposeful and strong. It changed the way she sat, the way she breathed. She was ready.

With her eyes closed, she felt for the threads of life that the plant exuded. It pulsed as it thrived, eager to reach the next stage of its life.

Plants were always eager for it. It was why she adored working with them so much. It was an infectious trait.

Working from the ground up, she gathered the bit of magic it would take to nudge the plant with her muladhara gate at the base of her spine. The bud increased in size, but minimally.

She moved on to her svadhishthana gate, settled in the depths of her belly. Pulling magic with it always gave her the slight feel of freefall. When she released the magic back over the plant, she could see the color of the petals would be red-orange, like a ripe peach. These two gates were what she usually used when she took in the energy from her feeds.

Further up, just underneath her ribcage, was her manipura gate. She'd never pulled magic with it, so when the magic listened, shock flushed through her.

"What is it?" Alessandro asked from the other side of the plant when she released her position in surprise.

"That was my manipura gate. It's never engaged in pulling magic!"

He furrowed his eyebrows. "Never?"

"No."

He let out a low hum. His eyes shone, but much like when he'd visited her in her childhood room, she couldn't tell which color they shifted to.

"How long have you been lining yourself with null charms?"

"Since I was nine."

"This is a good way to test what you've enhanced in that time. Try again."

She did. It still stunned her.

"Release."

Rowan poured the magic onto the petals and her breath hitched as the petals began parting.

He grinned at her. "Three out of three. Keep going."

The anahata gate, sitting at the center of her chest, caused the most change to the plant. It was where she called forth her sword of light. The bud went from the size of a mandarin to the size of a grapefruit.

Between her eyebrows, her ajna gate, like her manipura gate, was new to pulling magic. The action caused goosebumps to erupt along the back of her neck and down her arms.

This was strange. Too strange.

The last gate was her sahasrara. If this one pulled, Rowan was going to scream.

"Is that fear on your eyebrow, princess?"

She narrowed her eyes. "It's caution. That was six for six. If I pull from sahasrara..." Her words failed her.

He raised an eyebrow. "You *will* pull from your sahasrara. Little elf, you're Blessed. It's where the gods can reach you from the Celestial Realms."

Her breath caught in her throat. Then she let out a scream.

Frustration swelled in her chest.

Years. Years of being ignorant of her potential.

Of her truth.

She clenched her hands and stood. "I don't want to do this anymore."

He also rose to his feet. "What are you so afraid of?"

"I'm not afraid!" She snarled as she stormed past the threshold of her bedroom door. "I'm pissed."

The Dragon King appeared in front of her. She didn't let that stop her. He was in the astral plane. He shouldn't have been able to interact with the real world. But she slammed against his chest.

She glared up at him from her spot on the floor. "What the fuck!?"

He held out a hand to help her up, and she slapped it away, letting her head fall to the floor with a thud. Her vision swam with the force of it, but she had nowhere to vent her grievance.

He crouched down next to her head, propping his chin up on his hand as he looked down at her. "You're an interesting creature, Rowan Dahl."

She scoffed. "I'm not a cre-. Well. Shit. I don't actually know what I am."

"You're Rowan Dahl. What else matters?" He asked.

"Shouldn't I at least know what being Rowan Dahl actually means?"

"You don't know what being Rowan Dahl means?" He raised an eyebrow. "I've known you for all of three days and know exactly what it means."

He said it like a fact. Rowan took a deep breath, reaching up to wrap a finger around one of his curls. "I shouldn't be able to feel you."

"No. You shouldn't."

She dropped the curl, tucked her knees underneath her, and turned to him. "What does it mean?"

"Potential. Period. End of sentence." His eyes were so bright that even if she couldn't tell the color, they hurt her own to look at him for too long.

"I *am* afraid."

"I know."

"You're power and you're not afraid." She whispered.

"You're not afraid of me, either. It isn't power you fear. What in the world do you think you possess that is more frightening than me? I ask again, what are you so afraid of?"

Her eyes fluttered closed. It felt like it would relieve some of the sting of her confession. "I'm afraid if I go too far, that my family will realize that The Coven had a point, that I am a monster."

She felt him move to lay his head down next to hers. She opened her eyes and turned to look at him when he settled. Her lips were near his forehead, they were nose to nose, and she could feel his breath in the strands of her hair.

It lulled her eyes shut once more. How could comfort and danger exist so perfectly in him?

"There was a time when I was a kid. I burned down ten acres of the forest behind our house because my mom told me I couldn't leave the table until I was done with my food. In the Eastern Elven Kingdom, we use more candles than lightbulbs. I was so angry that I was shooting everything around the apartment in a telekinetic tantrum. One candle made it to the edge of the forest. It might have been a small, manageable fire, but my parents couldn't calm me down. The fire, already linked to my loss of control, spread fast. My dad, running out of options, slapped me. His face..." she sighed. "It was the first time he realized he was in over his head. That I was a menace to the carefully crafted peace of his kingdom. I saw the terror in his eyes. I knew he hated himself for hitting me. He was crying as he pulled me in, whispering sorry over and over again. I watched the forest burn. Heard the animals cry, and I promised myself I would be more careful with my magic."

"So, you made it your mission to be not only more careful with your own magic, but also to clean up the messes of everyone else's loss of control."

"It's gotten to the point I'm neurotic about it now."

"Lucky for the rest of us." His lips brushed against her forehead as he spoke. "You must know it is a safer world with your presence. You're not a monster, little elf. In fact, you're the opposite, a product of love. A type of love that won't shatter because you're a handful. The only way you will lose a family like that is if you walk away from it."

His words warmed her chest.

Growing up, she never found a place she belonged in the Eastern Elven Kingdom. Lexine was the heir apparent, and by far the most brilliant choice, too. She kept their people healthy with her gift of medicine. No one had her skill in diplomatic affairs. Axel bolstered their strength with strategies. Forces like the Coven hesitated acting against them because of the security measures her elder sister weaved both in the open through treaties and in the shadows through threats. Zeva had grown up in the libraries of the kingdom, gone toe to toe with every scholar and made it her personal mission to ensure the education of all elven children was on even ground.

Without realizing it, she had attributed her inability to fit in through the kingdom to being unable to fit in with her family.

But physical distance wasn't the same as emotional distance. How could she have forgotten about their love?

The warmth of their affection had allowed her to overlook the pain of the power test unit year after year.

In her mind, if she passed with her charade, no one could take her family from her. She wouldn't end up like those recruiters they'd sent to her.

Success stories of their indoctrination, each Coven-raised like she could be if she joined them.

Those people hadn't had families who threatened retaliation when the witches came for them. They didn't have a Master Japhet, who found them entertaining enough to mentor them through their worst years.

Somehow, they lacked substance, hardly more than NPCs to the game called life. They felt empty and disconnected.

Their presence reinforced her desire to avoid the Coven, rather than enticed her to join them.

Alessandro was right. She couldn't see her family letting her go. Even if she tried to walk away, she was sure they'd all follow and tackle her to the ground. Who was she to paint their love as superficial when they'd proven over a lifetime that they could and would go above and beyond to protect her?

Rowan took in the moment of feeling his magic brush against her face before she found her resolve once more. "Can you teach me?"

"Yes." The pressure of his body abandoned her, leaving her cold. "First step is getting your ass back in that room and trying again."

She squared her shoulders. "Okay."

He stood and held his hand out again. This time, she took it.

When she was back on her feet, his hand was at the small of her back, pulling her body flush against his and his soft, warm lips were on hers, eager and so hungry it stole all of her strength.

Desire hooded his eyes when he pulled back. There was a moment where she thought she saw something more of Alessandro than he intended for her to see. Black scales ran in streaks alongside his jaw, two great horns erupted from his forehead and his eyes were slit reptilian. Underneath the scales, she could almost see light dancing in a lazy wave.

She saw it only for a second before suddenly he wasn't with her anymore. Moisture tracked down her cheeks and when she pulled her fingers away from touching them, she saw blood. She'd had previous encounters with demigods. They could travel all over their realm unlike their full-fledged counterparts, but never had they made her bleed just by looking at them, and he'd been in the astral plane to boot.

It was a concrete fact for her then. Nothing she had run into before had been as lethal as the Dragon King.

XV

Alessandro was seething. Why had he done that? Blood had trick-led down her cheeks, but more concerning was the way she looked at him, as if she'd underestimated just who she was dealing with. It teetered on the edge of fear. He'd seen the look plenty of times before, but this was the first time that it made nausea instantly settle in his stomach. He wished he had more time to wipe it away, or question her about it, but there was an urgent knock on his door.

"Come in." He swung his legs over the side of his bed. His voice was gruff, and he didn't know if that was because of its lack of use, or his irritation.

Aqua stepped in, her long white nightgown trailing behind her. Ambrosia-laced wine he could smell even with her distance from him had her cheeks flushed. Her electric hair was down and it swept over her shoulders. The sweet scent of her arousal flowed into the room with her.

As one of his Elemental Generals, Aqua was one of the few dragons that he swore to keep out of his bed, so her demeanor made his entire body go rigid.

"My King, I've had a dream." Her voice trembled as she edged closer.

Growing hyper aware of his bare chest, the Dragon King created a distance from the bed and led the woman towards a small sitting area, making sure he took the armchair and she the love seat.

He almost didn't want to ask, but he had to rectify this situation if it was what he thought it might be. "What kind of dream?"

Her hazy eyes locked on him. "I believe," her voice was strained. "It was a vision of the past. Of you and the elf woman."

Alessandro raised an eyebrow. Aqua cast her eyes away and took a deep breath.

"You were engaging in coitus."

Well, fuck.

Alessandro winced, recalling the lack of tenderness or shame in the shared moments with Rowan. If Aqua had seen it, it wasn't a surprise she had been so heavily aroused, nor that she was drinking in excess.

It was a rare exercise to rut outside of the Thunder. The privacy of being a dragon made it favorable to be with another dragon who could be privy to all aspects of their lifestyle. Outsiders weren't as disciplined in keeping secrets.

Expectations for Alessandro demanded he keep his interests in the Thunder as he searched for his Dragon Queen. The idea of an outsider becoming his partner, even as a short fling, was outrageous.

"The way you looked at her." Aqua shot him an accusing look. "Your eyes were silver. Is she to be our Queen?"

Alessandro opened his mouth to deny the question, but her words seated themselves in his head and he leaned back. "Are you sure?" He asked. "Perhaps it was a trick of the light. Maybe an odd angle."

Aqua let out a disbelieving breath and her hand gripped the fabric of the nightgown on her thighs. "Alessandro, you and I know my visions are clear. Your eyes turned silver. You were nibbling all over her. I saw you kiss her."

He wondered how many women had to comment on his lack of kissing for it to be common knowledge that he rarely engaged in it. He could fuck all day and night, but kissing like he had enjoyed with Rowan was rare for him to indulge. Somehow it had become a marker that he was serious about courting someone and so he withheld it until he was sure he wanted to proceed.

He hadn't thought about the kisses. They had seemed natural with her, perhaps an unconscious realization that she didn't know of his aversion to the act. Anytime the scenes of their coupling played in his mind, they focused on her facial expressions during certain moments. How she had sunk to her knees and opened her mouth wide for him, or how when he had awoken the next morning it was to find her curled tightly around him, peace relaxing soft flushed face. It had half broken his will to leave without waking her up.

Silver. The color of any shifter's eye when they found a potential mate. It had happened without his knowledge.

Rowan Dahl was more dangerous than he had believed, and he did not think of her as a demure kitten.

Shit.

"You didn't know." Aqua's voice was soft. "How could you not have known?"

Alessandro growled, "I don't know. Isn't it supposed to hit you like a freight truck when you get the mating feeling?"

A bright blush lit Aqua's cheeks. He wanted to roll his eyes. Here she was confronting him about the event and she was embarrassed to hear him talk about it.

"The Houses won't accept an elf to lead us."

"I know that, Aqua."

"Then you must not see her again. We can't take the chance if your beast is insistent on it. He will mark her and the Houses will try to get rid of her and then there will be a cold war between you and the Thunder and there will be chaos."

He scoffed, "Is that a vision or your imagination running wild?"

"I'm a seer, but one doesn't require my particular gift to see where the path you're on leads."

"I will not allow it to go any further than it has." He growled.

Aqua narrowed her eyes. "So you won't see her again?"

Surprised by the vehemence, Alessandro responded. "I can't make that promise. Somehow the woman seems to have gotten entangled in the shifter attacks and I will use every source I have to make sure I get to the real culprit behind Elaine."

Aqua's lip trembled and her eyes watered. "Is this an excuse to see her? I don't mean to be so assertive, but Terra isn't here a-and Blaise would just kill her to get rid of the problem-" She flinched when he growled at her and she spoke her next words softly, "How can you not see that this is a problem, my king?"

Alessandro did. And that was what was pissing him off.

How could his dragon have been so incredibly wrong in finally choosing a mate?

He sighed and forced himself to calm down. "Allow me to think of alternatives."

"Perhaps I could help." Aqua looked desperate.

As gently as he could, Alessandro said, "I'll take care of it."

Aqua looked concerned, but she gave in and took it as her cue to leave. She bowed and whispered, "I'm sorry, Alessandro."

And he believed her. He really did.

-R-

The bastard really had left!

After promising to help her. After showing her his beast.

Her real annoyance had nothing to do with that, though. Her annoyance was that he'd kissed her, stirring up the succubus she'd been working hard to suppress all evening and then leaving her high and dry.

Without instruction Rowan wasn't sure what the next step was, so she gently placed the pot into the plant room, watched the cabin shuffle it around before settling it near the sky light full of subtle streaks of moonlight.

When she got back to her room, she checked her phone to see if the Dragon King had messaged her with an explanation for his abrupt departure, but besides a few texts from her sisters and a couple of friends, there were no messages.

Was he letting her stew? Next time she saw him, she would empha-size she definitely wasn't afraid of him, just surprised.

Bastard.

It was nearing midnight. She supposed it was time to turn in for the night, but the grimoire right beside the clock was mocking her. She only had ten more days with it. Didn't she want to know the se-crets it held?

She sighed and slid it onto her lap, relaxing against the collection of pillows littering her bed.

Even with Kin's and Dew's explanation on how to navigate the book, Rowan didn't have enough Coven history knowledge to figure out where certain entries should appear. So, still unsure, she opened it to the middle page.

This time it was an entry on how to get the most juice out of the eye of newts to get the best quality potions. She flipped the pages, finding that none of them had the feel of secret ancient knowledge she had assumed the pages would hold.

"Were you only meant to show Kin the relationship between shifters? Why would the Elder give you to me and not him?" She ques-tioned out loud, "Am I supposed to be researching a secret code she's left? Or is this really a show of good faith between the Coven and me? I feel like I'm losing a hold of myself. I don't even know how to use my power properly." She shook her head and turned the page, and then she stared.

There was a diagram of chakras neatly labeled. Underneath the di-agram there were instructions.

1.   *Now that you've determined which chakra points will put out your highest quality of magic, try using two at the same time. Some have found it helpful to envision push buttons at the chakra points they are intending to use, which they then try to press at a set rhythm of an eight count every second pressing a different button.*

2. *After you get a hang of two at a time, check back with me to see what's next.*

No way.

She cocked her head to the side and shrugged. Would it really hurt to try?

XVI

The morning was warm in the desert oasis the cabin had landed Rowan in. Though Alessandro could enter, as he had the cabin's permission, his fight with his dragon to stay standing there until she woke up was costing more than half of his concentration. If he went inside, he might as well shed his clothes to save them time.

It was a dangerous thing for the Dragon King to have so much of his concentration focused on one thing, especially as he was on high alert for intruders on his land.

Fucking pathetic.

It was what she had driven him to. He should have killed her as soon as he realized she had him acting in contradiction to his sane side. But he'd been weak.

He crossed his arms, gaze steady on the front door, waiting for her to exit. She could phase out within the confines of the house, but as long as he could still feel her magic present in the house, he would stay planted on the beach.

Except, he only could contain himself for another two minutes before he phased into her room. Cursing as he gathered his magic, he swore to tell her what he needed to, give her the material he'd gathered from Draconis' library and then leave.

His plans flew out the window as he came upon the mass of vines and black and orange flowers that erupted from the pot he had given her.

The woman herself was curled in bed around the vines, reminding him of how she had clung onto him and he had to shake that image away before temptation could send his plans to the endless hells.

He cleared his throat and watched with amusement as she shot to her feet, a dagger he hadn't seen nearby in her grip. She stopped mid swing once she realized who it was and her eyes lit up with recognition.

"Alessandro." She fell back to bed. "Give me like five more hours, okay?"

An unbidden smile pulled at the corner of his lips. She wasn't showing any signs of trauma or fear after he had revealed a portion of his true face. The smile fell off as soon as he remembered what his objectives were, and he stiffened again. "Princess Rowan, I have some things we need to discuss." He tried to use his commanding voice, but she was busy pushing the vines away from where she slept and curling back into a nest of blankets and pillows to pay it any mind.

"Princess Rowan? Discuss?" Her head poked out of the blanket cocoon she had made for herself.

"Yes. I've brought you this. Obviously, you've figured most of it out yourself, but there are a few more tips and tricks inside."

Her eyes were heavy with sleep, but she seemed attentive enough for him to present her with a binder he had stayed up all night working on.

She reached out and traced her name on the cover, a soft smile playing at her lips. "Are you breaking up with me before we even really start?"

He raised an eyebrow, unsure if she was just messing with him or if that was how she really felt. "I know I owe you a favor for you stepping in to help us, but this is the best I can do under the current circumstances."

"Yeah. I understand." She turned her gaze up to him. "Are they okay, your dragons?"

Startled by the question, he said, "Yes, a bit concerned about the future, but we will persevere."

Rowan nodded and held her finger up before she took off into another section of the cabin. Alessandro waited in his designated spot, afraid that if he moved he would do something foolish like give into the desire to chase her down and mark her there and then.

How had he missed this sign of longing before Aqua gave it a name?

She hadn't needed to use a single ounce of her succubus magic to ensnare him as he'd suspected. His dragon had done all of that work for her.

She came back with a small well-worn children's book, one that had a picture of an angry child at the front. He cocked his head to the side.

"For the fire-dragon that was with you yesterday. If you guys are going to work on your image issue, he's going to have to learn how to at least pretend to be in a better mood. He damn near ruined the effect of your heartbroken moment. This helped me deal with my rage over the Coven butting into my life. It's great."

He couldn't help the chuckle. "I'm sure he will appreciate it."

Blaise wouldn't, but it amused Alessandro.

Silence fell as they stared at each other. Her blue eyes showed her disappointment. Unlike her open seduction, she didn't voice it.

"Oh!" She grabbed his arm before he phased out. "Before you go, can you tell me about the bear shifter attack? Was there some sort of priceless treasure at the heart of it?"

Alessandro narrowed his eyes. "Yes." He said softly, "But one that had been with the Sleuth for a long time. It was their totem. The carnage stopped when we found it and repaired it."

Rowan bit her lip and asked. "Do you mind showing me?"

"This is a shifter issue. Outsiders like yourself shouldn't be so quick to become involved."

She looked mildly offended at the comment. "Outsider? Soon, this is going to be a problem for absolutely everyone. One of my best friends is a shifter. Should I wait for whoever is behind this to come after him to be involved?" She scoffed. "One incident is just an incident, but five of them are a planned attack. I fear that there are more waiting on the horizon."

He thought so too. However, with the injuries that seemed to be common for her, he didn't want her anywhere near the issue, even if it wasn't his place to say so.

It was infuriating.

He growled at himself, "There were no signs of an intruder. The bear who broke the totem was under some kind of hypnosis and I found him amongst one of the fallen. Their alpha informed me he kept shouting that he could hear voices from it. He said the voice of his dead mother pleaded with him to break it. The others tried to stop him, but he had a special ability; he could make anyone combust into flame without requiring physical touch. They weren't able to stop him."

Rowan frowned and put a hand on her chin. "Did you feel any foreign magical signature?"

"No. I raked the compound over. But unlike the attack on Draconis, there was no lingering magic."

"I couldn't find anything with the wolves either. Could whoever set Elaine on Draconis have learned their lesson about that?"

Alessandro felt the hair on the back of his neck stand. If this reasoning stood, it meant someone had infiltrated Draconis and seen Alessandro find the signature or witnessed Naseem complete his investigation. The barrier that had kept out Japhet, one of the most formidable witches of modern times, had failed to detect an intruder.

Yet, it was only speculation. The turn around time of the attacks had been so small that it didn't leave room for improvement if all the other attacks were to follow the same trajectory as the first.

"I'll review the camera footage at Draconis." He bowed his head and said, "Take care of yourself, Princess Rowan. If you continue down this path, you are in more danger than you have ever faced before." He almost phased away with those as his last words until she touched his arm to stop him.

"Hey. This feels a lot like goodbye for good." She whispered.

He remained silent.

"Not an 'I'll see you later after I settle my dragons and the world into peace'." Her eyes searched his, willing him to say more.

He forced himself to shake his head.

She was absolutely unabashed when she asked, "Why?"

He hadn't expected the question, or for her to actually expect an answer from him.

"Where exactly will continuing this lead us?" He leaned against her dresser.

"A very fulfilling sex life?" Her eyes flashed violet.

Alessandro crossed his arms and set a stony stare her way.

"What?" She asked, leaning against her pillow. "Are you insinuating I haven't delivered the best orgasms of your life?"

"My dragon wants to mark you." He grit out.

This made her sit up straight. She knew what it meant. If the sliding of her eyes to the doorway wasn't a big enough clue of her fear of it, the sharp increase in her heart rate was.

"So yes, you've given me orgasms I hadn't even dreamed of one day experiencing. But that is no longer enough."

It was only a moment of sadness that passed through her eyes before it turned to fierce rage.

"If you think the only thing I can offer is amazing sex, you're mistaken about who I am, Dragon King." She invaded his space and wrapped a piece of his hair around her finger. He growled when she tugged at it with a force meant to hurt. "But you're right, it's probably too much to ask for you to express any control over your beast."

Her eyes locked around his hand, which had encircled her wrist with a grip that would bruise.

"You're playing with fire."

"I don't mind a little heat." She snarled and used his forearm as leverage to reach his lips.

Her warmth pressed against his front, clearly as desperate as he was. Did she not realize she was in this as deep as he was? Or did she just not care?

He spun them so it was her back against the dresser as he fell deeper and deeper into the kiss. His promise to keep his distance was a memory from another lifetime.

Their tongues fought for dominance, as if the unruly specimen known as Rowan Dahl could ever truly be dominated.

"What do you say, then? One more for the road?" She backed away long enough to ask.

"Only one?" His hands were already pulling her shorts off as he backed her to her bed, her wings providing space for her to nestle into.

"How greedy."

"Ever known a dragon to be anything less?"

Unlike their first forays into the land of lust, he was moving languidly and slow. She bucked against him with her impatience, but he gripped her hips firmly in fair warning. "Patience, little elf. It doesn't have to be fast and hard for it to be pleasurable."

Her nose flared. "Is that what we're doing? Pretending? I've had enough of pretending to last me three lifetimes. Give me what I want. What I know you want."

His hand wrapped around hers as she tried to unzip his fly. "What you want is to feel good. Have I disappointed you yet? If it's going to be my last time in your bed, you're going to have to compromise. This is about both of us getting proper closure, isn't it?" He kissed her forehead, and he watched as color flooded her cheeks. A smile curled on his face. "Unless you can't handle a little intimacy."

"I'm not the one who can't handle their emotions." She huffed before relaxing against his hold. "Fine."

Through the cracks of her windows, bronze dawn sunlight crawled into bed. He watched as it caught in her hair, then in her eyes. The sun lit her up as if mocking him. He could never get inside her like it could.

He moved her to the shade as his hackles rose at the thought. He leaned down once more to recapture her mouth, one hand resting at the curve of her back, the other curling around the curve of her ass, down the underside of her thigh and hooking underneath her leg to bring her opening in line with his still clothed cock.

Her skin heated under his palms. Anticipation had her fingernails digging into his still clothed back in a delicious lick of pain as he deliberately took his time undoing the zipper of his pants.

She left the kiss, her mouth traveling to the spot under his ear that drove him mad.

His groan when she took the smallest bite was unbidden.

Did she know that if she went just a few inches lower and found purchase when his neck met his shoulder that she would claim him? Like he ached to claim her?

"This is torture." Her lips brushed the shell of his ear with her whisper.

Torture?

Yes.

She was.

Sliding home, Alessandro felt every single other thing besides the woman underneath him melt from his mind.

He seldom left her mouth as he rocked into her, hands exploring her curves, the dip of her back into the slope of her ass. His thumb worked her clit as he filled her. Each hit elicited a soft gasp from their kiss. He pulled back as he opened her wider and wider. The flexibility of the minx was pure seduction.

Color flushed her cheeks, the bridge of her button nose and her kiss-swollen lips. Her eyes glazed with lust, and he pulled all the way out before he slammed back into her. His hand massaged the back of her knee, and he felt her tighten around him at the action. He smirked, and she threw a smirk of her own back at him as she bore her weight on her forearms and her hips began rolling, making the sinking into her that much more powerful.

The movement pronounced her breasts.

Intrigued, he thrusted and watched her breasts bounce in perfect rhythm. Glowing lavender eyes watched him as her tail curled in between them and swiped against her clit as if saying she could bring herself to pleasure better than he could.

He bit the air with his annoyance and reached down to grab the extra appendage. Warmth radiated under his fingers, and she let out an inhuman sound that reminded him of a hissing snake.

Was that good or bad? He cocked his head to the side as he stroked the tail with a firm grip and smirked when he realized it was beyond good. It was something she wasn't used to. Her increased heat and slickness sealed the deal.

He slid a hand around to support her lower back as he rocked into her and worked her tail at the same time. Her mewls of pleasure had never been so breathless. They made his cock ache with its desire for release, but he was determined to get her there first. He tightened his grip on her tail as if it was his shaft. She let out a strangled sob and her legs were so tight around him that he could no longer move.

"Feels good, doesn't it?" He growled into her ear as her walls pulsed around him. "You hate it when my cock leaves you, don't you, little elf?"

Her nails slid under his shirt leaving trails of pain behind. She didn't answer, but her hips rolled around him barely letting him out before pulling him back in with incredible pressure. He managed to squeeze a hand between their bodies, finding her clit with practiced ease.

"That's right, grind your sweet pussy all over me. Come for me, Rowan."

Her mouth found purchase where his neck met his shoulders and she bit. His dragon roared his release.

The fucking little cheat.

She didn't even give him a chance to catch his breath as she toppled him back onto the collection of her pillows and began riding him, keeping his pace, but lost in her pleasure.

Her eyes were closed as she sought her own release, and he was breathless as her hips began rotating around him. Her moans shook the glass of her windows, and he saw in that moment the wild woman that Rowan truly was. He knew she could feel him growing larger inside her until her breathing came out short and he thought he heard a prayer of thanks being sent to the gods before he grabbed her hips and railed into her from below.

"I am the only god you fucking pray to." He roared.

She leaned forward to catch herself on his shoulders, wings enclosing them in a world where it was only the two of them. Her eyes were glowing so bright he was sure he would see stars if he closed his own, but he didn't dare look away because in the depths of them was something he hadn't expected, but was more than a little intrigued by.

She looked at him as if she'd been waiting her whole existence for him. She was mapping every detail of his face, her lips moving as if she was counting each of his eyelashes, committing him to the deepest memory bank she possessed. The expanse of what lay in her eyes made him finally see what his dragon desired. The long awaited resonance between beast and man shook him to the core.

He bared his teeth as he realized what he was giving up by walking away from her. No one had ever wanted him like she did. Even afraid of the commitment of the mark, her heart was shattering into pieces with his choice.

She needed time.

Time he could not give because his dragon and his sane side were now of the same mind.

He pumped in and out of her at the speed of a machine and, just like that, she closed the gates to whatever had encouraged her to bear herself to him. And she was screaming yes again, and he slammed deeper and harder into her. He felt her climax running down his thighs, mixed with his own, and the thought got him so turned on that he felt his fangs growing in his mouth.

She wasn't ready. That knowledge was the only thing allowing him to keep his genuine desires from becoming a reality. To keep from marking her, he had to get her sweet, open neck away from him, but he refused to stop fucking her.

He shifted her, so that she was face down, ass up, and he entered her from behind. The arch of her back and the round curve of her ass motivated him to smack it and his handprint glowed red on her fair skin.

She hissed her sound of approval. He noticed as he slammed in and out a small line of three beauty marks on her hip and he traced them with his fingers, lulling her into a false sense of security before he smacked her again.

"Fuck yes." She was breathless, and he was too. But they weren't there yet. He reached over to grab her shoulders to steady her, and then he pulled her down as he slammed forward.

It only took three more strokes, and they were both roaring their releases.

With one swift motion, he turned her to face him again. Her chest was red from the force, her eyes had spilled tears from their exertion and she looked so satisfied it made him cum again.

His fangs throbbed in his mouth and he leaned down to give in to the roaring demands of his dragon. He might have been able to keep him at bay if he had never seen that vulnerability in her gaze, the softness he hadn't expected, but he had and there was no way of unseeing it now.

She seemed to register what was happening. With her breathing ragged, she shook her head.

It astounded him that his beast listened to her when it had so easily overridden his own will on that beach.

"Goodbye, Alessandro." She laid a flutter of a kiss on his cheek and then phased out.

Alessandro roared from the bed once he realized what had happened. Where the fuck had she gone, naked?

XVII

T his time, when she popped into Chloe's apartment, Rowan did
so, dressed in a soft green lounge set.

Still reeling from the shock, Rowan walked through the rooms, realizing Chloe wasn't home. She made herself comfortable in front of
the TV and began flipping through channels that couldn't take her
mind off of what had just occurred.

Alessandro's dragon wanted to mark her. Something about her intrigued the beast so much that he wanted to chain them together for
the rest of their natural lives.

On principle as a succubus, she'd never really thought she could in-
trigue anything as territorial as a shifter. The idea of his rage if someone ever aroused her hunger made her tremble.

Julio and Kin had been the embodiment of hyper jealousy that she
associated with mated pairs, and she couldn't see herself willingly going through that.

It didn't seem the sane part of Alessandro did either, because he'd
showed up only to clear up the fact that while the beast wanted her
on the most primal of urges, the man didn't concur.

She wasn't good enough to be his queen.

On a deeper level, she knew she was not queen material for anyone,
let alone the oldest race of mystics, but that didn't stop her pride from
picturing herself leading them. She had a ton of attributes that would
allow her to fulfill the job if it ever came down to it.

Her control and strength with magic were above reproach. She was
scrappy enough that she could handle one or two dragons coming at
her. Her history with the Coven made sure she had a surplus of pa-

tience when dealing with obstinate people. She was proactive...though that sometimes looked more like recklessness.

She passed her morning away contemplating these thoughts before the lock on the door rattled open and Chloe entered, giggling in the arms of a tall brown-haired, blue-eyed man Rowan had been seeing with increasing regularity.

Chloe's good mood dropped to immediate concern as she took in the visage of her friend.

"Umm honey. Do you mind getting us some coffee from downstairs?" The blonde asked, dropping her keys off on a tray near the door.

"I don't mind at all." He dropped a kiss on Chloe's forehead, threw Rowan a soft look and shut the door gently behind him.

"That was cute." Rowan tried not to squirm under the tight embrace her friend gave her.

"What's wrong?" Chloe asked, cutting right to the heart of the issue.

"What gave you the idea that anything was wrong?"

"Oh Ro, you don't watch TV unless you're trying to ignore something going on in that crowded little mind of yours and you definitely don't do it anywhere but at home."

Rowan sighed. "Alessandro doesn't want to have sex anymore."

Chloe pulled back to look at her in the eyes, and she raised an eyebrow. "Want to try that again, but like with the actual meat of the problem?"

"Therapists suck." Rowan groaned and melted into the fluff of the couch, crossing her arms in front of her. "His beast wanted to mark me, so he thinks it's too dangerous to continue wandering into the lands of amazing sex in case he loses control."

"I've heard of a host and their beasts being at odds over small matters but never over choosing a mate." Chloe furrowed her eyebrows. "He must be quite stubborn."

"He is." Rowan scoffed, "And can you believe he told me I have nothing to offer but sex, so I'd make a terrible queen?"

Chloe gasped, "He did not!"

Rowan unwound her arms and scratched her cheek. "Actually, he didn't. Now that I'm thinking it over, I might have guessed what he was feeling—but he didn't deny it!"

Chloe leaned her chin on her fist. "Just because he didn't deny it doesn't mean you guessed were right, Rowan. In fact, it sounds like maybe you projected your own ideas onto him."

"I should've taken my chances at the Brood and gone to Louisa."

"But your first choice was to come here, almost as if you were looking for this conversation rather than retail or blackout therapy." Chloe grinned. "I'm quite proud of your healthy choice."

Rowan threw a throw pillow in her direction but it didn't give her the satisfaction she sought.

"I know being the youngest sister to three amazing women has given you the impression that you have to impress people for their approval, but in relationships as intimate as your insane sex one with Alessandro, you don't have to. Just being you is enough and his beast realizes it. I've worked with a couple of shifters and more often than not, if there's conflict between a host and his beast, it's due to the host side being slow on the uptake."

"The thing is that I don't want to be marked by a shifter. I have commitment issues!"

Chloe nodded her agreement. "Oh, I definitely don't think you're ready for that level of commitment. You haven't even explored your true magic limit with everything that's been happening to the shifters. Your relationship with magic is the most important one you've had up to this point. Until you figure out where you stand there, I don't think you'll be ready to explore a new relationship."

"You're right." Rowan grudgingly accepted the analysis and pouted. "By the time I get my shit together enough to even think about considering it, he'll have moved on."

Chloe patted her arm. "Now I know you're really bummed out. The Dragon King hasn't found someone to sit at his side for a couple hundred years. I don't think another potential mate is gonna pop up in the months it'll take to get where you need to be. My dad said no one has ever gotten an offer of the bite before, so keep that in mind."

Rowan blinked in surprise. "Huh?"

Chloe nodded. "Yep. you're the first person who has ever gotten his lamps to go off."

Something big settled on Rowan's chest as her cellphone's alarm went off and she stood. "I have to go."

Chloe glanced towards the clock on her wall and nodded. "Please be careful with the sphinx. Try not to let what just happened overwhelm you."

Rowan's bravado sounded false even to her own ears. "I'm a professional, Chlo."

The door opened, and the brunette walked in with three cups of coffee on a tray. He looked surprised to see her standing. "Leaving already?"

"Try not to cry about it too much, Tomas."

As *if*. If the sexual tension that had filled the room as soon as Chloe's eyes landed on her new boy toy was anything to go by, he was going to have a better time than she was.

She gratefully took the cup he offered and phased away.

-R-

Rowan was wary of returning home, but she needed to collect a few tools for the sphinx lair that Zeva had specifically requested.

It didn't take long to note two things.

One, the cabin had remained exactly where Rowan had last seen it, an oddity to be sure.

Two-there was a familiar energy pulsing from the direction of her bedroom. She bit her lip.

He had stayed. One half of her cheered, the other closed its eyes and held its breath.

She marched forward even as troubled as her mind was until she saw his broad back, taking up the space of her doorway.

Okay, he hadn't stayed. He was returning. Dressed in a pair of light jeans, brown boots, and a brown trench coat. His curls were still drying and the scent that radiated off of him could only be a fresh wash.

"I thought you would still be gone." His voice was gruff.

"I thought you would have stayed gone." She rebuked.

The smile he flashed her when he turned to look at her showed how much her back-talk amused him.

The poor fool.

"I needed to apologize." It was then that she noticed he was holding yet another plant. The vines that had grown around the room from his last one plant were still there. She'd only gotten to juggling three of her chakra points at once; she was unsure what would happen when she got all seven.

This plant, however, was in full health, gorgeous forest green leaves full of yellow and red dots. On the saucer a single black scale caught the light of the sun flooding the room now, it reflected dozens of rainbows. Her jaw dropped as she looked at it.

"Isn't this-?"

"One of my scales." He answered before she finished her question. "If you ever need me, a drop of blood on it will summon me."

Blue eyes widened with shock. "That's insane." She whispered. "There's no need to go this far."

"I was on the verge of merging our souls without either of our consent. It is the most heinous thing a shifter can do. You could order my head on a platter and everyone would agree it was the right decision, but because you are not a shifter and I don't foresee you taking that choice, this is the best penance I can give."

She let out a heavy sigh as she walked out of the room to put the plants amongst her growing collection at the entrance of the cabin. He fell into step behind her.

Before she surrendered it to the consideration of the cabin, she plucked the scale from the saucer. "After you leave, shall I act like we never met?"

She didn't turn to him as she asked this question, but she felt his tension.

"Yes."

She held her head up and gave a nod as she shot magic into the scale, turning it into dust that she blew from her fingertips.

"I didn't need you before. I won't need you in the future." She turned to face him, the tears of her anger rolling down her chin. "Fuck off, Dragon King."

Swirling rainbow eyes raked over her before the cabin itself ejected him from its walls.

There was the softest thrill of satisfaction in her as the view of the ocean swirled for a moment before settling into a view of icy mountain peaks.

-A-

Alessandro landed on the sand of the beach unceremoniously.

He laid, sprawled out, face up towards the sun, not quite knowing how to react to suddenly being ejected from the confines of the elf's home.

Anger so fierce it heated the blood in his vein swept through him. It reminded him of his youth when his celestial magic made its first appearance. Panic bled into that anger, chilling his blood enough to give him room to breathe. In the end, he settled on amusement.

He covered his face with his hands as he laughed. What the fucks were the fates thinking? Was it some sort of grand joke from the universe?

The woman never ceased to entertain. Fuck. He wanted her.

He rolled his head to dispel the tension that little conversation had merited and he phased from the beach.

Time to focus.

-N-

The Dragon King was upset. It was a minute observation on Naseem's part, but there was a certain ice in the rainbow eyes of his lord that he had only known to be there on rare occasions. He had expected it after Elaine had passed, but Alessandro had been more relaxed and less severe than Naseem had known him to be when his dragons failed to live up to his expectation of near perfection.

While the Dragon King examined the demonstration of the children's combat training, he weaved in and out, correcting gently and recognizing the students who had perfected their stances.

The children were nervous. They could feel, like Naseem could, that there was something off about their leader.

Naseem kept a close eye on the one who gave the most guff even to their most feared tutor, Terra, and noticed she was scowling. Her brown tresses, interwoven with hints of blue strands, whipped around her as she turned. Her eyes had one colored blue and the other brown. She would probably carry Water or Earth elements when her powers kicked in, or she could be like Stone and carry multiple at once.

If that was the case, Alessandro would take her under his wing and she would join a rare set of dragons who could one day be their Dragon King.

While Stone had been a studious and meritorious student, Talia Rain was easily bored, determined to do things her own way and often skipped lessons in favor of watching TV.

As Alessandro approached her, Talia's movements were perfectly precise. She scowled the entire time, obviously displeased.

Alessandro crouched down in front of her to get face to face, then with a one finger push on her forehead he threw her off balance.

She landed on the soft dirt and stayed there for a moment before she slowly sat up and glared at him. "What's your problem, huh?"

Alessandro leaned his head on his hand as he stared down at her. "I'm not the one who forgot to keep their core engaged and feet firmly planted. Forms only do so much if you don't engage the basics as well."

Talia moved in a dash and she was face to face with him, covering his eyes with her hands. "You look scary. Go away."

Naseem was moving to intervene, but Alessandro held a hand up in his direction. He didn't remove the girl's hands but stayed crouched there. Naseem watched in horror as Talia began to tear up and cry.

It was only then that Naseem noticed every child was on the verge of tears. As Talia wailed, it broke a dam of emotions and all fifteen kids fell into sobs.

Alessandro pulled the small dragons into his embrace and they sat there for ten minutes, just crying and holding on to one another.

Naseem recalled the first time Alessandro had met Stone. He'd been as gentle as he was now. Kids were his king's ultimate weak spot.

Alessandro whispered something to the group and then laughs bubbled up and it was as if it had never happened.

As they walked away from the group, Naseem asked, "What was that about?"

Grim faced Alessandro answered, "They're overwhelmed by the panic the adults are trying to hide from them. They know something is wrong, but no one will tell them what."

Right, and seeing their Dragon King upset had been the breaking of the hold on their emotions. "What did you say that made them feel better?"

"That my old knees were on the verge of giving out. Kids find old people hilarious."

It was a joke, but there wasn't a trace of humor on the Dragon King's face.

Naseem gave a grunt of understanding, though he didn't, and then said. "Since you're being so open, mind telling me what's happened overnight that you feel like a bomb about to explode?"

The Dragon King stopped mid step and turned to him. "The crown feels heavy today, that's all."

And Naseem knew he would get nothing else out of his king. He frowned, but continued following him through the cobbled streets of Dragon City.

XVIII

The winding paths of the labyrinth underneath the pyramid hadn't seemed like the best way to sneak into the sphinx lair, but Rowan trusted that the map Kin had procured for their break in would be accurate enough to get them to the dungeons. It was where Louisa thought the sphinx leader had locked himself away, preparing for his execution.

Rowan hadn't expected the ceilings to be so tall that they weren't visible as she looked up. She had never actually met a sphinx, and she wondered if in their beast forms they required so much space to move.

Ahead of her, Kin and Zeva moved with confidence. As they both enjoyed hunting treasure, they were the logical choice to lead their walk to avoid booby traps.

They learned their lesson at the beginning of the tunnels when boulders erupted from the sidewalls. If they hadn't been such excellent spellcasters, Rowan was sure they would have ended up as nothing more than piles of pulp.

"Okay, one more left turn and we should reach this 'Chasm of Eternal Pain'. Once we pass that, the dungeons should be right there." Zeva's tone was cheerful.

The way she had said 'Chasm of Eternal Pain' was a contrast to how dreadful the thing sounded. Her heightened senses could pick up the screams from the dark pit before they arrived. The bottom of the pit was too far to locate the source of all the noise.

Rowan turned to Louisa, whose breath got slow and deep. Her eyes were wide and glowing.

"There is so much blood down there." She whispered.

"You brought your hunger suppression tablets, right?" Rowan asked.

Louisa nodded and reached a shaky hand into her fanny pack to extract a small red pill. She was shaking so much that it slipped out of her hand. Rowan caught it mid-fall.

"Let me help you with that." Rowan suggested. Ever since the incident in Greece, Louisa hadn't seemed as controlled as she once had been with her cravings. She'd taken to carrying around hunger suppressant pills Rowan had only seen her take twice in their whole friendship.

Rowan waited until some color was back in her cheeks before she turned to Kin and Zeva, who were observing the chasm oblivious to the redhead's plight.

"There's a bridge, but it looks a bit worn." Zeva pointed to a rickety contraption of ropes and slabs of wood.

"Zev, we can fly. I'd suggest phasing, but there are some wards preventing that kind of magic in here." Rowan watched the realization hit her sister's face, lighting her blue eyes to an electric level.

Rowan wondered if the rest of her family was still so unaware of the different level Rowan was at now that the Coven rescinded their goal of attaining her as an asset.

"Oh my gods, yes! We are so going on all of those 'too dangerous' adventures dad barred us from." Zeva squealed, wrapping her arm around her younger sister. "Is this what true freedom feels like?"

Rowan snickered and then turned to look at the slowly recuperating vampire. "You good?"

Louisa gave a thumbs up.

Kin looked unsure, but his amusement replaced concern as Rowan picked Zeva up bridal style even though Zeva had a good four inches on her.

"Stop moving, or I'll drop you!" Rowan warned, as her wings shot them into the air. She wasn't used to carrying more than her own body weight around and it showed in their shaky flight path.

Zeva pouted. "I wanted to see if I could tell what's in the pit."

"It's at least three miles down. Even I cannot make out what is down there." Kin said from next to them.

"And he has better vision than a half-blind bat like you," Rowan teased.

Zeva pushed her glasses up on the bridge of her nose and huffed as she looked away, "Remind me not to do you guys anymore favors for the rest of the year."

"As the baby sister, I refuse to allow you to tell me no."

The ground was sand on the other side of the chasm. Rowan's boots sunk so low the sand covered the top of her foot.

Zeva frowned, "Let's stick to the walls, it's less likely to have traps."

The walls were cool to the touch.Rowan kept a guiding hand on them as she led the way up the sharply inclined field of sand that kept sliding under her feet.

It felt like a small lifetime had passed when they finally reached the apex, each breathing hard from the exertion.

Two giant cages of gold sat only a few yards away. They reflected the flames of torches lined against the cavern walls, giving them plenty of light to take in the sight.

One cage remained empty, but the other had a sphinx occupying it. The sphinx had the head of an older man, aged by the lines around his eyes and mouth. He was undeniably handsome.

He wore a white nemes headdress. The sculpture of the cobra that decorated it was as tall as Rowan. His great lion body was a dark brown shade sprinkled with random spurts of gray.

Rowan didn't know how to process the smell around him. Like some older scrolls that Zeva had discovered through her adventures, it was reminiscent of the era it originated from, something out of temporal space.

He was facing them by the time they made it to the bars of his cage, paws crossed in front of him as he leaned down so close she could reach through the bars and touch his sharp nose.

She didn't, though. Instead, she bowed her head and waited.

"Salam alaikum." The voice of the sphinx shook the sands under their feet with its deep octave.

"Wa Alaikum al-salam." Zeva spoke first, "Abanoub, I am Zeva Dahl. We are here to understand what happened two days ago. Could we trouble you with our questions?"

"Dahl." Abanoub whispered the name as if trying to remember where he'd heard it before. "You wish for me to retell the story of the worst day of my life?"

"Yes, Abanoub, attacks like the one you endured have been occurring too many times to just be coincidences. We believe something is connecting them, but your story hasn't been told to us in full."

"What does an elf want with the problems of shifters?"

Zeva turned to Rowan, clearly not expecting the question.

"Abanoub, as you know, the shifters are great in numbers, they along with the other mystic races and humans, have blended into society where there is nowhere that they're excluded from. This isn't a problem only for shifters, this is a problem for all races. We are already seeing the effects of the fear attacks like this have on our fragile societies. The dragons have shut their doors to outsiders. I have not faced wars of any sorts, but I listen to the stories of my elders and know that war kills not only people, but parts of their souls. I refuse to stand back and watch souls shatter."

Abanoub looked around at the collection of people. "A succubus, an elf, a vampire and a kitsune. Is this your army to fight against this?"

It was a bit troubling for Kin to be identified when he spent an enormous deal of effort to neutralize his scent, or magic signature, to the level of a common witch. Abanoub was unexpectedly sharp. Rowan chose to not draw anymore attention to her business partner and focused on the bigger issue at hand. "I don't need an army to get answers or to find a culprit. Peace is easier when there is one common enemy, isn't it?"

"They've attacked the world's oldest shifters. Do you think a mere person could do this to us? Do you truly think there is not an army waiting to fight back when they see you are in their way? Think carefully of where you want to land on this battle, little succubus. You may find that some of those you want to protect are the ones standing against you."

Rowan frowned. "Do you know who did this to you?"

"The gods." He let out a shriek, "The gods have done this all to us." He stood and his steps shook the ground beneath them all. "By my claws, my brothers fell. It is my fault, mine and the gods." His speech became unintelligible as he squawked.

"Hey!" From behind the cell a bronze skinned man was running towards them, changing into his sphinx form as he moved closer and closer.

Rowan looked from the oncoming threat to the crazed sphinx to her sister, who had taken several steps back.

"Can you take him, Kin?" She yelled over the squawks.

Kin sized up the oncoming threat, "Yes, but it'll be a tight squeeze."

She nodded and turned to Louisa, "Get in the other cage, and keep Zeva safe. The Atlanteans didn't finish cleaning this up."

"Rowan, he's ten times your size, he will kill you!" Zeva shrieked as Louisa began tugging her away.

"Listen to whatever Louisa says, Zev. I'm going to be fine. You need to give Kin room to move and I need to focus. Do you understand?"

Zeva's face was red with her anger, "I swear if you die Rowan Dahl, I'm so letting mom use the picture from my coming of age ceremony as your memorial!"

Rowan cringed. "You wouldn't dare!"

"Don't die then!" Zeva moved away with Louisa and only when they were safe did Rowan move towards the opening of Abanoub's cage and slide in.

Behind her, Kin erupted into flames. A giant albino fox with its paws wrapped in fire and five bushy tails stood in his place. He yipped at the charging sphinx two times smaller than himself, but the sphinx didn't stop. Kin took off to meet the creature, and the ground shook with the force of their mass.

Rowan turned her full concentration on the stampeding sphinx in the cage, shooting up to meet him face to face in the air, a claw slicing a tendril of her hair off as his paw missed contact with her head. His eyes became further dilated, eating the whites. His squawking grew desperate. "Abanoub, can you hear me?" She called, "If you can understand, blink twice."

The eyes didn't blink. But he had seemed lucid when they had first arrived. He was cognitive enough to recognize a succubus, an elf, a vampire and a kitsune, were in front of him. Could his mind have deteriorated from the trauma of killing six of his sphinxes? While there was that possibility, something was nagging at Rowan. Something was off with this scene.

She examined the bars of the cage, dialed her senses up despite the way the screeching already hurt her ears.

Yipping and growling came from behind her. Zeva's whispered prayers reached her. She concentrated past the squawks and heard what they had been covering; a squeak. A squeak like the one of a door in desperate need of lubrication. Nothing in the immediate vicinity would make that sound. The cage doors had both been closed and when she glanced down, that was still the case. She looked up towards the ceiling she couldn't see, but there was no noise coming from that direction either. She concentrated harder on Abanoub until she zeroed in on the source.

The cobra on his nemes headdress was moving. Wherever its head moved, the sphinx would follow.

Focusing on her target, Abanoub turned his full wrath to her, and he began an onslaught attack of claws or tail. Rowan decided for a bit of offense, and as she dodged his tail, she grabbed hold of it. She climbed onto his back, closing the distance between her and the snake. Her greatest advantage with the sphinx was that it couldn't reach its shoulder, no matter how it tried to get her by turning his neck around.

As she climbed along the fabric of his nemes, her arms, hands, and thighs burned with the exertion to keep hanging on. Just as she approached her goal, she felt him changing. Startled, she realized he was shrinking. He was going into his humanoid form and too quickly for her to do anything but kick off some feet away, barely regaining her footing before he turned. There was a gold sheen leaving his mouth before a spell hit her square in the chest and sent her flying back towards the bars. She realized she couldn't move. He was running towards her, eyes crazed, his arm pulled back and the first punch felt like needles covered his fist.

In the distance, she could hear Zeva screaming, begging for the shifter to stop his attack.

His hits came one after another, though each hit was weaker than the last. Louisa had seemed to notice it too, because instead of coming to her aid, she was trying to calm Zeva down and keep her in the relative safety of the second cage.

It wasn't long before the alpha fell to his knees and the paralyzation left Rowan. Pushing past the pain of putting up with his blows, she used her pent up energy, turned, kicked the headdress off and it flew to the other corner of the cage. Warily, she watched the cobra uncoil itself from the cloth of the nemes, its golden hood growing larger.

Her vision was blurry from the beat down she had just received, but she pushed past that pain and molded her magic to burst the metal into flames. She ratcheted up the temperature, the screeches from the snake deafening as the flames shifted from red to orange to yellow to blue when the snake reached its limit, melting into a pool of gold on the cell floor.

Spitting blood, she turned to the sphinx shifter and fell to her knees in front of him. Her energy was dangerously low, a hunger she knew she'd have to take care of sooner than later throbbed in her throat.

He looked up with glassy brown eyes. His skin was so pale he was nearly translucent.

"Are you alright?" She whispered, examining the hundreds of bite marks around the crown of his bald head.

He shook it and turned to the still fighting sphinx and kitsune. They had drawn blood, but not much. Their physical strength was on par.

"Tarik, enough." Abanoub's hoarse voice echoed in the chamber.

The sphinx immediately backed off and fell into a deep bow, his body morphing back to its humanoid shape. With his nearness, Rowan could make out his features more clearly. He was tall and lean with short, tight curls and bright brown eyes. In his simple black shirt and light jeans, he should've lacked genuine impact, but he, like Abanoub, smelled like long-lost memories that demanded attention.

She held her breath as Kin took a minute longer to begin his transformation. He leveled her with a stare that made her stand straight and set every ounce of dominance she had over the ruby red eyes that leveled with hers.

He let out a yip before finally following the sphinx's example. His face morphed into a harder and older version than his usual self when he changed back and he bent over to catch his breath. In her own weakened state, Rowan couldn't even make fun of his lack of prowess.

"Good thing we stayed against the walls." Louisa looked horror-struck at the many traps the two beasts had set off in their tumble. Spikes, and arrows and a swinging ax took up a lot of the space in the room.

Zeva rushed to Rowan, scowling as she took in her sister's wounds. For a moment Rowan could see her mother in her sister. "How am I supposed to talk dad into revoking his 'off limits' adventures if you keep going home all beat up?"

Rowan winced as Zeva tried to touch a fast swelling bruise under her eye.

"I don't have to go to Lexine for these injuries. Home care will be fine. Not to sound rude, but Abanoub's punches were pretty lame."

Abanoub, who was being helped up by Tarik, laughed and gave a groan. "Next time you try being poisoned by a cursed cobra for three days straight and see how your punches land, eh?"

Rowan shook her head, impressed by the realization that hit her. "You stayed in your sphinx form to keep from being completely consumed by the poison."

He nodded. "Though I can't hang on much longer. Maybe we can talk when I wake-"

Before he finished speaking, the sphinx passed out.

"Master!" Tarik yelled, surprised.

"Don't worry, we are traveling with the world's renowned poison expert, Louisa Monterrey." Kin reassured before he looked over Rowan's injuries as Zeva had and Rowan once again winced when he tried to touch the same spot.

"That hurts!" She cried.

Kin rolled his eyes. "Oh honestly, one would think you never get beaten up as often as you do if they only relied on your pathetic tolerance for pain!"

Rowan flipped him off, but allowed him to pick her up bridal style.

"You can stay here with us until Master Abanoub wakes up. Poison. It all makes sense now." Tarik shook his head as he picked up his frail body.

They followed Tarik through the caverns until the ceiling was visible. Sharp stalactites reached down to connect with a group of stalagmites on the floor, forming posts situated before an opening that led out into stone hallways and stone staircases so plentiful that Rowan couldn't keep track of their path.

Lucky for them, Zeva had solved enough mazes in her lifetime to keep a tab on them as she oohed and ahhed over the small treasures displayed along the walls.

The sun streamed in through a slanted skylight in the room they stopped in.

Ancient furniture and countless handmade rugs filled the space as Tarik moved to deposit Abanoub on the bed. Rowan noted the color had drained from the younger sphinx's face, leaving him ashen as he looked the man over.

Louisa, perhaps as aware as Rowan was of the man, ordered him to bring fresh washcloths and water as she examined Abanoub's wounds. Kin gently put Rowan down on an ornate chair and Zeva moved closer to the side of the bed.

She had enough energy recouped to walk without help, but, when Kin took it upon himself to actually be soft, Rowan milked each occasion for all she could get.

She watched from her chair as Zeva helped Louisa clean and place ointment over the puncture wounds with the supplies brought back by Tarik.

When they finished, Zeva returned to Rowan's side and Louisa leaned down, her fangs glinting in the rods of light still pouring in from outside.

"What are you doing?" Tarik hissed.

Louisa glared at the sphinx but indulged the question. "I have to know what poison he has in his bloodstream to transmogrify my blood cells for an antidote."

"The antidote will come from your vampire blood? Won't that turn him?" Tarik's face turned even paler, if possible. Rowan was sure he was seconds from face planting.

"He's not close enough to death to turn, and she won't give him more than what's required to cure him." Kin was the one to oblige him. "Tarik, we didn't come all this way to harm your master. If that were the case, we could've just waited for him to off himself tomorrow."

The words hung in the air, thick with tension, before Tarik allowed Louisa to continue with a reluctant nod.

Rowan watched with a careful eye as Louisa sank her fangs into the flesh of Abanoub's neck and gave a slight suck. It seemed the pills were still working as her red eyes remained in their neutral state. She straightened and swished the blood in her mouth as if tasting wine before spitting it out on a washcloth.

Her eyes glowed white before blazing lines mapped out each vein on every visible piece of skin.

Reaching into her fanny pack, she pulled out a knife. Made a small incision along her wrist and poured the free flowing blood into Abanoub's mouth.

A great jerk shook the bed, and Abanoub screamed in pain. Tarik made to stop the vampiress, but both Rowan and Kin pinned him to the ground before he took his first step.

"Give it a minute." Kin growled.

A few seconds was all it took for the shaking to cease and a few more for Rowan and Kin to let go of the young Egyptian.

Tarik roared at them, ready to attack, before a soft tired voice said, "Please Tarik, calm down."

Abanoub reached out his hand, which Zeva filled with a glass of water.

The glowing ebbed to a smolder and Louisa smiled down at Abanoub as it extinguished, "Feeling better?"

"Much." The sphinx answered, his face bronzed and much more handsome than Rowan had first realized.

Tarik moved to stand over his master's bed, tears rolling down his cheeks. "Father. You're okay?"

Abanoub furrowed his eyebrows together, and a hand reached down to pat his knee. "I think I'm better than I have been in years. Louisa, was it? Your blood is miraculous. I was certain there was no fix and you even rid me of the knee pain I've been contending with for half of a decade."

Louisa shook her shoulders in a cocky swagger. "I am pretty great. Aren't I?"

Rowan rolled her eyes. "Abanoub, would it be alright to ask you a few questions now?"

The man tensed, perhaps because of the habit of keeping sphinx business close to the vest, but when his shoulders relaxed Rowan knew she would get what she came for. "Alright, I believe you have earned it. What do you wish to know?"

Keeping in mind the prideful nature of alphas, she began, "What happened the night that asp first poisoned you?"

Abanoub's eyes glazed over as he recalled the tragedy, "That asp was supposed to be the gold-plated body of the asp Cleopatra — yes, that Cleo — used to poison herself. For centuries, Sphinx Alphas have given it to their replacements as a sign of the peaceful transfer of power. There's never been a sign of sentience, but some believe a fragment of the souls of our ancestors inhabit it." He cast his eyes to the ground. "The day of the attack, I felt as if our ancestors were rejecting me as their current bearer. It happened midmorning, on my way to breakfast. I felt disoriented and confused. This is one of the worst ways to feel when you're constantly keeping your beast at bay. We are at our deadliest during our adolescence and in moments of loss of emotional and physical control. By the time I got a bit of my control back, I had already done irreversible damage."

"Why didn't you remove the nemes as soon as you regained that control?" Louisa's question had Tarik on the offensive and Rowan watched as a knife slid out of his sheath, aimed at the vampiress' throat.

Kin caught the knife mid swing and set the sphinx with a fiery golden glare. Louisa, realizing what would've happened, stared slackjawed at the young sphinx.

"It is a fair question." Abanoub waved his hand. "Please, Tarik, control your temper. These are outsiders, unaccustomed to our ways."

Tarik cursed under his breath but retreated to a corner of the room with his hands stuffed deep into his pants and a scowl on his face.

Abanoub took a deep breath before continuing. "I didn't realize the asp was behind the madness. There was no pain in the initial attacks or even the discomfort that comes from the slightest mosquito bites. It was only when the asp injected me again that I realized what was attacking me. It was too late; no matter how much I willed my hands to remove my nemes, I couldn't. I ended up killing four more before the Atlanteans showed up with their holy water and forced it down my throat. It put me out of commission for a few hours. When I awoke, the Atlanteans were still on standby. They made me drink until they believed I was stable enough to be reasoned with. I tried to remove my nemes again, to explain myself to my betrayed sphinxes, but the words didn't want to come out."

"Tongue-tie curse." Louisa scowled. "The only reason you can tell us now is because Rowan melted the asp."

He nodded, "Yes. Once I reached the conclusion that once the Atlanteans left with the water, I would be under the control of the asp again, I decided the best thing was the execution. My family would be safe if I was gone. I vaguely remember making them lock the door of my cage, however the rest is a complete blur. I am not even sure I remember your approach."

"I understand you must be tired, Abanoub." The dark circles under his eyes and the way he had slowly sunk further and further into his pillows hinted at it. "But, I have one more important question. Does anyone else have access to your nemes?"

Tarik snapped his attention to them, and the wary gaze Abanoub threw at his son ignited a fury in response.

"Do you already have an idea?" Zeva asked when he didn't answer.

The sphinx clenched his jaw and gave one sharp nod. "Yes, but she is already dead."

Rowan felt the telltale sign of telepathy wrinkle the air. She watched the ping-pong match of words between father and son. Whoever Abanoub suspected had an emotional connection to the alpha. She could both smell and see the tears forming in the corner of his eyes.

Had she been one of his victims?

"There have been signs of manipulation in the other attacks." She whispered.

"What?" Abanoub roared, and Rowan felt a thrill of caution scale down her back. There was something otherworldly about Abanoub that she didn't quite recognize. Not quite on the level of Alessandro, but pretty damn close. Was he on the cusp of godhood? Is this how Alessandro had felt before he received his invitation?

"Each attack stemmed from someone within the shifter's pack. Someone who could do actual damage. But none of them can pinpoint who or what vaulted them down that road. Whoever did this to you could be on the same boat, Abanoub."

Relief etched the man's face, and it was only when Louisa's eyes motioned to something on his hand that Rowan took in the piece of jewelry.

It was unusual for shifters to marry when there was a possibility of a mate in their future. But some didn't receive the mating feeling until several years into their lives. Some grew lonely.

Rowan looked around the spartan room and noticed that there wasn't a trace of femininity in it. Had she died or was there something else going on? Knowing how touchy Tarik had already proven, Rowan watched his reaction when she asked, "Was it your wife?"

Tarik rolled his eyes as his father answered, "We were going through a bit of a rough patch."

"Amira was a human. She didn't feel comfortable living here among the sphinxes and had been trying to get father to move out with her to the city. She left last month after purchasing a condo with their joint bank account." Tarik clarified.

"Wait, she married you, the head of the sphinxes and wasn't willing to live with your people?" Louisa's unprofessionalism had always been a point of contention between her and her partners. They both glared at her and she held her hand up in self defense. "It's crazy!"

"It was shameful." Tarik hissed, "You might have loved her baba, but she was selfish to wish to take you from us."

Abanoub cast his eyes away, and Rowan tried not to compare her personal situation with Alessandro to this one. Still, she felt her back straighten defensively and only when Kin shot her a questioning look was she able to fully pull her mind out of those visions.

"May we search the apartment, Abanoub? We might find a clue."

Abanoub looked uncomfortable with the idea but sighed. "Yes. Tarik, get me the key."

XIX

H is dragon was driving him insane.

'*Rowan*' echoed in his head in a thundering heartbeat at any idle moment he could find. Only when he was engaged in something else could Alessandro find peace in his head.

As such, he turned his full attention to the ordeal of who had been behind their attack. In doing so, he discovered a report he must have overlooked when he had been more concerned about what the mutt's tongue had been doing all over Rowan's abdomen.

Concentrate.

"Stone, what is this about the change in leadership of the Coven being done in secret?" He asked his protégé when the young dragon stepped back into the library conference room with a bowl full of grapes.

The lean man peered at the report and frowned. "That's a report we got from Mateo last night. He was on watch when it happened. He thought it would be a bigger deal with a whole public showing, but Blaise thought that since Cherry Young had been basically running the show for the last year and with what was going on with us, they might have decided a huge ceremony would be in poor taste. I also thought it was weird, so I put it in my pile to investigate later."

Alessandro hummed as he fingered the piece of paper. "Summon Mateo, leave the grapes."

Stone frowned but swiped a handful of the fruit before he turned to do as bidden.

It didn't take long for the redhead to show up, not only paler than Alessandro had ever seen him, but shaking like a leaf and stinking of adrenaline and fear.

It didn't take too long for Alessandro to realize that he hadn't shown up alone, Blaise had also joined his underling with a mischievous grin on his face.

"Please, your majesty, anything but my wings. I don't heal as well as others of my kind. Have mercy."

Alessandro was careful to not show his exasperation to the kid. He knew the fear the younger generation showed him derived from exaggerated tales of the older generation who had seen him as his terrifying stage of unruliness. With Mateo's recent loss of control, he was sure his Fire General had amped up some relatively harmless tale of their king's wrath to include yet again ripping off the wings of some poor idiot who'd crossed him.

"I'll allow General Blaise to continue to take charge of your punishment for the time being, but this is regarding another matter. What exactly did you see at the leadership change for the Coven?"

The relief that washed over the boy didn't totally ease his tension enough to look directly at Alessandro, but he raised his head and he glanced at Blaise, who gave a nod of his permission to go into the tale.

"Well, it was weird. Security on the Compound rarely allows for us to hear or see much of what goes on from our watchtower, but that day the barriers glitched and we could see everything. I sent in a few of the bugs that were provided in case anything like that ever happened and recorded some footage of thousands of witches phasing in at the same time. Then the Elder appeared. She was there in full garb, with that freaky mask. You know, the one Elder Henrietta used to show up in when she was doing official Coven business? She walked around them for hours, making serious eye contact with each witch. At first I thought the equipment failed to catch sound, but everything that happened was in complete silence. There was only one clear shot we got of her passing by, but — and this is the real reason I reported it — I could swear that whoever was in the garb was not Cherry Young. I've seen her before and the witch has some serious weight on her chest. This person was flat."

Alessandro turned his attention to the video Stone had been queuing up as Mateo spoke. It paused at the clip where a figure in a hooded cream white and golden cloak passed by wearing a golden mask. He supposed it could be called freaky, as it covered every inch of the face, even the eyes, but the coverage didn't extend to the long blonde hair that peaked out around the shoulders that were not of Cherry Young.

His eyes drifted to the timestamp, and he could feel his scales roiling with his fury.

Alessandro hadn't meant to ice over the library, but with his dragon so volatile, it had been more of a surprise that he hadn't set it on fire. "This happened the night of the attack on us?"

Mateo gulped. "Y-yes, but I was trying to ensure that the audio wasn't a mistake before I turned it in. According to procedure, we have to take it to the techies to ensure it wasn't, and I didn't get it back until last night."

"According to procedure, you let your Generals know of any concern you put a chief priority on, but perhaps it fell under your priority to unseat your General from power. Is that what motivated you? You thought once you had my spot that you could turn this in as further proof that you deserved the position?" Blaise roared. Flames were dancing on his skin as he glared down at the much smaller fire dragon.

The tension that had left Mateo since the beginning of his tale was back in place, and he dropped his sight to the ground, a trick for younger dragons to calm older ones, but Blaise had no soft spot to exploit. "I swear, I was just trying to make sure that the silence wasn't a technical error! Unlike the heads of houses that refused us permission to move against the civilians, I know the importance of Draconis."

"Get the fuck back to the coliseum and wait for me. If you deviate, I will resort to our king's preferred method of punishment and tear your wings from your back in slices."

Mateo gave a small sound of a whimper and was gone in the next second.

"Fuck!" Blaise roared. His anger manifested in a fireball that shattered a stained window overhead.

Seeing the fire dragon so amped up made Alessandro redouble his grip on his own control and he removed his ice, hoping the protective spells on the books had withstood the instant thaw.

"If that's not Cherry Young, who is it?" Stone asked even as his fingers were flying on his laptop, his body already working faster than his mind.

Alessandro offered his commandeered bowl of grapes to the fuming dragon general.

He had half a mind to just show up to the compound and figure it out without all the stealth bullshit. But he couldn't risk showing any sign of hostility to the undisputed champions of non-shifters with their current state of affairs. He needed solid evidence something foul was happening with the Coven.

He felt the trigger of one of his barriers only seconds before the trespasser appeared before him.

Shock filled him at the sight of the blue-eyed beauty. Her body was fading slightly in spots where the sun shone just a little too brightly.

"Elaine?" Stone hissed.

"Why haven't you crossed over?" Alessandro demanded as she stepped into the shadows, anxiety written all over her face.

"I tried." Even in her ghost form, he could tell she was shaking. "But I saw what he had planned. I had to help the woman, the woman that healed me, but I can't find her."

"The ones responsible for Pan's Flute?" He demanded.

Elaine let out a breath that came out as mist. "Yes, my King, you must hurry, her family is in danger."

"The elf's?"

Elaine's form flickered. "I can't hang on anymore. Save her kingdom, Alessandro." Her last words hung thick in the surrounding air.

Her kingdom. The Eastern Elven Kingdom was in peril.

"Naseem, you're in charge. Aqua, come to me. I'm taking Stone and Blaise as well."

"Got it." Naseem's voice was liquid honey and the calming breeze Alessandro needed to keep from losing total control.

He felt the scales crawling along his skin, a sign of his rage. The anger he'd held onto since Draconis' attack finally had a source to concentrate its wrath on and his dragon was thirsty for blood.

Aqua appeared a moment later, looking flush with confusion, but just as Stone's and Blaise's beasts were showing their heads in iridescent opal and ruby red scales, her own cerulean joined the fray in patches on her flesh.

"We're going to the Eastern Elven Kingdom. I've just received a tip that the ones behind our attack are there, plotting something against the royal family." He held out a hand, and the book he still hadn't given to Blaise appeared. "This is the scent we'll be working off of to gather the targets."

Aqua looked like she was about to argue, but Alessandro's stern gaze quieted her.

"Great, now we can call it even against the elf." Blaise took the book and raised an eyebrow at the title. "Is this a kid's book?"

"It's a gift for you once we're done."

"For me?" Blaise demanded with disbelief before handing it off to Stone. "Last time I checked, I was a grown ass man."

Stone looked a bit troubled by the smell, but he kept quiet as he passed it to Aqua.

Once all his dragons had the scent, they phased out.

When the world reformed, it wasn't at all what Alessandro had been expecting.

"What in the endless hells?" Blaise lost his breath as they took in the sight of what had once been the Eastern Elven Kingdom.

A thin layer of ice covered the roads, the people, the shops.

Deep ice, his signature move.

Meant to protect and contain inorganic matter, using the spell against living people would produce harm.

"They're all alive. " Aqua noted as she examined one elf looking through a shop window at a green silk gown.

"How?" Stone demanded, looking towards his master.

Alessandro couldn't believe what he was feeling under the layer of the ice curse. "It's a protection rune." He looked around the ground for signs of their existence. His first instinct was to look for them engraved on the cobblestones.

"No way." Stone's eyes were on the trees that surrounded the entrance to the kingdom, particularly the roots. He took off into the sky and Alessandro realized what had caught the dragon's attention.

Blaise and Aqua joined him and Alessandro watched as Aqua paled and Blaise's eyes shone. Stone was speechless.

Alessandro didn't need to fly up to take in what they saw. He could feel the shape of Rowan's magic now that he knew where to look for it.

The insane woman had used the roots of the forest surrounding the Eastern Elven Kingdom to make a giant protection rune imbued with her blood as its nexus of power. He also came upon a more minor rune that was so clever he couldn't help but smirk.

She really needed absolutely nothing from him, did she?

He walked towards the center of the square where the smaller rune was exuding power. At the foot of a larger than usual hydrangea tree, in between a thick collection of colorful tulips, sat a man he had seen on the news coverage of the wolves in Greece. He had put up a struggle to get out of the wooden and magic bonds that shackled his hands to the trunk of the tree. His disheveled hair, red face and sweat drenched appearance suggested it. A trail of broken tulips ended where the witch sat. He huffed and puffed against the nulling magic holding him in place.

A Chloe Darling special.

"Dae Kang." Stone landed next to Alessandro.

Alessandro crouched until he was eye level with the man.

"I thought the Coven was no longer looking to recruit Rowan Dahl."

"Does this really look like a recruiting attempt?"

"Ah. So now it's time to take out the threat?"

"She shouldn't have believed she was safe. She should've kept her powers hidden. The Coven had no clue how much power she was hiding." He scoffed, "Stupid woman."

It was a quick punch, but it knocked the witch's head back as Alessandro's fist collided with his nose.

He let out a yelp of pain and whined for a few moments as streams of blood splurged from the break.

Blaise snickered.

Alessandro waited until the witch sat back up, his eyes wary. "Exactly what has the woman done to deserve such a response from your people?"

Refusing to answer, the man turned his face away.

Alessandro raised an eyebrow.

"If I were you, I'd answer before he loses the mask of civility." Stone warned. "I didn't think there was anything that would prompt the Coven to return to their barbaric methods of threatening loved ones."

"Barbaric? Your kind dares speak of barbarity?" Dae scoffed.

Warmth was exuding itself from Blaise, and Alessandro knew he was a ticking time bomb. Dragon pride made Blaise's affinity for fire strong. If the witch kept stroking his fire with blatant disrespect, Blaise would burn him to death.

"Now let me be frank. I know it is the Coven who is behind the attacks on the shifters. You are here to threaten Rowan Dahl because she got in the way one too many times. I'm just trying to reach a reason not to run you through with my claws here and now and start an all out war between your witches and the world."

"The Coven is not behind the shifter attacks." The witch hissed. His refusal was so vehement that Alessandro wondered if Elaine's message had been wrong. "The only reason I am here is to get the stolen Elder's Grimoire back."

Before he heard her. He felt her. Full of power and pissed off.

"Steal? Cherry Young delivered it to me." Rowan's voice shook with her indignation.

Alessandro turned and took her in. Of course, she had fresh injuries. It was apparently a thing she did, showing up beat up. A cut lip, swollen cheek, and a green-purple bruise bloomed on her temple.

In return she took him in, confusion and hurt front and center before she once again shuttered her feelings and showed him nothing but a slight mocking look as if she was saying, *I told you I needed nothing from you.*

His dragon reared.

He scowled and waved a hand over the bruises until they disappeared. "Defense is as important as a good offense."

She bristled. "My defense is great, or else I'd be dead ten times over. What are you doing here, Dragon King?"

"Must you be so hostile?"

"Yes. It's part of my defense."

He rolled his eyes. "We got a warning that your kingdom was about to be attacked."

"From whom?" She demanded.

"Ah, so that got through that little defense of yours, did it?"

"What in the endless hells?" Blaise's soft curse brought them back to the realization they had onlookers.

Alessandro took in Rowan's companions.

There was a black-haired man with golden eyes rimmed with red kohl. He could smell under layers of charms that he was a kitsune, a strong one at that.

Next to him was a brunette woman with cherry red eyes and an impressed smile that showed off fangs to denote her vampire heritage. The smell of blood he associated with the race was so slight, he nearly missed it. Was she starving herself?

Rowan stood protectively in front of what was obviously one of the other three princesses of the Eastern Elven Kingdom. He noted a lack of the succubus limbs Rowan carried, as well as the lack of concealment charms that would suggest she was simply hiding them. Were the sisters perhaps not fully related? She was a spitting image of Rowan, though her hair had an aquamarine streak and she wore round, golden rimmed glasses. Her face was taut with anxiety as she glanced at the witch.

She looked so much like Rowan that it was instinct to ease it. "As I was saying, I came to help, but your spell work beat me to the punch."

A glint of pride lightened her eyes. "Is that awe I hear in your voice?"

"Who thinks of such a defense?" Blaise asked, approaching and holding his hand out, "Princess Rowan, I am Blaise."

Rowan took the offered appendage. "Thank you for coming, Blaise. To be fair, the trap was a joint effort between my sister Axel and myself. She's creative with defense strategies and I am wicked good with magic."

"Makes me wonder how much you actually hid when we were in school together." Stone was next to approach. "I knew I caught you practicing higher level spells in the study chambers."

"Strange how each time you did, Louisa was supposed to be playing my lookout." Rowan sent a glare back toward the brunette.

"I was on vampire time, and you were asking me to pay attention during my equivalent of your crack of dawn!" Louisa snapped.

There was no real vehemence behind either woman, this was just their way of communicating. There was comfort and trust that came along with such a method.

"She tried her best to make up excuses for you." Stone grinned at the pair, "It took me months to figure out you couldn't harvest raw power from the conch of a mermaid if you played the right tune on a night of a new moon."

Blaise was unimpressed. "Alessandro, you know what I could've done with the money you dished out to send him to Spellcasters?"

"Hookers and blow?" Stone shot back.

"Enough." Alessandro cut through the argument before actual flames joined the mix. Unlike Rowan and Louisa, there was a history of actual vehemence between the two youngest of Alessandro's inner court. He'd had to intervene too many times where their mat time had turned a little too bloody.

Rowan looked impressed by the instant silence he received. "So, a little birdie told you my kingdom was getting attacked. Did they mention why?"

"No, but I have a theory." Alessandro looked down at the witch with teeth slightly bared. "Your role in helping the shifters is a threat to whatever twisted goal they have in mind."

Rowan's eyes widened.

"The Coven is behind the shifter attacks?" The kitsune asked for clarification.

All eyes turned to the only member of the Coven in their presence. Dae remained silent.

"But why?" Stone asked, confusion clear on his face.

"Because they are under the control of a man with the ability to weave illusions. They're so realistic that the entire Coven has fallen under the impression that the last words of Elder Henrietta were a warning. A warning of the shifters igniting a war that would destroy the world." The voice was inches from Alessandro's ear. His hand shot out in the direction it came from. A man, the spitting image of the witch kneeling at his feet, held his hands up in surrender.

The witch in his hold was stronger than the one on the ground by leagues. Alessandro slowly released his fingers from around the man's neck.

Upon his release, the second man gasped for air. Rowan instantly made her way to him, enraging the dragon in Alessandro, who hadn't deemed the man safe.

Control. He reminded himself.

She patted the witch's back, her eyes pitying. "Evil twin?"

Dae sighed. "He's bewitched by the False Elder like the rest of the Coven. I can't break his hold over any of them."

"Who is this False Elder, and why aren't you also under his hold?" Alessandro was hard to convince.

"Antoni Barros. He was part of the North American Chapter so my knowledge of him is minimal. I'm not being affected because of this." He held up a hand and a silver bracelet glinted on his wrist. "I had this on when he began hypnotizing everyone. There were a few others who resisted, he...punished them. I decided then to fly under the radar and figure out what had happened to Master Cherry."

"That's Chloe's magic signature." Louisa examined the piece of jewelry.

"Yes." he fingered the piece of jewelry and Rowan caught a fleeting look of tenderness before he snapped his attention back to Rowan. "She never came back from her meeting with you, neither has the Elder's Grimoire. I tried locating her through tracking spells, but when those failed, I turned to looking for the book. That's how I ended up here."

"Surely that's not an accusation I hear in your voice." The kitsune surged to stand between Rowan and the witch, his golden eyes glowing.

The kitsune's potential should have made him take the role of alpha for the cobbled pack, standing back until action was required. But intruding before danger escalated was an action for a second in command.

Alessandro was aware of Rowan's potential better than perhaps even herself, but she was not a shifter. To be considered an alpha by the beast of this kitsune, one of the most powerful shifters Alessandro had come across in a century, made the Dragon King question what he'd missed in his assessment of her.

Tension squared Dae's shoulders and, though he was several inches shorter than the massive kitsune, he raised his chin up in defiance.

Rowan peeked from around the suddenly enraged shifter. "Tone the hostility down a notch, Dae. When Kin's beast takes over, buildings crumble. My dad isn't a fan of eyesores on his land."

Dae clenched his jaw but bowed his head. "No. I don't think that Ms. Dahl had anything to do with Master Cherry's disappearance. Seeing her in action in Greece all but confirmed the reputation she's earned with the Coven. She can't help but play the part of the hero, even to her own detriment. Harming the rightful Elder isn't part of her M.O." He looked around at the still frozen people. "Barros is proving reckless."

"Elder Antoni, Dae. Do not take his name so lightly." The twin spoke for the first time since his brother popped into existence.

Dae rolled his eyes. "His name is Hye. I tried to give him nulling jewelry to counteract the effects of the illusion, but it didn't work."

"Nothing will, not unless this Antoni Barros lifts his spell, is nulled himself, or dies." Aqua's words were unexpected. Alessandro was sure the woman would've preferred to remain silent their entire visit.

"If that's the case, tell us where the bastard is and I'll have this all taken care of in a matter of hours." Blaise cracked his knuckles.

There was bloodlust in his Fire General's eye. Stone and Aqua had a similar glimmer in their own and Alessandro himself was itching to avenge the pride of his Thunder by ripping the man apart.

"They discovered me after that interview in Greece. I was supposed to paint the wolves to be rabid and out of control, to not let them know it had been Ms. Dahl behind getting them under control. But after the reaction to Draconis' incident, I knew I couldn't be a part of that. The Coven is supposed to bring the world together, not tear it apart like Barros wants."

Alessandro's eyes wandered to Rowan, who seemed to have softened even further towards the man. He tried to stamp down his infuriating irritation.

"I've spent the last day dodging witches. I haven't been able to figure out what's going on behind the scenes."

Dae glanced at his brother. "But he might know something that could lead us to Barros."

Hye snarled and said, "I will not turn my back on my oath. Unlike you, I have maintained my honor. I will serve the Coven until my dying breath."

Alessandro considered his options. He could rip apart Hye's mind and find the information he needed, but if there was already one set of hands on the witch's brain, he would leave permanent scars. Death would be kinder and dragons didn't kill without just cause.

With that being the case, he had only one other choice. He could send his dragons to find Antoni Barros now that he had a name. It might take longer than getting the answer out of Hye, but it would be less messy in the long run.

"Ro, is everyone okay, still frozen?"

Alessandro's gaze slid to Rowan's bandaged hands. She had used her magic wrong again and was paying the consequences. Yet, here she was pondering the length of the damage to assess if it was possible to cast the proper reversal of deep ice.

As its creator, he knew it was a challenging spell, even at full power.

"Oh, no you don't." Louisa crossed her arms. Her ruby eyes narrowed at Rowan. "Kin and I will take care of it. You need to recoup."

"You guys used as much magic as I did."

"Yeah, but we didn't take Abanoub's blows straight to the head like you did. In fact, why don't I take you to the infirmary first and begin with thawing Miasma or Lexine out? You could have a concussion!"

"I'm fine." Rowan hissed, fighting the brunette's wandering hands away from her face.

"No." Kin's voice was soft.

Something unspoken passed between the kitsune and the elf, and Alessandro watched as the fight drained from Rowan's body. It was yet another shifter characteristic, an alpha being talked down by a member of their pack. There was no hostility in Kin's resistance, just a statement of fact Rowan couldn't refuse. It was how Aqua should have approached Alessandro about his silver eyes, but out of all his generals she was the most anxious.

"Fine." She hissed. "But I'm calling Master Jah."

"He's with Halley." Louisa sing-songed. "Last time you interrupted their romantic time, I believe her words went something like, 'if you value your spine you'll make sure to only reach out in life or death situations, and I will be the judge of where it falls'."

Rowan paled at whatever memory occurred and Alessandro wondered if they were talking about Japhet and who the fuck Halley was if they were. Hadn't he basically confessed to being in love with Rowan?

"We can help." Blaise grinned, "I'm actually the uncontested champion of un-deep icing shit."

"Only because you won't count the last time I won." Stone rolled his shoulders. "If I win twice in a row, that means you'll have to swallow your pride."

Louisa perked up. "Do you have to be a dragon to compete?"

Blaise raised an eyebrow as his gaze roved all over the vampiress. "No, but babe, you're competing against dragons here. Vamps don't understand heat the way we do."

The woman began long-legged strides towards the nearest frozen elf and undid the deep ice in a matter of seconds.

"We better referee." Alessandro led Aqua away.

XX

"I'll go make sure our idiot doesn't go overboard." Kin said softly. "Rowan, if the Coven is behind this, they'll send a backup if they don't get their witch back. You should get ready."

Rowan nodded her understanding and with Dae beside her, they watched as the spellcasters moved from body to body after making sure whoever they thawed had no residual effects of being encased.

She would admit to feeling disappointed at not being able to throw her hat into the ring, but Kin had been right. She had to recover from her fight with the Sphinx Alpha and her succubus hunger was darkening the edges of her vision.

"Why did Cherry give you the grimoire?"

Rowan turned her full attention to Dae. The facade of a put-together witch slid off so completely she could hardly recognize him.

"She said it was a condition of my freedom." Rowan answered carefully, noting any change in his face as she spoke, "I tried to refuse, but she wouldn't hear of it."

"How did she appear when you last saw her?"

His strained tone and his glassy eyes tickled Rowan's inner succubus. Longing and worry, the kind reserved for lovers.

"Sad."

The words seemed to siphon more energy from the witch. "Tell me." He whispered to his brother, "Do you know where Cherry is?"

Hye's nostrils flared, "The False Elder is gone. Help me, Dae, help me and tell Elder Antoni you are on our side. We have always been of one mind. How can you be on the wrong side of this?"

Curses streamed from Dae's mouth as he stalked a few feet away to recollect himself.

Zeva spoke for the first time since they'd arrived back home, "Rowan, if they do come, the Coven has the media on their side. They're the most influential mystics to exist. They could paint us to be the bad guys here."

"Yep." Rowan let out a breath of uneasy breath. "Come on, I think they'll come from the south."

-A-

When Alessandro and the competing group made it to the throne room, the Bloody Elf was shaking the ice out of his hair.

His nose flared at the sight of the intruders. "Explain." The voice was low, full of threat if given the wrong answer.

Louisa stepped out from behind Blaise and the king released some of the tension.

"The Coven just threw a deep ice spell over the kingdom. Rowan is waiting at the south border for them to phase in and trigger intruder number six protocols."

"Nine." Kin corrected as he extended his forearm for King Kyron to grip and both men tapped each other's shoulders in greeting.

"Nine." Louisa corrected herself as she wrapped her arms around King Kyron, melting the rest of his tension. "I'm glad to see you're okay."

King Kyron returned the embrace and placed a soft kiss on the top of her head. "You've been gone for far too long."

"I know. Ma decided she liked your idea and is implementing our own family dinner nights."

King Kyron chuckled. "Perhaps one day we can simply invite her."

Louisa laughed, "I wouldn't put people I actually like through that. If you're thawed out, the jewelry may have worked for everyone else."

"Indeed, they did, little Lou." in the doorway was a stunning black haired elf. Eyes a shade of periwinkle that glowed when they landed on Alessandro.

It took a moment to realize what that meant and a moment more to recognize the woman from the tearoom in the cabin. He noted with confusion that she, like Zeva, didn't have the appendages that would denote her as a succubus. Her demonic levels were definitely higher than Rowan's. Her mere presence had Stone and his Elemental Generals straightening, their breathing coming out labored, scents tinged with arousal.

He wasn't surprised that she didn't affect him as well. His beast had already chosen the one and only succubus who could tease that reaction from him.

He took a moment to scan for a concealment charm like the one Rowan had worn the first time he'd met her, but there wasn't a single trace.

"Well, well, if it isn't the Dragon King." Her voice was little more than a sigh tinged with the slightest ring of a Spanish lilt.

"Ama." The warning came from the white-haired woman behind her.

He made the connection between this elf and Rowan as he had the one with her mother. Unlike Rowan's short white waves, this elf's hair fell past her shoulders. Her eyes were the sky blue of their father and she shared a similar nose to their mother. This woman's skin had seen the sun, it glowed bronze; her body was lean and toned where Rowan was soft and curvy.

She held no magic at her command, but she had a grip on a matte black tomahawk she kept at her side. Cords of muscles along her arm were proof enough that she could swing her weapon with serious strength behind it.

Her mother dropped the power she'd stirred up and brightened when her eyes caught sight of the Bloody Elf who was rolling his sleeves up as he approached the exit. Tattoos rippled as his muscles flexed.

"Wife." He said, dropping a firm kiss on the woman as he grabbed her hand, "Our daughter waits at the southern border. The Coven has gone back on their word. Shall we join her?"

Delight crossed the woman's face. "Yes, immediately."

"Well, only sort of," Louisa corrected.

King Kyron raised an eyebrow.

Kin explained and by the end of his story both the queen and king looked horrified at the implications.

Then Alessandro felt it. They had arrived exactly where Rowan had predicted.

He was stepping towards joining her when King Kyron shot him a wary look.

"Before you do that, I should let you know we are not cooperating with the Coven. We will take the young man into custody and they will more than likely try to paint us into villains. I believe it would be beneficial to split public outcry between your people and ours."

"It's a wise plan." Alessandro admitted and hesitantly said, "I'll remain in the shadows. If they try anything, I'll be here as backup."

It was to his total shock when Aqua stepped forward and held up a small green pill. "She's wounded."

King Kyron's nose flared. "Yes. That is a common occurrence lately. What is it?"

"A healing elixir. Mostly for physical wounds, but it'll also give her a slight boost in magic." Aqua answered.

The king beamed at the blue-haired dragon. "Thank you."

Alessandro couldn't help but notice the slight reddening of his Water General's face and then the heat that trailed out of his Fire General.

Noting the intriguing reaction, he sent Stone and Aqua to the West side of the castle and Kin and Blaise to the East to finish thawing out the remaining victims. He melted into the shadows and walked behind the three elves and the vampiress as they moved to meet Rowan and the witches.

-R-

Rowan wasn't sure what she had been expecting, but two of the highest ranked Coven Members seemed like overkill to her.

"All we have come for is the rogue witch." The woman taking the lead was tall with black hair streaked with silver. Her black eyes were sharp and beady as they regarded the two sisters.

Rowan knew Eve Tanoch could feel the edge of the barrier, but not the consequences of passing the threshold.

Rowan had only had the misfortune of meeting Eve once during one of the ex-Elder's visits. They had been best friends. Although Henrietta's nonchalance about the whole Rowan situation was amusing, Eve firmly believed Rowan was a threat not only to the world but to herself if not supervised carefully by the Coven. Her pale, ashen skin always reminded Rowan of a decaying corpse.

Rowan knew under normal circumstances that the witch's signature blood magic would have been tough to combat in her current ragged state, but in the Eastern Elven Kingdom, Rowan's arsenal of tools was extensive.

To choose to send Eve along with Dorin Indigo was a flex on Antoni Barros' part that Rowan couldn't pretend to miss.

Rowan had only heard stories of Dorin Indigo's adventures into dark magic. He didn't seem to care much about the worth of a life. To him, the greatest goal was finding the true limits of what magic could do and, as such, had gotten put on the Coven watch list, much like Rowan had in her formative years.

Unlike the Eastern Elven Kingdom family who threatened war if the Coven tried to take her, Dorin's people surrendered him without preamble.

She wasn't all that impressed by his buzz cut or his thundering dark blue eyes, but his body was a different story. White scars told of his violent past. Muscles under every inch of skin gave him a hardened warrior appearance that reminded her of the Dragon King. Her hunger throbbed, but she had to keep her cool.

She concentrated on the nagging feeling that the two witches were almost hollow.

Unlike Hye, who had seemed fanatic and crazed, the two witches didn't have eyes glowing with a mislaid sense of righteousness. Their expressions were little more than deadpanned, they weren't raising their voices. She wondered if perhaps their power affected the illusion. If there was doubt weaved in.

"Under the contract signed by both the Coven and the Eastern Elven Kingdom Chapter 3 Section 12 subsection B in the event of a witch trespassing onto Eastern Elven grounds without giving at least a two-day notice of planned arrival, the ruler of the aforementioned kingdom can choose what to do with said trespasser up to but excluding execution." Zeva cut in.

"The contract no longer exists, along with the lifted monthly check-ins." Eve sneered.

Zeva raised her eyebrows. "Actually, Chapter 23 Section 10 subsection C states that in the case of either party relinquishing their benefit of the contract, the agreements made in Chapters 1 through 13 will remain active."

"Enough with the legal mumbo jumbo." Dorin finally stepped forward. "Not sure you're aware, but we have new leadership. New leadership says we have to get the kid back. So move or I'll move you. I don't mind either way."

One more step forward and he would be in their territory. Rowan knew just what it would take to goad him, too. It was such a common weakness for most men with power who had to deal with women they viewed as a threat.

She smiled.

The challenge in her smile was like pulling a trigger as he shot forward and in a gust of wind from behind, her father erupted into existence, a sheathed sword pressing into the soft skin of the witch's throat as Dorin glared up from his position on the grass.

Rowan remained silent as Eve stepped forward to help. She didn't need to utter a single word to activate the barrier's consequence. Any magic used in the kingdom to affect the royal family was now hers.

Cold realization and instant panic hit the duo as no magic came to their beck and call.

"You're not welcome here." Kyron's voice sent a chill through Rowan's spine. "You have ten seconds to get out of my kingdom before I really lose my temper and unsheathe my sword. Let your people know I will show no more mercy to the members of the Coven. If I see you on my land again, I will ensure you don't live to see another day."

Dorin's moves were careful as he crawled back to the other side of the threshold, while Eve had to only take a step back.

"The Elder will come for you all." She warned, though still lacking heat, "You should have allowed us to take him."

Kyron barked a laugh, his eyes glowing with a life that Rowan had never seen. "I look forward to seeing him try."

When the two phased away, Kyron held out a little green pill Rowan recognized.

Her hunger throbbed loudly in her ears.

A small hand on her shoulder dragged her eyes to take in the concerned violet eyes of her mother.

"You know better than to do magic in these conditions, Rowan." Her voice was soft, but stern.

"It was an emergency."

Annabelle shook her head. "Go eat. Now."

Rowan's back went ramrod straight when she felt the familiar magic of Alessandro behind her. It called to her, familiar and fulfilling. It promised to soothe the ache.

Fists curled tight, she forced herself to leave it behind.

-A-

Alessandro didn't need the details of what happened after she disappeared.

He could practically hear the succubus' hunger reaching for him. His dragon overrode his will, urging him to pluck her up and return to his hoard. Before he could stop it, his hand reached out to nothing but air.

Her mother caught sight of the hand and let out a small breath of disbelief.

"That explains your presence." She crossed her arms. "She is not for you, Dragon King."

"I agree." He coughed awkwardly and motioned to the castle. "All is back to normal. I am here to discuss what happens to Hye Kang in your custody."

"We do what our Rowan excels at." Annabelle's mocking smile was so similar to her daughter's that he found it was endearing on the woman rather than challenging. "We fix him."

XXI

When Rowan hunted for her meals, she found there was excitement even if she sometimes arrived starving.

But now all the energy emitting from the grinding bodies of the nightclub she'd arrived in felt stuffy and tainted.

They were as appetizing as the remnant foods at a buffet's closing time.

It had been ages since she'd let her hunger get this bad.

Her head throbbed, her vision blurred.

Steeling herself, she plunged into the depths of the dancefloor that smelled of sweat and other bodily fluids. She found an unfamiliar repulsion to the scent that usually excited her succubus. She pulled a pretty blonde with a shimmering silver dress. Her eyes slid over Rowan, and a familiar gleam of desire lit them up.

She was at least three inches taller than Rowan, but she followed the pull of the succubus' hand as it settled on the arch of her back. "Want to fuck?" It was crude, but effective, especially when Rowan's power detected the spot on the woman's body that would bend her will. She slid her tail over the back of the woman's knee up to her hip, and traced a fingernail from the bottom of her ear to the tip of her chin as Rowan brought her face down to her.

"Woah, woah, how about an introduction first?" Good. She could consent. Rowan brushed her lips softly over the tip of the woman's nose. It was a rare place to find pleasure, but the diversity in her partners had been far-reaching.

"I'm what you've been waiting for." Rowan whispered. "Now, will you surrender yourself to me or not?"

The woman let out a breathy sigh before she melted.

It should have been sweet. The taste of sexual energy coincided with the scent of the individual and her chosen partner smelled like warm blueberries.

They'd moved away from the dancefloor into a dark corner of the club, where other couples were taking advantage of the lack of attention as everyone minded their own business. The woman gave up all control as Rowan's fingers worked underneath the dress. She was playing with Rowan's nipples as their tongues danced in rhythm to the music that vibrated their bodies.

She was a delightful treat but her succubus didn't find any nutrition in the soft sweetness the woman offered even after she shuddered her completion.

It wasn't enough. Rowan felt as empty as she'd begun. A separate set of hands came from behind. She turned to take in the sight of a black-haired man who swooped his head down for a kiss in an opening she hadn't meant to create.

Sandalwood was heady on the man's neck as the blonde, feeling left out, attached her mouth to Rowan's neck.

Pleasure assaulted Rowan as it normally would when engaging in this type of feast, but even with the added body and offered energy, it wasn't enough.

Two more hours of dissatisfaction were all the succubus allowed. Perhaps it was a matter of location? She glanced at the collection of people that had gathered. They were desperate for each other. Tits and cocks bouncing in a dance of uninhibited passion. She watched for a moment, hoping something would click into place and begin ebbing away at her hunger, but nothing changed.

She cursed as she phased to another club.

She lost track of time, her desperation for relief showing her the images of the last time she'd actually felt satisfied.

Or more precisely, who had brought about that satisfaction; Alessandro, the fucking Dragon King.

She'd be dead before she begged for him to help her.

Hadn't she said she'd never need him?

But soon her pride was deteriorating the longer she went without being fulfilled.

She called her mother to let her know she'd be going off-grid for a while and to spread the word to everyone else.

Rowan dropped into her first ever feeding frenzy.

Her mother had long ago warned that as emotion-based creatures, she and her sisters needed to protect their hearts from those who didn't deserve it. If they had the unfortunate luck of having their hearts moved by someone who didn't want them in return, they'd have to wipe the taste of that individual from their tongues with what she'd called a feeding frenzy.

Out of all the sisters, the only one who had needed to go on such a journey was Axel. Not only once, but three times. She'd hopped from town to town, building harems dedicated to the goal of making her forget.

The last time it had happened, Axel had been gone for a month. When Rowan hunted her down, Axel was so lost in pleasure that she reacted with vicious violence as Rowan dragged her away.

The harem joined their succubus in brutality.

Lexine didn't allow Rowan to leave the infirmary for an entire week when they made it back to the castle. The mission cost Rowan a broken arm, a concussion, and her hair.

Vain as it was, it was the loss of her hair that stung the most. She'd been growing it out for years, aiming to get it longer than Lexine's. It took a lot of coaxing from her eldest sister, and tons of styling sessions with Louisa to accept that she could rock a pixie cut which she had now grown out to reach her shoulders.

It was an entire week into her own feeding frenzy that Rowan felt the barrier around RLK Magical Disaster Services' brownstone shatter. Pain rocked her body with the force of the attack.

The dimming of one of her bonds followed.

Shock roiled through her as she pushed the male away and shot to her feet.

"Hey! We're not done." The man grabbed her tail as she began pulling down on the short denim skirt she'd worn.

Her hackles rose, and the punch met his nose before she could even think straight.

She barely checked that he was still breathing before she phased out.

When the world reformed around her, she was dumbstruck by the vision. At her feet were splinters of window shutters and glass shining with the reflection of the rising sun. The entire brownstone lay decimated. Sirens bellowed in the distance.

Her steps on the debris sounded just as distant as her magic crawled out of her to search for any sign of life without her bidding.

"Dew." She whispered. Pushing past the pain of molding magic to her command with her hunger at such a critical place, her arms rose. Kin and Louisa both phased in and each reacted at the same time she did, Louisa concentrating on putting out the fire as Rowan raised the rubble and Kin sprinted forward to reach the only source of life.

Dumping the rubble into piles around them, she and Louisa grasped hands while Kin began compressions with his pinky finger. He twisted magic to help boost healing along the body of the blue-haired fairy whose entire body had turned sooty from the fire. Focusing her above average senses, she waited to hear Dew's heart begin its hummingbird beat. Instead, Rowan listened to it slow and slow until it stopped.

Kin continued his attempt to revive her for a couple more minutes before he lowered his hand to the ground and cast his eyes away.

Rowan felt her stomach turn sour. Storm clouds rolled in from the distance. She tried to will her power back into her body, knowing if she lost control, she wouldn't be able to regain it easily.

But she couldn't tear her eyes away from Dew's body and different scenarios swirled in her head. What were her last moments like? Her fury grew. Thunder rattled her teeth.

"Ro." Louisa's voice was soft, her grip tight.

Rowan let out her held breath, snatched her eyes away from the body and dropped Louisa's hand. She wanted to walk off the excess energy coursing through her veins, but she was so angry, and the tears were so big and fat she felt like she was drowning as she kept her sobs locked away.

Was it the Coven who had attacked? She felt she knew it was, but she had no proof. That was until her trembling legs got her to the edge of the rubble, where she felt a familiar magic signature.

It wasn't a witch though, something as old as the dragon magic Alessandro used, but more divine? She stood over the nexus of power before she recognized it for what it was, a trap.

XXII

The twisted phase that whisked from her physical spot that dropped her like a sack of potatoes onto a cool metal floor.

Panic gripped her as, for the first time in her life, she didn't feel the threads of magic knocking to get into her pores. A bit like all the air had gone from the room.

Looking around, she realized she was in an enclosure. Golden floor, golden roof and golden bars that were all etched with inscriptions of a null spell. Inside of the cage, there was a camp bed and a toilet. Outside, there was a window that overlooked a line of evergreen trees less than five feet in front of the wall. They were so tall they kept the sun from shining at full power, but there were candles lining the walls of the room. Those lights lit up the second cage she hadn't noticed at first, and she realized she wasn't alone.

A red-haired witch with sage colored eyes stared over at her, horrified.

Still dressed in the same navy two-piece suit she'd worn to Rowan's office, Cherry scrambled to her feet, narrowing her eyes as if she wasn't sure of what she was seeing. Rowan supposed it could have something to do with the fact that Cherry had never seen her succubus out.

Her cheekbones protruded from her face, malnutrition as obvious as her injuries. She had bruises from head to toe. Some were fresh, some were fading.

"No." Cherry screamed, then clasped her hands over her mouth, terror bright in her eyes as they slid towards the still shut door before whispering, "You don't have the grimoire with you, do you?"

Rowan shook her head. "Is this the work of your usurper of a witch?"

Cherry's nose flared, and she nodded, "Though, I'm not sure I could call him a witch."

Rowan raised an eyebrow. "What would you call him?"

"Base evil." Cherry hissed, "How did you end up here?"

Footsteps outside of the room halted Rowan's answer. The door squeaked open and inside the flickering light of the candles, a man with long blonde hair and jade eyes stepped in. Dressed in white silken robes, his power thrummed even through the nulling cage bars.

Rowan had never known a witch to have so much raw power at their disposal.

His eyes were glacial as he looked down at Cherry who shrunk into herself and looked anywhere but at him. "What have I said about the level of noise you must maintain?"

Rowan watched, stunned, as the woman's eyes welled up with tears and the smell of her fear permeated the room.

"I take it you are Antoni." Rowan dragged his attention to herself.

He took her in, slowly. As he had about a foot on her, he bent down to examine her more closely. "You have been difficult to track down, Rowan Dahl. I saw the pictures, but I imagined you taller."

"I imagined you frightening, but all you look like is a coward to me. Can't handle a face-to-face confrontation, so you use tricks to trap." She looked around. "It's shoddy work at best, this cage."

"Shoddy work that will keep you in place while I fix what you have broken." He moved to stand as close to her as the cage would allow. A scent of fresh mountain air filled her nostrils, but it was hiding the smell of rotting meat. "And I will only ask you once to keep quiet while you're a guest. I despise unnecessary noise."

"Oh, a guest? That means I can leave, right? Cause this really isn't my kind of scene."

The man smirked. "Shall I break you like I've broken your companion?" He snapped his head back to Cherry, whose color drained from her face immediately.

She hated it. Seeing a man who thought his physical prowess could control a woman's will and actions. It filled her mouth with a taste of bile.

"Oh, I would like to see you try," She said with a laugh, "I really would like to see it."

The man examined her, understanding lighting up his eyes, and he gave a chuckle. "Oh, you're one of those, aren't you? A warrior trapped in the female body of modern times. Hiding your power behind soft curves and round cheeks." He stood to his full height. "I knew a woman like you once, and she had a glaring weakness. I wonder if you have it as well" He backed off and pivoted his attention to Cherry.

Panic rose in Rowan's throat as she figured out his train of thought. "Don't you dare touch her." She snarled and wrapped her hands around the cell's bars. Blinding hot pain shot through her already raw palms, up her arms and through to her head. For a moment, she felt as if she was flying out of her physical body and her vision filled with an unfamiliar landscape. She was sitting on the edge of a rock, the branches of a weeping willow dipping into the calm surface of an ocean, a reflection of a brown-eyed woman with sweeping brown hair that danced in the wind staring back at her.

Then she slammed back into her body, ears buzzing, aware that Antoni was undoing the locks on Cherry's cage. "I will shred you to pieces when I get out of here."

Antoni let out a laugh that chilled her bones before he stepped in

The sounds of skin on skin followed by the cracking bones were not as terrible at the shrieks of pain Cherry let out.

Rowan roared, fingers gripping the bars of her cage.

It was difficult to catch her breath when the begging began. Never in all her years of being harassed by the Coven could she have imag-

WHEN A DRAGON MEETS A PRINCESS - 218

ined wanting to defend Cherry Young. To want to take the pain from the witch and pour it into herself.

She fell away from the bars in horror as minutes later the man exited the cage, blood dripping on his robes and his knuckles torn to shreds from his brutality.

"Next time I have to warn you to be quiet, I might just kill her."

Rowan didn't speak as the witch left the room, the door shutting with a soft click.

She turned her attention to the puddle that was Cherry Young. She had fallen silent even before Antoni was through with his show of force. From the distance Rowan couldn't tell if the woman was even conscious, but the sound of her heart was pounding in Rowan's ears and she knew she was alive.

Antoni had already been on Rowan's shit list for his attacks, but now she would make sure it hurt when she took him down.

-A-

Alessandro didn't know what to make of the video that showed Rowan being phased out of existence as she walked away from her colleagues.

His initial thought had been that she had just phased out, unable to face either of them as she took in the fairy's death. But the looks from both the kitsune and vampiress told him immediately that something was off.

He rewatched the video before concluding that the way the magic folded around her was not of her creation. It was sloppy and forced, while Rowan's magic was usually fluid and natural.

Rowan Dahl, kidnapped, and local news had already aired bystander videos that caught the entire incident.

The kitsune, with his face morphed into someone unrecognizable to Alessandro, informed the reporters that the 'Dragon Hero', as they'd dubbed her locally, had stepped away in shock and that they wouldn't be answering questions until she returned.

"What are we going to do?" The fire-dragon asked.

Alessandro tried to keep the smirk from his face. The elf had earned herself a fan amongst one of his generals. It took a great deal of power to impress the hothead, but her stunt with the rune tree had stunned even him.

Briefly he wondered how many others in the Thunder would see her as an asset rather than threat and if maybe that would be enough for him to think sinking his fangs into her neck would be acceptable.

Then he remembered her mother.

'She is not for you.'

Still, he was indebted to her. The useless binder he'd gifted her was not an equal transaction.

"I'm going to the astral plane to check if she's safe. Guard my body."

Blaise nodded his acknowledgement.

Alessandro closed his eyes and let his mind wander, extracting his astral form until he was floating in a space of darkness. He recalled the way her magic felt when it brushed against his, the smell of her skin as it heated underneath his palms. He called forth the image of her eyes, chanted her name, even accessed the entire Blessed network to look for her unique signature of magic, which he thought he saw for a second, but it went out in the next breath making it impossible to lock onto her trace.

Frustrated, he called forth the memory of the vampiress' face. The connection was as instant as it should have been with Rowan. He floated over the rubble of the building, the woman an arm's length away from him, her eyes staring past him to the kitsune who was squatting to the floor.

Alessandro didn't need to get up close and personal to know what the man was doing.

"She can't be dead." Determination set on the vampiress' face as she spoke into her phone. "Our bonds are just strained. I swear I keep feeling her for the briefest of moments." She sighed after the person on the line replied. "Chloe, I have to go. Kin can't find her with a scry. We're going to try summoning her instead. But first we have to take Dew's body to her family. Can you ask Master Jah to set the circle up?" Ruby eyes filled with tears, she tilted her chin to the sky to collect herself. "Okay, see you soon. Love you, bye."

Alessandro stood for a few seconds by the vampiress' side as she composed herself before turning to the kitsune who was carrying a lacquer box. Inside, Alessandro caught the smell of death. His jaw clenched. Louisa's eyes watered again when she looked at it. This time, she let the tears fall.

"How are we supposed to tell them?" She asked, wiping her cheeks.

"Unfortunately," he threw a glare over at the cameras pointed in their general direction, "I think they already know. Come on, we'll head to EEK right after." He wiped another tear from the vampiress' cheek.

She snickered. "Please don't call it that to Axel's face. She will clobber us both."

"Yeah, I'm not interested in testing the berserker." He held out his hand before the two phased away.

Alessandro scanned the sea of reporters still standing and rolling film. Nausea rolled through him at the sight.

The decision to destroy the tech was an easy one to execute. With a snap of his fingers, each device gave a spark of blue lightning and died on the spot.

Satisfied with the shouts of frustration, Alessandro cut his connection and slid back into his body.

"I can't find her on the astral plane." He informed Blaise as he stood. "Her friends seem to think she's still alive, but scrying won't work. Are Naseem and Stone still with the witch?"

Blaise fell into step beside him by the time he walked out of his office. "Last time I saw them, they were comparing notes on Barros' recorded properties in the library."

"Have they seen the video?"

"Probably not. The only reason I ran into it was because I was scrolling through social media on the shitter and when I saw it, I knew you'd want to do something about it ASAP."

Alessandro tried not to let the image of Blaise in the bathroom enter his mind.

Together they passed through the covered walkways of the estate, passing dragons who seemed to sense their king was not in a good mood if the 180 degree turns were anything to go by.

Alessandro tried to relax, but as soon as the library's stone steeple came into view and a raised voice reached his ears, the tension snapped right back into place.

"You had no place saying that to him." It was Terra.

Terra who was supposed to be taking care of making backup plans in Dragon City in case everything went south with Draconis.

"It isn't our approval that matters, Terra. The houses will rebel against the idea."

"Are you insane? Do you know how long they have been trying to get him mated off? There hasn't been one dragon to get his headlights to go off, and the one shot he has at that bond you tell him to stay away from?" Naseem's voice cracked with emotion. An image of a young blonde woman flashed through the Dragon King's mind at the sound.

Being the only general who had actually received the mating feeling, Naseem saw the bond in a different light than any of his peers.

Clear on what the subject of the raised voices were concerned with, Alessandro put his hand on the knob until he heard a soft sob.

"I already said I messed up!" Aqua sniffed. "I'm the reason he's been unbearable since he last saw her! The pain it caused him to stay back while she put herself in the path of those witches woke me up. Now he's walking around here feeling so...*empty*. I just need you two to back me up and convince him she will be safe with our people. That we will have her back!"

Alessandro turned the knob.

Aqua shrieked in surprise at his sudden appearance behind her and snapped her head to look away. Naseem and Stone followed her example.

Terra grinned and shook her head, "Honestly, I leave for one week and you finally find us a suitable queen candidate, then you allow this knucklehead to convince you to not approach her?" She flicked Aqua on the forehead before forcing the younger dragon to turn his way.

"Suitable?"

She was more than suitable. But he'd be damned if he allowed the weight of that crown to dull even the smallest bit of her soul.

All he wanted now was to see what she'd do with her long awaited freedom.

Aqua rubbed the reddening spot. "You heard everything, right?" Her voice was soft, a tactic to make him feel pity for her.

She didn't need to. She had only done her sworn duty of protecting the Thunder, of acting as a check and balance to decisions that would affect more than just himself. "I did. But perhaps you should all recall that I don't give into your demands when it doesn't align with my aims. I have my own reasons for not going through with the instinct. We still owe her an actual favor that we can pay off. Rowan Dahl just got kidnapped in front of national TV. I have a good hunch Antoni Barros is behind it. What do you have on him so far?"

It took a moment for his words to elicit a response from his stunned dragons, but as was most often the case, it was Stone who was the first to react. He slid into a computer chair, his fingers waving over the table and bringing up holograms of several buildings, charts and scanned paperwork surrounding the image of a blonde man with green eyes staring off into space.

The witch, who had been standing in the background trying his hardest to blend into the bookcases, looked terrified when the Air General scooped him forward.

"Dae was just working on gathering information from his past." Naseem patted the witch on the back. "Go on, tell Alessandro what you found."

Dae gulped and pointed to his face. "Sorry, is no one going to mention why your eyes are glowing red?"

Alessandro was finding himself weary of the witch after allowing him access to the libraries of Draconis for the week that he'd been there. "It signifies I'm running thin on patience."

The witch took a deep breath and pointed to the hologram of the man. "He's originally from Macedonia, Greece, my neck of the woods, but when he was still in his adolescence, he left with his family to start over in South America. Even then, he honestly didn't show promise with magic until about two years ago, when he saved Henrietta Young during a demon exorcism." Dae looked disturbed by his next words. "Not only did he block the demon poison, but he also finished the exorcism himself."

Alessandro understood the disturbed look then. Demon poison had one known cure, celestial blood. Angels, who were made from the essence of celestial beings, were usually the ones who healed those victims.

"Well, since then, he has steadily built a following. As his control of magic has grown, he has surpassed many of the top spellcasters in the Coven. As far as his limits, I'm not sure he has any. He has shown an affinity for all four elements, a bit of clairvoyance and now, massive mental manipulation."

Alessandro frowned. "Does he live in a Coven compound like some elders before him, or has he taken a separate residence like Elder Henrietta?"

Naseem moved forward, and a list popped front and center, along with the holograms of a dozen houses. "He's not living at the compound, but with his growing following, he's also amassed multiple properties, whether gifted or bought. As far as some preliminary investigations show, he doesn't stay in one for too long. I've dispatched a pair of dragons for each location to keep watch. I've let them know of his ability to manipulate minds and they're all equipped with Darling nulling charms in case they make contact."

"Which of these is his first property?"

Everything but a cape cod two story home settled on a mountain side vanished.

"How did he get this one?"

"His parents passed it down to him. If you're thinking he uses this one most because of sentimental reasons, I thought the same. However, the scouts say it looks abandoned.." Naseem supplied.

"Are his parents still alive?"

"No." Naseem ran his hands over a keyboard suddenly available to him. "But this is the only land they left to him. They did own several in their lifetime. Did you want to look into those?"

"Yes, specifically the ones where he went through his latest accomplishments, whatever they may be."

Naseem's fingers flew across the keyboard, and Alessandro willed his body to relax. Despite the grim look of things, Alessandro merely had to recall how she had dodged his surprise attack that first night they met to find a bit of hope. If he hadn't kissed her, she might have made it a lot harder to kidnap her. If the witch kept his lips to himself, Alessandro was sure Rowan Dahl could survive through anything he threw at her.

XXIII

Rowan could hear the thumping of Cherry's heart slowing to a concerning rate even from their distance. She could smell death slowly creeping in from a dark corner of the room.

But, she had a plan. A tedious plan that had only been available to her because of the trap.

Antoni Barros, like most spellcasters, didn't comprehend nulling principles. But with Chloe, the most potent null in history, as her best friend, Rowan did.

First, any nulling object had to make at least a secondary contact with the target. This meant that standing on the floor with just her heels as a barrier, the nulling was successful. But, when she climbed on top of the camp bed, the nulling spell had to go through the legs of the bed, the two-inch mattress and her shoes to get to her. This made the spell ineffective.

Second, magic corroded physical elements. Gold, already a soft workable metal, didn't require more than a low flame to target the weakest points of the cage, their soldered joints.

The tedious part of her plan was the fact that the air inside of the cage lacked magic. To overcome this, she had to connect to the air outside the bars to gather magic.

Though small by nature, her hands were initially too large to fit through the bars without her skin touching the sides, which meant she only had four fingers available to channel the magic in as her other hand cast the flame spell on the joints. When the space got large enough for her to comfortably cast she could work faster but her succubus' starvation had her hands shaking so hard that they sometimes bumped against the metal and killed her spell.

She also had to deal with the fact that she couldn't just let the rods of the cage drop, as the noise they would make would alert Barros. So she'd created a bed of sheets to cushion their fall. As touching them to prevent them from falling nulled her as well.

She needed to remove only two more bars to have enough space to squeeze through, but she wasn't sure she could get out in time to save the woman.

"Don't you dare die." Rowan kept her voice calm and low.

"It wasn't so bad. This little life of mine." The witch's voice was barely discernible. "I think I'm ready."

Rowan growled. She willed the fire to burn hotter.

"The only thing I regret is never having a child." She laughed, "By my age, my grandmother had half a dozen."

"How many would you have wanted?" Rowan only had one more bar to go. She could keep the witch talking while she worked, she could get to her in time.

"Just one. To think the Young line will end with..."

Rowan didn't look over. She couldn't risk shouting to wake the unconscious woman. She was sure Barros would come, and she just needed one more joint.

With a soft pop, her freedom was at hand, her heart thumped hard against her chest as she gently placed the bar down next to the others before squeezing through the opening.

She winced when the magic the nulling spell had held at bay crashed into her, cramming her full of power in mere seconds. She used the magic to conjure two lock picks.

It wasn't her strongest skill, and under the pressure of Cherry's on-coming death, Rowan's nerves were so frayed that she slipped several times.

Axel's voice flitted through her head. *"One thing at a time. Don't worry about the future, just focus on the thing in front of you, then worry about the next step."*

A steady breath later, the lock gave way. She swung the door open and ran to the woman. The magic that she had just accumulated fled her blood, and she had to deal with it, slamming back in once she left that null cage as well. Dragging Cherry as gently as she could manage while time was against her was rough. She didn't have Louisa's or Axel's superstrength and the unconscious witch weighed more than she had imagined. The noise she was causing should have gotten their captor's attention.

As if summoning him through mere thought, she heard the door slam open behind her. But he was too late. Cherry's legs cleared the cage threshold, and she phased without a second thought.

Before her, the world reassembled into the hospital wing of the Eastern Elven Kingdom. A woman with hair streaked with all the colors of the rainbow screamed and dropped the papers she had been carrying as she had just tried to pass Rowan.

"Please help her, Miasma." was all Rowan said before she phased back to the room, facing down the blonde-haired man whose eyes widened at her reappearance.

Rowan snarled as she removed all the mental gates that held her magic at bay. She knew a threat when she smelled it and the witch was indeed powerful enough to claim the position of Elder. Magic that had already been pouring itself into her veins flew like a torrent through her so hard she could feel gashes on her skin open up.

The roots from the trees outside of the window shattered glass and broke through the concrete walls at her call. They began wrapping around him, but he summoned a fire shield that burned everything to a crisp.

Taking a deep breath, Rowan commanded the oxygen in the room to leave. His flames died, and the branches wrapped around his neck.

Antoni easily snapped the restraints, and he backed up into the hall-way, gasping for air as soon as he left her oxygen deprived domain.

She followed with her momentum, allowing the roots of the trees to pass through the foundation of the house up through the floor-boards to tangle around his arms and legs, reinforced with layers of branches.

Again he tore them away as if they were nothing more than strips of paper and he launched at her, his clenched fist landing in her solar plexus that both sent the breath out of her and her body flying back-wards through the crumbled wall. She tumbled to her feet and dodged a punch to her face that made her eardrum throb with its force. He was fast. And strong. He had held back when he attacked Cherry.

Rowan grimaced when he landed a kick to her side, but she used the opportunity to grab his leg and throw him off balance with a push off the floor.

As he landed, she climbed over him and grabbed his head.

He stared up at her bewildered and full of so much lust she felt the succubus in her rear its head. It had reached its limit.

Against her wishes, the being took the reins.

She leaned down and met his lips. It might have been a sensual kiss had it not been that when she pulled back, she pulled the threads of his life energy. She slowly inhaled the foreign feeling, and finally, af-ter days of being unsuccessful at filling her hunger, she grew stronger. She could feel her wounds healing, even those caused by the magic she thought would put her out of commission for a day at least. Yes. She wanted this life force, wanted the pain to ebb.

She sucked and sucked, watching as he grew pale and she got stronger. But she couldn't kill him. The still sane part screamed when the end of his life force was visible in red thread. Despite her anger and vow to kill him, she knew deep inside he needed to live to face the consequences of his actions.

It also did something to the man because he jerked so hard he pushed her off.

The back of her head bounced off the tree she landed against and her vision blurred as he towered over her and he reached a hand down so quickly she couldn't stop him. She saw too late that he was carrying a blade. As it sunk into her eye, she screamed. This wasn't her first stabbing. But she had never experienced the hot white pain that assaulted her.

Something dark was festering from the wound, a twisted form of magic that wanted to consume her.

Panic rose in her throat before the vision of Dew's body in Kin's hands slammed into her mind. She needed to be calm to avenge her friend.

Gritting her teeth and taking a deep breath as Antoni pulled his arm back to stab her again, she raised her own. The blinding light of the sword was enough to make him pause. She swung, aiming for his neck, blind with pain and rage. But he phased a few feet away.

He looked too sane to be Cursed, but perhaps that's how they all appeared before the object took them over. She'd only ever seen a Cursed when they were ready to move one, at the end of their lives.

No killing. She had to remind herself. She needed him alive. Past experience had taught her that if she didn't get a killing blow in the Cleansing wouldn't take hold. Her good eye locked on her target, and using his idea, she phased.

"What Cursed object do you carry, Barros? Is it behind the shifter attacks? Or is that your personal goal?"

"I am in control!" He hissed from behind her. "This is *my* vengeance."

She swung, but he was gone.

Dashing through the space of the forest behind the wrecked house, they phased around each other, slashing empty air with their weapons, until Rowan noticed his favoritism towards his right side. Had it not been for the many hours on the mat with Axel repeatedly criticizing her own favoritism for her right, she might have missed it, but again her sister's voice demanded she pay attention.

Plan in mind, she stopped phasing and caught another stinging blow from the blade with her left hand, the one she'd spent hours channeling magic through. With her right, she swung her sword from below his left armpit, taking him by surprise with the unconventional move.

"This is *mine*." She hissed.

She expected to feel resistance when she reached bone, but the sword sliced through with little more sound than metal biting air. Had her hatred for the man sharpened her sword?

His blood was warm on her arms and face even as he phased once more. She was faster though, and when she appeared before him. She took aim for his leg, only to pull back when she noticed that almost all the color had drained from his face.

She stayed her hand as he swayed forward and backwards until he fell face first in front of her, then disintegrated into dirt.

Fury tore through her at the realization. That last phase had been so slow because he'd sent a replacement in his stead.

She searched for any sign that he was still there, but his existence was long gone.

In her mind, she could once again hear Dew's last breath and nausea roiled through her.

She had failed to avenge her friend.

Frustrated, she bellowed and the magic she had gathered to fight the coward exploded from her like a sonic boom. Around her, the trees shook with the force. The earth quaked. The pain that her adrenaline had staved off from taking all those hits, the wound of her eye, and the overuse of magic all slammed into her, bringing her to her knees.

Fighting to catch her breath, she allowed herself to feel for the fairy who liked to bring her too many doughnuts and coffee topped by creative foam art.

She didn't have enough magic to phase. She barely had enough strength to turn her head when something in the corner of her eye caught her attention.

His arm had remained a few yards away and hope blossomed in her. He had done his little trick after she'd taken it. If she could survive long enough to recuperate some magic, she had a way to track the bastard.

Then she felt it. A familiar signature that made relief pump through her.

She looked up to the swirling rainbow eyes of the Dragon King and a collection of multi-colored dragons flying behind him, all staring down at her. She focused on him as she lifted her arms.

Red and silver competed for dominance as he took her beaten form in, silver overcame it all and he phased to her.

She wrapped her arms around his torso and sobbed so hard into his chest that he shook with its force.

He gently put a finger underneath her chin to lift it up and he looked her eye wound over. "This is damage from demon poison. We have to cut your eye out now before it spreads."

Rowan stiffened. "The whole thing?"

He nodded, losing a bit of color as he did.

"Well," She winced as a laugh tried to bubble up, "At least I took his arm."

Exasperation took over Alessandro's face. "I wonder why I even bother to worry about you, Rowan Dahl."

Rowan leaned against his chest, the assured safety in his presence allowing her to turn into a pile of jelly. "I need people to worry." She sighed, "I'm quite reckless."

Not quite unconscious, but very near it Rowan heard his command for his dragons to take the severed limb and put it on ice. And then she felt when Alessandro phased them out of the wooded area into an air-conditioned room that smelled heavily sanitized.

She opened her eye and noted that they were in a medical wing, but it wasn't like the Eastern Elven Kingdom's infirmary where there were separate rooms. This was one large open area with navy blue walls and gold trim, housing several huge gurneys. Heavy velvet curtains on tracks were the only offering of privacy.

"My King." Aqua appeared only a moment after Alessandro gently placed her on the edge of one of those gurneys.

Rowan wished she could've stayed awake even a moment longer, but within the safety of the Dragon King's warm and stalwart arms, she succumbed to the pain, hunger and darkness.

XXIV

Alessandro couldn't remember the last time Draconis had been in such a buzz. The presence of the elven royal family was the first of its kind.

Sure, the dragons entertained foreign entities, but none of them had been as free roaming, curious or as light bringing as Rowan's family.

Over the past week they had taken turns staying the night, dropping by with baskets full of elven artisanal snacks, fabrics, and fashion pieces the dragons adored.

Rowan was still unconscious, but that didn't surprise him. Demon poison was lethal. In all reality, she should've died minutes after the stabbing. The adrenaline would've delivered the poison anywhere her blood could reach, but the elf had a trace of divinity in her system that neutralized the poison.

It also helped that the blade had been subpar, only containing enough poison to take her right eye. Her left hand, which Aqua found injured on her initial check up, was poison free.

He had been ready to open a vein for the woman, pour his celestial magic in, to cut off the effects. But, once again, she didn't need him.

Alessandro barely had time to step into the medical wing, much less address where the hell she had gotten divinity from, as he dealt with the fallout of the Coven.

The shifter attacks had continued while Rowan had gone missing from the public eye. It saturated the media with hysterical anchors, putting out service announcements on how best to protect yourself from shifters who were all slowly losing their minds.

Antoni Barros' plans had come crashing down from his tussle with the elven woman. She had caused him enough damage to break his control over the illusion created for the Coven. Once the Dahls realized Hye had come to his senses, they'd coordinated with the dragons, Cherry and Dae to get Darling jewelry pieces in as many witch hands as possible.

Along with this responsibility, Cherry Young was fighting a deadlocked political battle against Eve Tanoch and Dorin Indigo, now two emergency elected representatives of the Coven until the dust settled on the shifter attacks.

Cherry desired to expose the truth to ease the declining relationship between the public and shifters, but the other two had voted against such action afraid of the loss of trust the move would bring to the Coven in its entirety rather than focus on the still missing Antoni Barros.

In response, the shifters were working overtime on compiling evidence Barros had left behind in the house he'd held Cherry and Rowan in, to build their request for Judgement whenever the witch came out of hiding.

Back in Draconis, the Eastern Elven Kingdom's doctor, Miasma, had been working alongside Aqua, who had never met her match in the world of healing. Their teamwork was responsible not only for getting Cherry back on her feet so quickly but also for realizing that there was a much larger issue for Rowan than just the demon poisoning.

Her years of misusing her magic had caused damage to all of her chakra paths. When she awoke, they would have to assess how far the damage had actually gotten. In the meantime, they'd had to bring Chloe Darling in to supply her with customized suppression jewelry to keep her power regulated as she slept. They'd lost power to the medical wing twice before they realized the problem was coming from its foreign guest.

'I'm quite reckless' kept rolling through his mind every time he thought of her.

The sight of her covered in blood, at death's doorstep, haunted him anytime he was too far to feel her presence.

When he'd toured the basement room with the two nulling cages, her escape method became clear and he couldn't help but admire the ingenuity in the woman.

How could someone so brilliant think they were reckless?

Now, an additional reason to refuse his dragon had cropped to the surface. The Draconian Thunder would undoubtedly benefit from her protection and influence, but the world wouldn't. She had so much to offer, the anonymity her life would require should she become the Dragon Queen would stifle her opportunities.

Yet, he wanted her every second of every damn day, and it was slowly driving him mad. A madness that had set plans in motion to take care of that issue.

More often than not, he would stand outside the doors of her private suite listening to her friends and family as they visited or getting quick updates on her status before moving on.

The only time he truly avoided the place was when Japhet visited. At least twice a day, the giant witch would show up, and each time he would ask to see Alessandro.

Each time, Alessandro would make up a believable excuse and the witch would retreat, but he knew eventually he'd have to face him.

As it was his turn to ask for a favor, Alessandro had a suspicion it would have something to do with leaving Rowan Dahl alone, and Alessandro knew he could make no such vow.

For the first time since she'd succumbed to her healing rest, Alessandro found her alone.

She was still unconscious, and he took the few precious moments of solitude to drink in her calm visage. Her bruises had faded, her cuts sealed. He took hold of her hand and dropped a brief kiss on her forehead.

He could allow the tenderness his dragon demanded he show his chosen with no eyes around to judge. He longed to curl his body around hers, which radiated such a seductive heat he might have given in if the door didn't slide open to reveal the sight of her mother.

"The silver in your eyes doesn't mean what I think it does, does it?" The woman asked, and he felt the tingling of pity edging her voice.

He didn't answer, but he also didn't let go of her daughter's hand.

Annabelle frowned and took a seat on the chair pushed up next to the bed.

"She will make a terrible queen." The elven-succubus' laugh was cruel. "She's too much like me to be any good at it."

He cocked his head. "You believe you are a terrible queen?"

"Oh, I know I am. The only duties I have kept are for showmanship. I am the wife of the king, mother to the heiress apparent, but I don't read to the children, arrange dinners and galas. I don't even really care for the people if I'm honest, and I know they don't really care for me. But we both love my husband, so we put up with each other. Do you think that is how a true queen should be?"

Alessandro didn't answer.

"I hoped if there was someone out there for her, they would be as free and wild as she is. But you, you're not what I hoped for her at all." Annabelle sighed, "You're rigid and cold. You might put out the radiant light that is my daughter."

"Ma, that's enough." The voice came from the doorway. Alessandro looked up and saw Axel entering with a pitying frown that suggested she didn't actually see the situation differently.

Annabelle scoffed, "I am only telling him what you all will be too proper to say. Rowan will suffocate in this life. What's worse is that, unlike our shorter lifespan, Rowan will have to endure it for centuries if she mates with a long-lived creature like a dragon. "

"That's her choice. You can't take it away from her!" Axel snapped.

Alessandro was stunned by the depth of emotion that came from the sister. Something else was happening there. He needed more information to know the full scope, but this wasn't simply an issue over Rowan.

Annabelle recoiled.

"Stop fighting." Rowan's voice was a rasp.

Alessandro turned to look at the woman as she squeezed his hand. He held a breath as her lashes parted to reveal a brilliant blue eye. She raised the hand she hadn't been holding to touch the suede eyepatch that covered the hole where her left eye used to be. "You really took out the whole thing."

"Are you in pain?" He asked, remembering to breathe.

"Does a headache from my screeching family count?" She asked with a smirk curling her lips.

"Malcriada." Annabelle shot up from the seat and glared down at her, "How long do you plan on lounging and being useless overall? I'm a very busy woman, you know."

It was such a different reaction than Alessandro had expected from the woman who he had found, more often than not, sniffling at her daughter's side.

Rowan waved her down. "Yeah, yeah. I'm sure the poker table really misses you. Could you go brush your hair or something? Have you been walking around Draconis looking like a troll the entire time I've been out?"

Annabelle relaxed. She laughed as she pinched her daughter's cheek. "I can't wait until you're cleared so I can slap the disrespect out of your mouth, little girl."

"Ow, Mami!" Rowan fought off the hand and tried to sit up before she landed with a hard thud back on the bed.

Alessandro gently removed the hand and glared at Annabelle, who shot him an impressed look. He turned back to Rowan. "Please let Aqua check up on you before you try to move around again."

Rowan sighed and nodded. "Fine, but keep that psycho away from me." She turned and stuck her tongue out at her mother, who flipped her off.

Axel pushed past her mom to kneel at the bedside, "I begged dad not to let her visit you, but you know he can't say no to her."

Rowan smiled, "I figured. How long was I out?"

"About a week. Now answer honestly, how much pain are you in?"

Rowan winced. "7 out of 10, mostly coming for my back. If I've been here for a week, that explains it."

"And your eye?" Axel raised an eyebrow.

"When I move the good one, the one that isn't there feels sore."

"It's going to take a while for the pain to fully recede," Aqua stepped into the room, relief clear in her eyes, "It's good to see you awake Princess Rowan, I would like to conduct a quick checkup if our visitors would kindly step outside."

Alessandro wanted to stay beside the woman who still hadn't let his hand go, but he saw the stubbornness trying to settle on the other elven women's faces. If he went, maybe they wouldn't fight the request.

"We'll be right outside."

With her awake, he had to fight back his base urge to stroke her cheek for reassurance. He wouldn't play with her feelings when he knew they wouldn't work from the start.

Rowan seemed to understand that restraint existed in him because she gave a firm nod and squeezed his hand once more before finally letting go.

-R-

Rowan's entire being was in pain. She hissed as Aqua's finger tips grazed over the eyepatch to remove it.

"7 out of 10?" Aqua raised an eyebrow.

"Okay, it feels like I'm going to shatter if I take a wrong breath." Rowan was willing the tension to leave her body. But any relaxation only added to the already insurmountable discomfort.

"Your older sister told us you don't deal with pain in the aftermath of battle very well, so we came up with this." Aqua motioned to the IV hooked up to her arm. "My pill in liquid form for you to administer with this button to help manage."

"You're a genius." Rowan sighed as the pain eased.

She still couldn't fully relax, but as Aqua went through her check-up, the pain just kept disappearing until she felt as if she were floating inches above her bed. But that couldn't be the case. Even with her muddled mind, she could tell the suppression necklace was a new design, and it almost completely cut off her access to magic.

She looked down at the simple golden chain. It smelled like Chloe, or maybe her friend had been to the ward recently because her scent of sour and sweet candies was as potent as her mother's and Axel's. Before she knew it, she was reaching for the clasp to allow more magic in so it could work to heal her as it always had in the past.

"No!" A whip of water pushed her hand away from the piece of jewelry.

Rowan furrowed her eyebrows and glared up at the dragon. "Hey, that's cold!"

"Sorry, Princess." Aqua looked panicked. Her wide blueberry hued eyes, flared nose and raised arms as if preparing for defense were Rowan's aids for determining so, but the painkillers were killing her follow through actions and she relaxed against her pillows instead of questioning.

"I shouldn't have done that." Aqua said after a few moments of silence. "I really am sorry."

"It's no biggie." Rowan waved the concern away and, in doing so, caught sight of the scar on the backside of her hand.

She had very few scars, Lexine and Miasma had always made it a priority to hide the less than graceful nature of the youngest princess from the people of the Eastern Elven Kingdom, but when she'd left the kingdom in pursuit of her magical disaster practice, she hadn't always reported her wounds to her doctors unless they became life threatening. She half wondered how angry they had been to discover she'd accumulated half a dozen as they tended to her.

"How is the pain?" In Aqua's hands was a small lacquer box she opened to show a collection of eyepatches of differing prints and shades.

Rowan could smell her mother all over the thoughtful gift and she couldn't help but smile. "The medicine has taken care of most of it."

She picked a cream-colored velvet one.

The dragon helped her slide it on. "At the rate you're healing, you should be eligible for a prosthetic in a day or two if you'd like. Although you do look rather more mysterious with an eyepatch." She handed her a mirror.

Horror struck Rowan. She'd never been so pale in her life. Large dark bags looked like bruises and her hair looked like it needed a serious wash and hours of detangling.

Alessandro had seen her in such a state. She groaned out loud.

"What's wrong?"

"He saw me like this." Rowan gently shooed the mirror away.

Aqua's eyes softened. "He checks in on you every four hours on the dot." She laid her hand down on Rowan's scarred one. "A man who wants nothing to do with you wouldn't do that."

Rowan clenched the sheets that had pooled around her hips. With the back of her hand, she rubbed her one good eye as she felt them sting. "This shouldn't matter. It doesn't matter."

Aqua looked as if she had slapped her. "I'm sorry, I'm sorry." She whispered before she stormed out of the room.

Rowan was utterly flabbergasted.

Annabelle, Axel and Alessandro all piled back into the room, staring curiously after the woman.

"What did you do to the poor doctor Rowan?" Her mother was the first to ask.

Rowan shook her head, just as confused, "Can someone catch me up on the ongoings of the world while I have been taking my nap?"

"No." Axel was firm. "Sorry, Ro, all of your doctors have advised against it."

Rowan glared at her. "And since when have we actually adhered to what my doctors say?"

"Since you permanently lost an eye!" Axel planted her hands on her hips. "Since you went into a coma for an entire week!"

"It's only an eye!"

Axel's nostrils flared, and she opened her mouth to retort before Annabelle gave her a hard nudge in the ribs.

Axel glared at her mother, but shut her mouth and looked away.

That sealed it. Something was definitely up. It was one thing for Aqua, a stranger, to keep her mouth shut, but Axel rarely kept anything from her.

"What?" Rowan demanded.

Annabelle sighed. "Your father wants to be here when we tell you. Can you trust us and not do anything stupid before then?"

Rowan wanted to fight against the demand. However, her eye was getting heavy, and the room was going out of focus. "When I wake up again, I want to know every-"

It was too much. She couldn't finish her threat. The room was too warm and her body too heavy.

XXV

The next time Rowan awoke, instant nausea had her lurching off the bed. Her legs gave out and in mid fall, whatever she had been force-fed exploded from her mouth and her nostrils.

One glance up showed Alessandro hurrying towards her from the armchair her mother had occupied earlier, his laptop crashing onto the tiled floor.

Rowan tried to get out of her own pile of sickness before he could reach her, but another wave of vomit hit the floor so hard that it splashed back up to cover her face with its ferocity.

Horror filled her when she could breathe again.

"Don't!" She squeaked when he got too close. "I just need a mop. I can clean it."

"You don't have to worry about that." He knelt down beside her. "Is it all out?"

Rowan hung her head and nodded.

"It's the medicine." Alessandro reassured patting her back, "And the fact that you haven't been eating. It's happened to me before if it makes you feel any better."

Rowan glanced up at him. "It has?"

"Yes, and I didn't just get myself. I got about half a city. I was in dragon form."

Rowan's mouth fell open. "What?"

He grinned at her. "And then I blamed it on Terra. We can't have the world thinking the Dragon King has a weak stomach."

Rowan giggled, "Who's Terra?"

"My Earth General and adopted sister. Her mother and father took me in when I was just a wyrmling."

She tried to imagine the powerhouse in the body of a child, but it was beyond her. She wanted to ask more questions of his youth to know him better, but that wasn't her place.

Rowan sighed, "I thought I could look cooler next time I saw you, and now I'm sitting here. In a pile of my puke."

"I think you're playing the cool card up a bit by continuing to sit in it when you can grab my hand and allow me to bathe you.'

Heat surged through Rowan, followed shortly by another wave of nausea. She snatched his hand and covered her mouth. It was all the nudging he needed to grab her and phase them into a pristine white tiled restroom where she puked until all that came out was clear stomach acid. The entire time, his hand rubbed her back in small circles and he held her hair out of the way.

When she was done, she sat in front of the door and watched through a heavy eyelid as he prepared her shower. She was so tired she wasn't sure she could stay awake much longer, but in the meantime, she wanted to absorb what he was doing for her.

All while dressed in a cream pullover, a pair of black sweats and- she couldn't believe she was witnessing it- slippers. She peeked out of the window and noticed the maroon sky bleeding into dark purple. Had he been preparing to stay the night at her bedside? In that chair?

Her heart lurched, and her stomach clenched.

"May I undress you, Rowan?" The words lacked the heat that she expected, considering the subject.

This was nothing more than him repaying her for saving the dragons. He had made it clear there was nothing else allowed to flourish between them. So then, why was he being so unbearably tender?

In response, she gave a solemn nod.

With each piece of clothing, more and more heat knotted in the depth of Rowan's belly. As his fingers hooked around her panties, she felt her uncontrollable lust overcome her utter embarrassment and she was slick with need.

She noted the tension on his shoulders as he slid them past her thighs, the increased grips on their sides as they passed her knees, and the smell of honey in the air as they finally cleared her body.

He was just as turned on as she was.

The realization pushed back her exhaustion. He still wanted her. He had just plucked her out of a pile of her own vomit, and here he was, full of desire.

Her inner succubus wanted out.

Her wings made an involuntary movement, pushing her away from the wall and right into his lap, the fabric of his pants hardly a barrier to his erection.

They both let out a small strangled sound as she scrambled to get off, her legs once again giving out before she could stand.

Alessandro slid his arms around her and pulled her into his chest.

Rowan could feel the tension he had carried was slowly evaporating the longer he held her. She buried her face into his neck and wrapped her own arms around him, allowing every dark feeling she had from the shame of losing the battle with Antoni, to the anger at not being better after a week and the sadness of never really having a chance at standing beside the man she currently held wash away. She could take what she could get from him. It was better than nothing, wasn't it?

"Just a little longer." His voice was full of emotion that confused and terrified her.

But she gave this to him and, if she was being honest, to herself.

This simple physical touch was more nourishing than what she had tried to gather for herself in her feeding frenzy. She was so fucked.

She wanted more. To fill herself up on him.

But she wouldn't be the one to ask.

She was Rowan Dahl, and she didn't beg.

"The smell is getting to me." She whispered when she reached her limit.

"Me too." He said, but instead of moving, he hugged her tighter.

She couldn't help it. She laughed and pushed at his chest. "Are you going to help me or not?"

He helped her to sit on the edge of the tub as it filled with near boiling water, just how she liked it. He made to clean the worst of the vomit off with a warm soapy towel, but Rowan insisted she be the one to do that. Once she handed it back, she had expected to be given a new washcloth and left to her own devices, but as soon as he began shedding his clothes, she knew she was going to have company.

A mixture of panic and thrill made her forget how to breathe when he grabbed the edge of his sweatshirt and pulled it off in one smooth movement. His curls bounced back into place before he summoned a pin to pull it all back. She preferred it down, and wild, but with it pulled up, the definition of his jawline and the bulging of his upper traps more than made up for it. She didn't know whether it was a disappointment or a relief when he moved to grab a container of bath salt to pour it into the stream from the tap.

She sank into the water, realizing just how large the tub was as it covered everything up to her shoulders. Relief from the salts washed over her and she watched sleepily as he reached up to remove the shower head from its holder.

It was an insane mixture of intimacy and a lesson in humility as he washed her hair. His fingertips left behind the sense of thousands of butterflies resting along her scalp.

"You're good at this." She sighed as he worked.

His hands paused.

"Keep going." She pleaded, and his thumbs rubbed the back of her ears.

Instant desire rushed through her at the simple touch. She felt her nipples harden so much they throbbed. She bit her lip to keep from crying out. Her breathing shallowed out as his touch lowered to lather her neck, then shoulders.

She needed to get her head out of the gutter immediately. In her mind, she began reciting company policies Kin had once forced her to write out again as punishment for taking over 45 IOUs in one month during their first year working together.

But then Alessandro's hands were on her back and she was so stunned by the amount of pleasure wrought on at the base of her wings that a moan ripped out of her.

His movements completely stopped, and she tried to calm herself down in the small eternity of silence.

"Your wings are like ours." He whispered. "I should've known it would be an erogenous zone."

Her mind was racing with only one thought.

Take. Take. Take.

It was a voice she didn't recognize, yet had known her whole life lurked within her.

Her succubus was awake. Yet, her body was in no state to take care of the feverish need building to heights she'd never reached before.

The contradictory nature of her situation made her feel as if she was being pulled apart in two different directions. Her vision blurred for a heartbeat before it was suddenly a mixture of reds and purples accompanied by the most delectable scent of heated honey from behind her.

She tilted her head back and licked her lips when she found the source. At the base of Alessandro's neck, a bright blade of white light called her name.

Against her tongue, she found her canines were suddenly sharp and growing. Her heartbeat raced as she turned to face him. If she just bit there, she knew it would bring him the greatest pleasure and give her some semblance of peace.

She entwined her fingers into his curls, pulled back with a slight tug to expose the entirety of his neck.

"Rowan. Stop." His hand was on hers, attempting to halt her. But his voice was full of husky desperation.

"This is what you want." She heard herself speak. But it wasn't her as much as the demonic part of her that only had one purpose; eat, by any means necessary.

Her marking him was what he wanted most. Even with his refusal to come to terms with it, she knew that his fulfilled desire would satiate her for a small eternity.

His smile didn't quite reach his eyes, which in her vision only lightened and darkened in hues of purples and reds rather than their lovely rainbow swirls. His fingers brushed against her forehead, which reminded her of the first night they met.

And then her world was once again black.

-A-

Rage ripped through Alessandro as he finished bathing the unconscious woman. His dragon was beyond furious at what had just transpired. He could feel his self control hanging on by the slightest thread, his scales fighting to overtake his sanity and wake the elf back up to demand she finish what she started, but anytime his fingers got near her forehead to undo the spell he summoned a knife to plunge into his thigh to keep a grip on his control. It made keeping her clean difficult.

"My king?"

Alessandro whipped his gaze to the man standing in the doorway to the bathroom.

"OUT!" He roared, shifting his body so Stone would not see Rowan's naked form.

"Ale-"

Alessandro sent a flurry of ice to force the dragon out of the room, too out of control to diminish his attack to warning.

A wall of stone erected to protect his protégé. Alessandro found he had never been so grateful for the woman who stepped forth once the wall crumbled with the hits of the shards.

"Help her." He demanded of Terra, who shoved Stone out of Alessandro's line of sight.

Terra didn't skip a beat. She had the woman in her arms only seconds before he felt the dragon was breaking past a threshold of his tight control.

Trusting no one above his Earth General, Alessandro phased to the one place he could pull his beast back from madness.

Gold twinkled and cold air washed over him as the world reassembled.

The immediate feeling of calm he had come searching for was absent. He hadn't expected the level of fury that his dragon reached, but Rowan was not in the right headspace to make such a decision.

He had prepped the cave for an occasion like this. For a sojourn into the old days, where he was more beast than man.

He wouldn't be able to leave until either he was back in control or until his dragon could work out the counter spell, which would almost certainly bring sanity with it.

Until such a time arrived, his beast was more than welcome to wreck their hoard. Anything to keep the world safe from him.

XXVI

S hattering glass and yells sliced through the air.

The sounds ripped Rowan from sleep in a rush of adrenaline.

Her eye snapped open.

Axel and Miasma were her only visitors, they were looking out of a window that offered a view of a darkened sky.

Pain she prepared herself for never came. Even the unbearable hunger that had haunted her was gone.

The only abnormal thing the elven-succubi felt was her limited access to magic. She despised it.

Pushing her discomfort down, she swung her legs over the side of the bed, getting the attention of both women.

"Princess!" Miasma gasped, already heading to check on her.

Rowan waved her down. "What's going on?" She approached the window and before either woman could respond, a torrent of wind shattered glass into the room.

Rowan raised a hand to erect a barrier out of habit. When no magic came, she glared at the useless appendage as her sister pushed her to safety while notably handling the good doctor with much softer hands.

She watched as the two women dusted fine shards off Axel's green tunic after standing back up. Oh-ho. There was something brewing there, wasn't there? Rowan itched to ask inappropriate, personal questions, but there was something more pressing happening at the moment than her sister's love life.

"Barros?" Rowan asked, forcing herself to choose to be a little more grown up than she felt.

"No, we gotta go." Axel held her hands out to both Rowan and Miasma, a blue scale in each palm.

"Are those..."

Axel apparently had no patience for silly questions; she cut Rowan off. "Aqua's scales? Yes. She gave them to me. Said they would phase us home when you came to after she finished dressing you. Now come on, before we get caught in the crossfire."

"The dragons are fighting each other again?" Rowan narrowed her eye.

Axel waved it off. "Nope, they're taking care of something else. Come on, you're in no state to help anyone out."

"Why not? I feel great."

Axel let out a familiar frustrated groan. "Why can't you just ask questions when we get there?"

Rowan spread her legs, grounding herself to her spot. "This might go quicker if you just answer my questions now."

It was rare for Rowan to argue with Axel. Neither Lexine nor Zeva had influence over Rowan's actions like their warrior sister did.

Perhaps it was because, out of all the sisters, Axel was the most like their father, or that she could physically subdue anyone who wasn't listening. Either way, when the two locked horns, things broke. Things like priceless artifacts, windows, or sometimes even bones.

Axel mimicked Rowan's stance, though she was admittedly more threatening with the extra four inches of height, as well as the definition of muscles underneath her contracted arms.

As Miasma had more often than not been in charge of healing Rowan and was prone to anxiety, she broke under the incurred tension. "We think this might actually be because of your presence."

Axel shot her an exasperated look. "We were supposed to wait for my father to tell her."

Miasma looked like she wanted to melt into the floor.

"Stop bullying her!" Rowan snapped.

Axel shot her a furious glare, but she stepped back to allow Rowan to take a peek outside.

A shaggy blue-haired dragon raced to put out small fires that roared to life over the lawn and up high on tree branches of massive oaks that dotted the pathways of Draconis. His magic became misdirected and landed a heaping water wave over another dragon, armed with shears, trying to keep a rapidly growing tree at bay.

Unlike the concerned pair in the bedroom, the dragons were having fun combating the wild magic in inventive ways.

"My presence?" She asked, confused.

Axel groaned when she realized Rowan was going to refuse to move until she got answers, "We think the magic is acting out because it's unable to get to you, so it's trying to overwhelm them."

"And there's a reason I can't just absorb the overflowing magic, isn't there?" She sighed and balled her fists up. "What is it?"

"Your body can't handle it at the rate it's trying to get in. It's like attaching a water balloon to a fire hydrant." Miasma's voice was soft and nervous. "With you awake you may regulate it, but without Ms. Darling here to null you out in case it gets to be too much, it could be dangerous."

Rowan cursed. What the hell was her body playing at, betraying her by breaking? Hadn't she been good to it? Given it all the cake and sex it demanded? Sure, she'd been an ignorant fool for misusing her power for years. But that hadn't been entirely her fault! She'd been doing better!

Perspective!

The word came to her in her father's voice.

She'd fucked up. Her succubi's energy had been too low to use the magic she'd dug out on that mountainside. She'd crossed a line and took in life energy rather than just the sexual energy she was supposed to. Her mother and godmother had warned her there would be consequences, and here they were.

There was a way to fix her gates. Much like a sprained ankle, she needed to take some time off pulling magic in order to rebuild them brick by brick. Back to basics.

The solution to the manic magic around them was simple. But it didn't include heading back to the Eastern Elven Kingdom. Like an improperly sealed hose with a nozzle, magic was trying to push through her to get out its normally open mouth, but was splashing out where it connected to the faucet.

She needed to pull out of magic's flow path. Normally a nulling charm should have done the trick, but her prolonged usage of them had finally exhausted their ability to keep her fully cloaked. It was lucky for her that her great-aunt Liza had left her the perfect tool for such an event. "Have there been sightings of my cabin?"

Axel raised an eyebrow, but she pointed to the giant house in the Estates that overlooked the forest behind and the city in front. "Apparently, it's been taking up space in your boyfriend's backyard."

"The entire time?"

Axel's knowing smirk was answer enough. Rowan tried not to react to the teasing, as she knew from experience it was her sister's way to sus out information she wasn't fully privy to, but she felt undeniably exposed. The Traveling Cabin only moved from place to place in regular practice because it knew that Rowan had yet to find a place to lay roots. Yet, if Axel was to be believed, it now took root in a portion of the Dragon King's land. Even after he'd made it clear nothing could happen between them.

Rowan turned on her heel and headed for the exit. "Come on, I need a quick catch up on our way over."

"Aqua said we should go." Axel reminded her sister.

"If the theory is correct, there's only one place that can take my share of magic. If I went home, the same thing you see happening out there would happen to our land, and the dragons are more equipped to handle magic than our people."

Axel let out an annoyed huff, but fell into step beside her.

"You think the cabin's time and space irregularities can absorb it?" Miasma asked as she joined her princesses.

"Yes." Rowan's conviction melted as quick as ice on the desert ground. "Well, I hope so. Where is the Dragon King? I assume he isn't here or he would've taken care of this."

"In his hoard. Good afternoon Princess Rowan, I am Terra." The voice preceded the entrance of Alessandro's stunning Earth General. Beige dragon garb draped around her body, adorned with colorful glass beads along her waist and intertwined into the tight curls of her honey hued hair.

Perhaps it was her title being used, or more the fact that Rowan had seldom met anyone that fit the description of 'queen' so well that Rowan bowed her head as a sign of respect for the woman. Beside her, Axel and Miasma followed her lead.

Terra gave her own curtsy back with a grace that could've rivaled Lexine, the most proper woman Rowan had ever known.

Behind her, Stone, Rowan's old classmate, grinned. "We were just on our way to make sure you could get home safe."

"We're actually heading to my cabin. I hear it's parked itself next to your King's house."

"Yes."

"Good." Rowan picked up her pace once more. "Let's walk and talk. Was it because of my succubus' actions that the Dragon King isn't here?"

She was half surprised to get a straight answer from Terra. Dragons, like the sphinxes, weren't open by nature. Even if they'd been nursing her back to health, Rowan didn't for a second believe that put her in their confidences.

"Yes. He has a failsafe way to check his beast when it gets out of control. He usually locks himself up in his hoard for a couple of weeks. However, with our current circumstances, I would rather it take a couple of days instead."

"What exactly are our current circumstances?" Rowan asked as they exited the medical building and spilled out onto the once immaculate green lawns and paved paths, now destroyed by the wayward magic, allowing Stone and Terra to lead them the way they felt best to get to her cabin.

"After Barros disappeared, the Coven decided not to air out their dirty laundry. In doing so, the tension between us and the non-shifters has only increased. Things have been getting more violent. We've attempted to improve relations by engaging in community outreach especially geared to the less fortunate, however the speed in which this is garnering results is less than nominal." Terra answered once again.

Rowan could get used to the straight answers.

"Well, when the world has known the dragons to keep to yourselves, it isn't hard to imagine why your help seems like an attempt to fool them." Axel murmured offhandedly.

"Exactly." Stone threw a side eye at Terra, packed with all the disgruntlement of a youth to an elder.

It occurred to Rowan that Stone was her age. He was next in line for the Dragon King's throne and Rowan wanted to know more about how it happened. She wanted to know everything about the world's oldest mystics, and she knew it stemmed from wanting to know absolutely everything about their enigmatic leader.

"We have our reasons to keep to ourselves, but dragons aren't the only ones being targeted. Wolves, who are notorious for their goodwill to non-shifters, especially those untouched by magic, have also been facing the backlash of Barros' actions."

Harris and Marissa Knox took a space in Rowan's heart, even though they'd only known each other for a few moments.

Rowan had a small army of people she considered hers from first contact, and the two wolf shifters had been her latest addition.

"So, you can only ease some of this antagonism if you find Barros, or if the Coven comes clean?" She asked to clarify how to best assist them in their goal of redemption.

The dragons were also apparently part of that army.

"Or if they leak audio and footage of Coven meetings. Something that should be impossible."

Axel's sharp gaze was on their two dragon escorts, reading every reaction to her words. Rowan recognized her sister's not-so-subtle method of digging for information for what it was; Axel wanted to know how they'd done it.

"It's helped not only with the anger towards us but also in digging up some leads of Barros." Stone shrugged, unabashed.

Rowan felt a flush of frustration course through her. "The arm didn't help?"

"No. He seems to be behind a protective barrier, and even with our work around in trying to track the magic signature before he disappeared behind it, we can't lock on. Still, it was an excellent cut. Your father's prestige on the battlefield translates into your combat skill, Princess." Terra's eyes roved the grounds as they got deeper and deeper into the Estate, her guard up.

Rowan wondered how much of that uneasiness was because outsiders were stepping into the more private side of the estate, and how much of it resulted because of the magic running amok on the grounds of Draconis.

There were several houses, many more than Rowan had ever imagined. They were mostly white stone work with terracotta roofs, each personalized in only a way that made sense to dragons.

Precious gems glittered from accent points along the clay trims. Gold and gem doors were a popular choice.

Dragons loved their treasures and nothing could point this out more than the sometimes gaudy collections that occurred in the bigger houses.

Rowan observed with a tad bit of jealousy as Terra wrangled the magic back into proper order. As they passed overgrown vines and small fires other dragons were failing to deal with, Terra's precise use of earth magic was as graceful as the woman.

Terra woman was powerful. As one of Alessandro's generals, it was a given. But there was an underlying aspect of leadership that she had. Stone, the true heir, lacked it.

Could it be that she was older and therefore more experienced than Stone? Or was it that Rowan had known him in his youth and had once helped hold him up for a keg stand?

"What are the chances you killed him during your fight? You always leave your opponents worse than what you look like, and you look terrible." Axel didn't pull her punches, emotional or physical.

Rowan threw out an elbow to her side that Axel easily dodged. "Unless we see a body, I'm not making any assumptions. But I think he was a Cursed."

"Cursed? Like Elaine?" Stone asked.

Rowan felt the bottom of her stomach drop. What had Alessandro revealed? Did his dragons know of her involvement? Had she trusted someone she shouldn't have with her secret?

But Stone's question wasn't for her. It was for Terra, who looked conflicted by whatever crossed her mind. Alessandro had said she was like his sister. Did she know?

"I didn't ask about specifics, but he said the curse had completely overtaken Elaine, half transformed into her beast form. How did Barros seem?"

Rowan chose her words carefully. "He was lucid. I could feel his emotions range." Yet, her sword, which could only bring harm to the Cursed, had chopped his arm off.

She'd summoned it purely based on the fact he'd had the stench of rotting meat, the stench that followed any of the other Cursed that came to her. If she was incorrect, she wouldn't have that arm. Yet, she couldn't just say this is how she knew. She didn't just go around spilling the secret her godfather had always pressed was imperative she kept.

That Alessandro had caught her in action as a Blessed was the only reason she ever let him know—then again, she'd never made the right call with that man.

"Then what makes you think he's a Cursed?" Terra asked softly.

"He smelled...rotten, and when he gave into the violence, I could almost swear darkness shrouded him."

"If he's a Cursed, we can tweak the tracking spell with the new information. Maybe he won't need to be connected to magic for us to find him." Terra's hazel eyes shone with new ideas.

"What exactly is the plan when you locate him?" Rowan asked as they turned the corner and caught sight of their goal.

Her cabin looked humble next to the massive manor that was Alessandro's home. Three times the size of the other houses, Alessandro's had a white stone floating fountain in the front, four detailed dragons spewing all four elements from their mouths to fall into four separate basins as they spun in a lazy circle. The exterior of the home used the same white stone, which contrasted with the dark shingles of the roof and up to the giant tower she'd seen as far as three blocks away from the steps of the medical ward.

Even though her cabin should've looked awkward next to the disparate architecture, Rowan couldn't help but admire the sight.

Somehow it fit.

"We want to call Judgment." Terra's answer made sense.

As the species of both magical and non magical descent built their new world of near inseparability, it quickly became apparent that cultures and sense of justice differed from species to species. Spells like phasing created a jurisdiction issue solved only by Judgement.

Judgement comprised elected representatives from every species that resolved to coexist. As of last count 356 representatives sat on the Judgement Panel and while not perfect, it allowed every species to have a voice.

With Antoni's actions having spanned to more than one continent, he fell into their purview.

It was only half surprising the dragons weren't just burning the man out of existence. They had a tendency to make aggressive responses to aggressive actions taken against them. It was what had kept them at the top for so long.

However, because the actions against them had highlighted their strength as a negative aspect, they had to approach it more conciliatory than normal.

Something the Thunder was so obviously at a loss with how to do.

Rowan herself, who normally took a softer approach, such as making herself smaller to avoid attention, found it difficult to picture doing anything other than running the man through with her blade so she could relate.

Dew's dwindling heartbeat still rang through her head.

With emotion heavy in her throat, she asked, "How is Dew's family?"

Axel shrugged. "You know faeries. They don't see death the way most of us do. Louisa said they didn't seem to take it too hard, and the funeral was more of a celebration."

Dew would've adored that. She had always done everything in her power to keep things cheery. It was a contagious desire that had made the office seem more like a family than a business.

She would visit Dew's mother when everything settled. She wanted to show Dew's entire family how much she adored the fairy.

"And since the Coven is in turmoil, I'm guessing that means Cherry hasn't recovered either?" She asked Miasma who looked startled to be addressed.

"No. Not really, there seems to be a block on her inheritance of the old Elder's magic."

"Tell her why you think that might be, Miasma." Axel encouraged.

Rowan couldn't wait to get her sister alone to tease her.

Miasma's eyes widened in obvious discomfort and her thumbs twirled around one another.

"Well, umm, I believe a portion of the magic trying to get into you is the Elder's."

"Witch magic in an elf?" Terra looked both horrified and impressed.

"Elven-succubus." Stone motioned to Rowan's wings.

"Fair point. Could there also be witch magic in your bloodline?" Terra asked, unsure.

"No." Rowan's eye lit up as a thought occurred to her. "But I think I might know why it would be trying."

She'd kept the Elder's Grimoire for over two weeks already. She hadn't gotten to use it as much as she'd like, losing two weeks just from falling into her feeding frenzy and recovering from her fight with Barros. Could the time limit have something to do with the Elder's magic? Did it come as a package deal?

Or, and Rowan suspected, this was most likely the case: Had Henrietta known Barros would take Cherry? Had Barros taken the expected Elder to steal the magic that she was supposed to have with her? To take it as his own? Is that why Cherry had asked about it as soon as she saw who dropped into that second cage?

The idea of that kind of power existing in someone as deranged as Antoni Barros was terrifying.

"Is that the only magic trying to kill me?" Could the solution to her problem be so simple? Why were there so many questions and so few answers?

"I don't think it's trying to kill you," Miasma spoke softly. "I think it just senses something in you that makes it feel like it belongs there. Like you're its proper home."

No way. Witch magic belonged to witches only. Though she could now pull magic through all of her chakra gates. Could that have something to do with it?

But maybe something in her blood or genealogy was of witch descent? She would have to look into that after she got the Dragon King back home.

As her priorities stood, the first was to get him back to his rightful place. After all, it was her fault he had to resort to locking himself away. Second was to check up on Kin and Louisa, who had been as close to the fallen fairy as she had been. Third was to check out what the hell was going on with her magic and fourth was to find the bastard who had taken her eye and bring him to proper justice and restore some of the peace he had sledgehammered out of existence with his actions.

When they stepped up to her porch, she turned and watched as the chaos died down.

A pair of nearby water dragons who had been trying to drown a raging fire in a pair of rose bushes looked disappointed to have their fun ended so easily.

"So this is the power of a space and time anomaly." Terra touched the wood of the wrap-around porch's banister and Rowan could feel the cabin's approval roil through their link.

Rowan smiled and turned the knob of the front door. What awaited on the other side took her breath away.

There were no walls or ceiling, just a glowing glass bridge that led the way to a giant stone pedestal. She had to get close to make out the scenic carvings of mountains flush with pine trees, the view of waves crashing on a glittering shore, and a field of tall prairie grass lazily blowing in the wind. Carefully, Rowan peered down at the endless void underneath the glass. Were those stars?

"It's been ages since I've seen one of these." Terra's voice echoed in the room as she entered behind her.

Rowan raised an eyebrow. "What is it?"

"A teleporter. It allows those without magic to phase, even in between dimensions." She touched the top rim. Inside the bowl, there were millions of shining particles that reminded her of small nebulas.

"It's beautiful." Axel peeked in from the other side, Miasma stood, clutching onto the warrior's arm for dear life. Her eyes avoided looking down. Was the good doctor afraid of heights? Why had she entered the room? Rowan didn't have time to contemplate further as Terra explained.

"They only work in places like the Traveling Cabin, anomalies of time and space. Like the Traveling Cabin, most places like that are particular of who they allow to enter. That's why they're so rare." The earth-dragon played with a wooden bangle on her wrist as she tilted her head up. "This could help you get into Alessandro's hoard even without his invitation."

Rowan gripped the side of the bowl before taking a step back. "If he has lost total control, what's the best way to calm him down?"

Terra raised an eyebrow. "Princess Rowan, you're the best way to calm him down. His dragon wants you as his mate. He won't harm you."

"But what if the dragon wants to mark me? Your king made it clear to me that if he had it his way, he would prefer not to."

Terra took a deep breath and glanced around the room. "May we have a word in private?"

Axel shot her a questioning look, and Rowan gave a small nod.

For a moment, she looked like she wanted to argue. Rowan had never seen her sister so protective. It hurt her pride to know it was because she'd allowed herself to get so injured.

But, she let whatever she was going to say slip away, leading Miasma, who'd shut her eyes and dug her face into her sister's shoulder, obviously uncomfortable with the height, back out onto the porch.

Stone looked like he also wished to dispute, but Terra shot him a simple look and that was enough to encourage him to leave.

"He told me you were his adopted sister." Rowan took charge of the confrontation she felt building in the woman. She searched for a flinch, a tick of a muscle, but the title elicited only relaxation from the woman. "But when you walked up with Stone at your side through the neighborhoods, I saw the way the dragons were with you. I understood, you're more than a sister to the king. You're his queen."

With the wind taken out of her sail, Terra's jaw looked slack. "Our relationship is not like that."

Rowan crossed her arms. "Terra, my father is one of the greatest kings of the Eastern Elven Kingdom. I know what it looks like when subjects lay eyes on their leader. You fill that role."

Terra squared her shoulders. "I can see where you might get that idea, but it isn't like Alessandro and I have ever had anything but sibling love for one another. When I was born, my mom and dad had already taken him in and considered him their own. He is as..." The earth-dragon searched for the right words, "...annoying and as overprotective to me as most brothers are to anyone else."

Rowan nodded, "Okay, so as his sister. I need you to help me protect him from a decision he really has no control over. How do I calm him down without giving him my neck?"

Terra let out a groan and Rowan watched, surprised as the facade of a cool and collected dragon fell as she grasped Rowan's shoulders and shook her. "Listen to me. He wants you. Both his dragon and his more sane side. What he's worried about is burdening you!"

Rowan's eyes widened. "What?"

"Gods, you two are going to be the end of my sanity!" She growled as she let Rowan go and began pacing the width of the bridge. "Once he marks you, I won't be able to say anything, so let me get it out now. Only you affect him the way you do. I was there on the mountainside. You want him as much as he wants you. I knew as soon as you two came together that anything that would get between you two would turn to dust. Even your stubbornness. I know you're not a dragon, so it might seem like everything is going too fast, too hot and that it's terrifying but, as a succubus you also have an alternate being inside you that lives for those base desires. Maybe ask what the fuck she wants instead of letting your stupid little insecurities have their way."

Tears forming in the woman's eyes startled Rowan. "When we are without a mate, we are constantly battling with our base desires. It would be pure anarchy if we allowed our beasts to have their way.

Alessandro himself is always fighting his beast unless they're in the middle of combat. It's been decades since he last knew real peace. You bring that to him. So as a little sister, I am begging you, don't be afraid. He'll take care of you. I vow here and now that if you take the crown to stand by his side, I will protect you. And if this doesn't sound like something you're interested in because you decide to hold on to your stubbornness, if you really don't want it, Alessandro won't mark you. Trust me."

Well, that wasn't as comforting as Terra was trying to make it seem, but as a little sister who would do anything to see her sisters happy, it was moving. "I'll trust your judgment, but if I come out with his mark, know that my first order as his queen will be to make you take all the responsibility, while I only take advantage of the perks."

Terra snorted, "I'm telling you, it will only happen if you want it."

That was kind of the problem, wasn't it? She *did* want it, consequences be damned.

Terra gave a soft smile as if reading her mind, "Just picture him in any moment you bonded. It should be enough to take you right to him."

It was surprisingly tough to figure out which memory she wanted to use. Memories of them in bed that overwhelmed her, but they didn't feel quite right. A vision of his distraught face as she destroyed his scale rolled into her mind. She supposed it was the most vulnerable she'd felt in front of him. Sure, she'd been angry, but the anger had nothing on her heartbreak. She closed her eyes to help empower the vision.

XXVII

Three days of knowing little peace. Alessandro was exhausted. His bones shook from the intense inner tug-of-war he'd spent three days engaging in with his dragon.

He was sane enough to know he wouldn't succumb to the rage lust that had taken his father, but there had been a few dark moments where he felt his will faltering. The first time it happened, he felt the wall he kept between himself and his celestial side crumble.

Panic from both the dragon and himself forced them to join efforts in reinforcing that wall.

With the wall refortified, the tug-of-war resumed.

He initially allowed the dragon to destroy their precious collection as an outlet, but when he turned the last chalice in the cave into a pool of molten gold, the beast had nothing left to distract him.

Three centuries' worth of treasures disintegrated in a matter of hours. He'd wished there was a way to physically get a hold of his dragon to let out his frustration with a good beat down, but as was always the case, Alessandro had to use words and reasoning. Something he lacked practice in even as the King of the dragons.

His dragon had developed a bad habit of responding with one word.

Rowan.

Then the dragon spent hours pushing images of his ultimate desire on Alessandro, nearly convincing him to leave the cave and just do what they both now agreed they desired.

But no. Rowan deserved more than the paltry benefits of being a mate to Alessandro, who so far had nothing to offer her. Nothing that she didn't already have or could get herself.

His dragon, enraged that he couldn't convince his sane side, spent hours trying to figure out how to release them back into the world. But the beast was all brawn, no brain. In physical combat, he was invincible, but puzzles were not his strong suit. He tried clawing the magic out of the cavern walls, blasting it with ice, fire, lightning, even tried biting at it with massive teeth, but the walls remained impenetrable.

Alessandro remained in his full dragon form through all of this. It consumed energy he wouldn't be able to replenish until he ate. Which is something he tried to entice his dragon with, to which the dragon replied with a chorus of 'Rowan'.

He felt the shift in the air. A sweet, familiar brand of magic caressed his icy scales. Her scent exploded from her, finally full of health, and his body sagged with the relief and peace at last washed through him.

-R-

There were sound of soft huffs and hot air brushed through the strands of her hair

Her eye opened. She had appeared on a single claw of the massive beast that was curled before her.

She had known Alessandro was colossal in his dragon form. She'd seen him fly overhead during her years of working in Black Cove, but nothing had prepared her to realize one of his claws was two times larger than her entire body.

It was impossible to tell the details through the darkness, but she could feel he had been sleeping before her appearance. She could hear the displacement of air as he moved his head to examine her.

"Alessandro?" She asked when a throaty growl gonged through the cave, making every hair along her spine stand at attention.

The dragon didn't speak, but a thin string of fire jetted from his mouth to light the several sconces around the cave.

The once immaculate collection was a mess. Metal treasures were bent or melted into silver and golden puddles. Rubies and other stones were now dust and intermingled with the torn fabrics of tapestries and furs.

He had been out of control. Yet, he seemed perfectly calm as he laid his head back down next to her and his nostrils let out warm air as he stared with large silver eyes.

She took a tentative step forward and returned to her original space when he let out another growl, one threaded with displeasure.

"My growl vocabulary is pretty limited, so if you could use words, I'd appreciate it."

The dragon huffed, and the ensuing gust pushed Rowan back a step.

"Well, at least now I know you can understand me. May I take a step towards you, or will you bite my head off?"

No answer.

Sucking up her uncertainty, she moved forward, taking slow steps until she could reach up and touch the bottom of his chin.

Black iridescent scales were ice underneath her touch. Two horns curved around his head and tipped into deadly points. Spikes ran along his spine just as menacing as the sharp tip of his tail. Though tucked, his wings reminded her of her own, soft, black and smooth.

Slowly his eyes closed, and he seemed to relax, which encouraged her to feel along the expanse of his face.

"You're beautiful."

She spoke after a while of letting him get used to her touch, to her presence.

No answer.

"Really." She insisted and spread her arms as she leaned against him, "But can I see you in a form that will allow me to hold you?"

She thought he might ignore her again, but then she felt his scales shift underneath her like the moving sands of a desert.

A moment later, her arms were full of a miniature version of the beast, a little rounder and softer, with eyes that were wider but still glowing silver as he looked up at her.

Rowan let out a laugh at the unexpected response. "You're adorable!" She squealed and rubbed her nose to his. A second later, she found him morphed back into his humanoid form, naked and rock hard, and his lips were on hers in a hungry kiss.

Rowan matched his energy. Pouring everything she hadn't said into their physical connection. How she was sorry to have crossed a boundary and forced his beast to take over, how worried she'd been to hear of his disappearance and how relieved she was that he hadn't lost himself to rage.

He pulled back after a moment and rainbow eyes swirled as they took her in. "You feel strong." His voice was hoarse with desire. Her own need rose to meet his, and she knew where this was going to end.

"On a scale of one to ten, how under control is the beast right now?" She asked as he peppered her cheeks and chin with small kisses and bites.

He chuckled. "I don't think I'd categorize how much he wishes to take you here and now as really sane, so maybe a three. I need to be inside of you."

Rowan moaned as his teeth applied pressure at the juncture of her neck and shoulders. She needed to focus, but her own second entity was bleeding, her vision red and purple once more. "If..." her words stuck in her throat as she felt the hunger of her succubus erasing her self control. "What if he pushes you to lose control again?"

His roaming hands froze at the edge of her sweatpants and his voice came out even more gruff than before. "I won't let him."

Terra had told her what she needed to know to take this next step, but she needed to hear it from his own lips.

"What's changed?" She demanded. "Why are you so willing to do this again after telling me last time would be the end?"

He cursed. "Because your succubus is giving us no choice."

That was certainly not the answer she was expecting. She blinked and cleared her throat. "Come again?"

"You imprinted on me." His fingers played with her tail, and her knees buckled at the unexpected pleasure. "You can no longer consume the sexual energy of any other than myself."

"What?"

"On that mountainside, when you held your arms out to me, I could smell it. Underneath all the blood, the scents of..." a growl of displeasure gonged through the cave, "...several partners. Yet your energy levels were depleted. Even what you got from Barros' life force wasn't enough and succubi can survive off that sort of energy for months." He took a deep breath and closed his eyes. "When we were in the bathroom, a hug gave you more than what they could. Your succubus chose me."

Untangling herself from his hold, Rowan let out a disbelieving laugh. "I think I can resist her as much as you've resisted your dragon. I'll just need to disappear for a few months on a feeding frenzy. I almost felt it regulate itself at the end."

His eyes were a soft lavender color as he looked away from her. "Is the idea of choosing me so repulsive?"

Her footsteps back and forth echoed, increasing in speed as her heart rate did. Was she going to be the first one to bare her soul here? Her pride wanted to see him hurt as much as she had when he'd walked away from her, but her succubus was damn near crying in her head.

She took three deep, calming breaths. "It is when you don't want me. It is when you're only doing it to save me from this perceived danger of starvation from my succubus. I don't need to be saved. I need to be cherished and respected."

Silence spread between them.

She bristled. "Look, you're in control of your dragon now, right? Let's head back out."

His fists clenched at his side. "Rowan, I'm afraid you don't understand. When a succubus imprints on a shifter, it only ever happens after they're mated because of the territorial nature of our beasts. Your succubus imprinted on me before we've mated only because my dragon is stronger than most shifters. Your succubus must have gotten confused, but an imprint .cannot be removed."

"What?"

His eyes were a steady silver, but there was pity in them as well. "How can you be so ignorant of what's happening to you?"

Fury ignited at the sore spot he'd just pressed. "Look, anything I know I've gotten from scrolls. Do you know how many scrolls there are covering succubus history? Like three."

His voice was much gentler when he spoke again. "Scrolls?"

A soft feeling of irritation mixed with sorrow filled her. "When my mother met my father, it was a setup by our clan. They wanted her to drain his riches dry, just as my grandmother had done to my grandfather from the Southern Elven Kingdom. They didn't expect for her to fall in love or choose him over their desires, but she did. As such, she, along with her progeny, is banned from lands held by any succubus."

His nose flared, and his chest expanded. "No one should have to live without the chance to know where they came from."

She shrugged, "I went 26 years with no need to know much about it. If I would've never met you, I'm sure I could've gone the rest of my life."

He reeled her back into his arms, a small crooked smile tugging at the corner of his lips, and she knew he saw through the lie she'd offered.

Of course, she craved to know the truth behind her succubus' side. She despised being ignorant over such a huge part of her life. But there was nothing she could do other than take it one day at a time and confront any hazards that came along the way.

His eyes pulsed red as he leaned down to capture her lips in a soft kiss.

She didn't have it in her to fight this, to fight him.

When he pulled back, his eyes raked all over her face. "If we are baring our souls here, I suppose I should tell you that this isn't a one sided dilemma. When you tried to mark me, it sent my dragon wild. The only thing stopping me from sinking my fangs into your neck is that you're healthy, strong, and that we're alone."

She bit her lip. "What does that mean?"

"I can't leave. My dragon is stuck, hovering too close to the surface, but I have an idea."

"Which is?"

"He might eventually calm down. In the meantime, you just come to see me whenever you need to fill up. You could continue living your life in a sort of ordinary way. We don't even have to have sex if you find someone to actually love out there. Before I locked myself away, I found I could transfer my energy through touch." A thrill of his energy seeped into her with a simple swipe of his finger over her arm.

Confusion threaded through every fiber of Rowan's being. "You speak as if you're planning on staying here for a long time."

He didn't answer, but his eyes were still flickering between red and silver.

Anger bubbled in her throat.

"The world without the Dragon King?" She demanded. "When the shifters need you the most?"

He chuckled, though she could feel it held no amusement. He was seething. "Now, now, little elf, as great of a beast as I am, the world would continue spinning. My heir can take on my duties with the backing of my generals. I only regret that I won't be able to take care of Antoni Barros. I planned on doubling what he took from you." His finger stroked the edge of her eyepatch.

"No." She whispered.

"Princess Rowan."

Irritation swelled through her at the obvious ploy to put distance between them. She reached down and grasped his warm, pulsing length. "You ever call me Princess Rowan again and I'll make your dick my personal chew toy."

His nose flared, but it seemed she had his attention. She relaxed her grip and, before letting it go, she gave the straining piece of his body a soft brush with her finger. Hunger once again burned hot in her veins.

She took a step back to cool her head. "This wouldn't be your home. This would be your prison." Her chin rose in defiance. "I couldn't just leave knowing that I could simply assure your freedom."

"This is anything but simple, Rowan. Assuring my freedom takes yours away." He tucked a stray strand of her hair behind her ear. "I've lived a long life. There's very little I haven't done or accomplished. You have yet to experience anything real. You've been busy hiding in the shadows because of the Coven. You deserve to flourish."

It might not be simple for him. But to Rowan, her freedom included the stubborn man. She still hadn't gone toe to toe with him. She had years before she would be strong enough to even dream about challenging him to a proper duel. And her bluster about the feeding frenzy? That was a straight lie. She would rather face demon poison again than go through that hell once more. Terra asked her to listen to her succubus, and her succubus was screaming in her head

Take. Take. Take.

As frantic as she has been in that bathtub. But with her recouped strength Rowan had a choice.

"Let me flourish with you by my side!" She hissed and exposed her neck. "Come on, sink your teeth in."

His breathing deepened. A growl emerged from the back of his throat as his head descended. But he didn't open his mouth, merely laid a soft kiss at the juncture. "You must go."

Panic filled her as the words rolled through her head. She knew what he would attempt before he did it, and she tore away the chain that held back the power she needed to stop him.

Magic tore through every pore in her body in a rush so painful, she fell to her knees as she tried to control it.

They had been right to be concerned. If she'd been asleep, it would have been impossible for her to reinforce the annihilated gates that allowed everything inside. But she was awake now. And though magic was a temperamental wave, she had the skill and strength to hone and control every particle, including the portion of Alessandro's that tried to send her away.

Alessandro knelt in front of her, silver eyes flashing red as he looked her over for any obvious wounds.

"*Fuck!* Why did it have to be someone like you?" He asked, sounding defeated as he dragged her back into his chest once more when he realized she was okay.

"I need you." She dug her face into his bare chest. "Please, Alessandro."

In her mouth, she felt her teeth lengthen.

Alessandro closed his throbbing silver eyes as if trying to gather his thoughts, but she felt the magic he was trying to pull together again.

She let out a frustrated growl. "This is my choice."

"It is the wrong one." He spoke with his eyes still closed.

"*My choice.*" She sunk her hands into his curls and tugged.

When his eyes opened to stare down at her, they were so bright when she blinked, she saw stars.

"Give me your neck, San." She whispered.

His breath hitched and he squeezed her tighter. "You can still run, little elf."

She cocked her head to the side. "I thought I informed you of my preferred form of cardio."

He let out a laugh as he tipped his own head to the side, revealing the roiling scales on the expanse of his neck. "Fine. Your choice. You go first."

Her vision swam with red and pink hues, her succubus so eager her heartbeat pulsed on her tongue.

Hoping her demon side knew what it was doing, she lowered her head, opened her mouth and bit down hard.

Blood rushed into her mouth, oddly cold. She sucked and sucked until she felt him go limp in her arms.

It was only when she was the only thing that kept him from crashing into the dirt floor that she knew it was time to pull away.

He was unbelievably heavy, and so her struggle to place his mouth on the juncture of her own neck took her by surprise.

"Graceful" He teased as he extended his own fangs.

"You did this on pur-" A sharp slice of pain that erupted from the bite mark cut her words off. Pain morphed into unbearable heat, as if every vein in her body was boiling.

Relief came as ice took the place of the heat, followed by a buzz of electricity that she could see arching off her body in blue lightning. It smelled like him, mint and honey.

"It should ease some of the discomfort." He whispered, extending his hand out to touch the arcs, and in it she could see frost where it touched him. "This is how I see your magic. Bright, clean, electric."

She smiled as he replaced the nulling necklace around her neck. It was for the best. She couldn't concentrate on keeping her gates up while she allowed the most intrusive bond she'd ever experienced to take root.

XXVIII

Visions flashed in her head. Places and faces she didn't recognize mixed with an odd assortment of stimuli so strong on her senses that she believed for a second she was there.

"They're my core memories. Parts of the past that have established the Alessandro, you know."

The first big moment of the Dragon King's life lay at the loss of his parents.

"It was rage lust." He said, as if watching the memories alongside her.

His father had been as rugged and handsome as his son, though in the memories before the loss of control he seemed sulky, pouting as his wife played with their son. Had he been envious of the attention Alessandro was receiving?

His eyes were slate gray, darker than the shining silver Alessandro had taken to staring at her with, but the same as the ones the child's, which peered shyly between his parents.

His mother had his full-bodied curls, clumps and clumps of it cascading around her shoulders, though they differed in color as she was a vibrant red head.

A vibrant red that matched the blood seeping around her body when Alessandro saw her fall after his father had snapped.

The handsome man had lost any hint of gray in his eyes. They had been black orbs that swept past his son, too weak and young to be a target for the rage that took him over as he fled from the home.

"He moved on and killed the neighbors. We lived in a village then, full of all kinds of mystics and humans. He took out half of the town before a group of shifters dedicated to taking care of the issue got a hold of him. At that point, I had been seven years old and, as the son of the man who had caused so much damage, the village turned its back on me. The shifters hadn't been aware of my existence before they left. With nowhere left to go, I began walking."

Rowan clenched her hands. How could they have failed him so hard as a child?

Her indignation fizzled out as a blanket fell around her shoulders.

In between reality and the visions, Alessandro had at some point phased them from the hoard into a neat, but lackluster bedroom with a bed covered in soft white sheets and an even softer comforter. Outside of the window, she could see the low skyline of Black Cove. Was it his bedroom?

He had also summoned and changed into a pair of sweats, much to her disappointment, and he sat cross-legged across from her.

She shifted the blanket over his shoulders before settling into his lap.

There had been tension in his body that melted as he wrapped his arms around her midsection, pulling her closer, his lips gently resting where her shoulder met her neck.

"Where did you go?" She asked, her fingers tracing the cords of muscle along his arms.

"Into the forest." His breath was warm, sending goosebumps down her back. "I was terrified. My mother spent years warning me about the monsters in the forest. I expected to be gobbled up by something much bigger than me in mere days, but in the end, I feared the villagers more. Anytime I went into town, they would chase me out with curses and beatings. Leaving was my only option. So one day I did, and it was months before I ran into another living soul. In that time, I had learned how to survive, learned through trial and error what I could eat. Time in the forest sharpened my hunting skills, and I was stronger than I'd ever imagined myself being. I liked the physical challenges I put myself through, jumping off cliffs and barely letting my wings out at the last second." She could feel his muscles twitching underneath her and she gave an appreciative mewl. He chuckled. "I also became friends with some of the wildlife. My best friend was a moose I met my second day in. We spent months walking the forest together until one day, when we were walking into one of the few clearings of that forest, a giant red and blue dragon swooped up and swallowed him whole."

Rowan gasped as the vision overtook her senses. The moose had been grand, a massive beast that put into perspective how big the dragon was, though as far as Rowan could tell, he wasn't as large as Alessandro had become in modern times.

Alessandro chuckled. "My reaction as well, right before I lost my cool. I attacked the dragon in my fury. He hadn't expected me to defend my territory. I was a small child who lacked proper nutrition and proper dragon upbringing, but I gave him a run for his money. I interested him even more by using more than one element. He was so shocked when I cast a water and earth spell. It gave me the chance to sink my teeth into his hide."

Rowan grinned. "So you've always been a badass."

His laughter rumbled against her back. "You got the biggest and baddest dragon in the world, little elf." A fireplace she hadn't noticed until then roared to life at the foot of the bed. Flames of every color danced within the grate and she rolled her eyes. What a showoff.

"So after you pissed him off, what happened?"

"I didn't piss him off, I impressed him. He calmed me down enough to stop throwing spells at him and brought me to a small upstart of a village exclusive to dragons. I didn't want to go. I liked my life in the forest, but he dragged me kicking and screaming until my adoptive mother, Anya, showed up. When she found out he had taken me against my will and beat me up, she was livid."

The woman in the vision was a spitting image of Terra, save for the blonde streaks in her hair. Her green eyes shone with the fire of a woman not to be trifled with.

"Her energy reminded me of my mother's. I instantly clung to her. She comforted me and asked if I just wanted to eat with them, then I could head back to the forest afterwards if I wished. When the dragon told her about my dual magic wielding, she commended me for my skill, but her offer still stood. I could leave if I wanted. So, I ate dinner and left. I came back every once in a while, especially when game in the forest became scarce, but pretty soon I was staying so regularly she had a bedroom made just for me in her small hut. It wasn't long until she met Phineas."

Rowan saw a beer bellied dragon with a wide smile full of good-hearted joy. He had no hair, but his sharp brown eyes noted him as a possible earth-dragon.

While she could sense there was comfort Alessandro felt with Anya, there was a mischievousness that he'd explored with Phineas who accepted the roaming street dragon as eagerly as Anya had.

"At that point, the village seemed to accept me as a part of their family and the dragon I'd attacked? He was their leader, King Titus. I avoided him the best I could when I would visit, but he always found me. He took it as a personal quest to train me. As a multi-elemental user, I was a potential replacement for him."

"When did he end up quitting?"

"He didn't."

A flash of a severed head startled Rowan.

"I killed him."

There was pain in his voice, and shame. She wanted to ask why, but she also knew whatever the answer, it would hurt for him to explain.

Instead, she wrapped her arms around his and laid a soft kiss on his right bicep.

"When I first received my godhood, I wasn't ready for it. Hells, I didn't even recognize it as celestial power. I just thought I was just progressing in my training. Then came the day when King Titus got a bit too greedy. I'd worked alongside him to bring the village up from 1,000 dragon shifters to over 20,000. He became drunk on his new power and began abusing it. These were in those days where mystics were still trying to get pieces of land under our control, chipping away at countries to build our homes. He sent us to wars with neighbors. He wanted an empire, and because I was so well-versed in magic, I could deliver anything he requested. In return, I gained the wealth and influence to provide comfortable lives for Phineas, Anya and their new baby Terra. Not that they were happy to be used by his majesty. Anya was especially vocal."

The next vision was inside of a farmhouse, the smell of blood thick in the air, so corporeal that she believed for a moment that she had gone back in time to experience that moment as if she'd lived through it. She understood. This was *the* moment. The one that would define him for the rest of his life.

"It was during a battle of one of these villages that his blood thirst got to me. He was in the middle of slaughtering a family of farmers who had no weapons to fight back with." The sounds of steel slicing into flesh and bones crunching surrounded her.

"Surrounded by men who didn't stand a chance at helping the children, I reached my limit. I was tired of the bloodshed. I subdued him."

At that point, Alessandro looked like he was maybe in his mid twenties. He hadn't fully grown into his head, and was so lean compared to how she knew him.

King Titus, in comparison, was tall, bulky and even though his greed defined him, he was no glutton for food. He was a weapon sheathed in skin, but he stood no chance against Alessandro's superior magic and speed. All Alessandro did was fend him off, away from the children and force him to go home, but he had created fear in the eyes of the king.

"That moment sowed the seed of my godhood into the minds of the soldiers who witnessed it. A couple of months went by. Each time I met my king, it was explosive, and then he tried to increase the taxes on our already poor people. People I'd promised would have a better life, a safer life when I recruited them for the kingdom. They still believed in the dream I'd sold, and by that point, I knew Titus wouldn't give them the future I'd envisioned. So we fought. I wasn't much for political bullshit—it still pisses me off to this day—and our kingdom was too young to really have cemented bonds, but there was a definite split, until he decided the only way to get me was by a surprise attack. He outfitted a couple of his supporter's kids with magic bombs. Terra had created a bit of a soft spot in me for children and he tried to use this knowledge to his advantage knowing I would let them get close. I survived, they didn't. His supporters had finally had enough. His action united both sides, and they all turned to me, the only one who had ever taken the brunt of his rage. On that same night when I visited him, I had 20,000 furious dragons seeping their years of rage into me and I beheaded him."

"Their will overrode yours."

He nodded. "Once you feel that kind of loss, it stays quaking in every single one of your cells. I wait every day for that moment to happen again. Everything I feel, I sift through again and again to make sure it's what I am truly feeling."

"It sounds exhausting." She sighed. "No wonder you're so cranky."

He let out an unwilling laugh. "You're one of the few things I don't have to do that with." He shook her leg.

"Because your dragons definitely would prefer a dragon mate?"

"Yes."

She laughed, "Well, I'm sorry to inform you that in due course, your dragons are going to be enthused for me to be your Dragon Queen."

His finger on her chin forced her to meet his silver eyes. "You don't have to take the position if you don't want to. How could I take away your freedom when the only reason you marked me was to give me mine?"

Now that she had his memories, she knew this was born out of a noble place within the Dragon King who had long since grown weary of the weight of his crown. Of a man who didn't want to drag her into something she wasn't totally sure she wanted.

But a deep part of her felt a sense of indignation she couldn't comprehend. Could it be a simple sting of pride? Her desire to fit into any role of power? Or could it be that now that she knew he wanted out, she wanted to save him, but knew she couldn't? The least she could do was share that burden. Her heart gave a painful lurch and she placed a hand over her chest to soothe it. At the corner of her eye she caught sight of a mark that hasn't been there before.

She swung her legs over the side of the bed and made her way over to his dresser mirror. She could feel his tension building behind her, could practically hear his dragon roaring his displeasure that she was putting distance between them, but she needed to see it in its entirety.

A mating mark. The mark that announced the claim they'd made on each other. It made them officially off limits.

Kin had his on the back of his neck. Two rings interconnected. Easily hidden and simple.

Rowan's was large in comparison as it ran along the entire underside of her collarbone. A hollow inverted triangle took space in the middle pointing down to her cleavage. A thin horizontal line slashed across it, ranging from one side of her chest to the other.

The sight of the mark ignited more visions. She hadn't realized the previous memories came with a hint of fogginess until the crisp memories of her took center stage. Since the moment she dodged his surprise attack, everything he experienced was suddenly in high definition.

Her body heated at the sight of her ecstasy and eagerness each time they met in bed. She could smell their combined lust, the heady tangy smell as they fell into each other. Every single time he saw her, it was a crisp picture accompanied by a feeling of constant free fall.

She glowed to him, like a walking drop of sunshine. She also experienced the sensation he got every time he had to walk away from her; it always felt like an ice bath in the middle of the arctic. It reminded

him of how it felt that day that he lost both of his parents, of the loneliness that it struck within him.

She gripped the sides of the dresser as the depth of his affection for
her overwhelmed her. It burned hot and cold so fast it was like experiencing whiplash. She made him feel like this and he still wanted her?

He was insane.

A laugh bubbled out of her.

She wasn't any better.

How quickly she had crumbled under the idea that they could be
together?

Her damn cabin was visible just outside of the window. It sat there,
mocking her with the truth.

She had committed to the man before her succubus had ever had
the chance to fall in line with his dragon's influence.

It must have been the first time she saw him flying overhead in
her first years at Spellcaster's Academy, way before Antoni Barros'
actions had forced her from her hidey-hole of averageness. Hadn't it
been since then that the idea of being with a meal more than once
physically made her ill?

Glancing back at him, she caught one last vision. Of her kneeling
on the ground on a destroyed mountainside, arms reaching out to him,
relief and joy at the sight of him. It was the moment he knew there
was no fighting against what she brought out of him.

Her legs ate the distance between them.

"I plan to be your equal in every way, Alessandro, in case that
wasn't clear when I sunk my teeth into your neck. If you are the
Dragon King, I will be the Dragon Queen. When you decide to step
down and just be Alessandro, I will step down and just be Rowan and
we can figure out the middle of what that may all mean together because you are my mate." She turned and pointed at the mark that had
taken place on his forehead. "You sunk your teeth into my neck too.
We're partners now, got it?"

His smile as he took in the mark over her collar bone made any sternness in her body melt. He was at pure peace while he examined the lines, unconcerned with her message.

She sighed and took his face in her hands. "Alessandro, we have to set our expectations. Focus."

He gently grabbed her wrist and ran his tongue along the center of her palm. She could differentiate the vision that hit her from his memories.

She was naked, holding onto the edge of the dresser. He knelt in front of her, face between her thighs, tongue inside of her.

He wanted to settle the mark with their bodies and Rowan's succubus needed no more encouragement to make her own presence and demands known.

It was easy to give in as she led the way away from the bed, eager to fulfill his fantasy.

As he stood to follow, his magic unfurled, coiling around her like a giant corporeal shadow. He slid the v-neck crew sweater from the medical wing over her head, eyes locked in on her tits as they bounced free.

Her eye followed his movement as he bent to take a nipple in his mouth, one hand working on her other breast, the other scooping a handful of ass and squeezing.

"Mine." He growled, eyes throbbing between silver and red.

Her nose flared as a foreign feeling joined what he was inciting.

Kin had once talked about the more risque benefits of a mating bond, the one that had interested her the most was the shared sensations they felt during sex.

Her imagination hadn't done the experience any justice. Confusion at the first hint of it when she could both feel the heat of his hardness, as well as the slick heat of her core. It threw her off balance. Her belly tightened with the overwhelming stimulus. Her breath came quickly as she tried to get accustomed to the feeling even as he increased both the pressure of his grip and the speed of his tongue. Or was that her?

Alessandro's teeth grazed the tip of her nipple, the only warning before a canine slipped and sent a delicious spark of pain to her core.

His reaction to the move was mesmerizing. He hissed and went tense for a moment before growling and standing at his full height to stare down at her.

"It's no wonder you like it rough, little elf."

The nickname ignited her irritation.

"What is it?"

Could he feel her emotions now?

She tried to move on by running her hand underneath his shirt. The feel of a ghost hand over her chest was exhilarating, but he halted it.

"Tell me."

"I'm not just an elf." She hissed.

His eyes swirled as they swept across her face. Confusion furrowed his eyebrows together and his eyes swirled with streaks of yellow. "I've called you that since the first day. Why haven't you said anything?"

"Because..." Her words faltered. "...Because if I brought it up, and I got even the slightest idea that you were trying to overlook the other half of me, my pride would allow nothing less than for me to walk away."

He bared his fangs, black scales rolled across his face, and his eyes flashed crimson. "I know you don't understand shifter customs. But mentioning walking away before the mark settles isn't something I'd recommend."

"You asked me to tell you!" She hissed.

"For the record. I only call you little elf because little elf succubus is a bit of a mouthful, and when we fuck, there's very little room for anything other than you in there. Your succubus is the reason you're able to bear me at my maximum. It's why, even though I can't seem to get enough, I know that it'll just take a moment for you to be ready for another go. You think I could disregard her?"

Her nails dragged across his ribs, and her nipples ached.

"Well, as long as you're obsessed with her."

"I am. I am obsessed with all of you." He crushed her mouth with his and the dresser dug into the small of her back.

She was breathless as he pulled away again, taking the back of her neck into his massive hand. An action that always made her succubus want to fuck him into submission. He halted her movements by pressing their bodies closer together, taking her ability to breathe. It was a reminder of how much of a physical advantage he had. It thrilled her. "Since the moment you tried to punch me that very first night, every single cell in my body has urged me to claim you as mine. I tried to warn you, Rowan Dahl. You stepped over the threshold again and again, thinking you were safe from my beast. But now you've willingly chained yourself up to me. You don't know what you've unleashed."

She raised her chin in defiance. "Now, now, let's not forget who claimed who first, Alessandro. Everything you do is because I will it. You are *my* beast."

This time she was prepared when he showed his true face. Despite the warmth of her bloody tears running down her cheek, she stared him down. She smirked and raised a hand to cup the side of his face. "There's my little terror. Now down on your knees for me."

His nose flared and desire throbbed off of him in waves intermingled with a violence that had his fist clenching and unclenching at the base of her neck.

He swore as her nails ghosted over the fabric that clung to his back. The sensations of what she was imposing on him with her actions assaulted her.

"Only ever for you." His words were a whisper in the stuffy air of the room.

She wanted inside of him. Or was that his desire? Dammit. Lust clouded her mind. She was close to her first orgasm and her pants had yet to come off.

Oh wait. There they went, along with the Dragon King, who kept his eyes locked on hers as he followed her command.

She bit her lip so hard she drew blood. She'd expected a fight. But he was eager to bend to her will. This kind of power he gave her fucked with her head.

He summoned a pin to pull back his hair. And she flicked it away. She wanted him wild.

-A-

Her tail slid from his shoulder to his cheek, leaving a trail of heat in its wake.

The woman was a fucking menace to everything Alessandro believed to be true to himself.

Here he was on his knees.

A candidate for godhood.

On.

His.

Godsdamned.

Knees.

Alessandro caught the extra appendage in his hands and eyed the visible shudder the touch brought her. He had to pause as the sensation he'd given returned to him. It was so similar to how it felt when she gripped his cock that for a moment, he lost the thread of where he ended and she began.

When he recollected himself, he gripped the back of her thigh and pressed his nose into her core.

Her scent was all flower and spice, her taste liquid fire on his tongue.

His hand stroked the length of her tail while he guided her leg over his shoulder, giving him more access to a nectar more addicting than ambrosia.

Her fingers tangled in his hair, her moans ripped through the air. The only reason she remained standing was because of his hold on her.

She was finally melting. Releasing some of that control she had over him.

It was becoming easier to distinguish his own pleasure from hers. He used it as a guide on how much pressure to use and when to ratchet up his speed all while his tongue became coated in the addicting notes of tang and heat that was all Rowan Dahl.

Focusing on the rigid bundle of nerves that had breathless vibrations of pleasure crashing out of her, he licked, sucked and nibbled until he could feel she was nearing the edge.

He pulled out the trick he'd been reserving for her peak as her heart rate reached a fevered rate. Ice coated his tongue, and she roared her release, hand pulling hard on his hair, legs trembling as she tried to figure out what he'd done. Her release coated his tongue, so abundant that the slickness slid down his chin.

He laid a soft kiss on the engorged bud and she pulled her hips back with a hiss, still sensitive.

Her chest was heaving. "Who taught you that?" she demanded.

He smirked, "Jealous?"

She let out a laugh of disbelief. "How could I be jealous when I'm reaping the reward of their hard work?"

Her lack of jealousy was surprisingly refreshing. He'd thought he liked the territorialism that came with his dragon lovers, but perhaps that had been because they hadn't found other ways to express that they cared for him.

Rowan had just thrown her treasured independence away for his freedom. She hadn't made a single demand in exchange, just showed up to drag him out of his self imposed cage, brought him back to the bars of his people's expectations and told him she'd be willing to wait right beside him until he could free himself.

His dragon had never been so right about anything else in his life. Rowan Dahl was the perfect beast to calm his own.

He laid a hand on the small of her back and pulled her forward, sealing her mouth in a kiss full of heat and the promise of so much more to come.

XXIX

"**O**f all the irresponsible directions you could have taken your life, you became the Dragon King's property?" Lilith was as enthralling as the mother of all succubi should be. She had full pouty lips, suggestive frosty amethyst eyes, and a voluptuous body enshrouded in barely there fabric that left absolutely nothing to the imagination. Rowan had never known her long silky black hair to know disarray. Though, as she paced the entirety of Rowan's kitchen, she was getting close.

She was the only other person Rowan knew to have the extra limbs of succubi, though she had four horns. Two that curved around her head and pointed straight back and two that pointed up. Her wings were massive, though she could call them forth or put them away with a special bit of magic her goddaughter had no access to.

When Rowan had asked why she was the only one to have the appendages, Lilith's explanation was unsatisfying. She supposed her mother and sisters' lack of extra appendages was because of their lack of magic. Most succubi held a ton of dark magic at their command. The more powerful their dark magic was, the bigger the markers were.

"Chew!" Axel growled as she, for the third time, hit Rowan's back to keep her from choking on her feast.

"Five days of non-stop sex." Annabelle sighed, "Maybe your father and I are due for a vacation."

Lilith slammed her hands on the table. "Belle, concentrate. We have to come up with a plan to rid your spawn of this dilemma!"

"I don't think it's a dilemma." Lexine was happily helping herself to a small portion of Rowan's meal. "While she was bedridden, you should've seen the way he looked at her through the door. It was swoon worthy."

"That man is the bane of my existence!" Lilith hissed.

When Rowan untangled herself from what Alessandro had called the mark's settling period—AKA five days of sex that only stopped for food, water and sleep—the last thing she wanted to do was to entertain the very irate mother of all succubi who had a past record of hating her mate.

She would have much rather phased out with her plate of protein to rejoin him in bed. But Terra had made it crystal clear that she wasn't to return to Draconis until the ceremony that would introduce her to the Thunder as their new queen consort.

Even though Rowan and Alessandro had agreed, they did indeed need to get back to their responsibilities that morning and as such had taken down the barrier that his dragon had put up the very moment they'd phased from the hoard to Draconis. They'd both been reluctant to let each other go through their last breakfast together. This resulted in Rowan eating most of her breakfast perched right on his lap.

It was when he'd fed her strawberries off his plate that they made eye contact. It was the flame on her fuse. The kiss, meant to curb her appetite only made her more ravenous and soon they were making out, ready to tear each other's clothes off.

Terra, who had the unfortunate responsibility of clearing the way for everyone else to show up, had to pull them apart. She reminded them as gently as she could, considering her skin was rolling with bronze scales, that they had things to do.

She killed the excitement by reminding them that a possible Cursed with a vendetta against the shifters was still at large. Then she led Rowan from the table, grabbing her plate of food and accompanying her all the way to the wrap-around porch of her cabin, which had yet to move even once.

After filling her in on what to expect over the next few hours, three wide-eyed dragons walked up to their King's porch, each holding two stuffed-to-the-brim banker's boxes. Terra informed Rowan that they were each full of time sensitive paperwork that Alessandro hadn't been able to get to in the two weeks he'd ignored his duties because he had been so busy dealing with her and the witch.

The cabin had changed location as soon as Rowan had stepped foot on its premises, dropping in next to her mother's garden where Lilith and Annabelle, Lexine and Axel were in the middle of tea time.

Rowan wondered how the hell Terra had overridden her ownership to the cabin even for that little command, but she didn't have time to mull it over as her godmother exploded into a fit of fury.

The scent of her nemesis all over her godchild had sent Lilith on a furious tirade of curses and death threats.

The mark on Rowan's collarbone constantly dragging the violet eyes of her godmother in and igniting them with rage.

Axel passed Rowan a glass of water to help her swallow a large bite of steak.

"What exactly did he do to you?" her sister asked. "You've never told us the story."

Lilith took a deep breath. "He's a constant wedge in my relationship with Luz. If I had it my way, I'd have taken him out the first time he did it, but he is under his protection."

Rowan highly doubted, even with all of her power, that Lilith could really beat Alessandro if he was really trying.

"He knows Uncle Luz?" Lexine gasped.

Lucifer was an eternal homebody. Rowan had seen him out of his corner of the endless hells twice in her life. Once for her sixth birthday, because six was his favorite number and on her graduation day from Spellcasters Academy.

Any other quality time they'd shared had occured in the halls of his black glass castle in his chosen corner of the endless hells where Rowan even had her own wing.

"Not as well as I do." Lilith snarled.

Rowan raised an eyebrow as she took the last bite of her collection. Was that jealousy she sensed from the woman? She never would've thought the woman even had the capacity for such a feeling.

"This was my choice, Auntie Lilith. I know it isn't what you wanted for me, but you are still invited to my formal introduction to the Thunder if you promise to behave."

Lilith's magic lashed out, grabbing a blue and green vase from the countertop.

Rowan dodged, and the glass erupted into shards against the wall behind her.

That was enough. "That was an antique!" Rowan hissed as she stood to her full height, though it was nothing on the towering form of her godmother. "Look, it's done. The alternatives are worse than the reality. I made a choice and you're the one always saying we have to pay the consequences for our decisions. You might have envisioned something different for me, but I'm not that five-year-old kid who needed you to keep me tethered to the ground when I couldn't control my magic. I am grown and I want you to see what I become because you were such a big part of my development. So will you stay and see what the product of your hard work is, or will you leave?"

No one had ever spoken like this to Lilith, especially not one of her succubi.

Her bottom lip trembled, carefully looking Rowan over, really seeing her for the very first time.

She took in the horns, wings, and tail that denoted her succubus descent, but her eyes almost always traveled back to the mark.

She held her hand out to the side. Rowan braced for impact, but instead of slapping her, Lilith summoned a small opalescent ball.

"If my lineage converges with that creature's we're going to make them realize how lucky they are. This is Odin's Eye--" She held it out towards Lexine. "--Work on this while Belle and I gather the wardrobe for tonight. Axel, you and your father go pick out the worm's present. Just remember, he's a dragon. If it shines, he'll like it."

Rowan beamed at the black-haired woman as she palmed the object, warm and full of magic. "And just how do you have Odin's Eye?"

"I won it during a poker match with the sloppy pervert." Lilith shrugged. "Do not make me regret this, Rowan Dahl. If he treats you poorly, I will take his head. As your godmother, it is my right."

A win was a win, right?

-A-

"Mother, you said you would control your cousin." Terra's voice preceded her appearance in Alessandro's fitting room.

Naseem worked in a concentrated flurry around him, closing the brown leather straps of Alessandro's traditional dragon garb. Stone was polishing the black and gold crown that the Dragon King hadn't laid eyes on in ages. Had it always been so bulky?

"I've taken care of it, Terra. She won't disrupt the ceremony." The soothing voice of Alessandro's adoptive father was a balm to the nerves that had settled in the pit of his stomach.

He hadn't realized how bad they'd gotten until that moment.

A part of him feared Rowan wouldn't show up. That she would conclude that their union was not what she wanted, that she'd acted out of some insanity.

All day he'd fought visions of his dragons turning to him with betrayal in their eyes. How could he have rejected one of their own for so long only to choose someone who wanted nothing to do with them?

"Well, well, no wonder you have everyone groaning in disappointment. You make a handsome mate, son." Phineas' hazel eyes twinkled as he took in the splendor of Alessandro.

Decked out in soft green and cream silks that matched the silks of both his wife and daughter behind him, the man wasn't half bad himself. There was a certain charm that the joyful man always seemed to exude, softening even the harshest of realities.

"I just need to work on being as charming as you and I'll be quite the package." Alessandro smirked as Naseem adjusted the final strap and stepped back.

Phineas let out a laugh from the belly and clapped a hand on his shoulder with affection, with his eyes on the mark on Alessandro's forehead he whistled, "I half believed this was all a joke, but that's a mate mark for sure. Where's your other half? I'd hoped we could get a sneak peek at her as repayment for raising you all these years."

Anya, who looked to be as regal as Terra, had her curls done up in intricate knots weaved with golden thread. She lightly slapped her husband's chest with the back of her hand. "You've repaid us plenty, honey." Her chestnut brown eyes traveled over his face and concern etched the slight crease of her brow.

Despite their many years on Alessandro, the couple had barely aged a day since she'd taken him in. Such was the gift of a long lifespan that the family now looked like a collection of brothers and sisters.

Anya didn't voice her concern. She merely raised a hand and laid it gently on Alessandro's cheek.

Tension released from his shoulders, and he nuzzled her palm in gratitude.

"The heirs of the houses have their people gathered and accounted for in the coliseum." Terra said with the slightest smile on her face. "Are you ready, my king?"

Stone raised the crown, and Alessandro knelt.

Like always, it felt heavy as it settled upon his brow. He despised the thing, but when all those in the room gazed at him with it on, it reminded him of its necessity.

He was their pride and hope with it on. Their protector, whether it be from the outside world or from themselves.

The stadium was full of as many dragons that could make it to the ceremony. The roar from the sheer size of the crowd was deafening as he made his way to the pair of matching thrones set on the raised stage at the center of the stadium.

Terra had outdone herself with the decorations. Where there was usually dirt and training equipment, she'd raised a garden of blooms that peppered the air with the sweet smell of nectar. The rows of bone white seating had never been brighter, each section draped with cotton linens. The crests of every family hung from each box, thousands of them reminding him how far a small village had come through the years.

From his first footstep into their view, a hush fell over the crowd. Terra stayed back to await Rowan and her family. His parents tore from his side as they approached their own family branch.

Aqua and Blaise stood at the base of the steps, joining Stone and Naseem behind him as they ascended.

His generals lined up next to his throne. Stone diverted to stand next to where Rowan would take her place. When he sat, Alessandro took in the faces of those looking down at him.

Some were eager, but he could sense the disappointment of many.

Facing the entrance again, he felt his dragon settle into the familiar cadence of Rowan's name. Though the marking had settled the more territorial aspects of his dragon, Rowan had not yet given him everything that a bond like mates required. She hadn't so much as grazed their connection with a curious tug, or given memories to it. She remained as distant as the day she told him to fuck off.

Yes. She desired him, perhaps more than she'd ever desired anyone. She enjoyed their time together. But that wasn't enough. He needed her trust, her devotion, her fucking heart on a platter.

When he felt her magic, as slight as it had become after her injury, his dragon relented in the chants. He relaxed into his throne, but it was a momentary condition.

His breath left him as he took in her visage.

Underneath an intricate golden wired corset, the woman wore black and blue swaths of thin fabrics that hugged every curve. His colors. How had she known? Had she seen it in a vision? They had never appealed so much to him.

Tendrils of white hair curled along her shoulders. Golden cuffs hugged the base of her black horns. They glinted underneath the flames of the surrounding torches. Her black wings acted like a cape as she kept them carefully tucked away.

For a moment he thought she'd found some way to heal her missing eye, but as his attention zeroed in on the new appendage, he recognized the starry iris as Odin's Eye.

His favorite part of her ensemble was the golden scale mail that made up shoulder and neck pieces. They framed her creamy breasts, showcasing their mating mark for the entire kingdom to see.

Without realizing it, he was on his feet and a wide grin that warmed everything inside of him took residence on her face. How could she look at him like that and yet keep what he needed most from her just out of reach?

Her full attention was on him and even the weight of the crown couldn't stop him from taking the untraditional action of leaving his chair to meet her at the bottom of the steps.

Before her, he hadn't known it would be possible for anyone to look at him the way she did every single time he met her. As if their separation was too long, as if he was the sun coming out after weeks of night.

It cemented his resolve.

He leaned down and captured her mouth in a kiss that put everything on the table. He was utterly hers. The rest of the world be damned.

The action set the crowd into a frenzy of whispers. The Dragon King had never been publicly affectionate with his candidates before. To witness it was a stronger confirmation that he had found his mate than even the ceremony.

Her magic, as diminished as it was, brushed against the bond. Sweet, sweet progress.

Peace only lasted the briefest moment as he felt three very familiar and concerning magical signatures.

His eyes cut up to where her guests had arrived. Family and friends along with a very cocky and impeccably dressed raven-haired woman with the wings, horns and tails denoting her as the mother of all succubi blood, Lilith. A stoic blonde-haired, blonde-bearded and blue eyed-man Alessandro hadn't seen out of the endless hells in nearly a century, Lucifer. And a wary, surprisingly sober viking of a witch, Japhet.

Terra was leading them to their reserved box, shooting him a concerned look when their eyes met.

He glanced down at Rowan, who had caught the tension and was following his line of sight.

"We're definitely going to talk about how you fit into all of those relationships. For now, shall we continue, Dragon King?"

He took her small hand in his. He'd never quite realized how much smaller she was. "Before you climb those steps, there's been a change of plans."

She raised an eyebrow. "What?"

"Rowan, this isn't your place. I'm no longer sure this is even mine."

Her bright blue eye filled with confusion, Odin's Eye reacted by glimmering.

He took a deep breath and looked around. Her confusion reflected in all the faces that stared down at them, the buzz of whispers growing into a roar the longer they stood there.

"I'm going to announce my retirement." Saying it out loud brought him a sense of relief he never thought he'd feel when he pictured this day.

Rowan's confusion melted into understanding. He could feel her prodding their bond, attempting to figure out what was happening.

"Right now?" She asked softly.

"Well, they are gathered." He shrugged.

She shook her head. "Oh my gods, they're totally going to blame me! Alessandro, are you sure? Or is this a side effect from the mark?"

He raised an eyebrow. "Have I not made it clear I am an over-thinker before I decide on a move? I told you in the cave that Stone could take my place with the support of my generals. It was the truth. I started planning all of this when you were lying on that hospital bed. I knew I'd reached a point of no return. My plan was to ask for your neck after the power was fully transferred. But you pushed my dragon too far by offering the bite."

She was ready to lash out, but he stopped her with a soft kiss. "My generals are aware of what this is. My heir is willing and ready to try his hand at power. It'll be a slow transition, so you will sit at my side during this period. It won't be traditional, and it won't be easy, but it is what is right."

She narrowed her eyes. "This really should have been a conversation."

He scoffed. "I tried to make it one, several times, but you kept jumping my bones."

She scoffed, "I kept jumping your bones? I was half convinced you were an incubus."

He grinned down at her and held his hand out. "What do you say, Rowan Dahl? Want to be my queen for whatever time my reign remains?"

"Well, they *are* gathered." She echoed his words and took his hand, "You're sure sure?"

"I'm sure, sure." He kissed her knuckles before turning and leading the way back up.

He could feel her shock over the declaration as they climbed. If nothing else, the bond allowed him to feel her emotions, and he'd gotten plenty of practice during their five day escape. He felt the moment her shock faded into nervousness. He squeezed her hand to remind her she wasn't alone.

Stone stepped up when they reached the top-most landing, a smaller version of his black and gold crown in hand.

Rowan gave his hand one last squeeze before dropping it.

He returned to his seat, silence returning as he shot a look around at the whispering crowd.

Rowan knelt before his heir, tilting her head up to meet his steady gaze.

"Princess Rowan Dahl of the Eastern Elven Kingdom, before the Thunder, before the Dragon King Alessandro, before our ancestors, we are here to welcome you into our ranks, not only as an esteemed honorary member, but as our queen consort." The stomps began small and slow from the bleachers. Stone beamed down at her as if pleased by the sound. "Will you accept the duties to support the Dragon King Alessandro's role through a dedicated study of our laws and culture to shape a more successful future of dragon kind?" Stone's voice thundered to every crook and cranny of the stadium as the stomps began gathering speed and more participation.

These moments made being their king worth it. Alessandro basked in the sound of his Thunder coming together.

"I will." She answered, casting the same spell with what Alessandro could feel was a monumental effort.

She masked her pain, and he had to clench his fists to stop from reaching out towards her. He would never cut her power in front of his people. They needed to believe she was as strong as she'd shown herself to be on the mountainside of Barros' hideout, even if their rule was to be short.

"In exchange, the Thunder pledges you our loyalty, our respect. I introduce you, from this day forth, as Rowan Dahl of the Draconian Thunder!" Stone roared, raising the crown high above his head as if to show it off to all those gathered.

Deafening roars ripped from his elemental generals. The roars of the Thunder topped the feverish tempo of the stomps joining in.

An unexpected wave of their faith washed over Alessandro, startling him.

Rowan Dahl had made an impression on his people. He wondered how much he had missed from the rumor mills as their prayers of gratitude passed through his ear. It was overwhelming.

Overhead, lightning ripped across the sky, bright and white with thunder that rattled his teeth.

Alessandro glanced at the direction the spell had emerged from and Lucifer discretely flipped him off.

His attention returned to Rowan, who bowed her head as Stone lowered the crown.

As it settled, through the continuing roars and cheers, Rowan unfurled to her full height, bearing the weight like a natural.

The generals each fell to one knee before her.

It surprised Alessandro as the entire stadium rose and silence reigned as the Thunder genuflected.

It wasn't a requirement or a custom of coronation, but a gift.

He stood once more and tucked her into his side.

"*Rise.*" His command gonged through the coliseum.

He took a beat to examine the faces that rose. There was still disappointment sown in here and there, but overall, the acceptance of an elven-succubus as their queen was unequivocal.

"The last couple of weeks have tested us as a people." He began, "But more than I could have ever hoped, I know you will be ready for the next test. Beginning today, I will begin taking a step away from my duties as your king."

Hisses of shock and mumblings began immediately.

He raised his hand to bring back the silence. "As I step away, Stone of the Draconian Thunder will ease into the role he has been preparing for over a decade. I was what you needed in the beginning days, but times have changed and to continue our prosperity, it is necessary that we change with them. I implore you to give him the support you've given me during my reign."

XXX

Rowan wasn't sure what the consensus of the dragons had been after Alessandro's announcement.

The unity that they'd shown in her crowning had crumbled into confusion.

She wasn't sure how to react until the sight of a familiar woman caught her attention and made her back straighten with anxiety.

There was a certain built-in hazard of being any percentage of succubus that created friction between a succubus and a monogamous partner's loved ones.

While Rowan had never faced it herself, she'd been part of Axel's countless recoveries from the backlash when her truth came out. Her dedication to being her sister's emotional support buddy in those cases was the true origin of her addiction to cheesecake and ice cream.

Terra and a couple of other Earth Dragons were finishing the touches on concrete slabs being floated out to make a makeshift dance floor, while Naseem and other air dragons floated tables and chairs to box in the space.

Rowan had been counting on the Earth General to be her second grounding point for this introduction, but it seemed she would have to rely solely on Alessandro.

Alessandro, who looked to be as at ease as a man who'd retired from 50 years in an office job rather than a king who had just upset the whole balance of his kingdom within a short 10 second speech.

"You're more nervous about this than taking the crown?" Alessandro teased as he took her hand in his.

Rowan scowled, "Well, you already know my family, and get along with most of them."

He scoffed, "Are you attempting to make how we get along with each other's family a competition, little elf?"

Some of the apprehension melted at the soft teasing and she grinned. "Just who do you think you took on as a mate?"

He returned her smile and tipped his head to the group who had grown larger the closer they got.

Anya, as warm in real life as in Alessandro's memories, had her in her arms before Rowan could curtsy.

The new queen consort returned the hug with just as much warmth, her face perfectly cradled on Anya's ample chest. She felt as if she'd known the woman her entire life from the visions Alessandro had shared. Rowan wondered if Anya felt just as connected to her as she did.

When Rowan pulled away, there was nothing but relief in the earth-dragon's eyes.

"Of course, we'd seen pictures of you, but I just couldn't believe it." The eldest of the three women that had followed Anya gasped, breaking the moment as she fluttered around Rowan, examining Rowan's wings more closely. "Look at this lovely sheen. What do you use? My wing girl has me on a salmon diet that's been killing my love for sea creatures."

"I heard that you and that no-good brat Stone went to Spellcasters together? Were you ever a thing? You kind of look like his type. Of course, the boy doesn't really have control once a pretty girl looks his way. You'd think he doesn't know that he's out of the ugly duckling stage from how he reacts to a little flirting." Said the middle, both more quickly and more unintelligible.

This earned the woman a growl of warning from Alessandro, who stood behind Rowan like a looming shadow.

"My goodness, you look just like your father." The youngest one spoke, attempting to break the tension, "'Cept the wings and tails and horns. Must come from your mom's side."

"Ladies, ladies, where are your manners?" Anya asked, shooing them back. "I'm so sorry dear, my cousins are just excited to meet you."

Rowan smiled. "To be fair, I'd be curious as well. To answer a few of your questions: I am on a strict multivitamin regiment as recommended by my eldest sister who is an amazing doctor and moonlights as an esthetician. I went to school with Stone. We were not a thing, though I always thought he always looked too long at my bestie. She's a total smoke show, right over there in the blood red dress. And the succubus is a gift from my mother and our ancestors."

This only encouraged an explosion of more questions from the women, and Alessandro let out a tendril of his power to cow them back in line.

"These are my aunties." He gestured to each. "Vera, Oksana and Galina." He pointed to the others behind him, "These are Galina's children, Alana." Alana was a pretty brunette with catlike hazel eyes that told Rowan the girl wished she could be anywhere else in the world. "And Helios." Helios was handsome, with sharp facial features. His hair, while cut short, was as curly and dark as any of his family. His lean frame reminded her of a professional swimmer.

He was carrying a dozing five-year-old half-dragon in his arms. The child had his blue hair picked out into a small afro, dressed in an all white linen two-piece suit. "His son, Ciel and mate, Opal."

Opal was a harpy, she had white plumage that trailed behind her and over massive thighs that narrowed into scaled legs and clawed feet. Her ice blue hair was up in a tight bun, neat and away from her no-nonsense face of sharp angles. Her eyes were bright as they took Rowan in.

She was on the defensive, ready to lash out if Rowan took a wrong step.

"I heard you were the only one in the Thunder that could relate to my position as an outsider taking a dragon mate."

Surprise widened Opal's eyes. "Y-Yes."

"Would it be okay to have you over for lunch at some point so we could talk?"

The words seemed to create tension in Galina that Rowan hadn't expected. Opal caught it and narrowed her eyes, irritation clear.

"I would love to." She answered, eyes unwavering from the woman.

Alessandro pulled Rowan back seconds before the two women were at each other's throats.

Feathers and hair flew in every direction as the two moved at speeds Rowan found impressive, considering they wore layers of jewelry and dragon garb that threatened the occurrence of a serious wardrobe malfunction.

Terra shot Phineas a look. "You said you took care of it."

"If you recall, I said she wouldn't disrupt the ceremony. The ceremony is over." He grimaced.

Helios sighed and held his child up to Alessandro, who took him without a second of hesitation. Rowan noted that her mate was so large the sleeping child could fit into the crook of one arm.

Phineas cursed as he and Helios reached in to tear the two women apart while hoots and whistles egged them on.

"That wasn't my fault, was it?" Rowan asked.

They took another step back as the fight fanned out to include bystanders who had their own grievances against each other.

"No." He scowled. "This happens every time they see each other."

"Should you stop it?"

"I don't get involved in the affairs of in-family power struggles."

"Even your own?" She raised an eyebrow.

He hesitated, "I'm not blood."

"Enough!" Anya's snarl preceded the emergence of two vines that snapped through the tiles and slapped the two women down to the ground, "It is my son's special day and you dare disrespect him by fighting over this ongoing petty dispute?"

"You bitch!" Galina screeched and from the buffet tables off to the side, fruits came flying, aimed at Anya's head.

Alessandro's reflexes saved Rowan from a stray orange, and the fight exploded to include Anya.

Irritation swelled in Rowan and she tried to tamp it down, but as her own family approached and she saw an apple hit her father, she'd had enough.

She fingered the necklace hidden underneath her neckpiece, but as she was quickly learning, she was going to have to rely on more than magic for a while.

Using the years of training with Axel and her father, she caught on to the rhythm of the fight. She found an opening to execute her plan.

A punch in the face from Galina, a slash on her back from Opal and a whip of the vine to her leg from Anya had her reeling in sharp pain for the briefest of seconds.

She stamped down the urge to hit back that was as ingrained in her as her tendency to reach for magic first and ask questions later.

She whipped her hair back and straightened the crown as she set a glare to all three of the women, who stood in shock.

"Sorry to interrupt this fight with my coronation." She cleared her throat and looked toward Alessandro. He stood stock still, his mouth slightly ajar. "I think I'd like a drink."

Alessandro let out a short laugh, beamed at her and took her hand, the sleeping baby still in the crook of his arm as they walked away.

-A-

Alessandro wanted nothing more than to whisk his mate away for maybe five more days of uninterrupted alone time to reward her for her brilliance in handling his family.

He glanced down to take her in once more and cursed when he saw the blood sliding down her face.

He was dabbing at the wound when her family reached them.

Lucifer looked unimpressed. "You can't even keep her from being mauled by your family? How will she fare against your enemies?"

The words packed more of a punch than Alessandro would have cared to admit.

"That was called respect for my decision, Uncle Luz." Rowan interjected.

"That was called weakness." Lucifer's eyes hadn't moved from Alessandro and he felt Rowan's irritation flare.

"This isn't even about me." She snapped and turned to the rest of her family. "Shots?"

"And carrot cake!" Axel held her arm out.

Rowan stood on the tips of her toes to give him a kiss before she and her family disappeared, dragging Lilith along as she glared at him, but didn't utter a word.

"She had my protection," Lucifer hissed. "Your nose should've smelled it my miles away."

Alessandro took a deep breath and motioned towards her retreating figure. "Lucifer, I claimed the woman five days ago. How strong is my smell?"

Lucifer narrowed his own eyes as he sought the scent out and shock eased some of the tension off his shoulders. "That can't be."

"She's like a filter for power, cleansing it out of any other ownership and claiming it as her own." Alessandro shook his head. "Her chakra paths are repairing themselves at a rate that within a month she will be back to one hundred percent. Before that happens, I need to understand what she is, because she's not just a succubus or an elf. What did you set up to protect her from?"

Lucifer's eyes pulsed with a sheen of red that Alessandro associated with the most reckless violence he'd ever witnessed.

"I was hiding her from my asshole siblings. She's the first demon Blessed. I'm going to have to figure out some new way of hiding her."

Alessandro frowned. "But she has divinity. They wouldn't harm one of their own descendants."

Lucifer narrowed his blood-red eyes and raked them over the dragon. "She's mostly a succubus. Any divinity you sense is negligible."

There was something about his tone that made the Dragon King's hackles rise. He was attempting to be duplicitous. But Lucifer never lied. Instead, he tried to shroud answers in shadows.

Alessandro cocked his head to the side and glanced back towards the collection of white-haired guests.

"It's faint, but she overcame demon poison. That's not negligible."

"Maybe the demon poison wasn't pure enough. You might have been mistaken. It's not the first time it's happened. You remember that hellish night when you swore three bottles of ambrosia-laced whiskey wouldn't affect you?"

He wouldn't take the bait. The one and only time Alessandro had truly allowed himself to let go with Lucifer, and the night that had sealed the friendship were the same. Though they argued often about the details, neither really knew the full story of what occurred that night.

All Alessandro knew was that when they awoke, they'd been in another dimension with a pack of satyrs and that never boded well.

Chasing away the images and the stench of that day, Alessandro focused on what Lucifer was trying to conceal.

It was easy to pick up on divinity once someone realized it was there. Alessandro had assumed the trace of divinity in Rowan came from her father's side as the idea that a succubus as strong as Annabelle, even without the usual markers of wings, horns and tails, having any divinity, was absurd.

A spell of misdirection protected her genetic status from much less trained spellcasters, but Lucifer's brand of magic was familiar to Alessandro and he navigated the spell to show him the truth.

Annabelle Dahl was a third generation divine.

Bright white specks colored her aura, and when he glanced over at her daughters, he realized why he had initially missed the presence of divinity. The first time he sought Rowan's magical signature, he'd noted that the colors of her demonic and elemental magic were brighter than usual. Lucifer had somehow hidden the white of divine magic behind them to saturate their appearance.

"What have you two done?" Alessandro hissed, turning his wide eyes to the devil.

Lucifer's nose flared, and his eyes flashed ruby. "You should have walked away."

Unaffected by the show of his anger, Alessandro pressed on, "How?"

Lucifer rolled his eyes, "When a mommy and a daddy..."

"Cut the shit, Lucifer. Rowan didn't know. Why wouldn't you tell her?"

Lucifer shook his head. "It should never have happened. When Lilith realized what she'd done, it was too late to reverse it. All she wanted was to see what a child between us would look like. What she did with Adam out of hatred, she wanted with me out of love. It fucked her up emotionally and you know how dangerous that is for someone with her power of creation."

Alessandro clenched his fists. "So, your little love child created an elf-demon-divine?"

"Yes, Annabelle."

"And Rowan is your great-grandchild."

"You can see why I am displeased with your attachment," Lucifer hissed.

Alessandro leveled him with a glare. "I don't recall you ever telling me you had a child, much less a great-grandchild. I might have taken precautions against landing in bed with her!"

Lucifer scowled, "No one can know."

"Shouldn't she at least know? And don't insinuate she does. She's my mate."

"Don't you start a territorial war with me, Dragon King. She is my blood." Lucifer hissed.

"Lucifer!" Alessandro was trying to hold back the urge to shake the man.

Lilith appeared beside them. "Would you two like a microphone to ensure everyone can hear your conversation?" Her face was splotchy with anger, her eyes rimmed red and glazed.

The child in Alessandro's arms wiggled for a second before his breath evened back out.

Alessandro glanced around and noticed there were several dragons coming close, as if trying to decipher the whispered argument.

"I would take several steps back if I were you, Janio."

The water-dragon, who had been the closest, did as bid. The rest followed suit.

"I suggest you recall that you're the one who sunk your teeth into our Rowan, even after you found the divinity present in her demon lineage. You were ready to take the consequences of that decision, and that shouldn't change now that you know where it came from." Lilith said evenly.

Alessandro let out a displeased growl. "It doesn't affect my decision in the slightest. But I'm sure it will affect her opinion of you when she finds out the truth."

Panic took over her face. "This doesn't concern you. You mustn't be the one to reveal it."

"Now that I know about it, I can't conceal it from her. She is my mate."

"Can you truly say that when you didn't know of our relationship with her?" Lilith hissed, "Your mark is unsettled, worm."

His dragon reared up in rage.

"Don't," Alessandro warned quietly, keeping his nephew in mind.

Lucifer's eyes widened. "What does that mean?"

The smug look the black-haired woman wore threatened to break Alessandro's control. She hadn't been sure until his reaction cemented her theory.

"She chose me." Alessandro spoke slowly. "I will not betray her trust to keep your secret. You have one week to figure it the fuck out and tell her yourselves."

The child in Alessandro's arms fussed.

He glanced down and sleepy blue eyes blinked open, as if making sure what he was seeing was true.

A giant smile took over Ciel's face, and he wrapped his arms around Alessandro's neck, choking him with his excitement. It melted the anger he'd felt growing out of check.

Alessandro chuckled as he tried to wrangle the child off. "Did you sleep well, little one?"

"Ciel is hungry!" Ciel crawled over Alessandro's head to sit himself on his shoulders, "Onward, Unc Sando."

Alessandro, knowing the only thing that stood between Ciel turning into an outright brat, relied heavily on how fast he could get food in his belly, laughed, "Alright, alright, give me just a second, okay?"

Ciel groaned, but crossed his arms over Alessandro's head and settled his chin into them as he waited as patiently as a hungry five-year-old could.

"Look, we're going to have to deal with each other more than we've ever had in the past, Lilith. I'd rather we work towards a more amicable future for Rowan's sake, but I'll never bow my head to your insensitivity, especially with her. One week."

And Ciel's small hands were pulling at Alessandro's hair to guide him as he turned.

XXXI

Rowan felt the moment the air became charged with danger. She'd been in the middle of shotgunning a pre-made cocktail with Blaise, Stone, and Louisa when the explosion of magic licked against her skin.

"What is that?" Annabelle hissed as she took a deep inhale.

"Smoke." Her father whispered. His eyes snapped to the entrance they'd used to get to the coliseum. It led out to the free weight room of their massive gym.

A body hurtled past the line of demarcation, a dragon who bore deep crimson slashes over his chest and arms.

Alessandro phased to catch him before he hit the floor, Ciel on his shoulders, looking down at the man with concern.

"Black Cove." The dragon growled. "The whole damn city is attacking."

Rowan watched as Blaise, Naseem, and Stone phased out without prompting.

Aqua phased next to the man and had already begun weaving spells of healing as Terra began yelling instructions to the remaining dragons.

Helios phased in next to Alessandro, collecting his son and placing a kiss on his forehead before depositing him into Opal's awaiting arms.

Rowan watched Opal fight back the urge to reach out to his retreating form as he followed a wave of dragons back into Draconis before she herself phased out.

It occurred to Rowan that if Draconis was being attacked the families had nowhere to go. Then she realized she'd never seen a dragon family in Draconis to begin with, nor enough space to house all of those who'd shown up for her coronation.

Her nose flared as something was on the verge of clicking before Alessandro phased in front of her.

His rainbow eyes swirled with hues of red. She'd never known the color to have so much range.

"I'll get back to you as soon as I can."

Confusion filled her before fury took its place as the world blurred from her vision before it reassembled to show the familiar shadow of the Eastern Elven Kingdom's castle.

Sidelined.

The hurt bubbled inside and she snapped her head to Louisa, who had appeared a second later, followed closely by her family.

"He said you need to stay here and protect your family," Louisa said before Rowan could even open her mouth.

Rowan narrowed her eyes. "Who exactly are your loyalties to, Louisa?"

Louisa leveled her with a stern stare before she wavered and groaned, "Fine, but no magic."

Axel grinned, holding her hand out and conjuring a giant tomahawk from mid-air. "Never needed magic myself."

Kin sighed, "I'm surprised I'm still alive after half the shit you two drag me into."

Rowan didn't need to remind him he was definitely not being dragged in. It was his defense mechanism.

"You're not going." Annabelle hissed, pulling on Rowan's arm. "You've lost your eye, your magic. Will you quit only when you lose your final breath?"

Rowan had never seen her mother so scared.

"My shifter mate is facing a psychopath who has a talent for making shifters lose control. I have to go."

"He's the one who sent you here!" Annabelle snapped. "Kyron, dile."

Rowan turned her attention to her father.

He was the only one who stood a real chance at stopping her. If he feared for her life, that meant she had been in a worse condition than she'd been imagining.

He cast his eyes to his hand. "You're not going." He reached down to the scabbard at his hip. "Not without Whisper."

Her jaw dropped. Never had she done more than sharpen and polish the heavy sword her father had taken into all of his battles throughout the elven-dwarf wars.

"It has some magic for defense, like your sister's tomahawk, but nothing like your own. Be quick, Rowan. Light on your feet, heavy on the hit."

She nodded and took the encrusted hilt. The magic licked against her palms, comforting, familiar.

Annabelle looked thunderous. She turned and stormed away. A flurry of Spanish Rowan had no hope of translating flying behind her. It was so rare for Annabelle to turn to what she called the tongue of her past that it had become a marker of her anger surpassing reasonable territory.

Rowan grimaced, "Sorry, dad."

He sighed, "I think I'll just have to treat her to that five-day getaway to make it up to her." He didn't look the least bit sorry about it.

Frowning, Lexine kissed her and Axel's brows. "Come back to us whole."

Zeva, who'd looped her arm around her father, simply waved and bit back a yawn

Rowan snorted and tipped her head to Louisa. They phased.

When the world reformed, Rowan found they were at the gates of Draconis.

The lights of the residences were out, but that didn't obliterate the view of thousands of Black Cove residents overwhelming the market street and squeezing through the hole in the barrier that was no longer charmed to keep intruders out.

Most of the trespassers were humans, but mystics scattered amongst them, varying in shape, size and race.

"Is that a fucking djinn?" Louisa cursed, pointing overhead at where Alessandro's black dragon form zoomed against the form of the djinn Rowan had ever only felt in the city.

"Yes. Yes it is." Kin rolled his shoulders. "Remember what I've asked you to do if I lose control, Rowan?"

"Something about owing me the rest of your life once I calm you down again?" She grinned.

He rolled his eyes. "Just remember your limited magic, alright?"

She waved his concern away and turned to Axel as the giant kitsune unfurled to his full size behind her. "Incapacitate only, they're under Barros' control. I can feel him somewhere in the middle, but the spell is taking its toll. He's too weak for me to pinpoint a precise location"

"You got it, boss." She saluted as she raised her weapon and began carving a path with the efficiency and grace of a dancer.

"I smell vampires." Louisa hissed from behind her. "And I don't think they're under Barros' control. They're just taking advantage of the chaos."

Rowan scowled, "You should definitely let them know why you're Rosario the Cruel's chosen heir. I got this."

Once having witnessed Louisa lose her shit on a vampire who had drawn blood without consent, Rowan was wary of accidental death resulting from her confrontation, but she also knew there was an instinct in the vampiress that she lost control of once incensed.

Light on her feet, Rowan plunged into the darkness of the body of moving victims and weeded out the weaker fighters, careful to hold back anything that would cause lasting damage.

Her swings were strong, her mind sharp as she distinguished the bodies of dragons who were taking just as much care. No doubt it was on Alessandro's command. It wasn't until she had to disassemble a knot of banshees screeching at the top of their lungs that she actually had to interact with the dance of the dragons during battle.

Unlike her style, which was airy and flexible, the dragons fought, grounded and powerful.

An air-dragon blasted the knot into the sky and an earth-dragon sent walls of earth shaped like hands to undo the banshees from one another and place a wad of grass in their screeching mouths.

"Nice." She praised as she dodged a swinging knife from a giant man and used her tail to swipe his legs from under him. Her free hand caught the weapon that went flying with his fall. A water-dragon dragged him to join the other bodies floating in midair, everything but their heads covered in turbulent water cells.

She grinned as she joined their ranks, cutting into the still overwhelming numbers.

It wasn't long before she ran into a form she recognized almost instantly. "Harris?" She asked, unsure as the giant white wolf was carefully holding his paw over the neck of a teenage kappa. She watched as he fell unconscious.

"*Princess Rowan.*" He took a deep inhale and his green eyes shone. "*Or should I refer to you as Queen Consort of the Dragon King?*"

"Sure, don't forget the bow when you utter it, though." She took a step back as a bear shifter jumped through and swiped three armed civilians deeper into the crowd.

The action created a ripple effect and, like dominoes, the civilians fell.

From just behind them, Rowan saw an incoming cloud of glowing sand being conjured by a bronze dragon she thought might be Terra. For who else had earth magic so strong that they could conjure a sea of sleep sand?

It was a rare piece of earth magic, and it usually took decades of training to conjure even one particle.

"*Get on.*" Harris lowered his head to allow her to clamber up on his back

She didn't have to be asked twice. They barely evacuated the area as Terra flew overhead.

The bodies behind them dropped.

Rowan's eye caught a shadow moving from one of the library's highest perches. The shape of Axel's tomahawk gave her away as she flung herself to intercept a flying hippogriff that was heading to stop Terra's progression.

Rowan's eyes locked on the plummeting duo, relief washing over her when Master Japhet phased in to pluck them both out of the air.

"*Hold tight!*" Harris' voice ran through her head, giving her only milliseconds to dig her fingers into his fur as he moved at the speed of light. Never having moved so quickly, nausea threaded its fingers into her.

"*Why are you here?*" Rowan had to ask through a link of low magic telepathy. It grated her nerves that even such a minor spell was costing her so much.

"*The Thunder declared they were receiving a new queen. The alphas of every shifter clan are here to meet her---well you, in the morning. Were you not informed?*"

Although she wanted to deny the knowledge, Rowan had to admit she'd only half listened to Terra's briefing on what the next few days would entail.

Her mind had been on less respectable matters, like getting Alessandro back in bed.

The thought of the Dragon King filled her with anger. How could he have looked down on her? After everything she'd done?

"*Maybe. It's been a lot. For now, I think you and I can take that djinn on so he can concentrate on the witch.*"

The wolf growled, "*A witch is causing all of this?*"

"Yes." Rowan answered, "I don't have the magic to counter him. But I have the knowledge and, with your help, the strength to take out what's stopping the Dragon King from taking care of it."

"Fine. Tell me what you need."

"Djinn cannot straddle the astral plane and the physical plane when wolf's teeth sink into their energy field. You can tell where it begins by that faint flow around its body. Don't aim for anything that will kill. Once you hold it firm, I can use some of this sand Terra has scattered around to knock him out." Rowan gripped his fur to emphasize how important her following words were. "The witch wasn't too happy about how our last encounter ended. As soon as we make ourselves known, I think he will aim everything he has at us. You'll have to be on the defensive as soon as you touch back down to the ground."

Harris let out a huff. "Just for clarification, how are we supposed to get up there? I can't fly."

"No. But I can." She patted his head. "And you don't have to be in wolf form for your teeth to be considered wolf teeth."

"Please don't tell me you're not suggesting what I think you're suggesting."

"Do you think I'm suggesting that I carry you up bridal-style?"

"Yes."

"Your mind reading skills are on point, Mr. Knox! Don't worry, you don't have to be naked. I have enough magic to get you into a fit perfect for the Alpha of the Mediterranean Wolf Pack."

-A-

His beast had smelled her the moment she'd appeared at the gates. The distraction had allowed the djinn he'd been wrestling with to get in a good punch and Alessandro cursed as restarted his wearisome incantations to bring the djinn into the physical plane all over again.

Troublesome creatures that the djinn were, Antoni Barros had picked the right nuisance to keep Alessandro occupied while his dragons fought off the hoards meant to keep him concealed in the middle.

But why?

Why had the witch decided it was worth throwing all his progress away in painting the shifters as the villains to this story just to turn all resentment against himself?

"Harris and I are tagging in, Dragon King." Rowan's voice rolled through his head, dripping with her anger.

It took a moment for him to understand why she was angry, but he didn't have time to defend the action that had set her mood.

Rage flared up in his gut, and a wave of nausea filled him as his jealousy spiked to heights he'd never imagined possible when he caught sight of his mate. The wolf's left shoulder pressed against Rowan's soft breasts as her wings cut through the air, dodging the flying foes that reached out to stop her.

That rage was short-lived as behind her, the center of the tightly packed bodies rippled apart. It lent the sight of a body so badly deformed the only way that Alessandro recognized it was Antoni Barros was because of the scent of rotting meat. It was the same as it had been in that house on that mountainside.

Even through his anger, he understood her plan at once. As he passed her, mid-transformation into his human body, he reached out a hand to pass through the strands of her hair. It was enough to ground him.

He should have realized like she had, the there was a wolf with a natural advantage near him. But he'd been used to being able to take care of things all on his own for so many years.

The woman was brilliant.

The woman was his.

Jealousy melted into pride as he called forth the magic of his land to go hand to hand with whatever Antoni Barros had transformed into.

-R-

As soon as the djinn caught sight of the wolf, its only natural predator, it retreated, throwing the bodies of other flying mystics towards the pair to encumber them.

Her wings were lithe and strong enough to get them through the barrage, even with her lack of training them. She was excited to test those limits as she barreled out of the way of a pegasus with fire in the depths of its eyes.

As soon as she saw a clear shot, she took it.

"Sorry about this." She fed into his mind and, using the momentum a necessary front flip had caused her, she flung him with all the strength her arms could muster.

His scream caught the djinn off guard, but the alpha was quick to understand what he had to do and he took a giant bite of air. He damn near missed the aura around the djinn's neck from his surprise.

Relief rolled through Rowan when the wolf remained in the air.

With the Djinn panicked and trying to swat the wolf from his neck, Rowan opened her pores up to the magic that had been knocking at her.

It burned, the resistance of her nulling jewelry against the power that she was allowing in, but she didn't care. She had to do this to buy Alessandro all the time he needed to fight against the hoards Antoni had sent after her and incapacitate whatever the witch had become.

She'd gotten a brief look at Barros as the bodies parted; she could tell that the being that had killed her friend was gone and what stood in his place could only be subdued by the power of a being as potent with magic as Alessandro was.

Rowan concentrated her sight on the lines of magic that were currently so chaotic around her. She'd never seen so many spells executed at once from so many branches of magic. It might have been overwhelming if she hadn't come equipped with Odin's Eye.

While she hadn't played with the supposed powers of prophecy it came with, she had been analyzing magic around her all day, playing and picking through the threads of the shifter, demon, and elf magic she'd come into contact with. She'd have to thank her godmother for such a useful gift as she dug out the thread of bright blue, the djinn's half elemental-half celestial nature, and looked for the golden thread of earth magic attached to the Earth General.

She hoped Terra wouldn't mind as Rowan phased out a share of her sleep sand. It was a social faux pas to intrude among another spellcaster's spell and use it as one's own, but considering the emergency of getting the djinn down before it could cast a wide enough spell to incapacitate the dragons, Rowan hoped a sincere apology would be enough to calm her.

Heat bubbled up behind her and Rowan tucked her wings in, sinking like a stone as a fireball from her left swept where she'd just been.

She took herself out of the dive as she'd finally gathered enough magic to enact the phase.

One second Terra's sand particles were sweeping over the bodies on the ground in a grainy cascade, the next they were midair, falling not only over the djinn but also all the other flying bodies of both dragons and the brainwashed victims.

Panic swept through her as she'd only gathered enough magic to phase Harris out of the way, but not the others.

Under normal circumstances, her magic would have replenished as soon as she used it, but with her current limits, she had to wait. Her neck blazed in pain as she tried to surpass her constraints. She fingered the piece of jewelry, getting ready to tear it off until she felt a swell of magic behind her.

She turned and plucked Stone out of midair.

"What the-"

"Cushion their fall!" She yelled over the screaming.

He glanced behind her, nodded, and zoomed past her with a pair of gorgeous opal wings. They propelled him faster than Rowan thought she could ever achieve, sending out a cushion of air.

Relief filled her, and she phased Harris to her side as she gently touched down back to Earth.

With the wolf's teeth removed, the djinn could safely return to the astral plane. She watched as it passed through every physical obstruction on its path back to earth until it completely melted into the ground.

Worn out by the pathetically limited magic she'd just used, she bent over to catch her breath, every muscle aching with the strain, her neck raw and stinging.

Harris was gagging beside her, trying to rid himself of whatever sensation the plan had put in his mouth and Rowan might have asked what it had felt like, but in the next moment Master Japhet phased in with Axel, forming a protective barrier between them and a new wave of bodies as they caught their breath.

Aqua popped in, her eyes wide. "Consort, allow me to heal your wound."

Rowan sat still as Aqua pulled out a roll of bandages from the pack on her hip.

The water dragon murmured an incantation over the dressing as another water dragon removed Rowan's neck and arm pieces.

Rowan unclipped the chain from her neck and wrapped it around her wrist, a swell of magic acted up in that moment, trying its best to get past her own barriers so fast and so hard it was a moment of terror where she thought she might drown.

She still had a long way to go to recover, but she was certain what she'd just done hadn't made her case any worse.

The rage of the fight continued around them as Aqua applied the bandages. A cooling sensation remained under their wraps even after she finished.

"Alright doc, am I clear to continue fighting?"

Aqua gave a reluctant nod of her head before bowing. "Stay safe, Consort." Then she phased out.

Rowan unsheathed her sword and tilted her head towards Harris, who shot her a wolfish grin before transforming and joining a bear shifter in subduing yet another citizen.

XXXII

Alessandro's dragon swam through a pool of bloodlust. The being that kept on regenerating kept him there.

The magic that the overtaken body of Antoni Barros wielded was familiar.

Alessandro now knew what the source of the power was, and also why it had such a strong interest in his mate.

The curse wasn't quite god-level, but it was so close that Alessandro should have registered its existence before it exposed itself. Tainted, but undeniably angelic.

Though rare, the few 'spars'—if that's what one wanted to call the all-out brawls—he and Lucifer had indulged in through their friendship had included magic.

They had always ended in a draw. Though Alessandro had a significantly higher magical aptitude, Lucifer was more creative than Alessandro could ever hope to be.

It was a trait that had passed down to his great-granddaughter.

The wild concept was still settling in his brain as he whittled the being down.

He had removed layers and layers of the witch's flesh from the source, which he now knew was a cursed weapon of an archangel.

Those parts he tore away were working on mending off to the side. Barros was in a stomach-turning but much more recognizable heap.

Lucifer had always been open about the issues he had with his siblings.

One had remained a gaping wound in the fallen angel's heart even centuries after her death.

Anytime he spoke of Uzziel, the archangel of faith, it had led to a night of debauchery that Lilith always blamed Alessandro for.

Uzziel had been one of the few angels who hadn't taken either Michael's or Lucifer's side in the angelic war.

Since their creation, Uzziel had followed Michael through training, work and play time. Many thought the two had become codependent to an eyebrow raising degree. As such, it had been a shock for everyone, including Lucifer himself, when Michael's shadow made her neutrality in the matter clear.

Uzziel *had* grown close to Lucifer during overlapping assignments on Earth, but her time with the fallen archangel was nothing compared to what she had spent with Michael.

Uzziel's decision came with the consequence of animosity from both sides, each thinking she was playing them for information. But she continued her work as if their silly little war was the last thing she'd ever have to be concerned about.

It ignited a movement. Those who hadn't felt as strongly about the issue—a question of what they were supposed to be doing because their creator had gone missing—followed her lead and resumed their daily tasks.

She maintained her decision until the day Lucifer and Michael met face to face in their creator's throne room.

Lucifer wanted to take the seat. He'd seen that the angels, without proper direction, were becoming destructive.

Michael wanted to leave it open for their creator. Desperate for his return, he'd seen it as his duty as the most cherished son to cull the humans who he thought were the source of their creator's displeasure.

Lucifer had his back turned, preparing to take the seat despite Michael's protests when Michael had reached his limit.

Uzziel broke her vow to not get involved. She stopped the swing of Michael's divine sword from taking Lucifer's head.

The others thought her intervention meant she had finally chosen a side, but, when Lucifer attempted to end Michael while he recovered from the shock of the interference, the archangel made it clear she still wasn't on either side by launching both Lucifer and Michael towards the walls on either side of the Hall.

Whether it was the violence Michael and Lucifer, two of their lord's favored angels, had shown to each other, or that they'd done it in the throne hall, their god decided it was time to make his reappearance.

His absence had been a test of their loyalty. He wanted to see which of his creations would stick to their lord's will if he ever disappeared.

Cast out of the celestial realms, Lucifer and his followers ultimately made their homes either on the earth itself or in the infinite circles of hell.

Michael and his side, in contrast, could not visit departed souls, limited to travel only in the confines of the skies or on earth.

Both sides shared the ultimate punishment of their creator's silence. Only able to regain favor if they completed tasks set to them by Blessed. Those treasured beings who could hear the words of gods.

Those who had maintained that they were not on either side could roam where they wanted and continued to communicate with their lord without restraint. In fear that they too would lose this privilege, these angels never told either side what their god said to them. They flitted around, listening to commands only they could hear.

As a unique case, Uzziel received a unique punishment. Confined to earth, and earth alone. The celestial realms and the endless hells both existed just out of reach.

At first, the archangel hadn't minded the punishment. She liked humans, took joy from guiding and caring for her charges during their natural lifespan. But, as time went on, humanity became more and more twisted. She lost her love for the fragile creatures, leaving her only one thing that brought joy—magic.

Despite there being an actual archangel of magic, no other was as well-versed in using it as she was. She used her skill to weave the most beautiful landscapes, awe-inspiring illusions and dedicated herself to more deeply understanding nature.

She created her own personal oasis on a deserted island through the means of this natural resource, still answering missions assigned directly from their creator without a fight until one day came when her answer was no.

Lucifer insisted no one knew what the command was, but Uzziel's outright defiance incited the wrath of their god.

Instead of having the freedom to move wherever she wanted to on Earth, their god sequestered her on her moving island. Within its borders, she could use her magic, but as soon as she stepped too far into the ocean, it would come to attack her.

Her god had turned her last joy into bars and chains against her.

The punishment enraged Lucifer, who hadn't seen the archangel since that fateful day where she both saved and doomed him.

He found the island, but by the time he'd arrived, the madness had already taken Uzziel. Isolation had done its worst. The results—a heap of wings on a glistening white beach, a trail of cooked blood leading to the drenched staff that had done the mangling. Buried deep, it stood upright, just a breath from the crashing waves of that too blue ocean.

It was Uzziel's last act of defiance.

The weapon had been a gift from their creator, just as precious as Lucifer's sword. It was a weapon that could transform into any form its owner wished.

Lucifer imagined the archangel had walked right into the ocean and, instead of fighting, let the magic tear her apart.

When Alessandro found out Lucifer had left the weapon there as a memorial, he tried to hunt it down to expand his hoard. In those days, he'd been young and didn't understand the sentimental weight some treasures carried.

It took him months to locate the moving piece of land. It had been so challenging that he'd almost given up half a dozen times.

The sight of the giant oak tree wrapped around an even bigger weeping willow at its very center was unique enough to make the hunt worth it. But that hadn't been his actual goal.

He combed through the overgrown flora in the middle of the island with only a hatchet, looking for it when he didn't find it next to the perfectly preserved wings on the beach. Roses and lilies thrived next to cacti and succulents of all shapes and sizes in the canvas of the deranged spellcaster.

It took weeks, as magic didn't work to its full capacity within the borders of the islands. Looking back, he was sure it was an unintended consequence of Uzziel's punishment.

In the end, his efforts proved futile.

The staff was missing.

That was no longer the case. It was here, finally within his grasp, somehow embedded inside of the witch that had thrown the world of shifters into a fiery storm.

It had overtaken that witch's will over for one reason.

It wanted Rowan Dahl.

It must have sensed her divinity during her fight with Antoni Barros, her angel-hood inherited from Lucifer. Her incredible control of magic must have reminded it of its original owner because to Alessandro, Rowan was, as Lucifer had described Uzziel, magic personified.

Even with celestial magic, he could not cleanse the staff, but he could trap it and it knew it.

Each time Barros regenerated, the weapon tried to split a bit of itself off to get around Alessandro to find a path to Rowan. It moved when she did, full effort fixed in her direction, but it was wary of having its physical form caught by the Dragon King.

It was in a desperate attempt that it hurled a collection of bodies, still under its control, at Alessandro. It had hidden a sliver of its form in the masses, passing through the bodies on its route to his woman.

He could feel her somewhere to the right, her magic close to both Japhet and Lucifer.

It had been a surprise that Lucifer had stayed behind to help Alessandro's people when Lilith had phased out without a second thought.

The fallen angel had been working through the shadows that crawled along the battlefield until he realized his progeny had shown up when Rowan faced off against the djinn.

He'd split himself into two bodies and stayed within phasing distance of both Axel and Rowan, keeping more deadly attacks from touching them like a living shield.

Lucifer locked onto the wooden sliver before Alessandro did, and he reflected it into the Dragon King's grip with a phase.

Triumphant, Alessandro released a small sonic boom, sending the bodies surrounding him flying at least ten feet back.

The sliver of wood, so small it could be called a splinter, burned against his fingers. The dark energy of the curse tried to crawl into his pores, yet, despite that he was mostly just a dragon, he was also a candidate for godhood. It had no way to overtake his own impenetrable will. His people had given him the power to overwhelm the curse of one powerful but very broken archangel.

He collected every atom that had the magic signature of the staff into his hand, reforming the weapon to its full, worn and beaten length before coating it completely in the most formidable encasing of deep ice he'd ever performed.

"*Pleaseeee.*" The sentience it had was disturbing. It tried to appeal to some morsel of mercy in the Dragon King, but in protecting Rowan Dahl, he had no mercy to give.

The parting of the staff from Antoni Barros had him entirely reformed on the ground in front of Alessandro. His cries were blood curdling.

This was the fate of those who didn't make it to a Blessed before the dark magic finally ate up everything the wielder offered. The body wouldn't fully disappear, but shrivel up in a state of consciousness suffocated by pain long after their vocal chords withered.

Around Alessandro, the Black Cove citizens were snapping out of the illusion.

Shifters and those who had come to their aid began dropping their attacks and calling out for medical attention for victims on both sides of the struggle.

Horror colored the faces of those overtaken.

Alessandro could tell the moment they all pinpointed the source of their confusion. The witch whose cries were as revolting as the state of his body.

He could leave the witch to eternal damnation. The staff wouldn't release its hold on him until it found a new wielder. As things stood, Alessandro would never allow that to happen as long as he breathed.

It would be a fitting punishment for the suffering creature after everything the witch had put his people through, of what damage he'd inflicted on his mate.

But it wasn't the most effective solution available.

There was one more option, one that would help shifter kind all over the world, not just the ones in Draconis.

-R-

"Rowan, I need you."

His plea was soft in Rowan's mind.

Rowan, who'd been helping an elderly Asian man to his feet, turned to find Alessandro's eyes settled on her.

Baby blue? She needed to get to work on a decoder for those emotions.

"Cleanse him."

Rowan felt her back straighten and her nose flare.

Cleanse him?

He who had taken her friend from her?

How had he even survived that takeover?

Even from the distance she stood at she could hear his cries of pain. Bloodcurdling. Devastating.

"*Kin?*" She called, seeking him out amongst the bodies.

From near Alessandro's yard, she saw the fox peek his head up.

"*I need a distraction and a face change.*"

The kitsune huffed, his attitude so clear even from so far that Rowan couldn't help but to smile.

"*I can handle the distraction.*" Louisa's voice came in. "*The vampires are ready to head to a more appropriate feeding ground.*"

"*Say when.*" Kin's voice was steady.

In a slight moment of hesitation, Rowan considered phasing away. Alessandro had never intended to have her in the battle. But this was bigger than their personal issues. "*Now.*"

The vampires Louisa had corralled and set straight erupted from a market street alley. The noise they made was a thundering screech as they scattered like roaches in different directions in the sky.

Eyes shifted to the potential new threat. Kin's magic slid over her face and even her clothes.

Always two steps ahead, he made sure she was completely unrecognizable as Alessandro phased her to join him.

He didn't meet her eyes, and she thought she could understand that it might give the charade up if he stared at this supposed stranger with the glowing silver she ignited.

Her eyes snagged on the wooden rod that was contained in a spell of deep ice. Dark curse energy oozed from it. Was this the weapon that had caused all this damage? Could she still cleanse someone who no longer had a cursed object in their possession?

Alessandro seemed to think so.

Taking a step back, lest their nearness gave any hint about her identity, she extended her hand.

The sword of light allowed her to see the genuine horror of what Antoni Barros had become. His gorgeous blonde locks were patches on a head so swollen she was unsure where any of his facial features had once been. His skin, sliced deep, made him look like the world's most grotesque blooming onion. The smell alone was almost enough to discourage her from approaching.

But she did, and her hand shook as in the air a familiar laugh she knew she would never have the pleasure of hearing again tinkled.

Thanks to this creature.

Her sword flickered, and she had to turn away to collect herself.

Her eyes snagged on a woman perched on a rooftop, tomahawk thrown over her shoulder, white curly hair shining in the moonlight. She had seen through the disguise and her blue eyes twinkled with a message Rowan didn't need to be telepathic to hear.

Could she live with walking away?

Barros' scream rocked something in her, something so central to her core that she knew that answer almost immediately.

No. She couldn't leave anyone to this fate.

At her side, her sword flared to a near blinding brightness as she recalled the beaming smile on Dew's face each morning she would greet her. She let her love for the fairy fill her and guide her mercy.

In one fluid move, she sliced through where she thought Barros' heart had once been.

As soon as her sword passed through, she felt the necklace around her wrist loosen. Her eyes traveled down to watch as it corroded, as if years were taking their claim to the material.

She braced herself for the pain she'd felt in Alessandro's cave, but all that came was a gentle heat. It traveled from where her hand wrapped around the hilt of her sword and it crawled up through her chest.

A foreign, yet all too familiar trace of magic reached from behind her.

Her gaze shifted to the staff in Alessandro's grasp.

A shadow of a body stood next to it, warm, inviting and were those angel wings?

Time had come to a halt around her. Barros' screams were silent. Several witnesses were in mid-step and Alessandro hadn't moved his gaze from the form of Barros to her.

Her free hand unsheathed Whisper, and she pointed it at the figure.

"Who are you?" She demanded.

The shadow stepped forward into the light of her sword. A ghostly smile stretched on a face that she'd seen in Barros' basement.

"There's no time, little one. Claim the staff before he breaks it." The voice was barely more than a passing breeze.

Rowan narrowed her eyes. "Why should I?"

"No time." The words continued even after the shadow disappeared and time rolled forward.

Her attention attached itself to the staff. The deep ice spell was deteriorating, but she could also see hairline fractures on the wood of the weapon. Was it simply a race to see which would fail first? What would happen if it was the ice that was lost?

She had nothing to prove she could trust the ghostly figure. She didn't even recognize it, but something about it had felt familiar. More compelling than that, it made her feel safe.

Gathering her courage, she reached out and broke Alessandro's spell. Panic widened his eyes as she took hold of the oddly warm weapon.

"Trust me." She squeezed her fingers around his.

He looked like he wanted to reject her request, but he grit his teeth and released his grip.

It made up for his decision to send her away by the smallest degree.

The darkness of the curse shot up her arm, but Rowan instinctively knew what she had to do as soon as her magic brushed against energy. She reached out towards where specks of the ghost had remained even after the power faded out and engaged her succubus like she had when she tried to suck Barros' life force out. She took in the scraps of energy.

As she did, she could feel the gates of all of her chakra points become as flexible as rubber.

For the first time since she woke up in Draconis' medical ward, she felt whole.

She could finally see why the energy had been so familiar. It had been her own. At least partially. There had been something foreign inside her for so long she hadn't known how to differentiate it until that moment.

The sound of soft laughter rolled through her head as the ghost emerged beside her, hands also on the staff.

"You're doing it!" The voice cheered. *"Just keep holding on!"*

Rowan didn't have time for questions. The darkness crawled further and further up her arms, down her legs, covering her until only her eyes remained unveiled.

"Uzziel?" The unexpected sound of her godfather's voice stole Rowan's attention.

It cost her.

Darkness enshrouded her.

The sound of the battlefield died away.

The scent of the blood and sweat neutralized to nothing.

She was slowly turning into nothing.

She felt the tendrils of fear entwine their way into her soul.

She wanted to curl up into a ball as visions of where the staff had been and what people had done with its power crept in, trying to eat away her own memories.

A vision of a woman sobbing for mercy and being sliced apart by a faceless body burned away the memory of the moment her father had first extended his hand with a plate full of cake and a pouch of juice.

The first time she'd bested Axel in a spar, and her sister had cheered in admiration for her cunning instead of getting angry at being bested shattered. A vision of burning buildings, the sharp stench of flesh in those flames assaulting her, took its place.

No!

She tried to hold on helplessly to a vision of Louisa singing karaoke on a bar's table top. Rowan herself had been taking part in a brawl that had broken out on the dance floor, singing along with her best friend. But it slipped from her fingers, replaced by a memory of someone being held face down in the water of a pristine marble fountain. A slice of air magic shredding the skin of the assaulter.

Rowan's fear hit a plateau at the sight of the spell work.

This was her bread and butter.

Curses, at the base of their being, were just bundles of magic.

Though there were no scrolls on how to cleanse curses, there were plenty concentrating on what they were.

The laughter was back again, wrapping around her, dropping bundles of energy as Rowan pushed the darkness away from her arms, legs, and soul.

The divine energy the ghost was leaving at her disposal was the hint she had needed. She could now see what she couldn't believe had always lived within her. Her own brand of divine magic, eager to be used. It was much smaller than the pools of her demonic and elven inheritance, but it certainly wasn't anything to scoff at.

At their core, curses were nothing more than parasitic dark magic, and now that she knew she had the opposing force under her control, she could neutralize it.

Recalling Alessandro's instructions of returning to basics, and the notes from the Elder's grimoire, she pulled the energy from the ley line overhead, filtering it through every single gate at once. She pushed out a spell of healing, interweaving her divinity as she overtook the particles of darkness. They receded as Rowan claimed every single atom as hers.

The world became visible, and she focused her attention on imbuing the memories it tried to take from her with power. They worked as a restraint when the curse energy bucked in rebellion and tried to spill out to find purchase on any of the onlookers around her.

The moment the last bit became neutralized, heat surged through the weapon. The power woven through the grain of the wood was overwhelming. It needed a wielder. It wasn't an everyday object. Created with a purpose, it needed somewhere to point its power, or it would fall into darkness again.

"*Mine.*" The words held power and the splinters and nicks on the staff began repairing themselves, leaving nothing behind but words of an unfamiliar language.

It was over.

Her eyes sought him out. Alessandro stood with his arms crossed over his chest so tightly that he was digging his claws into his forearms, trying to keep from reaching out to her.

She gave the barest hint of a smile before the ghost touched down beside her. The being had its attention turned to Lucifer, a small smile on the beautiful, haunting face before it burst into millions of fragments of light.

Rowan's hands shook and her eyes burned as she took in what she had just accomplished.

Behind her, a sound of pain made her back straighten. Shock was clear in Alessandro's golden eyes as they locked on the source.

Lucifer let out a soft curse and Rowan slowly turned to take in the rebuilt body of Antoni Barros. Bruised, unconscious and lightly bleeding, but totally whole once more.

The murmurs of the audience they'd had to the first ever successful cleansing made Rowan's eyes snap back up. She slid Whisper into the scabbard on her back, and after checking where Kin, Louisa and Axel were, she sent her mate a silent nod before phasing out.

XXXIII

The first time Lucifer overrode one of Rowan's spells, Rowan had been so discombobulated that she threw up.

It had happened during the only training session he'd agreed to give her.

Until then, Rowan had been perfectly unaware of the reason Lucifer was so feared in the depths of the endless hells that other underworld denizens gave his territory a wide berth.

In Lucifer's mind, there were only two modes of combat. On or off. It didn't matter that it was supposed to be just training. It didn't matter that Rowan was only ten years old and barely had control of her magic. Lucifer saw the threat of a dagger finding its way to the white plumage of his wings and he reversed the spell.

It had only missed because Lilith had been on the sidelines of the open field behind their imposing black castle. She knew her husband. Had warned Rowan and Lucifer both that a spar was a bad idea. But Rowan insisted it was the only birthday gift she was interested in.

Lilith phased Rowan out of harm's way and into her arms before she began a mad dash toward the safety of the castle.

Over the mother of all succubi's shoulders, Rowan had watched as her godfather, who had always been happy to play dolls and tea party with her anytime she asked, combusted into a cloud of darkness that billowed out over his lands. Darkness that contained screams and smelled sharply of blood.

Her image of the soft man turned upside down, she hurled her lunch.

It was the first time she knew true fear.

Now, sixteen years later, the feeling of his magic curling around hers and tugging her in the middle of a phase sent her heart rate skyrocketing.

Instead of the grassy Eastern Elven Kingdom grounds, Rowan landed on an abandoned, moonlit, white-sand beach.

It was abnormal. Even with the sound of the lapping waves hitting the sand, she could tell not all was as it seemed. She tuned in her senses, concentrating on figuring out why everything felt so off.

Then she saw it. A colossal oddity of a weeping willow intertwined with the branches and leaves of an oak tree. She shot into the sky, her breath catching. It was the same as it had been in her vision.

It was a tiny island. Behind the beach, ten acres jam-packed with thousands of species of flora flourished. Each limited to one specimen of each.

There wasn't a sign of a single animal. Not even an insect.

The magic of the island was just as strange. Sluggish and stale against her skin, it felt nothing like the effervescent magic she was used to. They were still on the world she called home. She could feel the familiar ley lines that attracted so many mystics to this realm set over her head.

Her eyebrows furrowed as she realized she hadn't felt them on the sand.

She glanced down at the beach, only to realize the island was moving. The difference was so small she would have missed it if she hadn't been concentrating on taking in every nuance of the place.

Her jaw clenched, and she touched back down next to her godfather, whose eyes locked on what she'd mistakenly assumed was a mound of sand. As the moonlight shifted like a spotlight, the white plumage of the stained wings became clear.

Rowan blinked between the wings to her godfather. "Those aren't yours, are they?"

His wings popped into existence behind him.

Unsure of what was happening, Rowan waited for him to talk, but he remained silent.

"What are we doing here, Uncle Luz?" She broke after only a few minutes of unbearable silence. She could see the place affected him. Tension lined his shoulders, and his hands and jaw were clenched.

"Uzziel."

It was the name he'd called when he'd seen the spectre. Rowan eyed her godfather uneasily. Had his voice broken uttering it?

"You knew who that was?"

"Bring forth the staff."

She'd never known him to be so short. Concerned by the sound of his heartbeat pounding in his chest, Rowan held her hand out, conjured the wooden weapon, and handed it over.

She still couldn't believe the lack of curses on the thing. As if it had never been part of ending hundreds of lives.

He held it horizontally as he ran a finger over the marks. "These etchings are the names of all the archangels that existed when our creator gifted her the staff." He said as he brought it up to her eye level, pointing at one full of curves and sharp points. "This one is hers, right next to mine."

Rowan's eyes slid to the wings. "Those are hers, aren't they?"

"Yes. This island was her cage once. In escaping it, she used this staff to mutilate herself."

Rowan's own wings quivered. They were so sensitive she couldn't imagine the pain Uzziel must have endured.

"I thought that was her end. But when you cleansed the witch, I realized she'd found her way into you."

Rowan's fingers settled over her heart where she felt a hole from where the foreign magic had existed for so long that it felt strange now that it was missing. When had the archangel settled there?

"What happened to her?"

He told her everything.

From her contrasting friendships with Michael and himself. To the similarities between Rowan and the angel. To the guilt he'd carried for centuries for not coming to her aid when she most needed him. He was only alive because of her interference. A choice that cost her freedom.

"How did the staff do this?" She whispered, crouched over the cuts of the wings that were building a morbid fascination within her.

"The staff can take any shape." He held the weapon for her to hold. "But only for its true wielder. You claimed it. It's now yours."

Rowan furrowed her eyebrows as she took it. She didn't have the first idea of what to do. Using the methods she used for her magic, she tried to imagine it changing shapes. She then tried filtering a bit of the reluctant magic into it, but it stayed in its initial shape.

"Blood?" She asked, turning to Lucifer, who'd remained silent.

His smile was sad. "No. Rowan, all you have to do is ask."

Rowan lowered the weapon so she could wipe the tears that trailed down his face.

"I'm sorry you lost her."

It was like breaking a dam.

He covered his face with both hands, his shoulders shook and his sobs rocked him from the deepest part of his soul.

Enraged by the injustice of Uzziel's fate, Rowan glanced down at the wings that hadn't decomposed with centuries of existing next to the corrosive air of the ocean. Then over to the flora, whose leaves shuddered in the light breeze.

It was as if time had come to a screeching halt once Uzziel walked out into the waves. It kept the horror alive.

Activating Odin's eye, she found the bars of the cage that had once contained the woman who'd helped her overcome the curses of the staff.

Determined, she ascended to the brightest point available. The apex of the criss-crossing spell of a god clumsy with magic.

Uzziel should have been able to break it if she'd been as well versed in magic as Lucifer implied she was. But, perhaps fighting the circumstance of her existence was no longer worth it.

Rowan gripped the crest and began the grueling task of tearing the threads of magic apart. Much like untangling a collection of necklaces. It was tedious work, but Lucifer joined her as soon as he realized what she was doing.

Together they undid it all by the time the sun reached the center of the sky the next day.

Sweating, hands burning from handling the magic of a god, they returned to the beach. As soon as Rowan touched down, the corner of her eye caught the moment her Cabin appeared, snug against the tree-line.

They fell into the two oversized chairs on her porch, as silent as they'd been when they were working.

Then Rowan heard it before she saw it. A seagull's call overhead.

Lucifer heard it at the same time.

They looked at each other before scrambling to the banister of the porch and looking up.

A flock of seagulls.

Rowan grinned and when she looked at her godfather, he was staring at her, half horrified, half awed.

"Uncle Luz?"

She was on the verge of passing out from exhaustion. The energy Alesandro had given her to Cleanse Antoni Barros was nearing depletion. She needed sleep she hadn't gotten on her five-day getaway to settle the mark. And she needed food.

But his next words turned her entire world upside down. "Actually, it's great-grandfather Luz."

Suddenly, she was as awake as she was confused.

He began a trek into the cabin.

"What do you mean?" She called, following through the front door right into the kitchen.

"Knew you were hungry." He mumbled as he made his way to the fridge.

"Uncle, Luz!"

"Great-grandfather."

"Demons and divine creatures cannot procreate." She slammed her hands on her counter. "I'm a succubus. You're an angel!"

"It wasn't a traditional creation." He pulled out her carrot cake and opened the lid. His eyebrow rose at the sight of the spoon inside. "This is concerning."

Rowan snatched the cake and picked up the spoon, pointing it at his chest. "Concentrate."

He let out a heavy breath and raked a hand through his long, blonde hair. "You're right. It shouldn't have been possible. But Lilith has never actually listened to the rules, has she? She refused the role she'd been created to fill. She refused to let the endless hells cage her as they were supposed to. And she did it once more when she created our daughter, Ellanora."

"Created? Alone? Auntie Lilith can't be a god."

He let out a scoff and a laugh. "No. If she ever became a god, the world would most assuredly come undone. But her intelligence allows her to skirt the expectations of the magical world. You've inherited that quality. Look at what you've done here. Look at what you did last night."

"How?"

"The same way she created the original succubi. Though, this time she used my genetic make-up, not Adam's. She disappeared for a year. I-I thought she'd had enough of my darkness and self-inflicted imprisonment in our castle. Then she showed up with a girl, just a year old. Golden-haired like me, violet-eyed like her."

Disbelief exploded in Rowan. She'd always known her godmother was self-serving, with little regard to anyone her decisions might affect. The only softness the woman ever showed was for Annabelle, Annabelle's family, and Lucifer himself. Rowan had seen her interact with the outside world, and the hatred she had for everyone who wasn't those select few.

To think she could do something as life altering as create an off-spring without input from the man she claimed to love above all else.

"How did you forgive her?"

He shrugged, "Love, I suppose. For her. I couldn't stand seeing her shaking, terrified of my reaction. But I also had a love for the child. Her magic was entertaining. She was a master of illusion. She encour-aged me to leave the endless hells and explore all the dimensions to satiate her curiosity. I was happy."

"Anytime we asked Ama about her, she'd redirect or straight up ig-nore us. What happened to her?"

"She still lives." He shrugged. "But she's been hopping dimensions living for herself only. When Annabelle was born, it was unexpected. Her fling with the Southern Elven Kingdom's ruler was a favor for all the other succubi, who she'd tried to fit in with even though she wasn't one of them. She stole most of the kingdom's gold by the time she was pregnant. Your grandfather, Lauricio, didn't really mind. He was old in age and had only one goal: to have a child. When Annabelle was born, Ellanora already had her next big adventure planned. It didn't include her."

Anger brushed every cell within Rowan. "What?"

"Even if Lilith had created her, Ellanora was little more than a pet in her eyes. She had me, her father, to raise her, and I did the best I could. In her mind, it wasn't a big deal to leave her daughter like she'd perceived Lilith to leave her. We didn't know about Annabelle until Lilith visited the one person who she'd ever loved other than me-Eliza Dahl."

"My dad's aunt?" Rowan's eyes widened.

"Yes. The Traveling Cabin settled in the endless pits of hell for a few months. Eliza was, well, for a lack of a better word, odd. I know my wife doesn't encourage confidence, but Eliza liked her. It didn't matter that Lilith verbally abused the woman as she tried to work out how to get the cabin unstuck." Lucifer tapped the counter lovingly. "I like to think the cabin knew my woman needed someone other than me to love her, and knew that Eliza could withstand her. Eliza also needed Lilith. She was an outcast in the Eastern Elven Kingdom."

"Wait." Rowan choked on a piece of cake she'd taken a chance on as her—she still couldn't believe it—great-grandfather, continued his story.

Lucifer poured her a large cup of milk to ease her distress.

"Love, love? As in, they were lovers?"

"Yes." He shrugged. "You're aware that we've had lovers throughout our marriage."

"Yeah, but not with my paternal great-aunt!" She hissed. How could he be so nonchalant?

"Well, Eliza was different. She softened Lilith's anger. Her passing broke her heart. I don't think she'll ever truly recover from her loss. For those years with Eliza, Lilith had patience. Enough that I could leave her and explore the world with my friend, your...mate."

Rowan took a deep breath. She was half afraid of the answer, but she needed to know. "Friend or friend?"

He let out such a raucous laugh that she got two more mouthfuls in as he recollected himself. "You're really not letting that mark settle, are you?" He shook his head. "You know that's got to be torture for him."

Her eyes narrowed, "Pardon me?"

"Lilith was the one who realized it. You're not offering the bond any part of you, nor are you asking it for anything. If you wanted to know, you could simply reach in and explore it, but you're afraid."

"I'm not af-"

"I helped raise you, Ro. I know when you're afraid, and you were afraid when you stood next to him on that pedestal, and then when you met his family, and even now that I've called you out on your bull-shit."

Rowan growled as she stuffed another bite of cake into her mouth to give her an excuse not to respond.

"You have spent less than a month at his side and look at you, acting like a little beast." He laughed.

Rowan sighed. "One day it'll be too much. One day he's going to give into his godhood."

"Ah, is that all that's stopping you? He's as stubborn as you are, Rowan. He doesn't consider the power his, as such he won't give in."

Rowan narrowed her eyes. "Are you okay with the mark now? I thought you were going to pop a blood vessel yesterday."

"It's hard to deny that the two of you work. As loath as I am to admit it. I've never seen him *happy*."

She rolled her eyes. "Well, I'm not. The asshole side-lined me."

Lucifer scoffed. "You came back. No harm, no foul."

"I call foul!"

"It is your pride talking. I've warned you to not let it get away with you."

"Hi, Pot. I'm Kettle."

Lucifer snatched the spoon from her hand. A tendril of a shadow crawled from his hand to hers. "Pride and fear are such an ugly look on you."

"When's the last time you saw your daughter?"

His nose flared. "When you aim to hurt, you really go for the jugular, don't you?"

"I apparently got it from my great-grandmother!" She clenched her fists. "How could you guys have kept this from us? I've begged to learn more about our past. I knew I wasn't normal from the day I set half of the forest on fire because I threw a tantrum. Hundreds of animals died because you guys didn't know what to do with me! Do-does Ama know?"

Lucifer's shoulders softened. "Yes. But only because of you."

"Me?"

"When you were born...Rowan, I didn't know your mother, much less your sisters, existed. But when you were born, you died. Lilith told me about everything in the same breath that she asked me to come to the Eastern Elven Kingdom to help save you."

"Died?" Rowan's eyes widened.

"When I came, I was too late. I tried everything to resuscitate you. You've always been small, but you were born early, too early. You cast magic from inside your mother's womb, trying to save her from an assassination attempt. It cost you your life."

How could they have hidden so much from her? "How did you save me?"

"I didn't." He shook his head. "I tried everything I could. I even tried using your sisters."

"My sisters? Lexine was six when I was born. What could she have done?"

His eyes misted over. "Before you were born, magic imbued your sisters. They were bursting at the seams with it."

Rowan leaned back in her chair. "What?"

"Lexine brought a bird back from the verge of death. Its neck had snapped when it fell out of its nest. It was barely a hatchling. Axel could lift boulders three times the size of her and at least 300 times her own weight. Zeva was fluently speaking 5 different languages at a year and a half old."

"I was still getting over the shock of learning that I had a full grown granddaughter, much less 3 great-granddaughters, when your father introduced me to them. I think he just needed someone to watch them while him and your mother grieved. Lilith had been in their lives for so long that they knew her as Auntie Lilith. They didn't have a great support system at that point. It was so early in his rule and the royals were not fans of his queen."

"Well, when I met them, I had a mad idea. Like blood, one of these girls had to have a good enough match for a magical transfusion."

Horror swept through Rowan. Magical transfusions were rare because the cost on the donor was too high. Whatever they gave, they never got back.

"You took their magic?"

"Not all of it."

"They're shades of what they had the potential of being?"

"Do you really think your sisters are less than just because they don't have more magic available to them?"

"No." She didn't. But she could only imagine the world if her three brilliant sisters had had more power.

"I thought it was what saved you. I was wrong. Uzziel gave me a vision of what had been happening just out of my sight. She was there that day. Saw your potential, the similar way in which magic responded to you. She fused herself to you. Took in your sister's energies and properly deposited them where they belonged. I didn't feel her once while she worked."

Her heart slammed in her chest.

A vision of a field full of bloody bodies and the sharp scent of burning flesh slammed into her. It was so similar to what the staff showed her.

Nausea crawled up her throat as she caught the barest scent of rotting meat before it faded.

"What am I?"

"You appear to be an ultimate siphon of magic. We knew you were different since that day your tantrum burnt the forest down."

Rowan's eyes fluttered closed. "We? As in everyone, including Lex, Zev and Axel?"

He gripped the corner of the counter. No denial or affirmation.

"Was the Coven, right? Am I too dangerous to be trusted? Do you now accept that Alessandro is my mate because he might stand a chance at controlling me? In case I let the power get to my head?"

"You already have him wrapped around your finger, Rowan. No one can control you, but you. But maybe he can make you feel less alone."

The word she hated most in the world.

Because for so long, she had indeed felt it.

Her succubus limbs marked her as differing from all of her family physically. Her magic widened that gap. She knew they loved her, that she could count on them for anything. Anything but to feel like she belonged.

It was why Louisa and Kin had become so important to her. They each understood the loneliness that came with their power. Each of them was an outlier.

An image of Alessandro slid into the forefront of her mind at this thought. The biggest outlier in the whole damn planet. A god who pretended he was still just a dragon.

One day, he would be unable to pretend any longer. One day, he would leave her. Gods couldn't survive on the mortal plane. This, more than anything, kept her from sinking into that desire he ignited in her, and she wasn't talking about that passion side of it. She'd enjoy that for as long as she could. She was talking about her desire to trust him with her insecurities, vulnerabilities—her entire fucking heart.

If he left her now, she would fall apart for a couple of months, maybe years, but she'd recover.

Eventually.

If she gave in and gave him everything that being his mate required she wouldn't.

Mortals, whether marked by and immortal or not, would deteriorate in the celestial realms. Her divinity would allow her to stay longer than others, but her succubus and elf side would wither. She would wither.

Yes. He could make her feel less alone, but if he ever left—she cut that thought off.

"I need some time."

"Ro-"

"Please. Just a little space."

"Okay."

Rowan felt the slightest brush of his magic against her head, a pat of comfort before he phased.

XXXIV

When Alessandro finally had time to make it to Rowan's side, night was falling all over again.

He called through their link several times, but she hadn't answered.

He considered giving her space to take in what she'd done by herself, but the thought of staying away longer than it took to get his dragons settled, the civilians treated and Barros into proper Judgment custody kicked his dragon into a tantrum.

He found her cabin settled on a beach he recognized at once. She was sitting in front of a pile of wings that refused to decompose onto the soft sands that Uzziel had abandoned them on.

Lucifer's scent was faint. He'd been gone for hours.

She didn't speak even as he settled next to her.

"Will you ignore me for the rest of our lives?" Were his first words.

She snorted.

"What's going on in that head, Rowan?"

Her sigh was weary. He didn't doubt she had yet to sleep.

"This won't work, Alessandro."

His nose flared. "What won't work?"

"Us." The word was nearly a breath. "You took my choice to stay and fight by your side. I'm not your queen. I'm little more than a precious pet."

He felt his breath leave at that declaration. "You know that isn't how I feel."

She snapped her gaze to him, Odin's Eye glistened like a tiny starry sky. "A queen's position is by her king's side."

"You are not the queen of a regular kingdom, Rowan. You are queen of the Draconian Thunder, and we don't play by the same rules."

He could feel her fury warm her before he could see it redden her cheeks. "What? Am I supposed to be subservient? A meek little damsel to be protected? I will never be like that, not even for you!"

She let out a huff of frustration, crossing her arms and looking away, disgusted.

He growled, "Do you really think I've taken hundreds of years to choose a queen because I have a lack of damsels in distress?"

She didn't deign him with even the slightest notion that she took in his words, but she was still there beside him, still willing to listen. Perhaps hoping that there was some reasonable explanation for what he'd done.

He couldn't ask for more from his obviously hurt mate.

Frustration welled inside of him as he realized the only way to explain it would ruin the surprise he'd had in store for her after the dust of everything settled.

"Give me your hand."

Rowan held her hand out but didn't turn to look at him

"Look at me."

She turned even further away.

His anger dissipated. He couldn't help but to find her annoyance amusing. And that is what it really was. She wasn't as furious as she was trying to make it seem. Even if their bond wasn't fully cemented, as Lilith had correctly assumed, he could feel her emotions as easily as his own.

"What the fuck is so funny?" She hissed, turning to glare at him.

He leaned down to steal the briefest of kisses before phasing them away.

Dragon City, the true home of the dragons, was in celebration mode.

On the top floor of the tallest tower, at the center of the city, were Alessandro's quarters.

There were no windows or walls, merely partitions of sheer curtains hung across a low suspended ceiling that gave him some semblance of privacy when he stayed.

The arches and columns that held up the roof gave him the views of the ocean one way, and an expansive forest the other.

The kingdom itself surrounded the castle. White stucco sidings and orange clay roofs were the most popular builds of residential areas, all tight together in the epicenter, and growing distant the further from the castle you got. It was the true inspiration for Draconis' architecture.

Rowan's breath hitched as she took in the sight of dragons flying over-head.

Tendrils of fire magic put on a dazzling display of colors that rivaled traditional fireworks. Music only a notch louder than the cheers that crept up from the crowds on the cobblestoned streets below.

"What the fuck?" Her voice shook.

"Dragon City. My home." He breathed as the magic his people offered him in exchange for protection settled in his bones.

Like in Black Cove, his magic extended over the land. He could feel the pulse of anyone tapped into the ley lines. It was so detailed that he could tell down to which spell was being cast and who had cast it. With the frenzy of celebration, he had to adjust his senses to concentrate on the woman beside him. The shadows from the fire of lit lanterns down below danced over her cheeks and wide eyes as they consumed the sight of his kingdom.

"Draconis is a front." Rowan gasped. "This is where all the families live."

"Yes." Alessandro answered, "And this is where I would have sent you had you not been with your family."

She raised an eyebrow, and he could feel her frustration growing once more.

If she had been a shifter, she would have understood him with a simple sift through their link. He had given her access to absolutely everything in his life when he'd offered his neck, while she had offered nothing.

He stamped down on his own annoyance with this. He'd accepted that this would be the case for as long as it took her to fully trust him.

Despite their undeniable chemistry and the fact that they'd crawled so far into each other, it was sometimes hard for them to tear apart; they'd barely known each other for a month.

To a shifter mate, that time wouldn't have mattered. To him, it didn't matter. As soon as he'd realized he could no longer disagree with what his dragon saw, he'd been completely and utterly hers.

Even with the many traits of shifters that she carried, she was an elf-succubus — he still couldn't believe it — -angel.

As such, he knew he would have to win her over the non-shifter way, and as frustrating as it was proving at the moment, he found that the idea fascinated him.

Placing a hand on the small of her back he motioned to the kingdom he'd planned to show her when they were on more sturdy ground, "While I was in charge of my dragons in Draconis, you would have been in charge of leading Dragon City. Of getting the defenses ready in case Draconis fell, like Opal and Phineas were."

She blinked out at the city and he felt the moment it all became clear. "You couldn't send me here because of my family. They can't know."

He shook his head. "No. They can't."

It was the reason he had an entire plan to introduce her to the place.

The smell of salt in the air preceded the tears that rolled down her cheeks.

She turned and wrapped her arms around his waist, burying her face into the space underneath his chest.

Caught off guard, he reflexively returned the embrace.

She'd been suppressing her emotions from the bond.

The fear and sorrow that washed over him as she released her hold on the dam she'd built slashed across his heart.

What could make her feel like this?

Alessandro pulled her in closer, rocking back and forth to soothe the pain.

"I'm trying not to fall here, San. Please stop being so fucking perfect."

He blinked in surprise and down at her. "What?"

She buried her chin against his chest to stare up at him. Her lashes dripped her tears, eyes shone red, nose slightly ran.

Alessandro had never seen a more perfect sight. He cupped her cheek and furrowed his eyebrows.

"Why haven't you given in to your godhood?"

"Because it isn't my power." It was the answer he'd always given. But her shining eyes, both the blue and starry one, required something deeper. Something he'd never admitted out loud. "People know that there are proper gods, those who spring from the celestial realm when enough humans practice their faith, and that there are made-gods, mystics who evolve from the faith of other mystics. What most people are unaware of is that no matter how they got into the celestial realms, they fall into two types of godhood. Do you know what those are?"

She shook her head, and the movement tickled. He ran his fingers through her hair as he continued. "There is the godhood of creation and the godhood of destruction. I fall into the latter category because my people gave me the power to bring about the destruction of King Titus." He sighed. "Gods of destruction are few, because the gods of creation usually enslave or eradicate them."

Her eyes widened.

"I don't and won't give into my godhood because I have no desire to live in that violence. And now you've given me another reason to keep rejecting it." He motioned toward the mating mark on his forehead. "As long as you keep choosing this, keep choosing me, I'm not going any- fucking-where."

"What if one day you are left with no choice?" She whispered. "What am I supposed to do if you're forced to leave?"

He narrowed his eyes. "Is that what's been holding you back?"

She gave a miserable nod.

"We can figure out the middle of what that may all mean together." Her words thrown back at her was all she needed to hear.

She closed her eyes and laughed. "This relationship is going to be such a pain in the ass."

"I realized that the moment you showed up to your coronation with the devil as your godfather." He groaned as he pulled her into his chest and kissed the top of her head. "But you're worth every growing pain."

He didn't have to see her face to tell that she was blushing. He could feel the heat against his sternum.

"San, say we were to make our way over to that giant bed in the middle of the room and you were to lie down while I rode your--"

"Ro, are you about to say something perverted to soften the blow of me saying something intimate?" He asked.

"I-I can be intimate." She pulled back to stare up at him. "Say we were to make our way over to that giant bed in the middle of the room and you were to lie down while I rode your....damn it."

He let out a sharp laugh. "Why don't you just tell me what you were really going to say?" He nuzzled her neck, and she squealed. "I prefer my insatiable mate, if I'm being honest."

She relaxed against him as his tongue snaked out and ran over the scar of where he'd marked her and she became putty in his hands.

"Say it." He growled into her ear, nibbling at the lobe.

Instead of speech, she fed him a vision. It was her first time giving anything to their bond. His dragon damn near purred in his head.

"Your wish is my command." It was only a moment as he tore away the flimsy cloth that was her skirt.

-R-

She let out a frustrated growl. "I liked that skirt."

"Pity." He didn't sound the least bit concerned as he stepped back.

Confusion laced through her until the feel of velvet on her side brought her attention to the curtains that were slinking around her body.

Her jaw dropped. What he had in mind began making sense as the curtains began knotting against her flesh, slowly raising her up, spread open for his viewing pleasure.

"Wai-" the cloth wrapped around her mouth.

His smirk was a challenge. She narrowed her eyes.

"I wanted to ride your face."

He positioned her shins on his shoulders, arms supporting her ass so she could control the movement of her hips. A thrill of pleasure launched from her belly as his tongue carved a trail of heat along her inner thigh through her entire opening.

Well, okay then.

She melted into the ride, the flexibility of the curtains giving her a bounce that aided her momentum as she began climbing the sweet hill of an orgasm. His hand was on her fucking tail and gods. She never knew how lucky she'd been to receive the gifts of her succubus blood until he showed her what their bodies could do together.

The closer she got, the tighter the curtain felt around her limbs, the sensations he felt as he shared her pleasure stacked up, making her body tighten in anticipation.

"Let go."

She didn't want to.

She wanted to hold on to that moment forever. Her breath left her body as he extended his fangs and lightly pierced her bud.

She saw white. Her climax was a geyser as her body shook for what felt like a small eternity before she fell limp against her bindings.

It was a moment of total relaxation that she regretted immediately as one of the several visions that had been haunting her all day slid past the crack of the mental shields.

A combination of flesh and blood colored the wall behind the crumpled body of a middle-aged human woman as a knife repeatedly plunged into her face.

She could hear the cracks and the squelch of the knife, but that wasn't nearly as horrifying as the voice that reached out for Rowan.

Help. Help.

She slammed her shields back into place as she came back to her own reality. Alessandro was stepping out from underneath her, curling her into his arms as the curtains unwound themselves.

Her essence drenched his face. A foreign feeling of absolute possession crawled inside of her as she curled her arms around his neck and trailed her tongue from where she'd claimed him up to the lobe of his ear.

"Give me a second, woman." He growled as his legs ate the distance to the bed.

She saved them the need by phasing them.

Admittedly, it was a clumsy phase as she missed by a couple of feet and they tumbled onto the floor where she climbed over him, taking his mouth in a breathless kiss.

"I want more." She sobbed, her frustration welling up inside of her.

She knew it was irrational. But the visions were undoing her. She needed to find something to anchor her. Shouldn't her mate be perfect for it? Why wasn't it working? Had she fucked it up?

He rolled them so he was on top. He was careful with her wings, concern etched on his eyebrow as he looked her over.

"Alessandro, I feel like I'm drowning." She wiped the tears that escaped from her eyes. "I can't block them out."

His eyes widened. "Who?"

"The cursed objects." She shook her head. "*All* the cursed objects."

Understanding relaxed his face, and he pulled her to sit cross-legged across from him.

"You're connected." His eyes began glowing golden.

He had answers?

She nodded. "I don't know how. I tried searching for the connection after I claimed the staff, but it's a solitary bond."

He let out a soft curse and took a deep breath. "When you hear them, do you feel like they're trying to drag you to them?"

"Yes. But there are so many that it feels like a tug of war."

He closed his eyes and bowed his head.

This was it. The confirmation she'd needed. She straightened her back and put her hands on his cheeks. "What is it?"

His eyes slid open and white light blazed inside of them.

Warm moisture slid down her cheeks as she locked her gaze with his.

Pain lanced through her. She winced, and his hands covered her vision.

Coolness dissipated the pain and when he pulled them away again, Rowan's stomach fell at the sight of the being in front of her.

She'd seen a brief glimpse of this that night he had projected himself into her room to work with the plant.

His scaled skin was as dark as the night sky, but as her eyes roved over every inch she realized, with the help of Odin's Eye, that what it was sheathing wasn't muscle and bones, but pure celestial magic.

His curly hair was so copious it curled along the floor underneath his thighs. It also had its own inner glow.

He was enormous, bending his head to keep it from hitting the ceiling. A head that sported a thick set of horns that curved alongside his head, ending at a point as sharp as her own. His eyes were still shining white and bright, but there was no pain as she took him in.

"As I thought." His voice gonged, layered with tenors so low it was inhuman.

When she next blinked, he was back in his regular form.

"Was that your god form?"

"Not entirely, I won't have access to that unless I fully take on the power, but the fact you saw even a portion would normally mean you've crossed into your own path to godhood, but..." he looked down at his hands and there was blood. "This means that you haven't."

Rowan's hands came away bloody when she touched her own cheeks.

"What?"

He let out a disbelieving laugh. "The objects think you're a god, one who has proven that she can cleanse them because you cleansed the staff. All because of your diet upgrade."

Realization lifted some of the anxiety she'd spiraled into. "Because you're connected to celestial magic. It doesn't matter if you use it, or if you don't. When I take energy from you, I've never differentiated where I took it from. Wait, cursed objects can communicate?"

"It was a theory. Until you just revealed that they're all calling to you. Now, it's a fact."

Surprise rolled through her and she shook her head, "But I could only cleanse the staff because I had demonic and divine magic available to neutralize the piece of demonic back into the divine it still had left...oh my gods."

"Yes?" His grin was mischievous.

She was too excited to roll her eyes at his corny joke. "I know how! I know how to cleanse them all! All I need is to access all of those other branches of magic I didn't have access to before. I already have elemental, divine and demonic. I just need to collect more, which I can do because of my insane godmother! The magic of the Elders was trying to get into me. Because I don't have to siphon just sexual energy like a regular succubus. I can siphon magic!"

He'd figured it out before her. She didn't contemplate it further as she reveled in the clarification of her truth.

So many parts of her abilities had never really made sense to her. She'd always thought it was because of her succubus side being

shrouded in secret. But her ability to calm the beasts of rage lust suf-
ferers four years prior had never sat right with her.

She recalled once holding Stone up for a keg-stand years ago. She'd
been searching for a meal that night, her succubus sifting through the
offerings, and she had felt Stone's desire. It hadn't been for her, but
she'd tasted it, curious if that was how the Dragon King would taste.
In doing so, she'd added it to a collection she hadn't realized she had
been building.

Years and years of sex with so many mystics struck her mute.

She didn't just have shifter, celestial, demonic, divine, and elemental magic; she had a slew of them. If she could just learn how to har-
ness them.

Convenient that she knew of someone whose magic knowledge was
even deeper than hers, and most importantly, could channel magic
through all of his chakra gates.

In the time everything clicked into place in her head, the Dragon
King had made himself comfortable by leaning back on his arms as his
eyes roved all over her still naked body.

Silver pulsed in his eyes along with the gold.

She really needed to work on that color key when she got the
chance.

She crawled forward and his eyes slid down to her nipples as gravity did its thing. "Oh amazing Dragon King, can this lowly girl ask a
favor? I promise it'll come with benefits."

Alessandro's nose flared as her hand slid from his knee and came to
rest on his upper thigh, close to where there was a pulsing white light
that let her succubus know just where to touch him to get the answer
she desired.

She used it as leverage to bring her lips just a breath away from his
own. Her succubus was out so much that her purple glow reflected in
his silver iris.

"I'm listening." His voice came out in a growl, his skin twitching
under her palm.

Her other hand entangled in his hair at the nape of his neck as she pressed her lips against his, making sure her breasts pressed against his chest.

Her tongue encouraged his tongue to join in a slow dance of dominance. He followed her lead. The heat radiating from his length was her cue to create a small distance between them.

"Teach me how to channel everything." She allowed her wrist to linger with pressure against the side of his cock.

He bucked against her, but she tugged at the collection of curls she had in her control.

He growled at her, but didn't move again.

Physically, he was her superior, but the dance of seduction was her native language.

"Fine. But I name my benefit." He hissed.

"Which is?" She asked.

Hus thumb against her lips were rough. "Wrap these pretty little lips around my cock and we can take it from there."

She smirked. "Your wish is my command."

XXXV

R owan awoke to the smell of croissants baking the next morning. Blearily, she opened her eyes to be greeted by the visage of the Dragon King sleeping.

Wonder crept in as she realized he had always woken up first and fell asleep last.

She took her time raking her eyes over the sharpness of his jawline, a contrast to the softness of his supple lips. He had high cheekbones fanned over by long lashes underneath a set of thick eyebrows and the lightest presence of scars from long ago fights.

Her gaze snagged on the inverted triangle with the horizontal line and she raised a hand to trace the lines.

Rainbow eyes swirled open underneath her palm and, embarrassed more than she liked to admit, she cast the same rune spell he'd used on her the first time they met.

Alessandro's eyes closed, the spell much stronger than she'd intended.

"Oh my gods, Rowan, why are you like this?" She hissed to herself as she tried to roll out of bed.

The move made her realize two things.

One, they'd fallen into unconsciousness with him still inside her again.

Two, he was still hard.

She knew she shouldn't, but the desire to bring herself to completion even with him still asleep rolled through her mind.

She groaned at her ethical dilemma, pressing her face into the crook of his neck.

She was more than sated from their activities of the previous night.

After he taught her how to lock her shields so the cursed objects couldn't get to her, she gave him a preview of what he was investing in by teaching her everything else she'd requested.

With the ample sunlight streaming in through the curtains, she fell back into that desperate feeling of when the mark had been fresh on her collarbone.

She traced the raised skin and her other hand found its way in between their bodies to her throbbing bud where it hovered with her indecisiveness.

She bit her lip as she considered how wrong it would be just to keep him inside while she finished herself off.

She didn't know her fingers had made their mind up before her brain did until they brushed over the heated skin on his lower belly and she hissed as their mate bond allowed her to feel the sensation rake along her belly even while he snoozed.

She lost herself to the pleasure as she moved against him.

Her free hand moved up to land on the back of his neck, and she laid kisses along his jawline.

It stirred him to consciousness.

"Fuck, Ro." He hissed as the pleasure skyrocketed in their bond.

She was still catching her breath as he rolled her to her back, careful to cradle her wings. He rocked his hips in a breathless pace as his teeth sunk into her neck.

Rowan cried out in shock.

"Best fucking alarm clock in the world."

Rowan dug her nails into his shoulders. Why was it so hot to hear him use foul language?

There was something seriously fucked up with her,

"How long were you using me like a sex toy?"

"Not long." She cried. "Fuck, San. Fuck."

He was slamming into her with abandon and she was vibrating with their combined pleasure, unable to ground herself enough to discern where he started and she finished.

But then she was finishing all over him and he looked like the cockiest dragon that ever existed as he took in the sight.

"You're beautiful." She whispered and was pleased to see the color bloom over his chest and race up to his cheeks.

Her stomach growled, and he let out a bark of laughter.

"Come on. I know you smelled that bakery downstairs."

-R-

"So how is this Judgement going to go?" Rowan asked an hour later.

They'd run into Anya at the bakery. Apparently, she lived in the house right next door. She had a whole breakfast spread set out for Terra and Phineas whose similarities shone in their state of hung-overness.

It was shocking to see the normally proper earth-dragon in mismatching pajamas, her hair underneath a satin bonnet, blowing the steam out of a cup of coffee, a pair of thick-lensed glasses perched on her nose that fogged up when she got too close.

"We have plenty of evidence from the second attack on Draconis from cameras around the city." Terra began.

"And the endless statements the citizens have turned into us!" Anya sighed as she poured her own cup of coffee. "They didn't hold back. They want him dead as much as we do."

Phineas let out a small groan of approval but couldn't lift his head. His mate looked more amused than annoyed.

"The initial attack is our weakest point. We have only hearsay. At best, we have circumstantial evidence of his involvement with Elaine. Apparently, a coffee shop downtown caught them on camera when they got coffee together once." Terra scowled. "If we can get Cherry

Young to testify, we think her story will include more details to further condemn him, but she won't speak. Dae Kang agreed to testify only if Cherry Young does and if he does, maybe his brother can fill in the gaps even further."

Anya leaned against the island as she sipped her coffee. "Well, he tortured her for weeks. It's surprising she's gaining as much traction as she has over the last couple of days."

Terra nodded her acknowledgement. "At least we have the alphas testifying, Stone will give our story since Alessandro wasn't present when it happened, your father will give his when Hye iced his whole kingdom and you're still giving your account of every time you showed up, right?"

The note of trepidation in Terra's voice surprised Rowan. "Of course."

Terra winced at Alessandro's growl of disapproval. "I don't mean to doubt you, but—we've never had to rely on anyone outside of the Thunder to take care of our issues. It's...."

"Humbling." Phineas stared up at Rowan through thick, dark eyelashes. "But you're part of the Thunder now, so if we go down, you go down with us."

Anya gave him a swift slap on the back of the head. "Why don't you just fall back to sleep, old man?"

Phineas rubbed the back of his head, pouting up at his mate.

"He's not wrong, Terra, I won't let you down," Rowan said softly, reaching a hand out to her.

Terra smiled and was about to reach out before Alessandro, who had Rowan perched on his lap as she conversed with his family, pulled her away.

Terra rolled her eyes. "Look, when the hard part is over, why don't you two leave for a week or two? Let Stone try to handle things solo and you two can focus on settling the mark?"

Rowan grinned. "I think a month is more realistic."

Alessandro let out a sound that reminded Rowan of a purr as he stabbed a few sausages on his fork and brought them to her lips.

"Please, I'm already feeling ill," Terra groaned, taking another whiff of her coffee to settle her stomach.

Rowan could hardly believe she was sick of them as she'd caught her staring at them more than once with an incredible softness that confirmed Terra loved Alessandro only as a brother.

Anya tsked and brought out a bottle of dark brown liquid with a hint of maroon at its center that Rowan recognized as ambrosia laced whiskey.

"Dear. Have mercy." Phineas groaned from his daughter's side, still unable to lift his head from the island.

"The only way to clear a hangover is with the hair of the dog. You two overindulged, so now you must pay the price for not knowing your limit." Anya's voice was nearly singing as she poured five shot glasses.

"I knew I liked you." Rowan beamed as Anya passed her two servings.

"Remind me to never leave you two alone." Alessandro reached for his glass before Rowan could take both of them for herself. "You'll drink the kingdom dry."

Anya's laugh was joy as she shoved her husband's and daughter's share in front of them. "To our new queen consort and our king."

Terra and Phineas groaned as they raised their glasses, nearly sobbing.

Chapter 23

"I only need twenty minutes." Rowan tried to reassure an irate Alessandro, who was glaring at her through the mirror.

"I can go." He tried to state rather than ask.

It was really such a shame that Rowan, a professional at getting her way, knew how to curb this attempt.

"If you wait, I will take you on a proper date."

His irritation fizzled out to fresh incredulity. "A date?"

Rowan turned on her vanity stool and raised an eyebrow. "Yes. You know we go out, get to know each other, get really lucky later on?"

He steadied his thunderous red gaze on her as he put a contemplative hand on his chin. "I'll wait, but I want to plan the date."

She sighed and raised her hands in surrender. "Oh, okay, if you must."

He narrowed his eyes. "Did you just trick me?"

She grinned, standing on the tips of her toes and laying a kiss on his chin. "I'll be back, okay?"

He growled. "Fine. But only twenty minutes. I still don't trust the witch."

She held a pinky up and he glanced at it, confused.

"Oh, come on! No way you don't know what a pinky promise is!"

"I've never made one." His sincerity melted her heart a little.

She shaped his pinky into a hook and connected her own to his.

When the world reformed, Rowan found herself in front of a black Victorian-style home so out of place in the middle of a cookie cutter suburb neighborhood.

She stepped forward and laid a palm against the barrier she could see as clearly as if it were solid with the aid of Odin's Eye.

She shot a tendril of magic at it to let the witch know she stood right outside.

The door creaked open of its own volition.

There was a certain smell of moths and flame that Rowan associated with Chloe and Master Japhet's home, but as she walked past the threshold, Rowan realized it might be all witches who carried this scent.

Her heels clicked as she walked through a cozy, dimly lit living room, past a set of curving stairs and into what she assumed was the kitchen of the home.

Cherry was lighting a cauldron when Rowan set her eyes on her.

The last time Rowan had seen the witch, she'd been a bloody mess, her face unrecognizable from Barros' strikes.

Miasma had never failed to erase every trace of Rowan's most troubling wounds; a deep slice that had reached bone after one of her most intense spars with Axel came to mind.

It was therefore a testament of the dire conditions the witch had been in as scars of her attack were still present even weeks after Miasma's treatment.

To Rowan, it didn't detract from the beauty Cherry Young held. In fact, it seemed to deepen her allure. There was now a certain air of mystery to her, a certain power.

"You're a week late. I was wondering if I'd have to go through with my promise." Cherry spoke without even a single glance up.

Rowan placed the leather-bound book down on the cluttered counter, "Wouldn't want you to flex your fragile power just yet, Ms. Young. Sorry it's later than promised. Life got in the way."

Cherry shrugged her shoulders, "So the news reports say. Every. Single. Day. You're making a name for yourself, Ms. Dahl. Do you know how much more powerful you could've been under our tutelage?"

Rowan's temper flared. "You ever going to let that go?"

"It was not a slight but an honor to receive the offer to join us." Cherry hissed as she snatched a bundle of lavender from a collection of dried herbs dangling from an overhead rack with a little more force than strictly required.

Rowan rolled her eyes, seeing this conversation going nowhere. With her end of the bargain fulfilled, she turned on her heel.

"Wait!" The witch called, her voice breaking.

Rowan turned with horror.

Cherry's arms were shaking on the counter as if she was bracing all her weight on her palms.

Her gaze locked deep into the steaming cauldron.

Nothing about the witch before Rowan was solid. She was on the verge of falling apart.

Rowan's shoulders relaxed, and she sat on a stool at the counter, waiting for Cherry to get it together.

"Thank you." The whispered gratitude made Rowan feel uncomfortable; she didn't know how to handle this version of the witch. "For saving me."

"Oh." Rowan shook her head, "You would've never been that hurt if it hadn't been for my mouth."

"He sped up the process, but in the end, Barros was going to kill me. I was one reason he ended up turning to that cursed tool." She hissed.

"Oh?" Rowan got comfortable in the seat.

Cherry glanced up and shock made her take a step away from the counter. "Your eye... is that Odin's Eye?"

"Yes. It is." Rowan said softly, "Is that a problem?"

Cherry took her in for the first time and her eye snagged on the mark over Rowan's collar bone. She'd taken to wearing low cut shirts in order to show it off. An unexpected sense of pride didn't allow her to do anything less

"You really are the Dragon King's mate, aren't you?"

Rowan couldn't help but smile at the sentence, "Yes. Yes, I am."

Cherry's shoulders sagged as she reached for a shaker to sprinkle sugar into her concoction.

"There was a reason Barros targeted the shifters." Cherry spoke slowly, as if she was unconvinced she really wanted to divulge this information.

Answers. Rowan loved straight answers, and it seemed the witch would give them.

"About four years before the first attack, Barros was trying to get attention brought onto a rise in rage lust cases."

Rowan relaxed into her seat. "Oh."

Cherry raised an eyebrow. "Were you also aware of the issue?"

"My company works on accidents brought about by wayward magic. We got more than a few cases called in that year." Rowan admitted.

"Well, the Coven was also aware, but used this information as leverage to build a compound on territory that the shifters disputed was theirs."

Rowan snorted. "Of course, put the Coven infrastructure over the safety of everyone else."

"That compound has helped over a thousand low-income Coven members get out of dangerous situations. And I didn't hear you kicking up a storm to do anything about it." Cherry hissed.

Rowan raised an eyebrow. "What would the words of an elf only slightly above average in terms of magical capability have done? I only had the option of actions, Cherry. Exactly how did you think the rise ended? "

Other than the bubbling of the cauldron, there was silence in the kitchen for the most tense of moments.

"How?" Cherry demanded.

"Confidential." Rowan shrugged.

"So there are no more instances of rage lust occurring?" Cherry's brows knitted together in confusion.

"We found out why there was an increase and we took care of it, but no, we didn't stop the instances of rage lust completely. We're working on it."

Cherry's nose flared, "I'm thinking that maybe you could be of help to the Coven at this moment."

Rowan let out a sharp laugh. "Say what?"

"You've debuted this week in the Mystic's Top 100." Cherry said, "You stopping the wolves in Greece was unexpected. You showing up to stop Black Cove's attack on Draconis amplified your power and position. You're currently good PR fodder, and like the dragons will surely use this to soften their relationship with the public, I'd like to propose a similar relationship with the Coven."

"You know that my relationship with the dragons is because their king is my mate, right? Exactly how could you offer something similar?" Rowan crossed her arms.

"Well..." It didn't seem that Cherry had quite had a proposal all planned out. "We could give you a leadership role."

Rowan sighed, "Cherry, I have not changed my stance. I want nothing to do with the Coven. There's too much history between us, especially if you take on the role of the Elder."

"I could leave it to someone else!" Cherry hissed. "Ms. Dahl. Judgement has been called for Antoni Barros. His testimony will tear our credibility to shreds. The accusations the shifters will throw at us will be detrimental to our operations. The Coven may have seemed like a source of misery for you, but we have helped more than harmed over the years."

"Yes, you have. But the moment you tried to infringe on my will is the moment you lost your chance of ever receiving my help. There's only one thing the Coven and you can do to survive the public outlash. Confess. Give your side of the story. Help the shifters point the finger in the right direction. Antoni Barros acted alone, and though he will apparently use rage lust as his excuse for his actions, he'll throw both the shifters and the Coven under the bus when he tells his side. Only your testimony will save the Coven Cherry, especially if you're the one in charge. How could anyone think that this was a Coven backed initiative if its current leader was a person he hurt?"

Cherry's eyes glistened as she shook her head. "That's just it, Ms. Dahl. He made me a victim. How can I take command of a force like the Coven when he exposed me as someone weak enough to become a victim? "

The image of her bloody body gave Rowan pause. She couldn't do this. Trick the woman who was still so obviously affected by the man into testifying, even if it would be better for the Thunder, for the people she'd agreed to lead.

Still, she had little mercy for the woman who'd been at the center of making her life hell for so long to offer words of comfort.

"It's your story, Cherry. You decide if you were truly a victim or a survivor." Rowan stood. "I'll see you around."

XXXVI

❦

"An amusement park?"

Alessandro grinned down at the flabbergasted face of Rowan as she looked around the sidewalk surrounded by rollercoasters and carnival games. The sounds of screaming riders and laughter screeched out as he produced two hats with "Jacques' Famous Fun-Ground" stitched in bright yellow letters.

"Only one rule, no magic." He said, holding one out to her while he placed the other over his head.

She narrowed her eyes. "Who blabbed?"

He lifted the bill of the hat to show off his mating mark as an answer. Though much slower than his memories had come to her, since their talk over his godhood, she'd let up on her blockage of the bond. He had seen a few recollections of what had been Rowan's core. Most notably of the bunch, a memory of a day in an amusement park where a costumed rabbit had scared her out of her mind.

Since that day, she hadn't been able to face returning to a supposed place of joy that she could only associate with terror.

"Today, we are conquering fear together." He placed the cap on her head, tilting it back so he could place a brief kiss on her forehead. "Even if that damned rabbit shows back up."

She wrapped her hand tightly around his and stuck to his side. "If that damned rabbit shows back up, I'm going to set it on fire."

Alessandro tutted. "No magic."

She bristled. "If you hated me, you should've just told me. I can take it. I'm a big girl."

"If I told you I hated you, you'd probably drown in tears," he teased, leading the way to a stand equipped with water guns and galloping horses.

Rowan sighed. "I knew taking you out of that cave was going to bite me in the ass one day."

He laughed and pulled a stool out for her to occupy while he took the one next to hers. "Would you like to wager?"

Her shoulders straightened, and she placed her hands on both sides of her gun. "What exactly did you have in mind?"

He knew it was a lot to ask for, but his dragon needed it above everything else. "If I win, we disappear for a month to allow the mark a chance to really settle."

She tried to read him, but her brush of magic was too familiar to go unnoticed by him. He tutted, "No magic, Rowan."

She frowned, but moved on. "And if I win?"

"What do you want?"

"We live in my cabin."

He found it entertaining that either way this went, he'd benefit. He hadn't really been too sure on how to broach the residence situation. Of course he'd expected they would live together, but as accomplished spellcasters they could both phase anywhere they needed to go in case the Traveling Cabin decided it wanted to keep bouncing from place to place.

"Agreed." He turned to the operator of the stand, a slack jawed centaur. He apparently recognized them both and with the media coverage over the attack, it didn't surprise Alessandro.

A quick scan around showed that the operator hadn't been the only one to make the connection. Even after he'd gone through the trouble of casting a stealth spell to mute their magic, he hadn't thought to change their appearance.

"Come on, sir, I need this to go my way, so sabotage him if you can." Rowan broke the tension.

The centaur shook out of his shock, then held up a filthy handkerchief to set them up. "On your marks…" He began, "Get set…" Rowan was all attention on the target.

"GO!"

The bells and lights exploded to life as Rowan's horse reached the finish line first.

She hooted with celebration, pumping her fists in the air.

He grinned as the spectacle that was his mate made the crowd second guess their assumption that the two were the esteemed king and queen of the dragons.

It was with fewer eyes overlooking that they worked their way down the carnival stands with new wagers at every stop.

A basketball throwing contest won her a shiny knife she'd noticed in his bedroom in Dragon City. He secured a breakfast in bed through a high striker round handicapped by limited use of his thumb and forefinger only. A ring toss won her a quickie in a secluded alleyway.

By the time they made it to their first roller coaster, Alessandro's arms were full of the oversized stuffed animals they'd also collected. Before strapping himself in, he turned to the ride operator, a teenage gorgon who was staring with open desire at the Dragon King.

"Protect those with your life."

The teenager's eyes widened, but she gave a firm nod.

Rowan grinned at him as the ride started pulling them along. It always stunned him, the joy he could make her feel by the simplest things.

Tilting her chin up, he sealed her lips with his just as they began their first descent. Butterflies flared to life in his stomach as he realized he was falling without control on his part. And wasn't that just how this journey with her had begun?

XXXVII

The press coverage was more appropriate for well-known award shows rather than the trial of a man whose actions had cost the lives of so many.

It was how life worked when so many mystics came together as they had to for Judgement. It was an open secret that the goal was to show everyone else up.

Rowan, as the unfamiliar face for the Draconian Thunder, wore silken traditional dragon garbs, drapes of blue and silver fabrics pinned around her body with tungsten jewelry on her throat, ears and wrists.

Her hair was pin straight, sweeping just past her shoulders, tinsel shining when light hit it at just the right angle.

Her mating mark was out on full display, matching Alessandro's as they led the collection of all the shifters who Barros' action had affected.

Her wings, tail and horns set her apart from the crowd of humanoid mystics. Years of living without the appendages hadn't prepared her to stand out so starkly.

Rowan was just grateful Alessandro commanded a lot of attention, regardless of his lack of extra limbs.

He was a sexy man. Dressed in a doublet-inspired piece that showcased the strength of his wide chest, his every move made him seem indecent. When Rowan first caught sight of him working on the thick braid, now contained in tungsten cuffs at every 3 inches, she'd dropped her purse.

Underneath the tight top made from the same fabric as her piece, his muscles had bunched and stretched. She demanded he take responsibility for getting her wet just by existing in that moment.

It cost them an extra thirty minutes, which they'd had to answer for when Terra cut them an exasperated look and nearly lectured them for what had felt like the hundredth time just that day until she realized all the other alphas had their eyes on them.

His magic was a second layer of protection to her quickly diminishing anonymity. Though it was not as overwhelming as when they were in Black Cove or Dragon City, magic shrouded him so thickly even those races who were notorious for having little to no access to magic felt it as he passed by the docks that allowed them access to the front steps of Judgement Hall.

Judgement Hall was the only building on a giant jutting black slab that had been stuck in the middle of international waters for centuries.

It was a quick way to distinguish low level magic users and humans who arrived through boats or jets rather than phasing in.

The actual building of Judgement Hall was a simple structure of several ornate support columns. They held up a stained glass ceiling depicting every race included in Judgement's jurisdiction

The sight of the building she'd only ever seen in articles and magazines struck her speechless. There had been no justice done to the details of the work.

Her eyes snagged on the depiction of a succubus and a pang of homesickness for a place she'd never known struck her.

Before knowing the family secret, Rowan had imagined one day she would meet her kin, but now that she knew there was no one she could call kin, who she didn't already know, those emotions had nowhere to land.

She wondered if she would catch sight of one as she scanned the many mystics surrounding them. The crowd was so thick she wasn't sure she would.

Past the columns, a sinking pit held assigned benches and tables for witnesses of the proceedings. The benches covered all 360 degrees of the middle of the floor where a platform held a stool for the use of the accused and a podium for the presenting of evidence for or against the defense.

Usually, the affected parties sat on the lowest section facing their trespasser and while the shifters were the main targets of these attacks, her family sat next to a small dark blue-haired fairy who turned large watery eyes to land on Rowan as soon as she began her descent.

The clicks of her heels sped up as Rowan all but dragged Alessandro down the stairs to reach the woman.

As soon as she reached her, the fairy had expanded her physical body so she could catch Rowan in a tight embrace.

Rain, Dew's mother, always smelled like her namesake. Rowan allowed the familiar scent to take her over as she hid her face in the ample bosom of the woman.

Her readiness to give forgiveness was too much for Rowan to take, especially when she hadn't even apologized yet.

"I'm sorry, I'm sorry." She chanted as the woman's grip tightened.

"Now, now, young Rowan, head up."

Rowan furiously wiped a tear away as she did as commanded. "I failed you, Rain."

Understanding shone in those haunting blue eyes. "Dew is in the next phase of her existence, young elf. I see her every morning on the blades of grass, sometimes on the pane of my windows. Next time just look and you'll feel her too."

It wasn't the same for those who were not fae.

She didn't have access to Dew like her mother continued to. Her loss was much more permanent, in a way more fitting of a punishment.

Still, who was she to deny Rain's attempts at comfort when it was her daughter?

"Thank you, Rain."

Rain gave her one last pat on the cheek before returning to her original size and zooming out of the way to reveal a breathtaking black haired woman with jade hued eyes.

She was in a silken green dress that fell across her body so snuggly it left nothing to the imagination. She wore a crown made of light bark on her head.

"Titania." Alessandro's displeasure with the woman was clear.

She didn't spare him a glance as she moved forward, eyes on Rowan's as she raised her hands to cup her cheeks.

Unsure of how to react, Rowan didn't fight against the force of the woman as she turned her head this way and that, looking for something specific.

"She's young." The woman hissed in disgust.

"Yes, my queen." Rain answered, landing on her shoulder. "But she is powerful."

The woman sighed and leaned in.

Alessandro had had enough. He placed his hand over Rowan's mouth a moment before the woman's kiss could land and pulled her back into his chest.

"*Mine.*" He snarled.

The woman turned her eyes up to him as if registering he was there for the first time. "Dragon King, it's been ages!"

"Why are you here, Titania? You're already falling apart." He demanded and Rowan noticed with a shock that the woman was indeed falling apart as an ear tumbled from her head, transforming into a pile of leaves on the floor.

A substitution spell combined with projection?

"I am here to deliver Favor."

Favor from any of the Fae was an invitation to visit Faerie.

Dew had told them once that she intended to apply a favor with the queen so that one day they could visit her home. Emotion swelled up in Rowan's throat as she pictured Dew leading her by the hand into Faerie rather than just by memory.

"There are other ways to deliver favor." Alessandro ran a hand down Rowan's arm and pointed at her wrist. "This is the only area I give you permission to place your lips."

Rowan bristled at the insinuation that he had a right to speak for her before her mate mark emitted a prickly sensation over her chest.

"*Your lips are mine. And mine alone.*" Alessandro hissed in her head.

"*Considering they're on my face, I feel like I should get more of a say on what I do with them!*" She hissed back.

"*Kiss her and I'll run her through. Would you like to be the catalyst of a war between Faerie and this realm?*"

Rowan rocked her foot back and stepped on his shoe. "*You're making me want to do it more. She looks like just my type, dark hair and gorgeous eyes.*"

He let out a growl of displeasure. "*I can stop a kiss of death on your hand. Your lips are another story.*"

"*Kiss of death?*"

"*It's what she's known for.*"

"*You could've started with that.*"

"*You could've just trusted me.*"

There was no way he was pouting, right?

She snuck a glance up and, though his face was placid, his eyes were rolling with red shards of light.

Remembering that he had a whole beast he was constantly fighting for control of his body over, Rowan smiled at the woman.

"I'm sure you understand."

The green eyes ran through Rowan and a tendril of foreign magic sliced through her in a painful slash over her stomach. It pissed Titania off, but she didn't argue, simply brushed her lips over the thin layer of skin.

Magic pulsed to life on the point she'd touched. Rowan blinked down at the dark mark that reminded her of a keyhole.

"Pass through any fairy circle to find us, young one. It'll only work once." Rain waved from her queen's shoulder. "Dew cherishes you."

The last words were a whisper on the wind as both bodies turned to a pile of leaves at Rowan's feet.

"Rowan?" Alessandro asked softly.

It made her realize she'd been stuck, staring at the pile, unable to move.

She sat next to her father, who took her hand and held it.

As the rest of the shifters filed in, Rowan's mind was numb.

How could Rain forgive her? Even if Fae saw death differently, Rain was still Dew's mother. She still had yet to forgive herself. How could the fairy?

She didn't realize tears were flowing down her face until Alessandro's thumb wiped the trail away.

"What do you need?"

She didn't know. But she couldn't continue to weep. She was the Dragon Queen! This was her first time in public while holding the title and she was wrecking their reputation more thoroughly than Barros had.

The crinkle of plastic brought her attention to her father, who slid out two packaged rolls from his suit's breast pocket and two pouches of juice. He set one pair in front of her and handed the other to Alessandro.

She had decided to not confront her parents over Lucifer's revelation. She didn't have it in her to hurt her mother by bringing up the woman who'd abandoned her as a child.

The only thing that had changed was her knowledge of her power. Over the last few days with Alessandro by her side, she'd already grown by leaps and bounds now that she had all the puzzle pieces and his inane ability to guide her.

Still, it wasn't until she witnessed his lack of hesitation in taking the offering that the fact that he was her mate settled in her mind.

The Dragon King punctured both of their juices and began opening his roll while she fumbled with hers. She couldn't see past the tears that had fattened up so much they threatened to drown her as they fell.

With a mouth full of strawberry cake already ebbing some of the pain, she slid her chair closer to him, decorum be damned as she leaned against his arm. She was slowly recovering her strength to see this trial through to the end.

Across from their section, Rowan caught sight of the Coven taking their seats.

Dorin Indigo and Eve Tanoch led a group of witches, but Cherry was nowhere to be seen.

Had it been too much? Had her trauma from Antoni Barros been too much to bear?

Rowan didn't look down on the witch for it, but it gave her a thrill of guilt for trying to use that to the Thunder's advantage.

"Hey, you didn't tell me we could bring snacks!" Louisa's voice slid into Rowan's mind.

Rowan turned her head to pinpoint where her friend stood. She wore a matcha-green off the shoulder dress that reached her ankles, red hair reached past her shoulders in soft waves, her makeup subtle except for the pop of bright red lipstick.

Rosario the Cruel was a sharp contrast in a no nonsense black three-piece suit. Brown hair pulled back in a tight, slick bun. She was all business. Though she also wore makeup, black lipstick was her crowning statement.

A wave of lust erupted from someone to Rowan's left.

Having gotten the nosey gene from her mother, she leaned back to glimpse who was sitting there and shock rolled through her at the sight of Harris Knox's silver eyes firmly locked on the vampiress.

Annabelle, the only other succubus present, had also turned to examine the originator of such uncontained lust and a mischievous glint took hold when Rowan glanced at her to check if she'd sensed the same thing.

"In our dear wolf's eyes, you might be the snack, Louisa. Exactly what happened there?"

Louisa, who'd been following her mother down the steps, snapped her attention to where Harris Knox was sitting. Either unaware or concerned with the attention he was gathering.

"Don't let my mom see!" Louisa's fear set Rowan into action.

Alessandro shot her a questioning look as she stood. "I need to talk to Knox."

She hoped by using his last name she would ease any jealousy that might flare up in the dragon. She was astonished that he gave a small nod and turned to talk to Stone, who had been whispering something to him.

Taking this golden chance of unhindered decision making, she began walking the length of the row, bringing the wolf's attention to her since she walked his way.

She stopped behind his chair. A soft knock to his telepathic walls allowed her access to say what she needed to without being overheard.

"You need to put the headlights away when her mother is present." She got right to the point.

His eyes narrowed in annoyance. *"I am not afraid of Rosario the Cruel."*

"You should be." Rowan crossed her arms, trying to decide how angry Louisa would be at what she was about to reveal. *"Her cruelty has in the past extended to her daughter."*

His nose flared, and he moved to stand, but she placed a hand on his shoulder to keep him in place.

"I know your alpha instincts are screeching to go rescue her, but this is not the time and place for it. We are still trying to convince the world shifters aren't willingly going to go into fits of violence. You going up there will most definitely end up in a physical confrontation and while I'm sure you could go toe to toe with Rosario physically, Rosario's loss will most assuredly be all of shifter-kind's loss. Louisa can handle her mother. She's been doing it for ages.

If you react, you're going to fuck up everything she's been working hard for over the last decade."

He let out a displeased growl. Rowan noted the tension in Naseem's back as Alessandro leaned forward to glance down at them.

"Still in control." She shot towards him and he relaxed back into his chair once more to continue his conversation. Only after Naseem's tension released somewhat did Rowan look back at the wolf.

She held out a conjured handkerchief and pointed to the corner of his mouth. "Just right there, Mr. Knox." She tried to smile as softly as possible as the next words she telepathically shot towards him were full of command. *"Turn around and keep your eyes off of Louisa Monterrey. You may contact her after the trial ends."*

He took the offered cloth and wiped at the corner of his mouth. His eyes returned to the hazel tone she'd grown to associate with the alpha. "Thank you, Dragon Queen."

"No problem." She chirped and began heading back to her mate's side while throwing back some last words. *"That handkerchief was for actual use. You were drooling."*

He let out a bark of laughter and Rowan turned her attention to her other concern, her mother.

"This is your only warning, butt out."

Annabelle gasped, as if affronted.

"You know Rosario will only try to lock Louisa away in a tower if she finds out."

Annabelle threw her a withering look. *"You never let me have any fun."*

"What will your silence cost?"

"I'm in charge of your bachelorette."

It was no actual loss. Rowan doubted the Dragon King had any intention of being at the center of the pandemonium that was a royal elf's wedding.

Lexine's wedding had been such an ordeal that even their cool and collected father had to take a walk to recollect himself after a meltdown surrounding the wrong utensils being delivered on the day of the event.

"*Fine. But no pressuring the Dragon King to ask for my hand just so you can throw it. Only if he asks for it himself.*"

"*Fine.*"

Annabelle's eyes twinkled, and she grabbed King Kyron's arm excitedly. "Do you think Rowan is more of a periwinkle or a baby rose kind of girl?"

King Kyron didn't miss a beat in answering. "Sage green."

Rowan didn't hear what her mother replied because, from the section across the way from them, Antoni Barros had appeared. He was being led in by two minotaurs, shackled with nulling chains around his wrists.

Even if she'd seen his reformation first hand, Rowan hadn't realized his arm had also grown back.

His blonde hair was dull, his skin a sickly green tinge, but he was whole.

His eyes found her as his guards forced him into the seat on the raised platform. His chains locked to rods on either side of the chair, which was bolted to the floor to keep him from moving too much.

Rowan's chin tipped up in defiance as hatred boiled deep in his eyes.

Alessandro growled beside her. She reached out and interlaced their fingers together, soothing his beast.

Fury filled the eyes of the witch and he bucked against his chains before one of the minotaurs placed a hand on his head to keep him from moving. A subtle threat that the man heeded.

Once the sections were full, an eerie hush settled over the collection.

A goblin entered the floor. Dressed in black velvet robes, his scaly green scalp held strands of black and gray hair, and on his large hooked nose, a pair of spectacles sat as he shuffled papers. He cleared his throat and, with a voice amplification spell, said to the thousands of spectators. "Today, we are gathered to decide the fate of a man accused of using the gifts of a god-level cursed object to manipulate the public's opinion of shifters. The actions of this individual have cost three hundred and seventy-two lives to be lost. We will hear testimony from Stone the Dragon Prince of the Draconian Thunder, Queen Consort Rowan Dahl of the Draconian Thunder, King Kyron of the Eastern Elven Kingdom, Alpha Abanoub of The Egyptian Sphinx Lair, Alpha Harris Knox of the Mediterranean Wolf Pack, Alpha Meadow of the Canadian Sleuth, Alpha Juliana of the Amazon Knot, Elder Cherry Young of the Coven, Dae Kang of the Coven and Hye Kang of the Coven."

Shock roiled through her. She snapped her head around the front tables trying to spot the copper red hair of the witch who had seemed so indisposed at her visit to take the position of Elder. She found her, dressed in the white robes of the Elder, with Dae Kang and Hye Kang on either side of her. Rowan couldn't recall ever seeing the woman more vibrant. Was this Elder magic settled? Available to her because she had the Elder's Grimoire back?

They made eye contact. Cherry's face softened just a fraction, and Rowan beamed at her. Cherry rolled her eyes and returned her attention to the goblin.

"Antoni Barros could not find witnesses to come to his defense, and as such, will give his defense testimony himself. As always, the podium has a spell of truth cast on it. Everything you hear will be the truth to the best knowledge of the witnesses. At the end, the Scales of Justitia will appear and each of the representatives will cast a pebble to determine if Antoni Barros' life will be forfeit or if he shall go free. We call now the first witness to the stand, Prince Stone."

XXXVIII

Alessandro had never felt the fact that Stone was still so young hit him until he was on that stand. Though in command of the situation, well-spoken and charming as always, the man lit up in a way that spoke of his youth. It took a long search through Alessandro's memory to recall when his heir had lit up like that.

In his early days, he'd been eager to follow Alessandro around like a second shadow. Had sought constant approval from the man who had seen potential in the kid even before he'd shown his double affinity for air and water magic.

Did Stone even want to be king? When Alessandro had informed him of his decision to retire, Stone had accepted it without a fight. But now that Alessandro thought of it, the young dragon had seemed more resigned than enthused.

Before he knew it, Rowan was called forward to give her testimony and while Stone waited by the podium to give her his hand to help her up, Alessandro was finding it hard to fathom that he'd been so blind to Stone's reluctance.

"Well done." Alessandro said as his heir retook his seat.

Stone looked abashed, as he always did when Alessandro paid him a compliment.

"One day you're going to have to teach me to talk like that." Naseem grinned at the young dragon, raising a hand to ruffle his hair.

Stone grinned and fluffed his hair back into shape as Rowan began her recounting of interfering with the dragons and the attack of Elaine after the fact.

She skirted around the fact that she was Blessed and able to purify Pan's Flute by implying the Dragon King's appearance had caused the water-dragon to return to her original form. Technically not a lie, but a definite mislead.

He hadn't given details to any of his dragons and he could feel the shift in Naseem and Stone as Rowan's story went into detail over the attack. Particularly how malformed and bloodthirsty Elaine had been.

"She regretted her actions." Alessandro assured them.

Stone's shoulders dropped, and Naseem shook his head.

He hadn't heard the details of what had happened with the wolves. Her description of the civilians jumping into the water to get away from them and the little girl she'd barely saved dug in the horror of the loss of the innocent.

Rowan's time with Abanoub was also new information and Alessandro wondered if, when the mark finally settled, he would see those moments in her exchange of memories.

Her eyes, which had been floating around the hall, just as much of a natural charmer as Stone was, landed on him and as she delved into the attack on the Eastern Elven Kingdom followed by her kidnapping, a vision filled his head.

The room was lit by wall sconces. He was behind the rods of a golden cage. The sounds of flesh against flesh reverberated in the room and his hands were burning, pain lashing through the rest of his body. He blinked, and the vision disappeared as Rowan went into the night Black Cove became Barros' target.

He tried to regain control of his dragon, but he wanted the witch dead.

It was suddenly an offense that the man was breathing the same air as his mate, that he was looking at her. The fury Barros had shown when he first saw her had grown each second she spoke.

"Alessandro, you're icing the Hall," Stone hissed from beside him.

He didn't care. Couldn't care. His woman was in the line of fire from that piece of scum and taking care of her was the only reason he existed.

Rowan snapped her gaze back to him, and he faltered.

"*I'm okay.*"

It was what he needed to ground himself.

He relaxed his grip on his chair, cursing when it snapped off.

Once again, she skirted the fact that she was the Blessed by alluding that the Dragon King called forth an unknown being and had the man cleansed. Historic magic, she called it, proud and awed, and he knew she still couldn't actually believe she'd done it.

King Kyron helped her down from the podium, his eyes shining with emotion Alessandro found he couldn't read as well as he could usually do with others.

But Rowan smiled and motioned to the podium before walking away.

Already known as the Bloody Elf, King Kyron was infamous, but he'd never given speeches as he would for Judgement.

It was short, sweet and efficient, but there was so much appeal that he'd passed down to his daughter that Alessandro heard a few sighs of longing.

Rowan snickered at his side when her mother gave a huff of displeasure.

When Harris was called forth, he and King Kyron took each other's forearms in the same greeting Alessandro had seen Kin exchange with the man.

When he sat, Rowan asked. "You know Knox?"

"He came looking for you when you were recovering. His daughter, Marissa, was apparently insistent. She gained your mother's favor, and we hosted him for a couple of nights."

Rowan scoffed and turned to her mother. "Since when are you good with kids?"

"Since it hit me. I'm really going to be a grandmother." Annabelle pouted, digging into her husband's side much like Rowan had done with her mate.

"*Are you going to tell me what's going on between you two?*" He asked, attempting nonchalance as he noted the annoyance that passed through Harris when he locked eyes with Rowan.

She sighed, and while Harris Knox spoke, she sent the story right to his head.

Alessandro couldn't help the grin. "*You should know by now that you can't thwart the mating feeling.*"

His hand caressed her shoulder to prove the point.

She melted into his side. He could stay there in that seat forever if she kept touching him and using him as a support. "*Yes, but we were both pretty damn stubborn about it and even when we both knew it was inevitable, you gave me the choice. Louisa deserves it too.*"

"I received another one of your memories."

Her eyebrows raised. "*What, which one?*"

"The one of you in that cage." He tightened his grip on her hand. "*I didn't really know what I was asking of you when I asked you to Cleanse him. When they convict him, I plan on volunteering to be the one to execute him.*"

"*To be fair, I didn't tell you.*" She tightened her own hold on him. "*If I could ask, could you let someone else do it? Now that we know Cherry is testifying, she will definitely bring up rage lust.*"

The words were like a hollow gong in his head.

"I'm still not convinced it was the best idea not to bring it up ourselves." He said.

"*I think you're just not accustomed to allowing Stone to take the lead. If he's your heir, you'll have to trust him.*"

"So if I run Barros through-"

"It will look like vengeance, like you're trying to shut him up."

"So who do you think should do it?"

Rowan's chin pointed towards the new Coven Elder as Juliana helped her to the stage. The Brazilian Knot Alpha had green hair and a black sheath dress reminded him of her form when she shifted.

The Elder's face glowed when light bounced off the several sets of scars. She sent Barros a frosty glare, her nose flaring when he leaned back in his seat, as if her presence was inconsequential.

Julianna shot Alessandro a slightly anxious look before she found her way back to her seat.

Cherry Young wasted no time in beginning her testimony. "On June 15th, Antoni Barros' chain of command marked him in the Northeastern Chapter of the North American Coven branch. Three months later, after walking out of a monthly meeting with RLK's Rowan Dahl—or as she is now know, Queen Consort Rowan Dahl of the Draconian Thunder—I fell into a dropped phase, a spell thought to be exclusive to Faerie denizens until I ran into the one created by Antoni Barro. He kept me inside a nulling cage for roughly two weeks. In that time, he used methods of torture to accumulate more power than he'd already had. Under the impression that I had already taken command as Elder of the Coven, he tried experimental and deranged forms of magic to retrieve the gifted magic the position brings. He grew more and more frustrated with each failure. Compounded with the interference of his plans for the shifters, he began losing control. Rowan Dahl seemed to become the focus of his rage and I became the outlet, each beating a further unraveling of the man who'd brought me there. During one round of mana extraction, he talked to himself. His motivations for the attacks became crystal clear."

The rustle of clothes and chairs was sharp, as everyone seemed to lean in to make sure they heard Cherry's next words clearly.

"About four years ago, a lynx shifter suffering from an uncommon condition known as rage lust killed his fiance, Tali Jessum. He told me this as he dug a needle into my vein and pumped me full of a potion that was supposed to make my magic easier to syphon off."

Her arms shook and her head bowed as she took a moment to compose herself.

Alessandro could smell the salt in the air as his mate was once again crying at his side. He brought her closer.

Across the room, he caught sight of Dae Kang at the table she'd left. His eyes were closed, arms and legs crossed as an attempt to stop himself from getting up, clearly so angry that if he did anything else, he would make his way to the platform and run a knife through Barros.

"That was the night Rowan Dahl popped up in that second cage. If you've had the unfortunate experience of trying to get Rowan Dahl to behave a certain way, you would know that it's impossible. But to cow her into obedience and fear, Antoni Barros used the information he'd gathered through my beatings and targeted her greatest weakness—her everlasting need to help others. He nearly beat me to death. I had already accepted my fate until I woke up in the care of the Eastern Elven Kingdom's best physician team. I was under surgery for two days as they tried to undo everything Barros had done to me. They had me as close to the condition that I'd been in before I fell into that trap. The only evidence remaining are these scars on my face and my vow as the new Coven Elder to denounce this witch and his actions. There is no room in our organization for those who do not prioritize helping those who cannot help themselves. It is the core of the Coven and I vow to refocus our attention on that idea during my time in the role of Elder."

"She didn't mention the rise in rage lust cases."

"No. She didn't. You made the right call, Stone."

"I could have made the wrong one. She could have made us look like we were hiding something."

"Then we would have dealt with it. We just have to get through Barros' confession and hope he's as close to a breakdown as he sounds. Don't focus on what could have been. Stay in the present moment."

"*Right. One step at a time.*" Stone's use of the words Alessandro had always repeated to him brought him a calm he couldn't have imagined.

One step at a time. If Stone decided he didn't want to be king, Alessandro would hear him out and one step at a time, they would figure everything out.

Gently, he squeezed Rowan's hand.

"*I agree.*" He said to Rowan. "*She should be the one to do it, if she wishes.*"

Dae Kang didn't make eye contact with Antoni Barros as he took the podium. His story was brief and factual, as if it was a waste of his time to be away from Cherry's side. The only new piece of information he gave was a recounting of his realization that Barros had set an illusion over the entire Coven and that while the wolves lost control, he'd interfere with a few close calls when the others weren't looking.

Hye Kang got through with his testimony, shining a light on how Barros ordered him to replace the fake nemes headdress that the Sphinx Lair had been using for centuries with the real one. Antoni Barros retrieved the genuine article from the pit at the base of the lair, retrieved by Antoni Barros himself. Hye admitted that Abanoub's wife had been unaware the trade had occurred. That she was the first victim without ever realizing she'd been instrumental in her own demise.

The mixture of sorrow and relief in the Sphinx Alpha was palpable in the air.

Tensions were high when the guards moved Antoni Barros from the platform to the podium. His gaze rested on Rowan and Rowan alone.

She was still curled into Alessandro's side, giving the impression that his glowering look had no effect on her.

It infuriated the man, and he took the momentary opportunity of when the minotaurs were about to attach the shackles to the podium to run towards her, emerald eyes wild.

391 - MIA BONES

Alessandro, Kyron, Naseem and Stone all reacted reflexively, all shooting to their feet. Rowan was faster than them all. From her seat, she threw a spell of gravity that had him pinned to the floor.

"You ruined everything, you fucking bitch!" He screamed as the minotaurs retook his chains and dragged him back to the podium.

Alessandro shook his head as he retook his seat. "You couldn't afford to let us look heroic for even a second?"

"You looked heroic." Rowan promised, giving him a small kiss on the chin. "But as your woman, I can't afford to look weak, can I?"

She really did just know what to say, didn't she?

Antoni let out a roar of frustration as the minotaurs finished chaining him in. "Want to hear my side of the story? Fine! I'll tell you. I lost the only good thing that happened to me because of these monsters. Four years ago, their true state of being known as rage lust was spreading like wildfire in between these shifters. They knew it, but they hushed up anyone who threatened to spill the truth. The cowardice and greed of the Coven cost me my fiance. She'd barely said yes before she got in the way of an infected jaguar shifter attacking a helpless kid. It slashed her to ribbons in front of me." He sobbed.

Rowan recalled the witch's words before he attacked Cherry, and her jaw clenched.

I knew a woman like you once, and she had a glaring weakness. I wonder if you have it too.

How could he have seen a trace of the "only good thing" that had happened to him in her and still have hurt her?

"How could you be so happy with a beast who can at any moment turn and run you through with his claws, just as they did with Tali? He doesn't deserve happiness. None of you filthy shifters hiding your beasts with the skin of humanity deserves to act like you're more than just the base monsters you are."

"Don't allow him to antagonize you." Alessandro sent a message to every single shifter present. "He wants to provoke us to lose control. But he doesn't know that we are more than that anger he's given into."

Those who had visibly had their hackles shaken tried to relax back into their chairs, scowls were the only hint of their offense.

"It is only a matter of time before you all show your true face, and now I've given the world time to prepare for that eventuality. The Coven was right about you, Rowan Dahl. You are a danger to the public. You are nothing more than a temporary fuck toy. They're using your goodwill with the public to soften their appearance. You're helping the wolves put on sheep's clothing and you will get hundreds killed with that decision. I hope when it happens you can find it in yourself to rise against them. Like you rose against me and stripped me of the power of the staff. I don't know how a Blessed could get their mission so fucking confused."

Gasps and whispers broke out amongst the onlookers.

Rowan maintained a cool facade through it all, raising an eyebrow as if confused when he hurled out that last accusation.

Well, that had certainly been unexpected.

The steam evaporated from Antoni Barros with her lack of reaction. He tried to stare her down, but as Cherry had said, Rowan Dahl was stubborn.

"Are you finished with your defense?" The Goblin, who had stepped back each time someone took to the podium, asked from behind him when no more words came.

Barros bowed his head and took a step back to allow the minotaurs to undo his chains.

"We will give Judgement members an hour to decide their vote." The goblin said, just as unaffected as Rowan was trying to seem, before he turned and walked off.

Conversation burst to life around them.

Alessandro glanced down at Rowan, who'd relaxed after everyone's attention left her.

"That fucking asshole. How did he know?" She hissed angrily. "Kin doesn't do sloppy work."

"I don't think he actually knows as much as suspects. The podium allows the witnesses to tell their honest belief of the truth, but beliefs are often unreliable." Kyron answered. "You did well, not rising to take the bait."

"I just want this to be over." She groaned, standing up and dropping a kiss on Alessandro's brow. "I gotta check on Louisa. I'll be back."

As she walked away, King Kyron slid his attention to him. "I take it she had talked you into not volunteering for his execution?"

Alessandro nodded.

"She can be surprisingly sharp." Annabelle sighed. "I am sorry for all that you will have to endure because of this."

Alessandro gave her a crooked grin. "We are strong, we will persevere. I have a separate query."

Kyron raised an eyebrow. "Are you finally going to ask for our blessing in your mating?"

Heat colored Alessandro's cheeks. "It did all happen suddenly, but this next part, I'm hoping, will happen a bit more traditionally to your people. I wish to ask her to marry me in the way of the elves. While I understand the overarching points, I would like to work out the finer details with your help."

Annabelle's eyes lit up. "Well, first, it is customary to ask for our blessing." She put a hand on her chin. "Usually you'd come with gifts to entice us. I am particular to the leather corsets of your people and my husband enjoys your pastries."

Alessandro let out a soft laugh. "I think I could arrange that."

King Kyron raised an eyebrow. "All I really want is for her to keep that joy alive. If you can promise me that will be your life's ambition, you have my blessing, Dragon King."

"Well, not mine," Annabelle scoffed. "I would like to be bribed. Not to make it into a competition, but Atlas gave me a stunning jewelry set that cost him a year's worth of wage. Come over tomorrow night and I'll show it to you while I give you a list of what's expected for the traditional wedding, okay?" Annabelle grinned.

It was so like Rowan's that Alessandro knew it would be hard to say no to her.

"I'll be there."

-R-

Louisa had her arms around Rowan as soon as she got close enough. "I know you're busy being a mate, but this has to be the last time I find out shit like this through a trial! When it comes time to volunteer, I'm raising my hand." Louisa growled.

Rowan found it amusing that Alessandro and Louisa, of all people, were on the same wavelength. "What he did to me was nothing compared to what he did to Cherry, it's her kill."

Louisa deflated but accepted her words. "He's demented. Seeing you happy with your dragon must've pushed him completely over the edge. It almost made me gag to see how cute you two are."

Rowan grinned at her friend when she pulled back. "It's obviously mostly me. So tell me, my dear little blood sucker, what's up with you and that tall, dark and handsome man I've had to threaten to behave?"

Louisa snickered and motioned to Rosario's empty chair for her to sit.

"Where'd she go?" Rowan asked as she settled the silken fabric of her dress around her thighs.

"Talking to some ambassador or something. I didn't really hear her because our wolf friend is drowning my own thoughts out with his." She sighed. "I honestly thought it was going to be just a one-night stand. I didn't think this would happen!"

Rowan scoffed. "Funny how that happens, huh?" She grinned, "But as you can see, it's working out well for me so far."

"Yeah, well, you have a set of parents that love you and aren't psychos half of the time."

"Definitely helps." Rowan cast a look at her parents, who were bowing their heads and talking to Alessandro conspiratorially. What was that about?

"So, what are you going to do about it?"

Louisa shrugged. "Pretend it didn't happen and try to forget him?"

"Ooh, you might have better luck than me. He does live like several continents away."

Louisa frowned. "You don't think it'll work."

Rowan shrugged. "I think you like him being in your head, seeing as you are quite adept at blocking out unwanted presences."

Louisa narrowed her eyes. "You're sounding a lot like a blonde woman I know."

Rowan leaned forward. "She makes fair points every once in a while. But if you want to get out of here and turn to our less healthy coping mechanisms, I know a bar in that town they get the boats from. We have about forty minutes to kill."

Louisa grinned. "That sounds fun. Do you have to ask your boyfriend for permission?"

"Woah, woah missy, you mean, mate?" Rowan corrected with a teasing grin. "No, I don't have to ask permission, but I am going to tell him."

Louisa let out a whipping sound.

"If only you could be so lucky." Rowan sighed dreamily.

"Louisa and I are sneaking away before the vote. Be a dear and cover for us if her mother comes looking, won't you?"

"Be a dear?" Alessandro asked with a raised eyebrow from his seat. *"I was unaware you were a sixty-year-old human woman."*

She winked down at him. *"I am just full of surprises, dear."*

"I want to talk about pet names when you come back. I refuse to be associated with game."

Rowan stood and held her hand out to her friend. Louisa stood and took it and with mischievous smirks, both women phased out.

-R-

When Rowan phased back in, she smelled of ambrosia laced whiskey.

"Did you go to a bar without me?" Annabelle hissed. "Kyron, put our pebble in the live section."

Rowan pulled a couple of shot bottles from the fabric of her dress and slid them over.

"Local brews." Rowan grinned.

"Considerate of you, daughter. Ky, you may put our pebble in the die section."

The goblin's reappearance at the podium brought a hush over the hall.

He snapped his finger, and an enormous set of golden scales appeared at his side. A smooth black pebble materialized at each table at the same time.

"We will now ask you to declare your decision. Whisper into the pebble 'live' or 'die' and the pebble will find its way into the proper basket."

Alessandro glanced down at the smooth rock before him. He could hear the whispers of those around him begin almost immediately.

Rowan curled her fingers around his as he picked it up.

"Die."

It felt wildly impersonal considering what the witch had put his people through. And he watched as the pebble shot from his hand and joined the overwhelming number in the "die" basket. Only three found their way into the "live" alternative.

It was nearly unanimous.

"Antoni Barros will face death. It is now that we will ask for an executioner from those affected by his crime. Do we have a volunteer?"

"*Let the witches have him.*" He passed to every shifter.

He saw a moment where the Sphinx Alpha looked like he wanted to rebel, but his eyes shifted to Rowan, who gave a slight shake of her head. He remained seated.

The other shifters, who had yet to really get to know his mate, looked astounded, and they all took their turns re-evaluating her.

Cherry Young and Dae Kang interrupted this by both surging to their feet.

Cherry leveled Dae with a look of displeasure. "It is my battle, Dae." She said so softly that Alessandro would've missed it if he didn't have heightened senses.

The witch clenched his fists and sat back down.

Cherry's eyes roved over the shifters who had remained sitting. When they rested on Rowan, she gave a small disbelieving shake of her head before bowing her head in a silent thanks.

Epilogue

Crashing to the floor of her wrap-around porch, the topmost plate Rowan had seen teetering too late went flying in separate directions. A sharp shard sliced across her shin.

Hissing in pain, she dumped the rest of the food as carefully as possible onto the small bistro table she'd dragged out from her kitchen.

The shrill sound of the alarm she'd set to signal when Alessandro was to arrive according to a very well paid off Earth General set her heart hammering into her throat.

Relax, Dahl! He's your mate, isn't he?

Snapping her fingers to send the shattered plate to the trash, Rowan struggled to find the sexiest way to greet her man. Changing pose after pose until she achieved the perfect idea by leaning against a banister on the porch with a flute of champagne in her carefully manicured hand.

His magic curled around her before he appeared. His hand gripped the hair closest to the base of her skull, tugging her head back before he completely dominated her mouth.

Well, what a pleasant surprise.

Rowan sent the flute of champagne flying so she could turn and fully receive everything he was pouring into her.

It was in taking this in that she realized he was enraged.

She tried to pull back, but the hand that wasn't tugging her hair to give him full access to her lips slid down to cup her ass and hold her hips flush to his.

What the hell had made him so desperate?

"Stop."

He went stock still at her telepathic command, but he didn't pull back.

He was panting, his heartbeat so loud it was ringing in her ears.

She pulled away to look up at him. Scales roiled to the surface of his face, and his eyes were glowing red, alerting his displeasure

"What happened?" Her hands cupped his cheeks.

"I received a memory."

Rowan raised an eyebrow. "What was it?"

"You lost your virginity."

"Oh?" She couldn't actually remember much from that night. Her succubus had furled to life with a bang in the middle of a high school party and, well, with the buffet of lust driven teenagers on the cusp of adulthood, Rowan had let control slip away.

"It was a fucking orgy." He growled.

She grimaced at the tone. "Maybe we should prevent my sex memories from transferring. That was one of my...softer nights."

"Softer?" The words escaped him like a curse.

"San, we were a bunch of teenagers. None of us had any experience."

"They worshipped you." He growled. "At that moment, they would have done anything you asked of them."

"Is that the problem? Because let me tell you, they're all like that. I'm a very skilled succubus! As the receiver of some of my best moves, you should be able to understand."

"That's exactly the problem!" Alessandro snapped. "If they even feel a fraction of how I feel...you aren't safe."

Rowan let out an involuntary laugh.

"You dare laugh?" Alessandro growled and Rowan noted the ice around him as if were his tell of coming close to losing control.

"I have to find humor in this or you're going to piss me off."

The ice grew, and her temper flared.

"How many times must I remind you? I am not a fucking damsel in distress." She hissed, snatching the bottle of champagne off the bistro table she'd spent so much time trying to perfect. The candles she'd lit seemed to mock her wasted effort. Disgusted, she waved a hand to put them out. "I'm tired of having to prove my strength."

"It isn't about you being a damsel in distress!"

"You're not safe." She mocked and shook her head, trying to remember why she went above and beyond for such an infuriating man.

Fucking mark.

"Did you set this up for me?" No trace of the anger he'd lashed out with was present.

Rowan looked up and noted that his ice had also disappeared.

"No. It's for me." She huffed. "I love setting out two dinner plates full of your favorite food that took me for freaking ever to find the ingredients for. I do it at least twice a week."

He crossed his arms and scowled down at her. "Is sarcasm really necessary?"

She huffed and looked away again, unable to think about staying angry at him when his forearms, biceps and triceps were all bunched in the position.

He crouched in front of her. "I'm sorry."

"For what?" She asked, unsure if she wanted to forgive him so easily.

His sigh was the longest she'd heard yet. Apologies didn't come naturally to him. "I just saw how they looked at you, and I could relate a little too much. The idea of anyone loving you the way I love you. It was unfathomable until I realized you have the power to make anyone fall."

She blinked down at him and heat traveled from the base of her chest to the very top of her head. She was sure if she looked up, there would be visible steam rolling off.

A slow shit-eating smile took up space on his face. "Are you blushing, Rowan Dahl?"

"That was the first time you've said it."

"It may be the first time I've said it, but I've felt it from the moment you called me after I closed the gates of Draconis."

She let out a disbelieving scoff. "You didn't even say goodbye after that call."

"If I have it my way, I'll never say goodbye to you."

This, more than anything else, deteriorated any anger she'd felt towards this man. She snapped her fingers, and the candles reignited. She beamed at him as he took his seat and revealed the meal underneath a silver plate cover, keeping his food warm.

A tomahawk steak the size of her head sat over a bed of different colored baked potatoes basted in garlic and herbs. His eyes slid to the touch that had actually taken her the longest to get a hold of. Mushrooms taken from the town he'd spent the first years of his life with his parents. They were characteristically bone white and as long as asparagus.

The sight of them transfixed him.

"Do you hate them?" She asked after he didn't make a single move.

"These are...rare. How did you find them?"

She waggled her eyebrows. "I have a source for all kinds of rare delicacies. Anya mentioned it was the only thing you ever asked her to prepare that she could not accommodate."

He fell silent again.

Rowan's heart sank. Preparing the mushrooms had been as tedious as finding them. "If they're not good, you don't have to force yourself to eat them."

"Thank you." His voice was softer than Rowan even knew it could go.

Relief made her smile. "You're welcome."

By the time they finished their meal, they had moved to the hammock, the distance of the bistro table top too far for either of their liking.

Using superior core strength, Alessandro placed the plates on the floor as Rowan held the champagne bottle they'd been drinking straight out of.

How the hell had she gotten here? And she wasn't thinking about the odd beach the cabin hadn't moved from since the night Rowan cleansed Antoni Barros. The wings still sat on the pearly sands, the weeping willow and oak tree monstrosity swayed behind them, growing at a concerning rate.

She was referring to the fact a man she'd never thought would know she existed had his arms wrapped around her and they were listening to the waves crashing in front of what was now their home.

"So I've been thinking." She began the proposal she'd been considering for the last couple of days.

"Ahh, I knew you were trying to get me drunk for a reason." He teased, hand playing with the snow white strands of her hair. Much gentler than when he'd first showed up.

"Since you are kind of handing off duties to Stone and the office is under renovation, we could go missing for a month. Let the mark settle."

He picked her up as if she weighed nothing. For a moment she thought he might have used a spell, but, as she had to keep reminding herself, he was the Dragon King.

He settled her over his hips, hunger blazing in the glowing silver eyes staring up at her, hardness just underneath the thin layers of their clothing.

"Woman, you were just born to make all of my dreams come true, weren't you?"

She grinned wickedly, "Of course. I *am* the Dragon Queen."

Instagram: @bynousette

First and foremost, Mia is a girl who seriously loves a happily ever after. Immigrating from El Salvador to the United States at the tender age of six, Fatima was completely unaware of how a box full of romance novels she, gifted from the mother of her childhood best friend, would eventually shape her biggest dream: To be a published author. After years of hauling around a fraying backpack full of journals scribbled with incomplete stories, it wasn't until she finally received her Bachelor's in English Literature-Creative Writing that she wrote her first full bodied story. As a proud Latina who is fighting to reclaim her roots to a culture she had at one point almost cut all contact with, she is dedicated to ensuring her works are weaved with love notes for her people. If she's not typing away in a Google Doc that keeps crashing, she can be found at the gym crushing PRs, on a patio day drinking with her best friends, collecting a new hobby, or hanging out with her two cute doggos Pika and Lady.